Praise for the Western Novels
of Richard Matheson

"The best novel I read last year."
— Stephen King on *Journal of the Gun Years*

"Some of the best damn writing Matheson's done in his spectacular career."
— Loren D. Estleman

"*Journal of the Gun Years* is a three-carat diamond. Read it and enjoy it without delay."
— Max Evans

"No one writes better."
— Richard S. Wheeler

"He is legend."
— Dale Walker, *Rocky Mountain News*

"A master storyteller."
— Joe R. Lansdale

"A credibility and honesty unusual in the genre."
— *Publishers Weekly*

LEGENDS
of the
GUN YEARS

RICHARD MATHESON

A Tom Doherty Associates Book
New York

LEGENDS OF THE GUN YEARS

Journal of the Gun Years copyright © 1991 by RXR, Inc.
The Memoirs of Wild Bill Hickok copyright © 1996 by RXR, Inc.

A Forge Book
Published by Tom Doherty Associates, LLC
175 Fifth Avenue
New York, NY 10010

www.tor-forge.com

Forge® is a registered trademark of Tom Doherty Associates, LLC.

ISBN 978-0-7653-2233-3

First Forge Trade Paperback Edition: May 2010

Printed in the United States of America

0 9 8 7 6 5 4 3 2 1

CONTENTS

JOURNAL
of the
GUN YEARS

For:

William Campbell Gault, William R. Cox, Henry Kuttner,
Les Savage, Jr., Joe Brennan, Hal Braham, Malden Grange Bishop,
Chick Coombs, Dean Owens, Bill Fay, Willard Temple,
Frank Bonham, Todhunter Ballard, Wilbur S. Peacock,
and all my other friends in the Fictioneers.

Happy memories.

BOOK ONE

(1864—1867)

It is my unhappy lot to write the closing entry in this journal.

Clay Halser is dead, killed this morning in my presence.

I have known him since we met during the latter days of The War Between the States. I have run across him, on occasion, through ensuing years and am, in fact, partially responsible (albeit involuntarily) for a portion of the legend which has magnified around him.

It is for these reasons (and another more important) that I make this final entry.

—————

I am in Silver Gulch acquiring research matter toward the preparation of a volume on the history of this territory (Colorado), which has recently become the thirty-eighth state of our Union.

I was having breakfast in the dining room of the *Silver Lode Hotel* when a man entered and sat down at a table across the room, his back to the wall. Initially, I failed to recognize him though there was, in his comportment, something familiar.

Several minutes later (to my startlement), I realized that it was none other than Clay Halser. True, I had not laid eyes on him for many years. Nonetheless, I was completely taken aback by the change in his appearance.

I was not, at that point, aware of his age, but took it to be somewhere in the middle thirties. Contrary to this, he presented the aspect of a man at least a decade older.

His face was haggard, his complexion (in my memory, quite ruddy) pale to the point of being ashen. His eyes, formerly suffused with animation, now looked burned out, dead. What many horrific sights those eyes had beheld I could not—and cannot—begin to estimate. Whatever those sights, however, no evidence of them had been reflected in his eyes before; it was as though he'd been emotionally immune.

He was no longer so. Rather, one could easily imagine that his eyes were gazing, in that very moment, at those bloody sights, dredging from the depths within his mind to which he'd relegated them, all their awful measure.

From the standpoint of physique, his deterioration was equally marked. I had always known him as a man of vigorous health, a condition necessary to sustain him in the execution of his harrowing duties. He was not a tall man; I would gauge his height at five feet ten inches maximum, perhaps an inch or so less, since his upright carriage and customary dress of black suit, hat, and boots might have afforded him the look of standing taller than he did. He had always been extremely well-presented though, with a broad chest, narrow waist, and pantherlike grace of movement; all in all, a picture of vitality.

Now, as he ate his meal across from me, I felt as though, by some bizarre transfiguration, I was gazing at an old man.

He had lost considerable weight and his dark suit (it, too, seemed worn and past its time) hung loosely on his frame. To my further disquiet, I noted a threading of gray through his dark blond hair and saw a tremor in his hands completely foreign to the young man I had known.

I came close to summary departure. To my shame, I nearly chose to leave rather than accost him. Despite the congenial relationship I had enjoyed with him throughout the past decade, I found myself so totally dismayed by the alteration in his looks that I lacked the will to rise and cross the room to him, preferring to consider a hasty exit. (I discovered, later, that the reason he had failed to notice me was that his vision, always so acute before, was now inordinately weak.)

At last, however, girding up my will, I stood and moved across the dining room, attempting to fix a smile of pleased surprise on my lips and hoping he would not be too aware of my distress.

"Well, good morning, Clay," I said, as evenly as possible.

I came close to baring my deception at the outset for, as he looked up sharply at me, his expression one of taut alarm, a perceptible "tic" under his right eye, I was hard put not to draw back apprehensively.

Abruptly, then, he smiled (though it was more a ghost of the smile I remembered). "*Frank,*" he said and jumped to his feet. No, that is not an accurate description of his movement. It may well have been his intent to jump up and welcome me with an avid handshake. As it happened, his stand was labored, his hand grip lacking in strength. "How *are* you?" he inquired. "It is good to see you."

"I'm fine," I answered.

"Good." He nodded, gesturing toward the table. "Join me."

I hope my momentary hesitation passed his notice. "I'd be happy to," I told him.

"Good," he said again.

We each sat down, he with his back toward the wall again. As we did, I noted how his gaunt frame slumped into the chair, so different from the movement of his earlier days.

He asked me if I'd eaten breakfast.

"Yes." I pointed across the room. "I was finishing when you entered."

"I am glad you came over," he said.

There was a momentary silence. Uncomfortable, I tried to think of something to say.

He helped me out. (I wonder, now, if it was deliberate; if he had, already, taken note of my discomfort.) "Well, old fellow," he asked, "what brings you to this neck of the woods?"

I explained my presence in Silver Gulch and, as I did, being now so close to him, was able to distinguish, in detail, the astounding metamorphosis which time (and experience) had effected.

There seemed to be, indelibly impressed on his still handsome face, a look of unutterable sorrow. His former blitheness had completely vanished and it was oppressive to behold what had occurred to his expression, to see the palsied gestures of his hands as he spoke, perceive the constant shifting of his eyes as though he was anticipating that, at any second, some impending danger might be thrust upon him.

I tried to coerce myself not to observe these things, concentrating on the task of bringing him "up to date" on my activities since last we'd met; no match for his activities, God knows.

"What about you?" I finally asked; I had no more to say about myself. "What are you doing these days?"

"Oh, gambling," he said, his listless tone indicative of his regard for that pursuit.

"No marshaling anymore?" I asked.

He shook his head. "Strictly the circuit," he answered.

"Circuit?" I wasn't really curious but feared the onset of silence and spoke the first word that occurred to me.

"A league of boomtown havens for faro players," he replied. "South Texas up to South Dakota—Idaho to Arizona. There is money to be gotten everywhere. Not that I am good enough to make a raise. And not that it's important if I do, at any rate. I only gamble for something to do."

All the time he spoke, his eyes kept shifting, searching; was it *waiting*?

As silence threatened once again, I quickly spoke. "Well, you

have traveled quite a long road since the War," I said. "A long, exciting road." I forced a smile. "*Adventurous*," I added.

His answering smile was as sadly bitter and exhausted as any
I have ever witnessed. "Yes, the writers of the stories have made it
all sound very colorful," he said. He leaned back with a heavy sigh,
regarding me. "I even thought it so myself at one time. Now I recognize it all for what it was." There was a tightening around his
eyes. "Frank, it was drab, and dirty, and there was a lot of blood."

I had no idea how to respond to that and, in spite of my resolve,
let silence fall between us once more.

Silence broke in a way that made my flesh go cold. A young man's
voice behind me, from some distance in the room. "So that is him,"
the voice said loudly. "Well, he does not look like much to me."

I'd begun to turn when Clay reached out and gripped my arm.
"Don't bother looking," he instructed me. "It's best to ignore them.
I have found the more attention paid, the more difficult they are to
shake in the long run."

He smiled but there was little humor in it. "Don't be concerned,"
he said. "It happens all the time. They spout a while, then go away,
and brag that Halser took their guff and never did a thing. It makes
them feel important. I don't mind. I've grown accustomed to it."

At which point, the boy—I could now tell, from the timbre of his
voice, that he had not attained his majority—spoke again.

"He looks like nothing at all to me to be so all-fired famous a
fighter with his guns," he said.

I confess the hostile quaver of his voice unsettled me. Seeing
my reaction, Clay smiled and was about to speak when the boy—
perhaps seeing the smile and angered by it—added, in a tone re-
sounding enough to be heard in the lobby, "In fact, I believe he
looks like a woman-hearted coward, that is what he looks like
to me!"

"Don't worry now," Clay reassured me. "He'll blow himself out of steam presently and crawl away." I felt some sense of relief to see a glimmer of the old sauce in his eyes. "Probably to visit, with uncommon haste, the nearest outhouse."

Still, the boy kept on with stubborn malice. "My name is Billy Howard," he announced. "And I am going to make . . ."

He went abruptly mute as Clay unbuttoned his dark frock coat to reveal a butt-reversed Colt at his left side. It was little wonder. Even I, a friend of Clay's, felt a chill of premonition at the movement. What spasm of dread it must have caused in the boy's heart, I can scarcely imagine.

"Sometimes I have to go this far," Clay told me. "Usually I wait longer but, since you are with me . . ." He let the sentence go unfinished and lifted his cup again.

I wanted to believe the incident was closed but, as we spoke—me asking questions to distract my mind from its foreboding state—I seemed to feel the presence of the boy behind me like some constant wraith.

"How are all your friends?" I asked.

"Dead," Clay answered.

"*All* of them?"

He nodded. "Yes. Jim Clements. Ben Pickett. John Harris." I saw a movement in his throat. "Henry Blackstone. All of them."

I had some difficulty breathing. I kept expecting to hear the boy's voice again. "What about your wife?" I asked.

"I have not heard from her in some time," he replied. "We are estranged."

"How old is your daughter now?"

"Three in January," he answered, his look of sadness deepening. I regretted having asked and quickly said, "What about your family in Indiana?"

"I went back to visit them last year," he said. "It was a waste."

I did not want to know, but heard myself inquiring nonetheless, "Why?"

"Oh . . . what I have become," he said. "What journalists have made me. Not you," he amended, believing, I suppose, that he'd insulted me. "My reputation, I mean. It stood like a wall between my family and me. I don't think they saw me. Not *me*. They saw what they believed I am."

The voice of Billy Howard made me start. "Well, why does he just *sit* there?" he said.

Clay ignored him. Or, perhaps, he did not even hear, so deep was he immersed in black thoughts.

"Hickok was right," he said, "I am not a man anymore. I'm a figment of imagination. Do you know, I looked at my reflection in the mirror this morning and did not even know who I was looking at? Who is that staring at me? I wondered. Clay Halser of Pine Grove? Or the *Hero of The Plains*?" he finished with contempt.

"*Well?*" demanded Billy Howard. "Why *does* he?"

Clay was silent for a passage of seconds and I felt my muscles drawing in, anticipating God knew what.

"I had no answer for my mirror," he went on then. "I have no answers left for anyone. All I know is that I am tired. They have offered me the job of City Marshal here and, although I could use the money, I cannot find it in myself to accept."

Clay Halser stared into my eyes and told me quietly, "To answer your long-time question: yes, Frank, I have learned what fear is. Though not fear of . . ."

He broke off as the boy spoke again, his tone now venomous. "I think he is afraid of me," said Billy Howard.

Clay drew in a long, deep breath, then slowly shifted his gaze to look across my shoulder. I sat immobile, conscious of an air of tension in the entire room now, everyone waiting with held breath.

"That is what I think," the boy's voice said. "I think Almighty God Halser is afraid of me."

Clay said nothing, looking past me at the boy. I did not dare to turn. I sat there, petrified.

"I think the Almighty God Halser is a yellow skunk!" cried Billy Howard. "I think he is a murderer who shoots men in the back and will not . . . !"

The boy's voice stopped again as Clay stood so abruptly that I felt a painful jolting in my heart. "I'll be right back," he said.

He walked past me and, shuddering, I turned to watch. It had grown so deathly still in the room that, as I did, the legs of my chair squeaked and caused some nearby diners to start.

I saw, now, for the first time, Clay Halser's challenger and was aghast at the callow look of him. He could not have been more than sixteen years of age and might well have been younger, his face speckled with skin blemishes, his dark hair long and shaggy. He was poorly dressed and had an old six-shooter pushed beneath the waistband of his faded trousers.

I wondered vaguely whether I should move, for I was sitting in whatever line of fire the boy might direct. I wondered vaguely if the other diners were wondering the same thing. If they were, their limbs were as frozen as mine.

I heard every word exchanged by the two.

"Now don't you think that we have had enough of this?" Clay said to the boy. "These folks are having their breakfast and I think that we should let them eat their meal in peace."

"Step out into the street then," said the boy.

"Now why should I step out into the street?" Clay asked. I knew it was no question. He was doing what he could to calm the agitated boy—that agitation obvious as the boy replied, "To fight me with your gun."

"You don't want to fight me," Clay informed him. "You would just be killed and no one would be better for it."

"You mean *you* don't want to fight *me*," the youth retorted. Even from where I sat, I could see that his face was almost white; it was clear that he was terror-stricken.

Still, he would not allow himself to back off, though Clay was giving him full opportunity. "*You* don't want to fight *me*," he repeated.

"That is not the case at all," Clay replied. "It is just that I am tired of fighting."

"I *thought* so!" cried the boy with malignant glee.

"Look," Clay told him quietly, "if it will make you feel good, you are free to tell your friends, or anyone you choose, that I backed down from you. You have my permission to do that."

"I don't need your d——d permission," snarled the boy. With a sudden move, he scraped his chair back, rising to his feet. Unnervingly, he seemed to be gaining resolution rather than losing it—as though, in some way, he sensed the weakness in Clay, despite the fact that Clay was famous for his prowess with the handgun. "I am sick of listening to you," he declared. "Are you going to step outside with me and pull your gun like a man, or do I shoot you down like a dog?"

"Go *home*, boy," Clay responded—and I felt an icy grip of premonition strike me full force as his voice broke in the middle of a word.

"Pull, you yellow b——d," Billy Howard ordered him.

Several diners close to them lunged up from their tables, scattering for the lobby. Clay stood motionless.

"I said *pull*, you God d——d son of a b——h!" Billy Howard shouted.

"No," was all Clay Halser answered.

"Then *I* will!" cried the boy.

Before his gun was halfway from the waistband of his trousers, Clay's had cleared its holster. Then—with what capricious twist of fate!—his shot misfired and, before he could squeeze off another, the boy's gun had discharged and a bullet struck Clay full in the chest, sending him reeling back to hit a table, then sprawl sideways to the floor.

Through the pall of dark smoke, Billy Howard gaped down at

his victim. "I did it," he muttered. "I *did* it." Though chance alone had done it.

Suddenly, his pistol clattered to the floor as his fingers lost their holding power and, with a cry of what he likely thought was victory, he bolted from the room. (Later, I heard, he was killed in a knife fight over a poker game somewhere near Bijou Basin.)

By then, I'd reached Clay, who had rolled onto his back, a dazed expression on his face, his right hand pressed against the blood-pumping wound in the center of his chest. I shouted for someone to get a doctor, and saw some man go dashing toward the lobby. Clay attempted to sit up, but did not have the strength, and slumped back.

Hastily, I knelt beside him and removed my coat to form a pillow underneath his head, then wedged my handkerchief between his fingers and the wound. As I did, he looked at me as though I were a stranger. Finally, he blinked and, to my startlement, began to chuckle. "The one time I di . . ." I could not make out the rest. "What, Clay?" I asked distractedly, wondering if I should try to stop the bleeding in some other way.

He chuckled again. "The one day I did not reload," he repeated with effort. "Ben would laugh at that."

He swallowed, then began to make a choking noise, a trickle of blood issuing from the left-hand corner of his mouth. "Hang on," I said, pressing my hand to his shoulder. "The doctor will be here directly."

He shook his head with several hitching movements. "No sawbones can remove me from *this* tight," he said.

He stared up at the ceiling now, his breath a liquid sound that made me shiver. I did not know what to say, but could only keep directing worried (and increasingly angry) glances toward the lobby. "Where *is* he?" I muttered.

Clay made a ghastly, wheezing noise, then said, "My God." His fingers closed in, clutching at the already blood-soaked handkerchief. "I am going to die." Another strangling breath. "And I am only thirty-one years old."

Instant tears distorted my vision. *Thirty-one?*

Clay murmured something I could not hear. Automatically, I bent over and he repeated, in a labored whisper, "She was such a pretty girl."

"Who?" I asked; could not help but ask.

"Mary Jane," he answered. He could barely speak by then. Straightening up, I saw the grayness of death seeping into his face and knew that there were only moments left to him.

He made a sound which might have been a chuckle had it not emerged in such a hideously bubbling manner. His eyes seemed lit now with some kind of strange amusement. "I could have married her," he managed to say. "I could still be there." He stared into his fading thoughts. "Then I would never have . . ."

At which his stare went lifeless and he expired.

I gazed at him until the doctor came. Then the two of us lifted his body—how *frail* it was—and placed it on a nearby table. The doctor closed Clay's eyes and I crossed Clay's arms on his chest after buttoning his coat across the ugly wound. Now he looked almost at peace, his expression that of a sleeping boy.

Soon people began to enter the dining room. In a short while, everyone in Silver Gulch, it seemed, had heard about Clay's death and come running to view the remains. They shuffled past his impromptu bier in a double line, gazed at him and, ofttimes, murmured some remark about his life and death.

As I stood beside the table, looking at the gray, still features, I wondered what Clay had been about to say before the rancorous voice of Billy Howard had interrupted. He'd said that he had learned what fear is, "though not fear of . . ." What words had he been about to say? Though not fear of other men? Of danger? Of death?

Later on, the undertaker came and took Clay's body after I had guaranteed his payment. That done, I was requested, by the manager of the hotel, to examine Clay's room and see to the disposal of his meager goods. This I did and will return his possessions to his family in Indiana.

With one exception.

In a lower bureau drawer, I found a stack of Record Books bound together with heavy twine. They turned out to be a journal which Clay Halser kept from the latter part of the War to this very morning.

It is my conviction that these books deserve to be published. Not in their entirety, of course; if that were done, I estimate the book would run in excess of a thousand pages. Moreover, there are many entries which, while perhaps of interest to immediate family (who will, of course, receive the Record Books when I have finished partially transcribing them), contribute nothing to the main thrust of his account, which is the unfoldment of his life as a nationally recognized lawman and gunfighter.

Accordingly, I plan to eliminate those sections of the journal which chronicle that variety of events which any man might experience during twelve years' time. After all, as hair-raising as Clay's life was, he could not possibly exist on the razor edge of peril every day of his life. As proof of this, I will incorporate a random sampling of those entries which may be considered, from a "thrilling" standpoint, more mundane.

In this way—concentrating on the sequences of "action"—it is hoped that the general reader, who might otherwise ignore the narrative because of its unwieldy length, will more willingly expose his interest to the life of one whom another journalist has referred to as "The Prince of Pistoleers."

Toward this end, I will, additionally, attempt to make corrections in the spelling, grammar and, especially, punctuation of the journal, leaving, as an indication of this necessity, the opening entry. It goes without saying that subsequent entries need less attention to this aspect since Clay Halser learned, by various means, to read and write with more skill in his later years.

I hope the reader will concur that, while there might well be a certain charm in viewing the entries precisely as Clay Halser wrote them, the difficulty in following his style through virtually an entire book would make the reading far too difficult. It is for this reason that I have tried to simplify his phraseology without—I trust— sacrificing the basic flavor of his language.

Keep in mind, then, that if the chronology of this account is, now and then, sporadic (with occasional truncated entries), it is because I have used, as its main basis, Clay Halser's life as a man of violence. I hope, by doing this, that I will not unbalance the impression of his personality. While trying not to intrude unduly on the texture of the journal, I may occasionally break into it if I believe my observations may enable the reader to better understand the protagonist of what is probably the bloodiest sequence of events to ever take place on the American frontier.

I plan to do all this, not for personal encomiums, but because I hope that I may be the agency by which the public-at-large may come to know Clay Halser's singular story, perhaps to thrill at his exploits, perhaps to moralize but, hopefully, to profit by the reading for, through the page-by-page transition of this man from high-hearted exuberance to hopeless resignation, we may, perhaps, achieve some insight into a sad, albeit fascinating and exciting, phenomenon of our times.

Frank Leslie
April 19, 1876

We are still here in this Valley, I think we will be here For Ever with those Secesh Boys keep us boteled up, the Sholder Strapps say we are at a Place called Al Mans Swich wer ever that is, I do not no, all I *Do* no is the Army of the Patomic is siting here, siting here and those Secesh Boys piking us of like Pigins on a log, I hate siting, siting, I feel tyd down like a prisner and I wish we just *Go*!! I hate to feel tyd down, by G———. I hate it! I think if we woud Go and Go Hard we woud thro those Jony Rebs back to Jef Davis Back Porch, that woud be the *End* of it, I rely feel that, *Do* it, *Do* it, dont just Sit Here like lumps, we her to suport the Artilery but all we are suporting our own rer ends while we *Sit* here!! Why think it all out, just GO!!!

My frend from New Jersy Albirt Jonson (I think that is a rong speling his Last Name) he took a Minie Ball in the rigt side this afternoon, it put him in grate pain, was holering and crying Some Thing awfil that I did feel sorry for him he was feeling so bad, it must have hurt like H———, poor Albirt. So a few of us Boys caried him Behind The Lines, we finily fond a waggin going North and placed him on it, caried him away poor fello, he was bleding Some Thing ferce, I hope he makes it—And as if that was not enogh the salt beef and patatos gave us last nigt made a bunch siker than Dogs, how we did "cast up acounts" over the Hill Side and down the

Creek was Some Thing awfil! How Ever at the start I did not feel sik but as more and more my comrads got sik after a time I did to and went the same road.

It did not make me feel beter to get a note from Mother, you woud think I took a trip for pursonel plesur here in Vergina insted of figting a D——— War! Why doesnt She leave me be not alway Scolding me as poring linamint into a sore with Ever Lasting Heranging, why did I leve the Farm when there is so much Work to do there, why did I enlist in the Army of the Patomic when there are lots of soldirs who can figt the War but No, no, no "Not enogh Good Men At Home" to help take care of ther Familes, My Lord She goes on and on and on, no wonder He went off to California (My Father) I think the Army of The Secesh less to face than *Her,* I mean I Rispect her and all but why does She never stop Heranging me, I am in a D——— War for G———'s sake, not for pursonel plesure!! Well that is that and we had beter move soon or I take my Rifel and go at those Rebs all my self and mean so in *Ernest*!!

September 14, 1864

Yesterday, this time, I thought we would be here forever. The problem this way: the Secesh Army planted solid on the Heights and regardless how our batteries fired at them—our cannons burning hot!—were so much dug in it did no good at all. This is a "key spot" Lieutenant Hale said; the Rebels need to hold it At Any Cost and no matter what we did, they held.

We started rushing them, charging the heights, bayonets in fix position, but a volley of fire burned at us and we were forced back in defeat, half dead and wounded on the field. Only our artillery at them saved any at all though it did hit some of our boys too. It was a bloody attack that was no use. I had 60 rounds of lead pills which, when it was over, I was down to 17 and I do not know if I had hit a soul, the smoke so heavy you could not see through it the boys in Grey were hid so.

At three o'clock this afternoon Lieutenant Hale collected a group—eight in all—and led us up the far slope of the Valley to "harass" the enemy. He said, "Come on, boys! Today we have a chance to fight our way to Glory!"

He was right, we *did*! It was a battle out of H——— but I came out without a scratch. I think my life is charmed because, when we charged up that slope, though it was far to one side, shot and shell ploughed up the ground in all directions; it was flying hot and heavy. Minnie Balls were buzzing all around us like swarms of angry bees! I felt the *wind* of them and some went by my ears so close they made me jump but not a one could touch me!

By when we reached the top, there was only three remaining, George Havers, me, and some fat man from New York State that I had not met. (How he climbed that slope not being blown to his Maker I will never know!) We got behind a fallen tree and, from that point, through clouds of smoke, could see the Grey lines clear as day. I said to Havers and the fat man we must fire at the Secesh batteries, but they were none too keen to lift their heads as bombarding shot was fierce and Southern Sharp Shooters doing their best to kill us!

So I had to do it my self though Havers, to admit the truth, did fire a shot or two. Mostly, it was me how ever and the first time I got value from the Sharps I picked up last month from the body of a killed Confederate. Lord All Mighty, how that piece can do! I aimed first for the Sharp Shooters, those I could see, and it was like I could not miss. I had 30 lead pills in my sack and there were not too many wasted! I shot at Battery Crews I saw and they fell also; Rebs were going down like sitting birds! I lost count at twelve what with smoke and noise and being worked up, I fell in what you might say was half sleep. I kept firing and firing and

Havers screamed, "God, boy, you hit *another*! God, boy, you hit *another*!"

When the firing at our lines grew thin, our boys came charging up and took the Heights and it was all because of me that we could whip them! Now they are on the run and I am happy as a clam at high water! I can say it if I want, no one will read this.

That is for now. I am glad I took this Record Book from a dead Rebel officer last week. I believe I will keep writing in it regular because . . .

Jim Brockmuller told me some boys have come across a Moonshine Still the Greys were running so there is going to be a lot of Liquid Joy tonight!

September 16, 1864

Early morning—the boys are sleeping off the battle for the Moonshine Whiskey Heights. I believe our officers were wise to let us drink after what we went through yesterday; anyway more fellows came to drink than expected—good news does travel fast!—and no one got enough to hear the owl hoot. It made our bellies warm though and our heads some light.

I can not sleep for thinking of the man I met last night. His name is Frank Leslie, a Reporter for *The New York Ledger*. He had heard about my part in the battle and came to ask questions to write about it in his News paper. I can not get over it. A story in a News paper read by thousands. About *me*. The folks in Pine Grove will be some surprised to read it, I imagine. Specially Mother: may be she will sing a warmer song now. And Mary Jane. It thrills me to think about her reading what I did. I would not show her this Record Book (or show it to any one) but if a News paper man wants to write about me I can not stop him. So long as I do not have to see or talk to all those people who read it; I want to be *Private* Halser all the way. But I do not object to a story in a News paper.

After he had introduced him self to me, Mr. Leslie said that several of the boys had "witnessed my heroic action" (as he put it) specially Private George Havers, Mill Town, Pennsylvania; that was nice of George, I thanked him later.

"He tells me that you turned the tide of battle almost single-handedly." Those were his words. It happened that I shot down nineteen Rebels, killing eleven including two officers, "throwing such confusion and dismay into the Southern ranks that they began to waver," as Mr. Leslie stated it. (I wrote down that hill of words soon after, so not to forget them.)

"Tell me, Private Halser," Mr. Leslie said. "What were you feeling during that engagement?"

"I was not feeling any thing," I answered. "I had little time for feeling."

"You felt no fear?" he asked me with surprise.

"No, sir," I told him. I explained that I do not know what that particular "emotion" feels like; he was even more surprised to hear that. May be I am odd, I fail to know. I was not even able to "build up" what I did. I suppose that was a dumb thing but I did not want to lie to him; not for a News paper. I had to tell him, in all truth, that I have had a lot of targets more hard to hit in my life. I agree they were not shooting back (which counts for *something*) but they were a H——— of a lot smaller and moving faster.

"To what do you refer?" he asked. Lord, to talk so savory!

I told him when I was a boy in Pine Grove (that made him smile because I believe he thinks I look like a boy now, though nineteen) I had to supply my family with meat, my father being dead. (I did not reveal the truth about Father as I do not believe Mother would be pleased to see it printed in a News paper.) Any way, with five brothers and one sister plus Mother that was some degree of meat to provide. So I had to learn to shoot All Mighty Straight All Mighty Soon or we would starve to death once Father was gone. Specially with the cock-eyed Ballard I had to use; it drifted like a d——— boat!

I told him how I learned to shoot when I was ten. He was right surprised by that. I can still see the expression on his face as he said, "*Ten?*"

"Yes, sir," I answered. "I was small for my age and all the bullies in the country side had them selves a frolic on me. I was black and blue so much some people thought I had a unknown disease."

I went on to tell him that, for Xmas 1855, my Uncle Simon gave me his worn out Maynard for a present and I made use of it first rattle out of the box. I practiced regular and it was some hard doing as well as my chores because I had to keep firing the same lead balls again and again. I did so, how ever, and in not too much time I learned to down a small bird on the wing.

"That was when I gathered all the bullies of the area to watch me shoot," I said to Mr. Leslie. "After that, the black and blue spots started fading."

We talked a while more and, at last, he asked what I planned to do with my self after the war was over. I told him I am not certain save one thing—I will not let my self be tied down but will live a fast, exciting life of some kind, that is for dead sure!

March 9, 1866

Another day gone off where ever days go when they end. It is some hard to recall when life had some excitement. H———, it is some hard to believe it *ever* had excitement. Here I am at home, the farm, the d——— chores—when I do them—Mother at me all the time to do more, do more. I have got to get out of here soon, I *mean* it.

I am sitting by candle light, writing in my Record Book. It started good in the War but is some thing to make a man sleep now. I feel tied down with ropes. I want to get away but Mother tells me (enough times to bury me) there are things I must take care of, I am the man of the house, she needs me, the family needs

me, may be if Father had not run off to California—words, words
shoveled at me night and day.

I feel my life is wasted. I am stuck here on this d—— farm in this
d—— community, I agreed to marry Mary Jane come Spring; I
do not even know how that took place, I swear I never said the actual
words, "Will you marry me?" but, some how, it has happened. I do
not know where we would live; Mother no doubt expects on the
farm. I would not want that but do not like the thought of trying to
work in Pine Grove either. I mean I love Mary Jane and all but feel
sick inside to see myself a married man and father growing old in
this dead place. What else can I *do* though?

Well this: I am thinking of leaving Pine Grove to go out West.
We hear each day, it seems, how much is going on out there. There
are new chances and all manner of excitement. I have got to give it
serious thought.

March 11, 1866

Just helped Ralph to bed. He is a good lad and I do not think will
tell Mother what happened tonight at the *Black Horse Tavern*. It
was good luck she was sleeping when we got home or I would be
on the taking end of a "word hiding" right now I am certain; not to
mention what poor Ralph would have to endure, being younger.

Ralph came to town to fetch me as Mother was angry at my absence all day and knew I was somewhere in Pine Grove drinking
and playing cards as I do, so she sent Ralph to bring me back for
a "good talking to" as she likes to call it—several hundred times a
week.

I was playing Seven Up with several of the boys when Ralph
came in. He walked behind my chair and said, "I have been looking for you, Clay."

"Good, you found me," I told him. "Now go home." I had been

drinking my fair share of whiskey and, what with losing cards, was feeling not to happy with my lot.

"Mother says she wants you to come home," Ralph said.

"Tell Mother I will come home when I am ready," I responded. "Now get out of here."

The other boys piped in and said the same, for Ralph to clear out, he was ruining the card game.

Ralph is not easy to push, how ever, and kept on ragging me. Mother says the north field needs plowing out for rocks, you promised long ago to do it. Mother says the roof is leaking and one of the windows. Mother says we need meat and on and on.

Finally, he started pulling at my sleeve and riled me proper, so I gave him a shove and he slipped on a wet spot on the floor and landed on his elbow. I guess it hurt something bad for he began to cry even though he is sixteen. At which the boys at the table started jibing him for being a Cry Baby. I told them to "lay off" but they continued doing so.

At this, Ralph got all wrathy—he has the Halser temper like us boys all do—even though he is as skinny as a corn stalk. He jumped up and to the table where he slapped the cards from Bob Fisher's hand, who had been the worst one, pretending to be Ralph and crying like a infant.

This got Bob Fisher good and mad so he got up and, when Ralph had a swing at him that missed, he punched Ralph on the nose and made it bleed.

I could not let that happen to my brother so I dropped my cards and jumped up. Bob turned just in time to get it on the jaw from my fist and go flying back, falling over Ralph.

This made Hannibal Fisher mad to see *his* younger brother hit so he jumped up and hit me on the head. I returned the favor, punching his left eye so he fell across the table we were playing on and knocked the cards and money all to H———.

Every one got wrathy then and I was fighting four of them.

Ralph was on my side, I guess, but little help. Every time he tried to give me aid, I got an extra blow or two because he hindered more than helped. I did the best I could, gave my share of hits and bruises, but there were too many what with Ralph no help and soon the two of us flew straight out through the bat wing doors and landed on the street. Ralph had bleeding from his mouth and nose. My head was ringing but I tried to make him stay outside so I could go back in and give a better account of myself, but Ralph insisted he would go along and we would "clean" the place out. I decided it was wiser to forget it, talked him out of it. He is a good lad but a bad joke as a fighter.

It is sad when a tavern dog fight (which I lose) is the best thing I have known in months!

March 14, 1866

I have just come back from Mary Jane's house and feel I have to say I am some low, fiendish being straight from H———!

That poor, sweet Angel of a girl deserves a better fellow than me. I love her dearly and admire her and she is ever kind to me—so why do I feel like a trap is just about to clamp shut on me? What is wrong with me? What is wrong with living here in Pine Grove for that matter? It is . . .

H——— and brimstone, I can not even finish that remark! Pine Grove is the dullest, dumbest place on God's Green Earth! I have got to go out West! I need to make my mind up—*do* it! I am not afraid to go, that is not it. It is because I do not want to make Mary Jane unhappy. Not to mention Mother who keeps talking of the wedding all the time now and how Mary Jane and me will share the farm and if I want to I can build a separate house and we will all be together—GOD! The more I think of it, the worse I feel!

Does Mary Jane complain how ever? No, not her. She is so sweet and understanding. She is an *Angel* and I know she had other offers. Why does she want *me*? She is such a fine person yet wants no more than to be Mary Jane Halser, make a happy home for me, bear and raise my children, and live her span by my side. What is wrong with that?

I have got to resolve my mind soon. I can not do this to her. Am I the master of my life or not? Do I want a life of excitement or not? *Am I going to go out West or not?*

If only some thing would make up my mind for me.

March 21, 1866

I can not believe it, looking back. It came so sudden and without a hint.

I was in the *Black Horse Tavern* playing Seven Up with several of the boys. Also in the game was Scoby Menlo, son of Truman Menlo, owner of The Pine Grove Mercantile and Shipping. I had not seen much of Scoby since the War but heard he was a hot head and a scoundrel; several of the local girls were got "in trouble" by him and their families paid off by his father.

I soon found out the truth of the report about his temper. I am not the coolest head around but he was worse. I had enjoyed a winning streak and built my pile to more than forty dollars. I was feeling good, thinking Mother would be pleased to see the money; I would claim it was an old loan paid to me or unexpected money from my Army pay.

Menlo was feeling other wise from me. His face got redder as we played. He slammed his cards on the table when he lost, and cursed, and drank his whiskey down like water.

Finally, it came. He glared at me and said, "I think some body at this table cheats at cards."

It did not take a college man to know he meant me since I was the only one who had a winning pile. I tried to ignore it though because I felt so good; I was some whiskey laden as well.

It did not end at that how ever. Shortly later, Menlo spoke again. "No one wins so much at cards unless they cheat," he said.

I could not pretend I did not understand those words and felt a low fire catching in my belly. "If you mean me," I said, "not only are you dead wrong but I want you to apologize for what you said."

He made a snorting noise like that was some joke I had spoken. The fire in my belly rose, I looked him in the eye and told him, "I believe you heard."

He stared at me, his cheeks a little redder now. I noted how his eyes reminded me of Beulah's (our pig) and considered telling him so.

"Yes, I heard," he said.

"Then do what I ask," I said.

"Apologize to you?" he answered with a sneering smile. "A card cheat?"

"You say that one more time," I told him, "and I will wipe the floor with you."

His face looked white now; I recall how fast the color left his cheeks. "Wrong," he said. His voice was shaking. *"I am going to wipe the floor with your blood."*

At that, he unbuttoned the front of his coat so I saw the handle of a six-shooter under his belt. He started reaching for it.

As quick as thought, I knew all talk was ended for there was no point in telling him I was not armed because he meant to kill me where I sat. That so, I leaped up fast and dived across the table at him, grabbing at his right hand and, by fortune, getting it before he could pull the gun free. He fell back on his chair, me on top of him, and we began to wrestle on the floor, he trying hard to get the gun so he might shoot me dead. I said nothing as we struggled for the will to murder was as clear as writing in his eyes.

I do not know how it happened but the gun went off like thunder; still inside his trousers and he screamed in pain. I jerked back and I saw a red stain at his stomach, spreading on his shirt so fast I knew the wound was fatal. Menlo tried to stand but had no strength to do it and he sat down, weak, his right hand over his stomach. He made a sound like he was going to cry. "You b——d," he said. "You killed me."

Moments after, he slumped back on the floor, cold dead.

I stared at him, heart beating so hard it hurt my chest. I had never killed any one face to face and it was terrible to know I had.

No one made a move. I can not guess how long we stood, silent as a cemetery, looking down at Menlo and the puddle of blood around his body.

Then Donald Bell (the bar tender) said some thing about the Constable. At his words, I felt an extra blow of fright inside my heart because I knew Scoby's father having so much power, he would see me hang for sure.

I turned and ran outside to jump on Kit. I rode home in a lather and told Mother what happened. She was no help to me, only saying, "I knew it. I knew it—" following me around the house while I gathered some clothes and my Record Book and flung them in a sack. I told her I had to take Kit but she did not seem to hear my words. She kept saying, "I knew it. I knew it—" like that would help me. I felt sick to hear her so uninterested in what happened and gave up trying to explain.

I did not want to wake my brothers or Nell so kissed their cheeks as they slept and turned away from them. I tried to kiss Mother but she pushed me off, looking angry though tears ran on her cheeks and saying those words again. I came close to tears my self at that. "Well, goodbye then!" I shouted. "If that is all I mean to you!"

I wanted to stop at Mary Jane's house to explain what happened but, near Pine Grove, I could see an armed pursuit preparing and was forced to pull the horse around and gallop for the Wabash River.

I have stopped to rest Kit for a while and write this down by moonlight; I will be an easy target if they see me.

God have mercy on me, it is done now. I am off the plank and have to swim alone. I wondered what will happen to me. Will they over take and capture me? Will I hang for Scoby's try to murder me? Where will I go now?

D———! The answer is so clear, I feel a fool for even wondering. *West!*

July 12, 1866

I am in Morgan City, Kansas. I have only the dinero (which means money, I learned) to sleep tonight and buy some food but still feel *good*. This place is Alive! It may be just a dirty trail town but I never saw the like, so Pine Grove seems as far away as Russia!

There is one Main Street. On each side sit saloons, gambling houses, dance halls, cafes, theatres, stables, horse trade corrals, stores, hotels. Not one building looks like it will last a year, all give the feel of being built last week.

And the men and women! Every kind a person could imagine. Cow boys with their Ten Gallon hats, merchants in their white shirts, buffalo hunters in their bloody ones, gamblers in their fancy duds, the street seems never empty of them! Also women like I never saw in Pine Grove. Dance hall girls and actresses and "worse," not many high tones here though you see a few. But I like them all and like this town! It took me long to get here, had to sell my saddle, then sell Kit, work at different jobs but here I am and mean to stay.

I know that I am going to find a life of excitement now!

July 14, 1866

Did not have one shin plaster in my pocket so have taken work in a saloon, *The Red Dog*. I am clean up man and—may be—relief bar tender. It is not what you would call a "fancy" position but beggers can not be choosers—as Mother liked to say—and I am in the begger group all right until I earn some dollars.

The regular bar tender is a tall, thin fellow, Jim Clements by name. He gave me a dollar of his own to find a place to live so I am going to take up in a boarding house run by a Mrs. Kelly, not bad.

I start tonight.

July 16, 1866

I can not believe it! I have seen it happen after only four days here!

I was talking to Jim Clements while behind the bar; just brought out a tray of glasses from washing them. I told him how exciting Morgan City was compared to Pine Grove and he nodded at my words.

"Yes, that is how it is in cow towns," he observed. "All this H—— raising is common because these towns are made so cow boys can blow off steam at the end of cattle drives."

"I never saw so much going on," I said, "not since the War."

And that is G——d's truth! Cow boys crowd the streets by hundreds, some big drive having ended. They fill saloons and gambling houses and what Jim calls "Pleasure Domes"; that is a funny name for crib houses.

"These cow boys have a lot of 'pent up' action in their blood," Jim said. "They want to have them selves a blow out before riding out for more long months of hardship on the plains." He reminds me, by his words, of that reporter in the War, what was his name? I will look it up, hold on.

Frank Leslie.

Any way, we talked on and I told him that I like the West a lot but cow boy life did not appeal to me.

"No, a man has to have a taste for it," Jim admitted.

We went on some more about Morgan City. Since its money comes from "walking beef" as Jim referred to them, and from the men who "walk" them, no one aims to see the town "domesticated" as Jim called it. Even the peace officer is told by Main Street owners not to step on cow boy toes.

His name is Hickok called "Wild Bill." It seems I heard of him but I am not sure. Jim says he came out from Illinois and was the scout for a General named Custer. Jim says he (Hickok) has built him self a reputation as a man to be accounted for in any "show down." Still he does not make efforts to preserve the peace except for may be outright murder. Which occurs a good bit here, Jim said. "A word and a blow too often turns into a word and a shot—" was how he put it.

And, of all strange things, he said it and—in *seconds*—that very thing took place in front of me!

A big, tall, ugly cow boy started arguing with some man Jim said (later) worked in a livery stable down the street. I could hardly believe what they argued about. Like this—

"And I say cows is stupider—" The cow boy.

"And *I* say *horses*—" The livery stable man.

"Well, what do *you* know?" said the cow boy. "I *live* with the G—— d—— stupid critters and I say horses can read *books* compared to cows!"

"Well, I take *care* of horses night and day and nothing on this whole wide world is dumber than those G—— d—— buzzard heads!" the other man replied.

I thought it all right and funny and was chuckling (so was Jim) when, in a flash, the two men started cursing at each other, then shoving, then the cow boy pulled his gun and shot the livery stable man right in the chest. There was a cloud of dark smoke but I saw the livery man knocked back on the floor. The cow boy fired his gun so close it set the dead man's shirt on fire.

I admit I stood behind the counter like a statue. I know what killing is. I shot those soldiers in the War and, though not intended, had to do with Menlo's death. But that was over *something*; Menlo called me a cheat at cards and made the threat of wiping the floor with my blood. This was over *nothing*, the brains of cows and horses for G———d's sake! Still the livery stable man is no less dead than if there had been reason to it.

Jim has seen this kind of thing before, it was clear: he filled a stein with beer and leaned across the counter to dump it on the dead man's shirt, then did the same again and put the fire out. All the time he did, the ugly cow boy was glaring around like daring any one to say him wrong.

Jim was first to speak. "You better clear out or you'll likely be arrested, charged, and hanged," he said.

The cow boy did not like to hear this; he looked like a red-faced savage, I believe the blood lust had got into him. "Don't tell me to clear out," he said.

"You better pull your freight," Jim told him. His tone was peaceful and did not seem distressed but there was a look in his black eyes that did not mean well for the cow boy, I believed.

The cow boy did not see the look. "I am warning you, you skinny, no account b———d," he said.

"Would you rather I sent for Hickok?" Jim asked.

"Sure, you yellow-livered son of a b———h," the cow boy said. "Get somebody else to help you."

Jim only looked at him. The cow boy had a mean smile; he was full of "forked lightning." "If you had the guts of a pig, you would meet me outside, man to man," he said.

"Is that what you want?" Jim asked.

"Come outside and I will meet you smoking," was the cow boy's answer.

Jim did not reply but reached beneath the counter and picked up a .41 revolver kept in case of someone trying robbery. The cow boy twitched, then stepped back, Jim slipping the gun beneath his waistband and, with no word, heading for the bat wing doors. The cow boy looked some stupid watching; I think he was amazed that Jim accepted him. Then he cursed, and spat, and said "All right!" and swaggered for the doors.

I hurried after them and got a spot outside the door.

It did not last long. Jim and the cow boy stood about nine feet apart on the street off the plank walk, looking at each other. The cow boy said, "You b——d! *Die!*" and grabbed down at his gun. Jim reached for his, the cow boy pulled first but was shaking, I believe. There was a roaring shot from his gun, then another from Jim's and, for moments, I could not see clearly for the cloud of powder smoke. Then I saw the cow boy on his knees, thrown back. He made a sound of pain and fell to his right side, cursing, and dying.

Jim incurred a powder burn across the left sleeve of his shirt. He rubbed it as he walked past me, saying, "Never leave the counter untended." I watched in awe as he returned to his spot and put the .41 away, started pouring whiskey for a customer. He is a chunk of steel and anyone who strikes him will strike fire, that is sure.

I could never be as brave as that.

August 9, 1866

It has been a slow few weeks. I am beginning to think excitement is not ahead of me after all. The job is boring at *The Red Dog*; there is nothing to it which I do not mind but it is dull. If Jim was not there I feel I would move on.

I like him though and believe I can account him as my friend. He does not say much of him self but I have learned he comes from Pennsylvania, fought in the Army of the Potomac, incurred a shrapnel wound at Gettysburg (has a scar on his back, he told me), never married, is a loner.

He is nice to me. I do not know how old he is (thirty-five may be) but he is like a sort of father. He has bought me dinner twice,

gives me good advice on how to get by, and there was the day we
took that ride together on rented horses I liked a lot.

Still, life in total is dull. I almost feel the way I did in Pine
Grove. Morgan City is a wilder place but not that wild; that cow
boy thing I saw is all there was. I am twice now to the Golden
Temple but did not like the girls each time, they are too rough and
out spoken for my taste, also one stole a dollar from me, I am sure.
Jim says what can you expect from them?

Now what?

August 11, 1866

Finally some thing different in my life.

Last night was my night off so I went to the Fenway Circus
which has stopped in Morgan City. I was much pleased by the
chance as I have not done much of pleasure since arrival having to
collect hard money after taking part in that game of Black Jack
I was lucky to come out of with my teeth.

Any way, I was excited and went running down the street to
town edge where the circus was set up. In dashing on the grounds,
I bumped into a tall man in a black suit and, as luck would have
it, it was no man else but Hickok, a tall fellow with drooping mustache, not bad looking—but what a temper! I thought, first, he was
going to shoot me, then kick or hit me but he settled for a "dressing down" my ears have not heard since that Sergeant, training for
the War. Hickok has more than guns in his arsenal, he has cuss
words in such number and array as few men possess and I believe
he used them all on me at once.

I did not like it, made me simmer some but, after all, he is the
Marshal and had two guns. I had nothing. If there had been a
weapon in my pocket, I might not—H———, what am I saying? I
would have "called him out"? Not likely for his pale blue eyes are
not too pleasant as they bore at you, so I let him have it out and

took it all without a peep. As said, I did not like it, who does to have your skin flayed off by someone's tongue, still what could I do?

When he turned and stormed away from me, I took a breath; which was how I saw a woman nearby, smiling at me. I suppose she saw the whole event. I did not think what to do until she said. "Don't let him bother you. He has a hard job and his nerves are rubbed thin."

At that I smiled back and we introduced our selves. She said her name was Hazel Thatcher, she and her husband are perform-ers with the circus, doing bare back riding. She was fine looking I saw, with a head of red hair very handsome. We had a chat, quite nice, then she held her hand out, said she hoped I would enjoy the show. She seemed to hold my hand a little longer than I would suppose but decided that was imagined.

Enjoy the show I did! Well worth each penny of the dollar and fifty cents though I have little dinero to spare. I confess I spent a good deal of the show looking for the arrival of Hazel Thatcher and, when she arrived, all the time she was performing staring at her in her costume which was less than eyes could believe! She is one grand figure of a woman, that is certain, every curve complete. Her costume, as noted, brief as law will bear and all the men went crazy over her, whistling and stamping; no louder than a certain party in the front row, initials C.H. She is graceful as a bird as well. She and her husband, Carl (mostly her, he seemed less lively), did leaps, and somersaults, and capers on the back of a galloping horse to much thunderlike clapping; my palms were red and stinging after they went off.

Following the performance, I sat a long time in the tent, not wanting to depart, savoring the show like some kind of feast I was digesting. In truth, I hoped (did not admit to my self at first) that Hazel Thatcher would appear so I might tell her I thought she was a fine acrobat and beautiful lady. She never did show up though and, at last, the workers told me to be on my way, they had to "strike" the tent.

I went outside, the grounds were dark and no one anywhere in sight. I strolled across them and, in walking around a wagon, of all things, came upon Hazel Thatcher and her husband. I saw then why his movements were not lively in the show—he was drunk, she leading him, one arm around him; I could smell his breath from feet away.

I felt embarrassed to come on them in that way but Hazel Thatcher seemed pleased to see me, asked right off if I would help her take her husband to their wagon.

I said I would be glad to, grabbed his left arm while she held his right. His legs were made of rubber it appeared and various times he almost fell. He kept muttering, "This is not necessary—" in a kind of dignified voice; but it *was* necessary since he would have toppled if we had not held him up.

"This is very nice of you," Hazel Thatcher told me as we led her husband.

I still was embarrassed. "I am very glad to help," I said.

"This is not necessary," said her husband.

"He has been feeling pain from a broken leg which never healed right," Hazel Thatcher told me. "That is why he drinks a little more than good for him."

I nodded.

"This is not necessary," said her husband as he almost fell again.

It took a while to get him up the steps of their wagon and I wondered how the man was able to perform in such a state until Hazel Thatcher told me he had started drinking heavily after the show was ended and I recalled that I had sat inside the tent long enough for a minister to paint his nose.

At last we got Carl Thatcher on his bunk and he went off to sleep, was snoring in a second. Hazel Thatcher thanked me and

I said that I was pleased to be of service, started to back out of the wagon when she asked me to help her light the hanging lantern which I did.

I confess to being raptured by the sight of oil light on her face. Her skin is very white and clear, eyes green as jade with long red hair falling on her shoulders. I have never seen a woman so beautiful in all respects. I stared at her, she smiled and touched my cheek. "You are very handsome," she said.

I had no reply, I felt a stupid boy again. Hazel Thatcher smiled (what teeth!) and asked if I would care to have a cup of coffee with her. Well, to tell the world I would have said "yes" if she asked me if I cared to have a cup of poison with her. "Yes, thank you," I replied.

She told me sit down at the table (very small) and I did while she removed her cloak. She looked around then, I had made a gasping noise because she still had on her costume and the sight of her white shoulders and bosom tops caused me to catch my breath. She smiled at me, leaned over and kissed my cheek (she did!). "You are very sweet and young," she said, those were actual words. I remember shivering though far from cold.

I did not hear her words too well as she prepared the coffee, I was too entranced in looking at her, I mean close up she was so remarkable to look at, she made me feel (the only word that catches it) *hungry*. I did not hear the snoring of her husband which was loud, I was so much fascinated by her looks, the truth is I have never seen the like, not ever.

What did she say? (I said nothing, a staring lump.) I think she said her husband once was a star performer in a Europe circus, drank occasional but not much. His wife was killed in an accident during a performance and he had lost interest in life, began to drink for real because he thought her death his fault. The circus let him go, then another, and he ended up in the United States where he took a job with another circus, his reputation as a bare back rider ahead of his reputation as a drinker, in this country any way.

He kept on drinking and that circus let him go and the next one hiring him was Fenway Circus where he met Hazel Moore (her previous name). They married and, for some while, he seemed better, taught her all the bare back tricks and things looked bright. But he started "hitting at" the whiskey vat again and now is hanging by a thread since he managed to be close to sober for performances and Fenway is a small circus any way. (I guess I did hear almost every word in spite of staring!) So it was not his leg he drank for, I learned.

Hazel Thatcher told me all these things without a single cruel word and I do admire her for that, not tearing at her husband who could not defend himself but being thoughtful of the reason for his weakness.

I would not say more if I was telling this to some one but this is my own Record Book and no one will ever read it being my private concern. So I continue and reveal that Hazel Thatcher (I feel dumb to call her full name as things are) asked me if I cared to have a "jot" of whiskey in my coffee which I said I would not mind. We talked and talked (I do not remember much of that, mostly she asked questions, where I came from, what I had done, what I planned to do) and it was not too long before she added coffee to our whiskey, then forgot the coffee all together.

By then, my head was numb, the wagon seemed to move some under me and, in the lantern light, I thought Hazel the most matchless woman in the world and told her so.

I remember she was holding both my hands on the table, tears in her eyes. "Oh, Clay, it is so hard to be without a man because my husband only cares for drink," she said.

"I'm sorry, I am sorry," I told her.

She drew my hands closer to her self, it was a small table so I could lean further. "I am so lonely all the time," she said, tears rolling down her cheeks.

"Oh, I am sorry," I said. I wanted to say I would take care of her but even roostered as I was, I knew my self to be a clean up man in a saloon and no more.

"Thank you, my dear," Hazel said. She lifted my right hand to her lips and kissed it. Then she kissed my left hand. Then she leaned forward at me. "Please," she whispered.

What I was feeling at that time! I bent forward and her warm, red lips pressed to mine, I tasted her breath, then again and harder; I have never had a girl (woman) kiss like that.

I jumped a little as she pulled back, pushing up the table where I saw she hooked it up, then, with a sigh, fell against me and held my arms and we were kissing fierce, my arms around her and her lips came apart and—Oh, I must pause!

All right, to the finish. (I will burn this Record Book before a human soul shall read it!) We kissed and kissed and Hazel drew down her costume so her b——s were bared, all white and heavy and, before I knew it, we were on her bunk, both n——d as our days of birth. G—— in Heaven, she is such a gorgeous female and her body is—well, private Record Book or not, I can not put it down what happened. All I will say is I lost my head and every thing and did not even care her husband was asleep and snoring only several feet away from us, the wagon rattling, rocking as we—did not even *care*!

I remained with her until the middle of the night and four times "claimed" her; or did she claim me? She is some fiery person, those two girls in The Golden Temple seem like dull goats. To be honest, it was the first time I could think of Mary Jane and not feel bad because I know she could not give me any thing what Hazel did because she is a different sort; I will not go into fine points but I *will* say Hazel—

(*Here I must omit three paragraphs which, in their vivid clinical description, are unsuitable for the general reader. F.L.*)

I returned to my room at nearly five o'clock and slept like two men in a grave yard. Now it is past one o'clock, afternoon, I have to go to work soon but must write down what I remember.

I suppose she is much older than me but I love her. I love
Hazel Thatcher and can not wait 'til I see her again!

+━━━━+

Later: same day. It appears that many things can happen at the
same time.

When I went to work tonight it was to find the *Red Dog* burning. Jim was across the street, watching it so I walked over to him
to ask what happened.

Much to my surprise, he told me he had set the fire him self! He
said the owner of *The Red Dog* (Mr. German, I have not met)
played poker with him last night and lost a pile but did not care to
pay it honest there fore hired some trail bum to bushwhack Jim.
The trail bum was stupid, missed, and Jim "took care" of him, then
went to the saloon, threw down oil lamps, setting them ablaze. He
said he would shoot Mr. German like the cur he is (if he could find
him) but it would likely bring on wrath from Hickok who is paid by
men like Mr. German so he set the saloon on fire instead.

I asked Jim what he meant to do now for employment. He
replied he planned "returning to an earlier pursuit"—stage coach
driving, said if I am half the rifle shot as I have told him (clearly he
does not believe it) I could hire out as guard.

I might do it but for Hazel. I would rather have a job so I can
stay nearby her. I admit the idea does appeal to me—being guard,
I mean. But Hazel first and fore most.

August 12, 1866

What did I write the other day? Let me look. That many things can
happen at the same time. What I meant—a person's life goes on
and on the same and then, no warning, every thing is changed.

Now another. I went to the circus to see Hazel, took a while to
get her to my self because of Carl, he was not very drunk tonight.
I told her about the coach guard job and said I did not mean to

take it for I wanted to be with her, asked her to find out if there was some job I could do with the circus so we could be together when ever Carl is drunk or may be she might think to leave him some time if it worked out, her and me.

We were out behind the tents and Hazel was so quiet I wondered what was wrong and asked. I heard a sound of her swallowing in her throat, that is how still it was. Finally, she drew a long breath in and said, "I can not let you do that, Clay."

I failed to know what she was meaning.

"Don't you see how painful it would be for me to have you around when I am married to Carl?" she said.

I began to say again about her may be leaving Carl but she pressed hard against me, hugging me. "Oh, no, my darling," she declared. "You have your own life to lead."

I tried to answer but she went on. "You are much too bright to waste your life being a circus roust about," she said.

"I don't mind," I told her. "It will be—"

"No, no." She shook her head, then kissed me on the lips. "I can not permit it. You have a full life ahead of you."

"But, Hazel—"

"Please, my darling, no," she said.

"But I love you," I told her. "I want to be—"

"And *I* love *you*," she said, "with all my heart, Clay. That is why I can not do this to you."

"But—"

"For another thing, I am too old for you," she said.

"No," I said, protesting. "We could—"

She stopped my talking with another kiss. "No, no," she said. "I could not bear to see you looking at me as the months went by and you began to see me as I am."

"As you am?—you *are*?!" I asked; I was so worked up by then I could not speak a proper English.

She held me tight, I held her tight. "Just remember me as one who crossed your path," she said.

"But, Hazel!"

"No, no," she said, and kissed me once more. "Go quickly," she told me. "And do not look back."

She was the one who went quickly, with a sob, into the night. I stood there feeling sick. I wanted to run after her and make her change her mind but I was not able to move, I felt my legs were anvils.

I do not understand. She says she loves me and I love her; isn't that enough? There is an aching in my chest; I wonder if hearts really break. Oh, G———, I feel so miserable! Is poor Hazel in her wagon now, crying? Does her heart ache too? She is doing this for Carl, I know it. She is sacrificing her self for him, so bravely.

I will never be the same again.

My hand is shaking as I write this, still weak from what happened but I want to put it down while still fresh in mind.

What did I say a few months back?—several times while writing in this Record Book, it seems. That I wanted excitement? Well, I have got it and double.

In truth, I never thought the like would happen. My writing in this book has been enough to put a reader (if there was one) to dead sleep. First it was exciting to ride the driver's seat with Jim, armed with pistols and my new Winchester (I am glad I got it rather than carrying a shotgun as suggested by some including Jim), but soon the jolting on my backside and eating dust became a pain.

Also nothing happened, I mean *nothing*. We picked up passengers and shipment, carried them from place to place, stayed overnight at road ranches, or long enough for meals, changed teams at relay stations, traveled thirty-five miles about each eight hours and that was it. The closest to excitement came that time I thought a road agent was stopping us and got ready for action to find out it was a cow boy whose horse had stepped into a chuck hole and broke its leg so had to be shot leaving him afoot. That was my excitement since I started in August as noted in this Record Book.

Again, as in *The Red Dog*, if it was not for Jim I would have quit. But I have written endless of his skill and handling as much as eight "ribbons" at once, and skill at cracking the whip so close he can remove a small fly from a horse's ear never touching the ear. Also have written endless of our talks, and how we know each other well, and are good friends so no more of that.

We were talking when it happened, coming down a grade from Black Rock Pass about seven miles from Fort Dodge. As I recollect, we were discussing Hazel. I was telling Jim I had recovered from the pain but still feel Hazel is a fine woman who is sacrificing herself for her husband.

"Yes, I know the kind," Jim said and I could tell he understood.

I noticed then that he was glancing around. "What are you looking for?" I asked.

"Not for. At," he answered.

I looked around but did not see a thing. "At what?" I asked.

"Twenty or so Cheyenne," he answered.

I felt my heart bump at these words and looked around more carefully. I saw some movement in the distance; horses and riders it appeared.

"Did they just show up?" I asked.

"No," Jim told me. "They have been trailing us all afternoon."

I was amazed to hear that, which makes it certain I will never be a stage driver or guard of any value. I felt a fool to hear it but pretended not by asking Jim why the Red Skins did not rush us if they wanted to—they had us beaten in numbers.

"They will probably make their move before we get much closer to the Fort," he said.

His words came true before another fifteen minutes had gone by. I felt myself shiver as the Red Skins started riding in at us, galloping their ponies. I raised my rifle but Jim said wait 'til they were closer which I did.

Soon the Cheyennes—twenty-one—were galloping across our path and moving in a line like a traveling circle which, in time, they started to draw in like a noose around our coach. I raised my

Winchester again but Jim said not to waste my powder as the "breech clouts" were still not close enough to us. I thought they were; they were no further than those Secesh soldiers I was able to hit during the War, still it is true these targets were moving more.

"Pass down mail sacks to the people and tell them to barricade them selves," Jim told me. He cracked his whip and the team of six (I wished there were eight) leaned forward in their traces, moving faster.

I put my rifle in its boot and started handing down the mail sacks to the four passengers, telling them—as Jim told me—to look to what ever weapons they might have as it was likely they were going to have to defend them selves.

Before forgetting, I must put down that, though this was the first time I have been in mortal danger since the War (the event with Menlo happened too fast for me to feel anything), the emotion I had in those long ago days came rushing back full force— no fear what ever; I felt keyed up and anxious for the battle to commence. It is only now I see how dangerous it was and find it strange I did not feel it as such.

Then I was all pitched up for the fighting. I remember shouting at those Red Skins as they rode in their moving circle, getting closer and closer. "Come on, you b——s!" I yelled. "We are ready for you!"

Finally, they did—with a series of blood-curdling "whoops"—and the battle was on! "*Now* start firing!" Jim shouted. "And show me how good you are!"

It was a fierce battle because those Red Skins do know how to ride and they can duck while riding which makes shooting at them not an easy task. They also shoot not bad for savages; I wonder where they got their rifles and who taught them.

Jim drove the coach as fast as the team could pull it, cracking his whip across their heads so that it sounded like the firing of a pistol. The coach creaked awful as we sped; there was a woman passenger inside who screamed in fright. The rocking and skidding did not help my shooting either, nor the shooting of the passengers; I do not believe their firing hit a single Red Skin.

So it was up to me and I must say I did all right! I kept on firing at those Cheyennes and that Winchester is some good weapon! No matter how those Indians galloped or dipped or ducked, I kept on hitting them one by one; I think it all took place in only minutes too, though noisy minutes what with the thunder of the hooves, and wheels creaking, and the woman screaming, shots, and howling Savages, it was a scene straight out of H———! Yet even so I gave seven of the Red Skins one-way tickets to their Happy Hunting Ground, finally—I believe—impressing Jim with what I told him I could do but he had never seen me do. For he yelled and whooped him self and even laughed once which I hardly ever hear him do.

The last Cheyenne I got appeared to have a charmed life for he kept on riding at us with a lance to throw. I kept missing and the woman in the coach was screaming out of her mind before the Red Skin was only ten feet or so away and I was able to shoot him off his horse. He went tumbling and another Cheyenne pony trampled on him. After that, the Indians slowed down and gave up; may be he was Chief or some thing though he had no Head Dress on.

Speaking of charmed lives, mine held up; well, almost. In the War, despite the Minnie balls around me and many explosions, I was not touched. This time, with only twenty-one Red Skins, I took an arrow in my right leg underneath the knee which is odd because I never felt it 'til the Cheyenne left us be. By then, how ever, I had lost some lot of blood (my boot was full of it) and things began to swim around me so I almost toppled from the seat to my death, I am sure, under heavy wheels. Jim grabbed me by the belt and held me from falling while he drove. That is one I owe him as he no doubt saved my life.

He also may have saved my leg (the Doctor said) for, when the Indians had moved off, Jim stopped the coach to bind my leg and "cauterize" the place the arrow went in. He broke off the back part of the arrow, pulled it out, then opened a bullet and poured its powder into the wound. It is lucky for me I was almost "out" any way for if I knew what he was going to do I would have given him a fight. Because when he set fire to the powder, I had a pain as I have never known in all my life, and screamed just like that woman (I am not ashamed to tell it), and passed out cold. Jim put me in the coach, my leg wrapped with his bandanna and drove me to the Fort where now I am.

I am writing this from bed. The Doctor says my wound is not too serious but I will be "out of action" for a while.

September 19, 1866

Jim came in to see me, brought some candy and a news paper to read. There is a little story in it of the "Indian Attack On Stage" and how a "Mr. Cley Halsem" shot some of the "pursuing Savages" to help "save the day." Give credit to that Cley Halsem, he is one fine shot, who ever he is.

Jim said the company has replaced me as guard on his run which does not please me but he said he talked them into giving me a post as helper at the Blue Creek Way Station. The work will not be hard, they told Jim, odds and ends, and when I have recovered from my leg wound I will get back my job as guard, I hope with Jim again; he says he will request it.

I start at Blue Creek next Monday so guess all is well for now.

+>→→<+

Little did Clay know. F.L.

October 8, 1866

Another rotten day. Leg hurts like H——. Zandt knows I have been hit there by an arrow but does not seem to care a d——, has me on my feet constant, day and night. He woke me up last night after sleeping only two hours, said a coal oil lamp exploded in the Station house, wanted me to clean the mess. I tried to tell him I was tired having worked since six o'clock yesterday morning but he shoved me hard and said, "I vant it *now*, vare stayin?—(what ever that means) so had to rise to do it. He is a real b——d for certain.

October 10, 1866

I swear he did it on purpose, knocked that deck of cards all over the floor just to make me pick them up.

October 11, 1866

He yelled at me in front of all those people because some one had knocked the soap on the dirt instead of putting it on the dish out-side as if it was my fault. I know he did it to "show off" in front of two lady passengers to make them think how big a man he is. I hate him.

October 13, 1866

I think my leg is getting worse. I limp more now than when I came and it aches some thing fierce, some times bleeds a little, cracking open. You think that means a d—— to Zandt? "Vat are you, *cripple*, Halzer? *Move!*"—and shoves me on the back.

Lying here, never more "washed out" in all my days. A spider crawling on my leg, I am too tired to brush it off.

October 14, 1866

Heard today, from a passing driver, that, before I came, there was a Mexican named Juan who was helper. Zandt made his life so miserable he took off one night without pay or belongings, never has been seen again. I can understand. I would leave my self but my leg is hurting terrible and I could not walk. I would not steal a horse, that is too dangerous out here, better kill a man than steal a horse. I do not have enough dinero to buy a stage ride out allowing Zandt would let me go. So what can I do?

He rags me some thing awful. Mother was a angel compared. He limps like I do but worse when I am around with people watching. If it was not for my d——d wound I would go at him full tilt. The way it is, I will be lucky if he does not ruin my leg for life.

I can not go regardless but if I could I do not think I would; that would be running from him and I will never do that from a bully.

Oh, the H——.

October 16, 1866

Too tired to write. Zandt has been at me all day. I have been working like a mule since five o'clock this morning, now is past eleven at night. I must *sleep*.

October 17, 1866

Some thing new, worse. I am ready to do some thing *hard* in return, I swear I am. Leg aches like a tooth ache but I can not pull it out like a tooth can be.

Today, when the afternoon run from Leonardville came by, Zandt grabbed me in front of every body and wrestled me, threw me on the floor. I landed on my left elbow which is swelling and now also aches. D—— him any way! I wish I could pump lead into him like I did those Cheyennes! He is too big to fist fight. G—— d——, he is a son of a b——!

October 19, 1866

I do not know how much more I can stand. I feel close to murder. Zandt is the worst bully I have known in my life. Menlo was a comrade compared. Zandt does all these things:

1. He over works me.
2. He under feeds me.
3. He makes fun of my limp.
4. If I feel sick or weak, he mocks me.
5. He shoves me around and hits me on the back a lot.
6. He rags me in front of passengers and wrestles me, knowing I am too weak to resist.
7. How to say this? There is some thing "odd" about him. When he is not ragging me or bullying and has a few drinks "under his belt," he puts an arm around me, hugs me like a girl and says I am "a good-looking young fellow." Once touched me in a certain spot.

I made it certain I will not stand for this. That only makes him wrathy and he throws me around some more. Today he flung me down so hard my leg wound cracked again and blood leaked out.

I am getting close to some thing and do not like what I feel close to. I will not run off no matter what, like some cur with my tail between my legs. Yet I am not strong enough to give him back his own "brand" of medicine.

Some thing has to break.

What Clay could not have known, which I have now established, is that Emil Zandt had been an officer in the Prussian Army and been dishonorably discharged for attempting "liaisons" with certain of the more youthful men in his command.

Additionally, it should be noted (since Clay does not), that Zandt was a giant of a man, some six feet four or five inches in height and weighing in excess of two hundred and fifty pounds. As stated earlier, Clay Halser was no taller than five feet ten and, at the time, because of his hampered convalescence, weighed at least a hundred pounds less than the hulking German.

Lastly, it is noteworthy to observe that Clay rejected the notion of retreat; typical of him. In retrospect, it seems that, surely, there was some way he might have backed off from the situation. As it turned out, although his consequent action is understandable (if not justifiable), it forged yet one more heavy link in the chain which was, one day, to hold him fast in its tangled length.

October 23, 1866

It is ended and I am not sorry. If I fry in H———— for it, I will not say that I am sorry for what happened.

It started as the night stage from Stockdale came in so the passengers could warm them selves and eat some food. It was bitter cold with whistling wind and people came in quickly, stood before the crackling fire and warmed their bodies while I helped prepare the food and drink.

As always, Zandt began to "put on" for the passengers, the women mostly (there were two), showing them how he could rag me as he chose. He had been drinking all the day and put his hand on me once, which I knocked off so his face got red with anger; he was in a black mood.

He was never worse, pretending to the passengers he was a rogue and full of fun instead of the b————d he was. He kept punching my arm and slapping me on the back, knocking me off balance, being "jovial" as he said.

When every one was eating, he began to wrestle me and hold me tight to make me look the fool I was, so helpless in his arms. His face was red and white in patches, and his whiskey breath steamed on my face, and made me sick.

I got so mad I twisted hard and was able to break free which surprised him, I believe; he did not realize I was some stronger in spite of little sleep and food.

"Zo," he said. "You are ze little *worm* tonight." He laughed to show the people he was playing at a game but I knew he was not playing, not from the look in his red pig eyes, like Menlo. I had never noticed 'til then.

He moved at me and I backed off. "Zo," he said. "You think you can outvit me."

He reached for me but I slapped his big, fat hand aside. This made him frothy that I gave him back so much because it hurt his pride; he did not like to have me giving back what he liked "dishing out." He kept moving at me and I told him leave off, I did not want any more.

That made him crazy, I believe, to hear me talking up in front of all those people, mostly the women. He lunged at me and I dodged side ways, knowing if he caught me he would do his best to hurt me and could squeeze so hard with me in his arms he might crack my ribs.

"Oh, leave the young man alone," one of the women said.

That got all Zandt's bristles up for sure. He did not pretend he was all jovial now. He looked as mean as he was feeling and that was much. He began to stalk me around the room, ignoring any one who said to stop.

He jumped at me, I side stepped but he stuck his leg out so I tripped. I fell down on my right leg and the pain was like the arrow sticking in there when it happened and the powder being burned there. I cried out and he laughed at that. "Vot's the matter, little boy, *hurt* your self?" he said.

I pushed to my feet and he stepped in, started pushing me around, jostling me, and slapping me across the shoulders, "straight arming" my chest, and knocking me backward 'til I hit the wall. By then the pain in my leg was crazing me and, as he stopped in front of me, I made a fist of my right hand and hit him in the face as hard as I could.

That broke the dam. Jumping at me with a curse, he started squeezing me so hard I could not breathe and knew I would pass out. There was nothing I could do, so had to jerk my knee up at his ——— and hit him there as hard as possible. He cried out, backing off, and clutching there in spite of ladies watching. "Zon of a b———," he muttered, "zon of a b———."

He leaped at me but I jumped to the side and he fell on his knees, slipping. The pain of that was too much for him and he bellowed like a bull. Staggering up, he turned away from me, at first to my surprise, then cold dismay as I saw where he headed—to the counter where he kept his horse whip underneath.

Snatching it up, he shook it loose, glaring at me with his pig eyes, breathing heavy.

"Put that away," the stage coach driver said. "There are passengers here."

Zandt gave no attention to him, his eyes intent on me. I started easing toward the door but he was shrewd and cut me off, a mad smile on his lips. *"Zo,"* he said. "You want to *run?"*

I knew he had me and I wondered what to do. I can not say I was afraid but knew that he could cut me to shreds with that whip of his.

The stage coach driver moved at him. "Zandt, *stop* this," he declared.

The next instant, Zandt had brushed him aside like a child and the driver was flying across the room to almost crash into the fire place.

"Now, *girl man,"* Zandt said, and began to flick the whip as he stalked me like his prey.

I did not say one word, knowing it was useless. I kept my eyes on him as he came nearer.

"Now I crack your crust, you little scum," he said.

The whip end shot out, snapping like a pistol shot near my face.

"Stop it!" cried a woman which made Zandt the madder; now his face was closer to purple than red.

He started cracking out the whip end harder, snapping it closer and closer. I tried to grab it but it only tore a chunk of skin from my palm. The passengers were all up from the table now and backed against the wall, several calling for Zandt to stop which he would never do at that point.

Suddenly, the whip end lashed across my neck and I felt fiery pain.

"*Got* you, girl man!" Zandt cried; I never saw a look so wild, not even on the faces of those Cheyennes.

The whip end snapped again and tore a piece of shirt arm off me and the skin beneath. Fury made *me* crazy now and I began to hurl things at him, dishes, candle holders, fire irons, stools, any thing I could lay hands on. Some hit him, making him more angry yet. The whip cracked faster and faster, tearing at my clothes and body so it felt like slashes of a red hot poker on my flesh.

When the whip end caught me on the cheek and gouged out skin, I lost my mind, it made my right eye hurt so much. With a cry that sounded like some wounded animal, I raced across the room and dived across the counter. Scrambling down some feet, I reared up quick and grabbed the shotgun off the wall. Zandt thought me still where I had disappeared behind the counter and he cracked his whip there, ripping out a piece of log wall.

He was turning to me when I fired both barrels to hit him straight on in the chest and stomach so he fell back with the cry of some dumb brute and, I believe, was dead before he landed.

In the deathly stillness following, all the people stared at me. I did not say a word. I felt a little sick but I was glad that Zandt was dead and still am glad. I put down the empty shotgun and poured my self a drink of whiskey though my hand was shaking so much I could hardly manage.

I regret the need to kill another man who did not have a weapon—unless one thinks the whip such. But there was nothing else I could do, I had to save my self, he would have blinded and crippled me. Every one in that room said I had a right to defend my self so I do not feel worried over that. I will surrender myself to the hands of the law and feel certain of a fair trial under the conditions of what truly happened.

I have not been "up" to writing several days. It is not my Record Book was taken; I have kept it hidden under my shirt. No, the reason I have not been able to write is I am so shocked by what has happened all I did was sit and stare in dumb amazement at the wall.

I am to hang.

Hang.

I can not believe it even now that I have put the words in my own hand. I sat in my cell day by day waiting for the judge to come so my trial would take place. No one (certainly not me) believed I was in danger. Even the Marshal—a man named Dolan who is kind to me—believed the trial would be short and in my favor.

No.

The trial was short all right but not in my favor. I had no defense, it turned out. Not one of the passengers or driver or guard who saw what happened at Blue Creek that night were any where near, so all the judge could see was that I shot a "Un-armed" man with a double shotgun charge; so I was guilty—murder—now to hang.

Hang!

I am still in a daze about it. My head feels numb, my stomach seems empty like hollowed out. In less than two weeks, the hang man will be here and I will drop, my neck will—J——s! It is not fair! I did not murder Zandt! If I had not shot him, he would have whipped me clear to death! That is no guess but certain! I am not the kind to kill a man in cold blood! I am *not*! I shot those soldiers in a War, I made Menlo shoot him self by accident (in self defense) and that is *it*! No murders. None. I was defending my self. *Defending* my self!

Oh, to H—— with it! To G—— d—— H—— with every body!

November 21, 1866

I have got a cell mate, a Texan near my age. His name is Henry Blackstone and he told me he has been "in jug" a lot of times. He was found guilty of robbing a store and murdering the clerk which he claims he did not do for the good reason he robs only stage coaches.

He also seems entertained by my anger. He says he has no bad feelings against me but finds my "distress an amusement" because I believed I would get a fair trial.

I was reading about the trial in the *Riverville Clarion* today, raging at the lies and half lies in the story. To read it, you would think I was a heartless brute who decided it would be a good joke to kill Zandt. Finally, I flung the paper off from me but Blackstone only smiled, lying on his bunk. "Do you really expect to find the truth in a news paper?" he asked. He shook his head. "You never will, old fellow." That is what he calls me.

He seems so calm and easy going about every thing, it is hard to believe he is, also, sentenced to hang.

November 24, 1866

I talked with Henry today; he says to write in my Record Book to say Hello. To *who*?

Any way, he says we have no chance of beating the hang man's noose so might as well "accept our fate." He says that young men like us never have a chance because the world is against us. I never thought of it before but, when you think about what brought me here, it was not justice, that is sure. Coming west because of Menlo is another thing. Henry says it was a "bad break" as in a game of pool, nothing more. We are the kind of people who get bad breaks all the time, he says; that is just the way it is and nothing we can do about it. Even G——— does not care what happens to people like us.

I hate to believe that but what else can I do? It seems to make sense when you think what has happened to me. The only thing left is to die "without a murmur" Henry says; show the dirty b———s we will not crack in front of them.

I think I would rather try to break free on the day they mean to hang me, force them to shoot me down so death comes fast.

November 25, 1866

No, I will not die without a murmur! I am going to scream out curses at the b———s! I will tell them what I think about their G——— d——— d justice!

November 26, 1866

Henry and I talked today of cutting our arms some how and cheating the hang man and "justice" but decided it was better to let them see how brave men can die.

November 27, 1866

I have decided not to make a sound, just stand there glaring at every body, showing how low I think they are.

But there is the hood. How can I glare at them . . . ?

November 28, 1866

I intend to *scream* at them, the stinking b——s!

November 29, 1866

One of the prisoners is sick (a Mexican) and there is fear that he has come down with small pox. There is a panic rushing through the town; we see them in the street talking of it. A small pox "epidemic" (Henry's word) could wipe out the town. It would not be the first time such has happened.

I hope it does. That is what *I* would call justice. Let the whole d—— town go with us!

November 30, 1866

I could not believe my ears when Henry offered to take care of the sick prisoner. He told the Deputy his father was a doctor so he knows what to do. The Deputy has gone to ask Dolan if it is all right. The Mexican's cell is a mess, smells awful.

I suppose Henry feels if he is going to "swing" any way, he might as well die by small pox as by "strangulation" (another of his words). I think I would prefer the rope as faster.

"I thought you said your father was a cow boy," I asked him a few seconds ago.

"I did," he answered, smiling.

He is very odd.

◆━◆━◆

Later. Still feel dizzy from the speed of it. I feel I may wake up and find it is a dream. I have had dreams like it every night lately which is why it seems unreal.

It went like this. The Deputy came back to say that Dolan had accepted Henry's "generous" offer. Henry said (to me) he knew they would ahead of time because it would give them some chance to "isolate" the disease, as he said, where if they had to go near the Mexican them selves or leave his cell uncleaned, the small pox might spread.

The Deputy took out his gun and pointed it at Henry as he unlocked the cell door. Henry smiled and held his hands up in the air, saying, "I am not going to try to escape."

"I know you are not," the Deputy replied.

He took Henry to the Mexican's cell and unlocked the door. Henry went inside the cell and leaned across the Mexican who was lying on the bottom bunk. The Deputy remained in the door way of the cell, gun in hand.

Henry put his palm on the Mexican's brow and felt the skin. He made a humming noise and shook his head. He put his fingers on the man's neck and prodded. Then he whistled softly and looked around at the Deputy. "Yes, it is small pox all right," he said.

The Deputy got a look of dread and took a step back, lowering his gun.

The next instant, he was knocked back by the wooden slopbucket which Henry had, some how, got hold of and hurled through the door way. The Deputy cried out in surprise (and, I must add, disgust) and lost his balance, falling against the cell door on the other side.

Before he could recover, Henry leaped across the space between them like a panther; I have never seen a person move so fast who never seemed to want to move at all. Snatching up the fallen gun, he laid the barrel sharp across the Deputy's skull and knocked him senseless.

He took one breath, then grabbed the Deputy's keys, and ran back to our cell. He unlocked the door and flung it open, grinning at me. "Time to make tracks, old fellow," he said.

I admit to being so surprised by what happened I could not move, staring at Henry.

"You want to *hang?*" he asked.

He did not have to say another word. Pulling on my boots, I shoved the Record Book under my shirt and left the cell. We ran to the Marshal's office where, as luck would have it (for Dolan, Henry said), he was out at lunch. We each took a rifle, Henry a Sharps, me a Winchester, I pushed a Colt under the waist of my trousers, and we went outside, Henry wearing the Deputy's jacket, me a blanket wrapped around me for the cold.

There was a horse tied up down the walk and we took it, riding double out of town. I find it a joke now that I hesitated about stealing it, thinking it is bad to steal a horse out here. Then I realized I was supposed to "dangle" any way and could not be hanged twice, so rode the horse without another thought. By fortune (and the cold) no one much was outside in the street and we rode from town without a hitch, trotting the horse first, then galloping when we were out of town.

It was a strange feeling to be free and a wanted man at the same time. Still, the joy of having clean air (even icy cold) in my lungs and being in the open weighed over the bad. I had to laugh and seeing how my breath steamed like a kettle made me laugh harder. Henry asked me what was funny and I told him after all the trouble he went to getting us out, we might both die of small pox any way.

"He does not have small pox," Henry told me.

"But I heard you say . . ."

"That was to trick the Deputy and turn him off from what I was planning," Henry said.

"Then what *does* the Mexican have?" I asked.

"Chicken pox," Henry answered. "People always get the two mixed up."

"How do you know that?" I asked.

Henry smiled and told me that he rode once with a doctor who told him all about it. "Before I robbed him, of course," Henry said.

May be it was not that funny but it struck me so and made me laugh until tears ran down my face.

Then I asked him how he could know it was chicken pox all the way from our cell. He said he couldn't. "That is the risk I took to get a chance at breaking out," he told me.

That sobered me so I asked him what if it *had* been small pox.

Henry smiled. "Old fellow, that is the game we play," he said. "You never know what card you will draw."

I write this in a hut we came across, thank G——because it is so cold outside. Henry is asleep. (He smiles in his sleep.) He says we might as well team up a while as both of us are "fugitives" from the sentence of hanging. I can not see a better idea. He saved my life so I owe him some thing in return.

Besides, he seems a steady person all in all.

One of the more ironic statements in the journal. F.L.

┽══┽

So began a new phase in the life of Clay Halser, his period of adventuring with Henry Blackstone.

Blackstone was a strange young man, a unique product of his times. On the face of things, he seemed as lighthearted a person as Clay had ever known. According to Clay's entries during this time, Henry Blackstone smiled almost constantly. (As noted, Clay even saw him smiling in his sleep.) Nothing seemed to bother him. Yet something festered underneath. The War and his background scarred him in some way Clay was never to truly comprehend. Behind the beaming countenance and pleasantries, there lurked a violent amorality.

Clay was witness to this in the first community they reached, and it is an interesting insight into his sense of values that he would not condemn Blackstone's action, even though he clearly disapproved of it.

December 8, 1866

Henry killed a man today. I do not know what to make of it. He saved my life and he is certainly good company. Still, I feel uneasy in his presence.

Here is how it happened.

We reached this town at two o'clock in the afternoon.

It was terribly cold (still is!) and we were glad to reach some shelter. The town is called Miller's Fork and I guess it is in Kansas although we have ridden far enough South to be in the Nations, I believe.

We had some money Henry had taken from the Marshal's office when we escaped and we went to have a bath and get our clothes washed. We had a nice sleep in a warm bed, then a hearty supper of steak and eggs, then a few drinks at a saloon. Henry said that all our needs were now accounted for except for one and suggested that we make our way to the nearest w——— house for an evening of "dalliance," as he called it. I agreed and we asked the bar tender where to find one. He told us and, after one more glass of whiskey, we headed in that direction.

It was our misfortune—actually, it was the man's misfortune—to run into a huge man coming out of the w——— house as we were going in. He reminded me of that b——— Zandt because he was so big and ugly in his manner.

"Well, what have we here?" he said. "Don't tell me you two boys are going *inside* this place?" He blocked our way and looked amused.

Henry only smiled and asked him if he would kindly get out of the way.

"I don't think that two young boys like you should go in *here*," the man said, laughing. "I am going to tell your Sunday School teacher you are sneaking off to 'cat cribs' when her back is turned."

"Get out of our way, please," Henry told him.

"Oh, no. You are too young."

Those were the last words the man ever spoke in this world. I did not notice Henry drawing. The first I knew, a shot was roaring in my ears and the big man was falling on the ground with lead in his chest. He twitched once and was dead.

Henry looked at me with a smile. "Let's go in and find some women now," he said. He did not seem concerned about the man.

I thought we should run for it but Henry gave three dollars to one of the w——s and she told the town Marshal that the man had drawn on Henry first and Henry had killed him in self-defense. Which may be the case, I suppose, in fairness to Henry. His eyes may be quicker than mine and maybe that man was just about to go for his gun.

We stayed at the w—— house for the evening but I did not enjoy it much because the killing had disturbed me some. It seems to me that Henry shot that man without a thought and never gave a hint that he intended doing so. I owe Henry my life, that is certain. Still, I am a little restless about his way of thinking.

✛══✛

Later: I asked Henry before he went to sleep why he had killed that man. I was not easy about asking but had to know.

Henry was not disturbed by the question. "I asked him to get out of the way and he wouldn't," he answered.

He explained to me that he can be so cheerful all the time because he never lets anger stew inside him. He told me that, if he had been Zandt's helper, he would have shot him the first day, in the back or in the front.

"Never bear a grudge, old fellow," he told me. "If a stranger starts to rile you, kill him right away. That way you get it 'out of your blood' so to speak and are not poisoned. I am not talking about friends, of course."

I was glad to hear that as I guess (I hope) I am a friend of his.

✛══✛

The entries in Clay's journal through the winter and into the spring of 1867 are cut from the same cloth. Constantly in Henry Blackstone's company, he began to manifest that infirmity of character which had turned him toward indolent pursuits instead of honest labor following the War. He never worked, drank a good deal, learned to play cards almost like a professional, and generally caroused through the Indian Nations, Texas, and New Mexico. When things were lean, he was not above a crack at highway robbery, on at least two occasions assisting Henry Blackstone in stagecoach holdups.

None of this is stated as condemnation for he, later, more than compensated for these youthful digressions from the law. It is merely noted to "flesh out" the picture of the young man he was at that point— becoming fully acclimated to the Western mode of life but yet to earn—or be given the chance to earn—the opportunity to prove himself a law-abiding citizen.

An illustrative entry follows.

February 22, 1867

Almost "bought it" tonight. The two of us have never been in such a tight before. How we got out of it, the Lord alone knows.

We were playing poker with some Mexicans on the outskirts of town. I don't even know the name of it except to say we are in Texas.

Henry and I were winning like there was to be no end to it. It was after midnight when he and I began to realize (we think alike, it seems) that, short of some miracle, those Mexicans were not going to let us leave the game except with empty pockets and slit throats.

It was not a cheerful situation to be in, a sod hut on the high ground near a muddy river with the only light a candle on the table and our only "companions" five Mexican b——s who would steal pennies off their Mothers' dead eyes.

Henry moved first. Fortunately, I know how he does things now so when he yawned and stretched, I felt my muscles snap to, ready for the play.

It came fast. Shooting out his hand, Henry doused the candle flame and flung himself to one side of his chair. I did the same.

The dark hut was a scene of shouts and curses. Fiery gun explosions followed and I felt the hot wind of lead around me. Henry dove through the window opening a second before I did.

It was good luck for us that the moon was not in sight but bad luck that some s—— of a b—— had taken our horses while we were playing cards.

"The river!" Henry said and we legged it down that slope as fast as we could.

By then, those Mexicans were out the door and shooting after us. I discovered later, to my surprise, that those were the first shots they had gotten off. The shots inside were snapped off by Henry, trying to kill a few of them before we lit out. When I told him that the slugs almost got me instead, he laughed and reminded me that a miss is as good as a mile.

We reached the river bank a few yards ahead of the Mexicans and plunged into the current which was COLD!! I pulled out my revolver and fired off a few shots at the Mexicans but it was too dark and the river current very fast. I held my gun so I wouldn't lose it and we fought our way to shore a distance down the bank, it might have been a half mile.

We found ourselves near the town and ran toward it to steal some horses to replace our own. Our clothes got stiff before we reached it and we moved like wooden creatures held by strings. Then, when we were cutting out two horses from the first house, a pack of hounds came at us. They tore at us insanely, ripping open our clothes and skins. The seat of my trousers was torn out and my rump bit hard. Henry shot one of the dogs and we got on the horses and rode, not bothering to look for saddles.

That was the most agonizing ride in the history of my life! My behind was bare and bloody, freezing cold and pounded to a pulp on that horse's bony back. I think I picked a nag that had not seen a square meal for a month or else was ninety years of age for I felt every bone it had.

As if that was not enough, the Mexicans caught sight of us and took out in pursuit. They would have caught us too if a storm had not come up.

Lightning crashed and I saw clouds like black mountains in the sky. Thunder began and then more lightning. A tornado of wind commenced that not only almost blew us off our horses' backs but almost blew our horses over as well. Finally, hailstones as big as peaches started pounding us before it started raining so hard that it was like riding underneath a waterfall. I swear I thought the Lord above was punishing us for the life we were leading.

Henry must have thought the same thing (though not as seriously as me) for he looked up at the sky and shouted, "Well, old fellow, about the only thing you ain't seen fit to hit us with tonight is *boulders!*"

At that moment, we were riding through a draw and several boulders from above started rolling down at us. We barely managed to escape them. I was scared white but Henry laughed as hard as I have ever heard him laugh. He tipped his hat to Heaven. "Called me on that one, didn't you?" he shouted.

We are taking shelter in a cave now, drying out our clothes over a fire. Henry is asleep as I write. I thank the Lord I keep this Record Book on my person now and did not leave it in my saddle bag.

+>=-=<+

What Clay refers to as a "bad chill" (probably pneumonia) plus complications from his still not completely healed shoulder wound compelled him to slow the frenetic pace of his schedule and take a job on a New Mexican ranch, first as cook's helper, later as a cowhand. Out of friendship, Henry kept him company and the arrangement worked out reasonably well until late September when Henry shot one of the cowhands over a card game in the bunkhouse. Forced to flee, he left the ranch accompanied by Clay who had, by that time, regained his health.

I am on the run again with Henry. He killed Ned Woodridge last evening while they were playing poker. He said that I did not have to light out with him as it is his own trouble but I decided that I owe it to him still.

The chase was not too bad. We got away from the cow boys who were led by Baxter. (*The ranch's foreman. F.L.*) We did get a shock as we were riding though. Suddenly, our horses reared back, terrified, as it appeared that we had galloped straight into an Indian witch!

It turned out to be a dead papoose. We had ridden into an Indian burial ground without knowing it. The papoose had been tied to a tree but the fastening had come loose and the body swung to and fro. It was a grisly sight with its face shriveled up and staring at us, looking very strange with all the beads and ornaments attached to it.

We rode another hour or so and came upon the campground of a group of men, outlaws as it turned out. To my surprise, Henry said hello to their leader Cullen Baker. They have ridden together in the past.

I have heard about this Baker. Everyone says he is a murderous "desperado" but he strikes me much like Henry. He does not seem aware of his renown and is affable. Like Henry, he smiles a good deal.

I do not know what to do now. Henry has declared that he intends to join forces with Baker and ride with him again. I do not believe that I am up to living that kind of life again. It is exciting, sure enough, but hard to sleep, never knowing when John Law might pick you up. That time in jail, thinking I was going to hang, was enough for me. I do not want to be a cow boy or a cook's helper, that is for sure. Neither do I choose to be "gallow's meat."

It seemed today as if it wasn't going to matter whether I decided to ride with Henry or not!

All of us were riding up a hill and I was thinking how to let Henry know that I was going to split up with him when we heard a noise in the distance that sounded like rolling thunder. The difference was it made the earth shake underneath us.

As we reached the top of a hill, we saw what was causing the noise. Hundreds of stampeding buffalo chased by several dozen Comanches. Seeing us, the Red Skins left off chasing buffalo and started after us. Deciding that caution was the better part of valor, we turned tail.

Those Indians rode too well for us, however, and it became clear that a stand would have to be made. Spotting a deserted trench house in the distance, we rode like H——— until we reached it. Leaping off our mounts, we pulled them inside and slammed the door shut just before those Red Skins reached us.

I can not say if they were drunk or crazy or what but those Comanches sure did want our hides for supper! They kicked and hammered at the door and dove in through the window. Only our constant, accurate fire kept the battle on an even keel. There must have been twenty-five to thirty of them and they just kept coming at us like they were determined to kill us to the last man.

Once, in a lull that lasted a few minutes, I heard a bugle call and told the others, with excited pleasure, that the Cavalry had come to save us. They laughed and said it was an Indian doing it who had, likely, stolen the bugle from a dead Cavalry man. "They like to blow bugles," Henry told me. "It fires them up."

I guess it must have for the next attack came right away. It was a mean one. We fired our guns until they were burning hot to touch. Indian bodies were stacked all over. Our horses screamed and bucked, knocking their heads against the roof of the house. There was so much powder smoke that it was hard to see or breathe. The Comanches yelled, and pounded on the door, and jumped in through the window even though it just meant jumping into lead. I must have shot down seven or eight of them. You did not have to have good aim either. You could not miss them.

Finally, they had enough I guess and what was left of them rode off. (Which was a good coincidence as we were down to nine more shots between us.) Two of Baker's men were killed and nineteen Indians, six inside and thirteen around the house. One of our horses was also killed but, I am glad to state, my "charmed life" has reported back for duty as I did not get so much as a scratch.

When we were leaving—Henry riding double with Cullen—I decided that it was as good a time as any to declare myself and told Henry that I had made up my mind to get myself another ranch job. This is not true but I did not want to tell him that his mode of living is not to my taste any more.

He did not take it hard, only smiling and saying, "Sure thing, old fellow. Good luck to you—" as he rode off. I thought our parting would make him a little sadder than that.

I am sad about it. Even though Henry is a strange person, he had always been a good friend to me and I am sorry I could never repay his favor by saving his life. I do not suppose I will ever have the chance now.

Adios, Amigo! It has been good fun but our paths go off in different ways now.

+>=<+

About a week later, Clay came upon the camp of an old man with a small herd of cattle. The man had been lying in his bedroll for three days and was close to death.

I buried the old man today. He did not have much of a chance to live, I think. I took care of him as best as I could and he seemed grateful. He said that I could have his herd of cattle if I would write a letter to his son in Missouri and tell him what had happened. I promised that I would. The old man's name was Gerald Shaner.

Now I am a cow boy once again. I can not seem to get away from it. I hate those long horns like the plague and now I have to nurse a herd of them across the plains. I say "a herd" but there are only twelve of them! I say "I have to nurse" them but, of course, I don't. I could let them wander off to live or die but that would not be smart. I can use the money they will bring me so I am going to drive them to Hickman which is about a hundred and twenty miles southwest of here and hope to sell them. That is my plan.

＋＞─＝─＜＋

As indicated earlier—and a leitmotif throughout Clay's account—his plans "gang aft astray." Judging from a percentage viewpoint, one might declare that Clay's plans were altered by outside influences more than not. This fact strengthens my contention that he was, indeed, a "product" of his times, being led with almost preordained inevitability toward his destiny. This is not to say that he did not have a mind of his own or make decisions on his own. Yet, caught up by the violent wave of the period through which he lived, he could do little more than "keep his head up," swimming short distances in various directions even as the wave bore him on toward his appointment with fate.

The next entry of note occurs almost two weeks later as he nears Hickman with his herd of nine cows, two of them having been lost to Indians, one to a pack of wolves.

I came up on the camp at sunset yesterday, the men there working for a ranch called The Circle Seven.

Their foreman, a man named Tiner, was affable at first, inviting me to light and have some food. I accepted gladly and counted myself fortunate to have come this way. He told me that Hickman is just a day's ride away and I decided that I was a lucky fellow to have made it.

Then he surprised the H——— out of me by telling me that, since I was new to these parts and a "one-man spread" I only had to pay them ten dollars to move my herd across their range. He told me this was Circle Seven land and strangers were required to pay for its use.

I was angered by this and told him I did not have a one-bit piece to my name. This did not disturb him. He said that I could pay my way across with one of my cows.

"How can you rake me down like that?" I asked him. "You know that I can get more than ten dollars for one of those cows."

He said that he was sorry about that but that, if I wanted, he could have the cow cut in half or thirds and take ten dollars worth of it for payment.

Something about the way he said that riled me good. I got up and mounted. When he told one of his men to cut out a cow, I told him to keep his d———d hands off. He paid no attention to me and sent the man to do what he had ordered.

I suppose I am crazy but I got so mad at this, I saw red. I told that cow boy to stay the H——— away from my herd. He acted as if I wasn't even talking and started after one of my cows. I pulled out my rifle and shot the ground up by his boots.

That did it royal. The next second, lead was flying and I was forced to ride for my life. I tried to drive my herd off on the run but wasn't very far before they caught me and shot my horse out from underneath me. I had to leg it to a pile of rocks and take cover. It was almost dark by then and although I took a shot or two at them, I don't believe I hit a single target.

Now it is morning and my herd is gone and so are all the Circle Seven men as well. I have no horse so it looks like a long walk ahead for me. If I ever run across those cow stealing b——s, I will let air into them so help me G——!

※—＞═══＜—※

No further entry appears for five days. Clay's walk across the New Mexican prairie must have been an arduous one. Cowboy boots are hardly designed for hiking (he knocked the high heels off the first day so he could move more easily), and Clay, though healthy, was not accustomed to walking great distances. By the time he reached the property of the Arrow-C ranch, his feet were swollen, blistered, and bloody. He was taken into the ranch by one of the cowboys, fed, and put up for the night.

The following day, he met Arthur Courtwright who probably had more to do with what Clay Halser became than any other individual.

October 20, 1867

I have decided to stay at the Arrow-C and work for Mr. Courtwright.

He is about the nicest gentleman I have ever met and I like him a good deal. He is British and has only been in this country for nine months. He is twenty years older than me but we talk the same lingo. He makes a body feel at ease and has charm enough to talk the birds out of the branches. He seems to have taken a shine to me, I am glad to state. I spent most of the day talking to him.

He told me that his family is a "venerable" one. (I think that is the word he used.) He said that they go back in English history and were, at one time, famous, and rich. Now, although the fame in history is still intact, their riches have faded. He took what was left of the money and "came to The New World to recoup the family fortune" as he put it.

A Hickman man—named Charles McConnell—who Mr. Courtwright met in St. Louis convinced him that this area was ideal for his purposes. Taking McConnell's word at face value, Mr. Courtwright came here, bought this ranch and started a supply store with McConnell in Hickman.

Since coming here, however, he has discovered that the "path to wealth" is not to be an easy one. There is a man named Sam Brady who controls the entire range, holding the best springs, streams, water holes, and grazing lands which makes his ranch (The Circle Seven!) the most powerful around.

I asked Mr. Courtwright why the small ranchers did not join forces to break Brady's "strangle hold." He answered that, until he came here, Brady owned the only supply store in Hickman. Either the ranchers went along with him or they got starved out.

Now that Mr. Courtwright and McConnell have a "rival" store, the tide is changing but it is just beginning to change. Most of the small ranchers are buying their supplies from the Courtwright-McConnell store now and Sam Brady is beginning to hurt. Mr. Courtwright fears "a major conflict" some time soon. He hopes to avoid it but doesn't know that it is possible.

I got the feeling that he feels a little doubt about his partner although he never said it in so many words. I don't even *know* McConnell but I feel doubt about him. I mean, why didn't he tell Mr. Courtwright he was sticking his neck on a chopping block by coming here?

I don't know why Mr. Courtwright told me all these things. He said that he could trust me and asked if I would stay and help him. I said I would be glad to do so and would never stand back in a tight place. I would help him even if it was just because he asked, I like him that much.

But for a chance to get back at those Circle Seven b———s, I would take a situation in H———!

┼━━━┥

What Clay did not realize was that, by taking employ at the Arrow-C he was doing just that; taking a situation in H———.

So he began to work for the Britisher Arthur Courtwright whom he came, quickly, to revere. Clay never mentioned his own father or expressed any sense of loss at never having had a father-son relationship. It seems clear, however, that, in Courtwright—who, by all reports, was a man of infinite charm, patience, and wisdom—Clay found the father he had never had.

He also found, within the month, the young woman he was, consequently, to wed.

November 28, 1867

Mr. Courtwright was kind enough to take me with him today into Hickman where we had Thanksgiving dinner at the home of his partner, Charles McConnell.

I cannot say I like McConnell worth a d——— although I would never say this to Mr. Courtwright if my life depended on it. I think McConnell is not to be trusted. I found out, to my surprise, that he was, at one time, Sam Brady's lawyer! This is not what I would call a good "omen." If a man can turn on one he can turn on another. If he ever proves to be false to Mr. Courtwright's trust, I will kill him.

That would not be so easy to do however. I do not mean as a physical act. (McConnell is a weak tub of a man.) I mean it would not be so easy to do because of his daughter, Anne, who I met today.

I don't trust myself any more where it comes to the heart but I have the feeling that I could fall in love with Anne McConnell very easy. There is something about her that reminds me of Mary Jane Silo. (It is hard to believe that it is getting close to *two years* since I saw her last!) She is very pretty and has a gentle smile that pleases the eye.

I must not let myself be fooled however. I thought I was in love with Hazel Thatcher. What is more, I have had many females since (all w——s) and may not have the ability to feel an honest emotion.

I do feel *something* though—and something powerful. I hope I am not fooling myself to believe that she feels something too. I can not believe, however, that the looks and smiles she gave me were without meaning.

I *do* believe that her father does not care for me. When I was looking at his daughter, I noticed him frowning. I guess he knows that I am only a common ranch hand and wants more for his daughter. Because Mr. Courtwright is his partner though and Mr. Courtwright likes me, McConnell can't say anything right out.

I don't believe that Mrs. McConnell noticed anything of what passed. She is Anne's stepmother and seems very retiring in nature.

━━━

Clay's ability at character analysis deserted him on this occasion as a later entry makes vividly clear.

December 14, 1867

God All Mighty, what a strange H—— of an afternoon!

Mr. Courtwright sent me in to Hickman to deliver a message to Mr. McConnell. He was not at home but Mrs. McConnell was.

It is not often that you smell whiskey on a lady's breath. A w——'s yes but not a lady's. I smelled it on Mrs. McConnell's breath however. Her eyes had a faraway look in them and she moved oddly.

I did not know what to say when she told me to come inside the house. I thought, at first, she meant for me to sit and wait until her husband got home so I could deliver the message to him personally. On second thought, that did not make much sense but, by then, I was already in the house.

Mrs. McConnell embarrassed me by offering me a drink of whiskey. I said no thank you and she had one any way. I sat on the sofa which she told me to do. I tried to be polite and make conversation with her but it was hard.

Too late I remembered Hazel Thatcher and that night in the wagon as Mrs. McConnell put her hand on me. I don't mean on my *hand* either! I was so surprised I must have turned into a statue!

She started saying things to me that I can not put down even if this *is* a secret journal! I mean I never heard such talk from a female, not even a w———! I tried to get up and excuse myself but she wouldn't let me. I know I was blushing because my face felt as though I was holding it a few inches from a red hot stove.

Then she cursed and pulled open her dress and buttons popped all over. She had nothing on underneath and I near to froze when she held her bare b——s in her hands and told me to ———!

I couldn't even speak I was so startled by the turn of events! She was grabbing me and telling me she wanted me to — her right there on the sofa in the full light! I swear to G———, fighting those Comanches was a sight easier than fighting off that woman.

To top it all, Anne came in just then! Seeing her, her stepmother cursed something awful, then ran upstairs and slammed a door. I stood dazed and looking at Anne, believing that she was going to tell me to get out of the house and never come back.

To my surprise, she asked me to sit down. She was blushing too as she sat across the parlor from me and told me that her stepmother is "ill" and that she would honor me if I would not say anything about what had happened as it would break her father's heart. I agreed and, shortly after, left. When I did, she kissed me on the cheek and said that she was grateful to me and hoped that we might see each other again under "more pleasant circumstances."

I take back what I said. I *do* love Anne McConnell. I believe that I must ask for her hand in marriage.

It is going to be d———d awkward though. I mean, for G———'s

sake what am I supposed to say the next time I see her stepmother? It is such a dreadful problem, I can not even ask Mr. Courtwright what *he* would do though I am sure that he would give some good advice.

December 15, 1867

A few lines remaining in this, my first Record Book that I found on the belongings of that Confederate officer more than three years ago.

I am going in to Hickman in a few days to pick up some supplies for Mr. Courtwright. While I am in town, I will buy myself another Record Book.

BOOK TWO

(1868—1873)

✦═◉═✦

If the purpose of this work were to present a story of young love in the West, circa 1867–68, a modest volume in itself would be prepared from this period of Clay's life during which he came to know and love Anne McConnell. Like all young men in any given period of history, Clay rhapsodizes endlessly about his loved one's beauty, and charm, and the total wonderment of their feeling for each other.

Whenever he was not actually working for his employer, Clay was seeing Anne or dreaming of her, filling countless pages in his second Record Book (sixty-eight in all) with youthful outpourings.

As to his "courtship" of Anne McConnell, it consisted, as courtships usually do, of walks and rides together, dances attended, visits at the McConnell house or at the Courtwright ranch. Clay says nothing more of Mrs. McConnell except to note that he almost never saw her after the unsettling incident in the McConnell parlor. Doubtless, she remained to herself whenever there was any possibility that their paths might cross.

Anne's father continued to object to her relationship with Clay but never strongly enough to make a difference—especially when it started to become apparent that Courtwright's feeling for Clay was that of a man for his son which, of course, considerably illuminated Clay's potential as a son-in-law.

All in all, this was a time of happiness for Clay. He had found a home, a father, a bride-to-be, and a potentially stable future. So wrapped up was he in these individual pleasures that he even forgot his animosity toward The Circle Seven ranch, feeling that "fate" had more than compensated him in other ways.

As indicated, however, this is not a story of young love but a tale of mounting violence in which Clay was to enact a bigger role with each succeeding year.

Accordingly, we skip, in time, to August of 1868 when Brady made his first clear move to break Courtwright's increasing control of the small ranchers in the area.

August 12, 1868

The "conflict" Mr. Courtwright foresaw when I first met him seems to be beginning.

This afternoon, Sheriff Bollinger came out to the ranch with a warrant for Mr. Courtwright's arrest. It has been obvious to all that Bollinger is Brady's pawn but no one thought he would make it as clear as this.

Bollinger told Mr. Courtwright that Brady was claiming ownership of the Arrow-C. He said that Brady had a paper from the ranch's former owner which signed over the ranch to him in payment for a debt. Mr. Courtwright explained to the Sheriff (I would have chased him off the ranch) that this was "ancient history" as he called it. He said that the former owner had never filed for the land whereas he had. This made Brady's paper "invalid." Bollinger allowed as how that might be true but Courtwright had to come and face trial any way.

I told Mr. Courtwright (taking him aside) that he should not surrender himself to the Brady forces but he said that he had no fear as he was in the legal right and they would not dare to hurt him openly.

I did not like it. There was no reason why this claim on the ranch should be brought up again. I suspected Bollinger and followed him and Mr. Courtwright at a distance.

My suspicion proved a true one. I saw Bollinger draw his revolver and point it at Mr. Courtwright. Later, Mr. Courtwright told me that Bollinger said the warrant was only a ruse. There was to be no trial because he was never to reach Hickman alive. When asked what had happened, Bollinger was going to say that Mr. Courtwright had tried to escape and that he had to shoot him.

He will never say it now, by G———! He will never say another lie to anyone. I grabbed my rifle and aimed as fast as I have ever aimed in my life. Before he could pull the trigger, I blew him off his saddle. It was a lucky shot. I got him the first time.

I rode down to Mr. Courtwright who was very white and shaken. I told him that, from now on, I would not let him put himself in such danger. He did not argue with me. All he kept saying was, "I had no idea they would try a thing like this."

+≻———≺+

A month later, a second "arresting party" rode out to the Arrow-C, led by Bollinger's brother who had been appointed as the new Sheriff.

September 13, 1868

Brady made himself as clear as day this afternoon.

Mr. Courtwright, Tom (*the foreman of the Arrow-C. F.L.*), and I were having dinner when a group of riders pulled up at the ranch house. Tom and I put on our guns and went outside to see what was going on.

It turned out to be *another* Sheriff Bollinger (the former one's brother has been made the Sheriff) and four of his Deputys. He said that he was here to take in Mr. Courtwright for the murder of his brother.

"You are not taking any one," I told him.

"I will take him a corpse or a living man," he answered.

"Take *me*," I said, "for *I* am the one who shot your brother."

He looked at me in surprise. Later, Tom said that, even though I am twenty-two years old, I look like a boy and this was what set back Bollinger. "*You?*" he said.

"*Me*," I said. "As I will shoot down any s———— of a b———— who tries to murder Mr. Courtwright."

Bollinger started cursing at me but Tom told him to get off the Arrow-C unless he was prepared to sling lead for the privilege.

Bollinger said no more. He looked at us a while, then pulled his horse around as did his Deputys. Something warned me that he had some other play in mind so I said, low, to Tom, "Pretend to turn away."

We did that and, from the corners of my eyes, I saw Bollinger go for his gun.

"Down!" I cried and threw myself across the porch, snatching out my revolver. Tom ducked behind a porch chair and lead started flying. Tom and I had the advantage being in the shadows of the porch. Tom brought down one of the Deputys, and I killed another, and wounded Bollinger. The group took off at high speed. I am sure they will be back.

Mr. Courtwright had been watching at a window. He told me afterward that he was much impressed by my "instinctive prowess" (his words) with the hand gun. He said that I should practice at it and become "adept" as I am certain to be one of Brady's "principal" targets now.

I have never thought about the hand gun much. I have used it, of course, but never given it consideration as a weapon, preferring the rifle. I can see, however, that there are times when one must defend himself at close quarters and a rifle is useless for that.

I suppose that I had better practice some and try to get a little better.

╪══╪

"I suppose that I had better practice some and try to get a little better."

With these simple words, Clay embarks on his brief career as one of the deadliest gun fighters ever spawned by the frontier. I am certain that he had no conception of his future when he wrote those words. Thinking, no doubt, that he was, merely, developing a skill that would help him to protect his employer, he could not have dreamed of the violent path down which he would be led by this mastery.

A mastery he acquired with almost consummate ease, I would add. Where other men might have had to practice for years, Clay became incredibly "adept" in a matter of months. Possessed of near to preternatural reflexes (eyewitness accounts of his gun battles verify this time and again) and a virtually infallible sense of direction, he discovered that his ability increased by leaps and bounds as he learned "to start my lead pump fast."

Learn he did, using a five-month period of stalemate between the Brady-Courtwright forces to refine his natural skill at drawing and firing accurately at high speed. Although he learned to do this ambidextrously, he elected—after much experimentation—to confine himself to the "cross" draw, wearing his scabbard on the left side, the butt of his revolver reversed; he preferred, at this time, a Single Action, .41 caliber Colt.

That he soon would have use of this newly developed skill was a fact not lost on Clay as he wrote, during the winter of 1868, "There is going to be powder burned soon."

March 23, 1869

I am writing this on a piece of brown paper that I took from the store a while ago. Later on, I will write these words in my Record Book.

We are under siege. It has been going on since morning. We are in the grain house out in back of Mr. Courtwright's store—Mr. Courtwright, McConnell, Benton, Stanbury, Grass, and myself. All the rest are dead and Mr. Courtwright's store is nearly burned to the ground. This is the first time I have had a moment's breath since morning. It is only for a moment too. We will have to make a break for freedom soon or die.

Bollinger (that b———!) and his men waited until we were in Hickman. He must have been planning this for months. It came as a surprise to us since we had been looking for an attack on the ranch.

We were in Mr. Courtwright's store getting supplies when Bollinger came in and said I had to surrender myself for the murder of his brother. I refused, naturally. This did not appear to surprise him. He said that he had done his duty now and whatever happened afterward was on our heads. He left the store and, five minutes later, the firing began.

Bollinger must have had thirty or forty men out there because the lead came flying hot and heavy, breaking all the windows and making Swiss Cheese of the walls. I grabbed Mr. Courtwright and pulled him down behind the counter. He never showed fear. I admire him the more for that. He has behaved with courage all day long which is more than I can say for that sniveling son of a b———, McConnell!

Any way, although we were much outnumbered (there were nine of us to begin with), we kept Bollinger's forces off because of our accurate rifle fire. I got a Winchester Repeater from the rifle cabinet and was able to hit many living targets in the next few hours. Once again, my "charmed life" is in evidence and, although things look grim, I feel full of cheer and am confident that we will get out of here safe and sound.

About four o'clock, we had lost three men and decided to retreat to the grain house which is made of stone as the fire set by Bollinger's men was getting too hot to bear. While we were running, poor Tom took a slug in the back of his head and died in a second. He was a brave man. The rest of us got into the grain house alive although Grass and Benton are wounded, Grass in the right leg, Benton in the left thigh.

It is almost dark now and we are going to have to make a run for it shortly. If we can get to the ranch we will be all right.

⊹━⊱

Later: We are at the ranch. Mr. Courtwright has a slight wound in his arm but is otherwise untouched. I have no wounds at all.

We broke out after six o'clock. It started raining and the fire started smoking quite a lot. As wind began to blow the smoke across the yard, we ran out, one by one. I was close behind Mr. Courtwright as we dashed across the yard and over the wall. There was a perfect hail of lead but we were untouched except, as I said, for a slight wound to Mr. Courtwright's left arm. Poor Glass was killed however and Stanbury is a prisoner.

So is McConnell but I don't give a d—— about that. He refused to leave the grain house, crying and pleading with us to surrender so the "bloodshed" would stop. Finally, I shoved him in a corner and we took out.

After making the wall and going over it, we ran through the back alleys and found some horses tied up in front of *The Latigo Saloon,* which we quickly "commandeered" and used to ride back to the ranch. Mr. Courtwright says that he will send them back tomorrow, which shows what an honest man he is even at such a time.

I do not know what he is going to do now. The store had more than two-thirds of his money in it and is a total loss. He says that he will not give in to Brady though for which I admire him even more. Still, what is he going to do?

I do not know how I am going to see Anne now as I can not ride into Hickman any more without risking life and limb.

As for her father, I hope they hang the b—— by his——! He is a miserable coward and nothing more.

‡⇥═⇤‡

*What Clay did not know at the time was that McConnell, after being
captured by Bollinger, was given a choice of helping Brady deal with
Courtwright or being killed. Being, as Clay accurately appraised, "a
miserable coward and nothing more," he quickly agreed to help Brady
in order to preserve his own existence.*

March 27, 1869

I am writing this before I leave for Hickman. I may not come back
alive but I do not care as long as I get whoever is responsible for
Mr. Courtwright's death.

I had been up for two straight days on guard and had fallen
asleep in exhaustion. While I was asleep, McConnell rode out to
the ranch and told Mr. Courtwright that Brady wanted to parley in
town and declare a truce. (Benton told me this.) Mr. Courtwright
had been terribly upset since the attack on his store and wanted to
believe that what McConnell said was true. Immediately, he had
his horse saddled and started into town beside McConnell.

When I woke up and found that Mr. Courtwright was gone, I
saddled fast and rode for Hickman, feeling a cold weight in my
stomach because I knew, somehow, exactly what had happened.

I found Mr. Courtwright at the bottom of a draw, his body riddled
by lead. There were hoofmarks all around the spot and I calculate
that four men must have been in on the murder, one of them Mc-
Connell.

I brought Mr. Courtwright's body to the house and, I confess,
spilled hot tears every foot of the way. I have never known a finer
man in my life and say openly that I loved him and respected him as
I would love and respect a father. D—— his killers! I will find
them if it takes me twenty years! And if I die in getting them, that is
all right too.

I am leaving now. G—— help those who murdered Mr. Courtwright for vengeance is riding after them.

╪═══╪

Later: I rode to Hickman and went first to the McConnell house. Anne opened the door when I knocked and told me that her father was not there.

I did not believe her and pushed inside. I searched the house from top to bottom and found him hiding in the cellar. He had a Derringer in his hand but did not pull the trigger, knowing that he was a dead man if he did.

I told him that I wanted to know who had been with him when he murdered Mr. Courtwright. I heard Anne gasp when I said that, then she said no more.

McConnell started crying and begging for his life. He swore that he had had no notion that Brady meant to murder Mr. Courtwright. I yelled at him and asked him what in H—— he *did* think Brady meant to do! He could hardly answer me, he was so scared. He swore on his Mother's grave that he had not drawn a gun but had ridden off when he saw the three men waiting to kill Mr. Courtwright.

I asked him who they were but he would not tell me, saying that his life would not be worth a plugged nickel if he told. I put my Colt against his forehead and swore that I would drench the cellar wall with his brains if he did not answer. Anne began to cry and grabbed my arm. I pushed her off and told McConnell again that I would kill him if he did not tell me who the men were.

He answered that the three hired by Brady were not from Hickman. He said that they have been staying at the hotel but he did not know if they were still in town.

I was going to kill him where he stood but Anne was pleading for his life and, despite my fury, I could not make myself kill her father in front of her eyes. I left the house and went to the hotel. The clerk told me that the three men were not checked out but were not in their rooms. I went to the cafe but they were not there either.

I found them in *The Latigo Saloon.* They were standing at the counter, drinking and laughing, bragging about the "Limey" they had "put to rest" that afternoon.

As soon as they said that, I pulled out my gun and pushed in through the bat wing doors, firing and snapping as fast as I could until the gun was empty. They did not expect me and not one of them had time to draw, but I do not feel remorse about murdering them the way they murdered Mr. Courtwright. One of them was wounded, lying on the floor. I reloaded my revolver and stepped over to him, putting a ball between his eyes as he begged for his life. I left the three of them dead and rode back to the ranch.

There is nothing left now but to leave. I can not ask Anne to go with me and doubt that she would if I did ask. I feel numb inside. It is impossible for me to believe that everything has changed so much. A week ago, my life was perfect. Now everything is ended and the world seems black to me.

I will leave in a . . .

✦━✦━✦

Anne just left. She rode out from town to beg me not to leave. She said that she and her father will testify on my behalf. I do not believe that McConnell will do anything of the kind no matter what he told her. I *do* believe Anne though. She said that she will tell the jury at the trial exactly what her father said about Brady making him go out to invite Mr. Courtwright into town for a parley and how the three men were waiting on the trail to murder him instead.

Still, I am not sure. Brady still controls the town. If I surrender myself to Sheriff Bollinger, what is to prevent them from murdering me as well? It is true that, if I run, I may be running from the law until I die and I do not want that. Anne believes that I will be acquitted and says that she will marry me afterward and we will leave Hickman.

I do not know what to do. To give myself up to Bollinger would be like putting my head in a noose. There must be some other way.

✦━━━✦

The "other way" Clay chose was to surrender himself to the military post at Fort Nelson (two miles outside of Hickman) hoping, by this stratagem, to stay out of Brady's hands while, at the same time, remain on "the right side" of the law.

It soon became evident that he was not, in this way, to escape Brady's influence. The commander of the fort—a Captain Hooker— turned out to be one of Brady's "under-the-table" confreres who saw to it that Clay was imprisoned in a "bull pen" stockade, a small open area surrounded by high walls on which sentries were posted twenty-four hours a day. They "ironed" Clay—put shackles with chains on his ankles and wrists—and kept him staked to the ground all day every day, no matter what the weather. During this period, two toes on Clay's right foot became frostbitten, then gangrenous and had to be amputated by the post surgeon.

The trial was endlessly—deliberately, I feel—postponed in the hope that Clay would die of natural causes prior to the need for a trial. When his dogged will kept him alive, the trial was started.

Clay was forced to walk to the courthouse and back, the ankle irons rubbing at his skin until the flesh was lacerated, bleeding, and infected. All hope deserted him as, first, McConnell, then Anne, left town without testifying on his behalf as promised. The trial was brief. Clay was found guilty of murdering the original Sheriff Bollinger and sentenced to hang.

Now in the custody of Bollinger's brother, he was mercilessly abused until he told a fellow prisoner that he anticipated hanging "with pleasure" so that his "torment would end."

One night in February, 1870, Bollinger, raging drunk, burst into Clay's cell and beat him almost senseless. He had just received no- tification from the office of the territorial governor that every man involved in the Brady-Courtwright War had been granted amnesty.

*Under the circumstances, Bollinger did not dare to murder Clay and,
having beaten him savagely, threw him on a horse and sent him
packing.*

*Barely conscious, slumped and bleeding on the saddle, Clay rode
off into the darkness, heading toward the next phase of his life.*

May 17, 1870

I have been in Caldwell now for two weeks. It is no great shakes of
a town but it will do for a while. My money is holding out all right.
I win a little at cards and lose a little. I can probably get by for
several months without a job. I do not care to work right now. I am
not in much condition to do so. I have not learned to walk very
well yet with those two toes missing. Also, my ankles are weak and
I get stiff in my back when the nights are cold. I am in great shape
for a man of twenty-five years.

I am sitting in my room, writing in this book again. I decided
to give it up after leaving Hickman. I did not care enough about
day to day living to keep a journal on it. Now I feel a little better so
I will start writing again.

I will not try to fill in the details of what happened to me after
I gave myself up at Fort Nelson. (*The facts about this period were
told to me by Clay, in person, at a later date. F.L.*) I will start here
at Caldwell with a "new slate." Not that I am a new *anything* myself.
Leg wound, shoulder wound, missing toes, rheumatism, (I suppose that sounds like a poem!) from lying on that d——d ground
so many days. It is amazing I can deal a hand of cards.

This town reminds me of Morgan City. It is similar in nature except for more permanent residents—about seven hundred. Morgan
City only had four hundred. The look is the same, however, and the
purpose. Caldwell is a cow town. I am told that more than a quarter
of a million head of cattle move through its stockyards during shipping season.

The providing of entertainment for the men who drive the herds is Caldwell's main business. On South Main Street are four solid blocks of saloons, gambling and dance halls, fleabag hotels, cafes, and w—— houses. The population of this "infamous zone" (as some old galoot I was drinking with called it) consists of w——s and horse thieves, drunks and murderers, cappers, deadbeats, and pick-pockets, and close to a hundred gamblers, members of the so-called "circuit." It is a grand place to bring your mother for a visit.

If I could become good enough at cards to make a living, I would be pleased to join the "circuit" myself.

+≻━≺+

As the concluding sentence of this entry demonstrates, Clay, in his early days in Caldwell, despite a revival of his sense of humor, seemed to be retrograding toward that mental state which had given him trouble following the War and during his period of adventuring with Henry Blackstone.

Devoid of ambition, he passed his days without accomplishment, rising late and spending his afternoons and evenings playing cards and keeping company with the denizens of the four-block area along South Main Street.

This situation continued until one night when, while playing cards in an inebriated condition, he lost almost every cent he had and was forced to face the prospect of earning his keep once more.

While in this state, he took a conversation with some never-to-be-identified bartender and took a fateful step in the direction of the career which was, soon, to make his name a byword in the West.

July 9, 1870

I have been thinking over seriously what that bar tender told me last night.

He said that Caldwell has no law to speak of. Not that this was much of a shock to me. It is clear the town is not conducted on the order of a Sunday School. Still, I did not realize that the Marshal—a man named Palmer—has no control at all, being merely a pawn in the hands of the local "merchants" who pay his salary, allow him to stay alive.

From what the bar tender said, Palmer is a coward and will do anything to keep from following the former Marshals into Boot Hill. (Four in all.)

The man in charge of everything is named Bob Keller. He is the owner of the *Bullhead Saloon*—the biggest in the town—and the president of The League of Proprietors—a fancy way of saying "saloon owners."

I asked the bar tender if there are any Deputy Marshals and he said that there are not. I am thinking of applying for the job. If I can get in "on the deal" it will be fine with me. I am sure there is enough money floating around to keep me from starving. I am also sure that they could use a good man with a gun to help them keep the peace during shipping season.

✦—✦—✦

As is evident from this entry, Clay's motivation for desiring to become a Deputy City Marshal in Caldwell was hardly of the highest caliber, being more in the nature of a search for an easy meal ticket than an ambition to foster law and order. (At the same time, it is not surprising that Clay had no respect for the principles of law and order in the West, having been "stung" by them more than once.)

At any rate, learning a week later that the position of Deputy Marshal was one which was handed out by the town council, he headed for the courthouse to consult the head of said council, Mayor Oliver Weatherby Rayburn.

July 11, 1870

I took a stroll to the courthouse after lunch today. It is a raw pine structure on the edge of town.

There was a dried-up old man on the porch as I arrived. He was sitting on a rocking chair, moving back and forth. He looked a hundred years old. His derby hat was too big for his shriveled head.

I asked him if he could tell me where to find Mayor Rayburn. The old geezer answered that he was "said dignitary." (His own words.) I will try to remember the words he used for he could sure spit out a power of them.

"May this ancient worthy inquire what he can do for you, young man?" he asked.

I told him I had come to apply for the job of Deputy City Marshal.

"If it is suicide you seek," he replied, "why not drink or ——— yourself to death for it is infinitely more pleasant to pass on that way than with an aggravated case of lead poisoning."

It took me several moments to haul that in and sift out the sense of it. Then I told him that I did not intend to commit suicide but planned to rock on a porch myself some day, my old head shaded by a derby hat. I said that I did not choose to do manual work and was not good enough to be a professional gambler. (The fact that I was applying for a job was proof enough of that!) As I had some skill with the gun and did not buffalo easy (I told him) I figured I would not do too badly as a Deputy Marshal. I assured him that I did not plan to cause a wave of goodness and light to wash over Caldwell but only wanted a "bread and butter" position.

He allowed as how he "apperceived my point of view" but could not promise that Marshal Palmer would receive the news of a new Deputy Marshal with smiles and songs. "Not to mention Bob Keller and the League of Proprietors." He said that he liked me, however, and would appoint me if that was what I really wanted but that staying alive afterward was my problem.

I accepted and, I must say, for the first time since the attack on Mr. Courtwright's store, I felt a "tingle" of excitement. I hold that tingle precious after more than a year of deadness and would have gone on even if the job was not a paying one.

The mayor swore me in and told me to report to Marshal Palmer, who would more than likely be found at the *Bullhead Saloon* playing cards and drinking as a good, obedient peace officer should.

I went to the *Bullhead* and found the Marshal who is a rednecked, heavy man. I introduced myself and told him that I had just been appointed as his Deputy.

I can not say that my news went over big. Palmer looked at me as if I had just come crawling out of the nearest rat hole. The men who were playing cards with him seemed amused to hear it though, chuckling a good deal among themselves. One of these was Bob Keller, a big man with dark curly hair who, I guess, you would call handsome. All he had to say was that I limped kind of bad and did I think I could make my rounds without falling down?

I told him that I thought I could and Marshal Palmer got his voice back long enough to tell me I could take the night shift starting at six o'clock and lasting until midnight.

I played the whole hand like a farmer with hay seeds in his hair and I am sure they think I am some poor lad who has gone demented. From the way they started laughing when I left the saloon, I expect it was the joke of the year for them. This amuses me as I know what they do not—that they have got something on their hands a little more than expected. Not that I am going to turn on them and try to be a Big Man. But neither am I going to let them hurrah me. If they give me enough respect to get by on I will play along with them.

After I left the saloon, I took a walk around the South Main area, checking every entrance, front and rear, of every building. After that, I spent the last of my money on a shotgun and a saw which I took to my room. I have cut the barrel short and will take it with me on my "rounds."

I have also cleaned my revolver with extra care and spent about thirty minutes practicing my draw. I was pleased to see that I am not as creaky as I expected.

Now I am ready for my first time on the job as Deputy City Marshal of Caldwell, Texas. I do not think I will have too much trouble when they find out I am not planning to step on any toes.

+⟩━┼━⟨+

Later: The job is not going to be as easy as I thought. I was prepared for a little trouble but not for what happened.

Promptly at six o'clock, I began to walk (limp) my rounds. I had pinned the badge on my shirt and, I must say, got many goggle-eyed stares from people I passed on South Main. I guess I am the first new "law man" they have seen in a month of Sundays.

All went well for about an hour. Then I heard the sound of gun shots coming from the *Bullhead Saloon* and, running over, saw what appeared to be a drunken cow boy staggering around inside, firing his revolver.

I say "what appeared to be a drunken cow boy" for, on the verge of going in, I got a prickling on the back of my neck and decided that I wasn't going to go in by the front way after all. I ran around the building as fast as I could and went in through the back.

My hunch proved correct. The drunk was only a ruse. Waiting in a front corner was a second man, gun drawn and cocked. The picture was clear to me. While I was trying to arrest the cow boy, the second man would give him back action and disarm me, maybe even kill me if I resisted.

Seeing this, I stepped in from the back room and held my revolver pointed at the second man, my shotgun at the first. "If you boys are itching to meet your Maker, now is the time to do it," I told them.

At that, the play was turned. That cow boy was no drunker than I was. He and the second man dropped their guns on the floor and raised their arms at my command. I glanced at Bob Keller who was sitting at a nearby table. (Palmer was "elsewhere.") I smiled and said, "Your boys will have to do better than that."

I do not know why I did not let it go at that. Bob Keller laughed and said that I had caught those men fair and square and there would be no more "horseplay" at my expense. He invited me to join him for a drink and I could tell, from his expression, that he expected me to do it.

I guess I am strange but I would rather have died than give him satisfaction at that point. He just *knew* that I was going to feel relieved and have that drink with him to be everlasting grateful for his kindness.

The look on his face when I told him that I couldn't have a drink with him until I had put the two men in jail was something to keep me warm on winter nights! His mouth fell open and he looked as if he had been kicked in the stomach by a mule.

He caught himself and smiled but I had won the hand and he knew it. He did not say any more as I marched those b——s to jail and locked them up.

That was not as easy to do as it is to write. It took me twenty-five minutes to find the key to the cell. That jail looks as though it hasn't had a cleaning in years, its only prisoners being spiders. I will have to clean it up, I can see. I had to laugh when the "drunken" cow boy sat on a cot and made a cloud of dust rise from the mattress that caused him to cough until his face was red.

Well, I have done it now. I could have "won over" Keller, I believe, but I had to do it my own way. Maybe I can settle things with him later. Right now I am sure he would be happy to see me take a one way ride to H—— on a runaway horse.

All in all, a good day!

+>==<+

It is worth a comment, at this juncture, to point out Clay's intuitive ability to "smell" a perilous situation.

From a practical viewpoint, there can have been no logical reason for him not to enter Bob Keller's saloon when he saw what appeared to be a drunken cowboy firing indiscriminately.

Only if we look toward that sense which is "beyond the senses" can we explain Clay's action. This "extra" sense seems to have been part and parcel of the makeup of every successful gun fighter of that period. It is as if they had built in antennae which enabled them to "pick up" impulses of danger whether they were visible to them or not. This ability served Clay in good stead many times in the years to come.

As to his intention to "settle things" with Bob Keller, this was not to be, the entire situation altering radically the following day.

July 12, 1870

Things have sure moved fast since I had that talk with Mayor Rayburn yesterday!

I was in the jail this morning, sweeping up, when Palmer burst in, fortified by a breakfast of whiskey. Obviously, Keller had given him the word because he tried to order me to let the two men go and, when that didn't work, told me I was "discharged."

I know this kind. McConnell was exactly like him, all bluff and bluster and jelly for a spine. I told him he had better go back to Keller and tell him he had failed to follow orders properly. (It seems, no matter what my intentions, I end up "crossing swords" with Keller!)

Palmer started losing nerve and yelled at me in a voice that started sounding like a woman's. "You get out of here!" he cried. "No one wants you! Get out, d———it!"

I reached out and ripped the badge off his vest.

"No," I said. "*You* get out before I kick your ——— to Kingdom Come."

He turned as white as a snowflake and left the office, moving backward. The next I heard, he had saddled up and ridden hell bent for leather out of town. I guess he knew his life was worthless from the moment he had failed to follow Keller's orders.

I finished cleaning the jail and took another walk to the court-house. The good Mayor was still in his rocking chair. I think he has taken root there. I told him that since the position of City Marshal of Caldwell had been "vacated" unexpectedly, I was applying for the job.

He looked at the Marshal's badge which I had pinned to my shirt and nodded. "Since there seems to be no throng of applicants waiting to compete with you," he said, "I guess that your availability will decide the issue." (Lord, how that man can spiel!)

Then he leaned forward in his chair and said, "Young fellow, take it easy now and maybe you will see the Autumn."

I walked to the *Bullhead* and went inside. Keller was in his room so I went up and knocked on the door. He was with a woman and didn't like being disturbed. When I told him I was the new Marshal, that topped it. "The H——— you are!" he said.

I guess I could have made some effort to unruffle his feathers. That was the time for it. There is something about him that rubs me the wrong way though. No matter what I mean to do, every time I see his face, I could not say a kind word if my life depended on it.

And it may.

◆━━━◆

The facts now stated were told to me by Clay at a later date, there being no way he could have known about them at the time.

After he had gone to Keller and informed him of his new status as City Marshal, Keller went storming to Mayor Rayburn who, not surprisingly, was also on his "boodle roll." He ordered Rayburn to get rid of Clay but Rayburn, old and tough—if not above whatever financial chicanery he could get away with—replied that Keller would have to do it himself. There was no point in Keller arranging the "advent" of a new Mayor either, he added, because the new one might be even less co-operative than he.

He told Keller that it was better to leave well enough alone. Clay was far superior to Palmer and, during their peak season, a dependable

Marshal would be valuable to "hold the cover on the boiling pot." As for Clay's antipathy toward Keller, that would pass and things would simmer down.

This proved to be an error in judgment on Mayor Rayburn's part. He did not take into consideration—perhaps the concept was beyond his limited intellectual means—the inimical chemistry between Clay and Keller.

Sometimes, two men cannot get along no matter what the circumstances. Why this is so is grist for a full-scale study in itself, being a matter of so many infinitesimal details and their admixture that no "pat" solution can possibly be advanced as to why such a clash occurs.

That it does occur is evident. Clay and Keller probably could not have made peace with each other if they tried. Some fundamental alienation existed between the two which, in time, resulted in one more step of the progression—or, some would say, retrogression—of Clay toward his ultimate station as one of the West's most noted men of violence.

<hr />

Clay's initial days as City Marshal in Caldwell were not easy ones. His journal entries made it clear he felt compelled to prove that his authority was valid. With Keller doing everything in his power to thwart this effort, it turned out to be an onerous one indeed.

Clay began to experience, for the first time in his life, the uncomfortable sensation of knowing that his life was in jeopardy twenty-four hours a day. Shots burned by him in the night, fired from alleys or darkened windows. Near accidents occurred with horses, wagons, and falling objects. On at least one occasion he found ground glass in his food, on several others, scorpions in his bed, once, a rattlesnake.

This proved to be a far cry from the sort of excitement to which Clay responded. His "tingle" soon degenerated to a cold sweat, his pleasure at having achieved the position of City Marshal fading steadily. His nerves began to fray, his temper shortened.

Then, one day in September of that year . . .

Got a nice surprise today. While I was making my rounds, I ran into Cullen Baker and several of his cronies coming out of a saloon. He did not recognize me right away, seeming to see only the badge which made his features harden when I addressed him.

Then he remembered me and we shook hands. I invited him into the saloon for another drink but he said that he and his boys had to be on their way. I think his feeling toward me was un-friendly even though I tried to make him feel at home.

That is not important though. What is important is that, when I asked him where Henry was, he said in Kellville recovering from some minor buckshot wounds. Kellville is only forty miles away!

I have sent a letter with the evening stage and hope that Henry will receive it soon and answer me. I asked him if he would like to come to Caldwell and be my Deputy. I told him that I realized he had no love for the law (nor do I) but that being Deputy would be a good "cover" for him so that he could be safe from any warrant put out for his arrest. Also, I wrote that if he wanted action, this is the place to find it as a daily food.

G———, I hope he comes! It would be grand to see the "old fel-low" again! It would also be a relief to have someone like him back-ing me up. I am getting tired of being alone. It is not good for the nerves.

⊷═━═⊷

The passage of several weeks of silence just about convinced Clay that either Henry had not received his message or did not choose to reply, feeling that Clay had betrayed their friendship by becoming a "law man." In this, he underestimated Henry. To Blackstone, friendship was the only verity to be respected. He had no regard for anything else, least of all the law. It did not matter to him, therefore, which side of it he lived on. If "going honest" was what his friend requested, he would be pleased to do so.

Henry has come! G———— d———— but it is good to see his smiling face again! He has not changed a bit!

I was leaving my office when he came in.

"Well, old fellow," he said, "here I am."

I was so happy to see him I gave him a bear hug. He laughed and said to take it easy because his buckshot wounds were giving him a little bother.

I apologized and shook his hand. (*Wrung* his hand is what I did!) I had no idea how much I needed someone. When he told me he had come to be my Deputy, I felt a heavy weight fly off my back.

We talked a while and he told me what he had been doing since I last saw him. It was not much different from what he and I had done. How he can look so unchanged living like that is amazing to me.

He told me that he had read about my "exploits" in the Brady-Courtwright War which surprised me as I did not know that the papers in New Mexico had written about it. (How could I have known *anything* being staked to the ground every day?) He said that he had stopped in Hickman to say hello but found that I was gone. I told him all about it and he said that if he was ever back that way, he would shoot Bollinger for me.

I took him to the courthouse and told Rayburn I wanted Henry sworn in as my Deputy. Needless to say, the Mayor was rocking. He never even slowed down as he swore in Henry.

Henry and I walked back to South Main and went into the *Bullhead*. There, I introduced him to Keller. While that was still fresh in his craw, I told him he was going to have to move his faro tables out of the back room and put them in front where I could keep an eye on them. A lot of cow boys have complained to me that they were fleeced. His is not the only place that does it naturally but, since he is the biggest (and my favorite victim!), I figured an example should be set.

I really had the b——— off his balance today! To begin with, he is not sure at all how far he can push me. On top of that, Henry bothered the H——— out of him! I can see why. Henry looks so young—younger than me now—and standing there, smiling like he does, with a shotgun cradled in his arms, he must have set Keller's teeth on edge.

Maybe I imagined that but, whatever the case, they carried those tables into the front room and Henry and I left. We went across the street to the *Palomino House* and I bought him the biggest steak they had. Lord, but it is good to be together with him again!

+———+

Keller, now more anxious than ever to dispose of Clay—though un-willing to attempt the job himself—began to work on Lieutenant Al-fred Gregory, the hot-tempered son of the General who commanded Fort Morgan, a nearby military post.

Gregory was well known in that area as a troublemaker. Hand-some and arrogant, the victor in a score of past gun duels, he provided the ideal pawn for Keller's game.

Telling Gregory that Clay had voiced hostility toward him, he en-hanced the plot by implying that the talk about Clay's prowess with the hand gun was without substance, no one ever really having seen him use it. As for the stories circulated by Henry Blackstone regarding the "murderous swath" Clay had cut through the Brady-Courtwright War in New Mexico, they were obvious fabrications put forth by Blackstone, with Clay's blessing, to bolster Clay's position as Marshal.

The first encounter between Gregory and Clay came about as follows.

November 19, 1870

I was standing at the counter in *The Virginia Saloon* tonight, hav-ing a drink with Henry when Lieutenant Gregory came in.

I knew as soon as I saw him that he had made up his mind to

test me. Even as he started toward me, I made up *my* mind to try something I had never done before.

He stopped behind me and I turned to face him. Henry did not turn but watched us in the mirror. Knowing he was there gave me confidence that no tricks would be played on me.

"What do you want?" I asked Gregory.

"I want to know if you are really as fast with a gun as I have heard," he replied.

"There is only one way to find out," I said.

"That is why I am here," he answered. "I intend to prove to every one present that you are nothing but a bag of wind."

"Prove away," I told him.

"And after you are shot down, I am going to cut out your tongue and make you eat it before you die."

"Sounds as though you have quite an evening planned," I said. I did not look around but I knew Henry would be smiling at that.

Gregory waited.

"Well?" I asked. "What are you waiting for? If I am to have my tongue for a late snack, we had better get to it."

"Fill your hand," he said.

"I will not pull down on you first," I told him.

"You are a coward then," he said.

"No," I answered, "I am just too fast for you and think it only kind to let you take first crack."

That did it. I saw him start to draw in his eyes, long before the message reached his hand. I did not give him any time but snatched out my Colt and laid it across his skull as hard as I could. He went down like a sack of grain.

I finished my drink. Then Henry took one of Gregory's legs and I took the other and we dragged him out of the saloon and down the street to jail.

He opened his eyes as I was locking the door of the cell. I never saw such hatred in a man's face, not even Keller's. He told me that the next time we meet, the only possible exchange between us is one of lead.

I believe that I will not be able to buffalo him a second time and will keep my eyes on him in word and action.

Henry said that he did not know why I did not kill Gregory. I told him that I wanted to see if I could buffalo him as I had never done that to a man before. Henry asked me if I wanted him to kill Gregory in the cell but I told him no. I think he would have done it too.

Henry is as strange as ever.

┼══════┼

The "show down" between Clay and Lieutenant Gregory came following a blizzard.

I wonder if the reader is aware of the fantastic violence of the so-called "Norther" of the plains. If not, it might not be amiss to append here a brief description of same selected from an article written by myself some years ago.

"The sky is a sunless gray and a deep, incredible stillness fills the air. Horses and cattle are restless, snorting and moaning in anticipation of something terrible about to happen.

"Suddenly, their breath goes white, all warmth swept from the air as a cloud of white appears on the horizon. Soft and fleecy-looking, it approaches quickly, rising and spreading. Soon the wail of wind is heard, the icy juggernaut drawing closer and closer.

"In the flash of an instant, it hits, a brutal "Norther"—blinding, smothering waves of fine white snow. Livestock turn their backs to it, covered, in seconds, by a blanket of white. Men, women, and children rush for shelter, unable to breathe outside, their nostrils clogged by freezing, driving grains of snow, their eyes stung and blinded.

"The wind increases steadily, an Arctic banshee howling across the land. Nothing can be seen but one, continuous, glittering whirl of particles. Powdery snow rushes over everything. Great drifts begin to form. Horses and cattle shiver helplessly, their mouths and eyelids frozen shut, icicles hanging from their jaws."

Such a blizzard hit Caldwell in December of that year leaving in its wake a vast, white, mantling silence.

Soon afterward, the incident which became popularly known as "Snowballs and Lead" occurred.

December 20, 1870

Henry and I were in the office, sitting by the stove, when we heard some horses stop outside. I was comfortable and sleepy so I asked Henry to see who it was.

He got up and went to the window.

"Gregory," he said.

That woke me quick enough. I got up and went over beside him.

Lieutenant Gregory and three men, one of them a Cavalry Sergeant, were just dismounting. They saw us looking at them but made no sign that they had. Their breath steamed as they stood outside, waiting.

"We have to go outside?" Henry asked.

"Don't you want to?" I said.

"No," he replied. "It is too cold. Can't we just shoot them down from here?"

"Henry," I said. "We are law men. We are supposed to *not* shoot people if we can."

"I thought you said this job was going to be fun," he replied. I glanced at him. Naturally, he was smiling.

We looked at Gregory and the three men for a while. I guess they thought we were trying to figure out a way to get out of it.

"If we can keep from going out a little longer," I said, "they will freeze to death and we will not have to face them."

"I hope so," Henry said. "I hate to go outside when it's cold."

"Well," I said after a few more moments, "we had better go out anyway."

We put on our coats and hats but no gloves.

"The odds are not good," I said. "If we can keep from shooting, we had better do it."

"Anything you say," Henry told me but I knew that he was hoping there would be gun play. There is a difference in his smile when he is ready for action. I did not notice it in the old days but I do now.

We went outside and stood on the plank walk facing the four men across the hitching pole. There was snow on top of it and I scooped up some and started packing a snow ball while we talked.

"Well," I said, "don't you think it is a little cold for this sort of thing?"

"Don't worry," Gregory said, "you will be frying in H——— pretty quick."

"Has it ever occurred to you that *you* might be the one to fry?" I asked.

"No," he said. "It is going to be you and your G——— d——d, grinning Deputy."

I looked at the other men. They did not seem as sure of the play so I decided to work on them. If I could separate them from Gregory, there would be less of a problem.

"You boys look sensible," I said. "Why are you here? This is not your ruckus."

None of them spoke but I could see, clear enough, that not one of them wanted to fight.

"We are not here to listen to you, you yellow b———," Gregory said. I saw him pull back the flap of his coat and start to draw and I let fly with the snow ball. It was a risk but it worked. The snow ball hit him on the hand and knocked his revolver into the snow.

The Sergeant knew what I was trying to do right away. It is strange how he and I seemed to understand each other without a word between us while, after seven months of talk, Keller and I are further apart than ever.

Any way, the Sergeant understood that I was trying to avoid spilling blood and, as quick as he could, he snatched up snow, rolled a ball and heaved it at me. It hit me on the chest and splattered over my coat.

That opened up the situation fine. Those other men were glad to grab up snow and, in a matter of seconds, the air was thick with snow balls flying back and forth. Everybody started laughing. Henry got a real kick out of it and laughed louder than any of them. We started having a H——— of a good time and I figured I had saved some lives.

Henry broke it. I do not know if it was an accident or not. I am afraid it wasn't because Gregory had called him a G——— d———d, grinning Deputy. Henry kept throwing snow balls at him. Gregory was not returning them but he was not shooting either even though he had picked up his gun and put it back in its scabbard. He was smart enough to know that it wasn't four to two in his favor anymore but two to one in ours.

As I say, Henry broke it. First, he knocked off Gregory's hat. That was not too bad as I had lost my hat as well as the Sergeant and one of Gregory's other men. But then Henry hit Gregory full in the face with a snow ball and blood started spurting from Gregory's nose as he staggered back. It must have hurt him something terrible.

"You G——— d———d s——— of a b———!" he cried. Suddenly, he did not seem to care what the odds were for he snatched at his revolver.

I guess that was what Henry was waiting for. He outdrew Gregory and shot him dead between the eyes.

In that moment, all the fun and laughter ended. The three men went for their revolvers, I drew mine and gun fire exploded all around. It did not last for more than five or six seconds, I believe. When the cloud of black smoke drifted off, Henry and I were still on our feet, untouched, but, except for us, only the Sergeant was still alive and that was because I had tried to knock him down without killing him.

I put my Colt away and moved to the Sergeant. The snow was red with his blood.

"I am sorry it went this way," I said. "You saw I was trying to avoid it."

He nodded but could not speak because of pain. I helped him to his feet and started leading him down the street toward Doctor Kiley's place. Henry went with me.

As we passed the *Bullhead*, Keller and some other men were standing outside. Keller glared at us, disappointed that we were still alive.

"The next time you talk anybody into coming after me," I told him, "I will come gunning for you after I have killed them."

He did not say any thing. He jumped as Henry kicked some snow across his legs and shoes. He would not fight though. Henry kicked some more snow at him and he backed away. When Henry picked up snow, Keller went into his saloon fast. Henry threw a snow ball after him which sailed over the bat wing doors. I hope it hit him on the back of the head but I doubt it.

The next time I *will* go after him, the miserable s——— of a b———. The Sergeant died tonight. It is a waste of a good man. I promised him that I would write to his wife in St. Louis. I wish I knew what I could say to her that would make it easier.

<hr/>

The duel in the snow was the first gunbattle of Clay's to be publicized to any extent.

While some notoriety had attached itself to his part in the Brady-Courtwright War, word of it was not as widely promulgated as word of this particular encounter.

Why this is so is anybody's guess. My personal feeling is that the details of it had a certain extra color to them: a good-looking young Marshal trying to avoid bloodshed by attempting to convert a moment of sanguine threat into one of schoolboy jollity and, failing that, making it obvious that the attempt had not been motivated by cowardice

*by revealing himself to be a deadly gun handler and, with his Deputy,
killing three men and fatally wounding a fourth, all at close range.*

*Whatever the reason, the story of "Snowballs and Lead" spread
around the country like wildfire, catching the fancy of a man who,
more than anyone, was to catapult Clay's name into national promi-
nence.*

April 17, 1871

Henry and I were having breakfast at the *Palomino House* when
this dude came in and walked over to our table.

He introduced himself as Miles Radaker, the editor-publisher
of a New York City magazine called *The Current Observer.*

I asked him what he was doing so far away from his home digs.

He told me that he had come out West for a number of reasons.
The main one was to meet me.

"What for?" I asked.

"You are too modest, sir," he replied. "Do you not realize that
your name is on everyone's tongue back East?"

"Why?" I asked.

"Because of your heroic exploit in the snow," he said. "Not to mention your daring accomplishments during the Brady-Courtwright
War on which I have been doing considerable research."

"Is that right?" I said.

"That is pre-eminently right, sir," he replied. (He and Mayor
Rayburn ought to get together!) "People back East are entranced by
frontier activities and read every word about them they can lay their
hands on. And you, sir, are just the sort of man they want to read
about."

He sounded weird to me so I did not have too much to say to
him. I left, soon, to go to the office. Henry stayed behind. I wish I
could have hidden underneath the table and listened. Henry said,
later, that he started telling Radaker one "whopper" after another

about me. For once in his life, he said, he did not smile but kept a serious face.

For instance, Radaker asked him how many men I had killed.

"Well, sir," Henry answered, "not counting Rebs and Indians, seventy-five. No, make that seventy-six. I forgot the one he shot this morning before breakfast. He likes to do that as it sharpens his appetite."

How he could keep a straight face through that I can not imagine. When he told me all the crazy things he had said, to Radaker, about me, I laughed until my sides ached.

What is most amazing, Henry said, is that Radaker believed every word!

—◆—

Here, Henry Blackstone (and Clay) revealed his basic naivete.

I know Miles Radaker and, if there is one quality he does not possess to any degree whatsoever it is gullibility. Obviously, Blackstone, thinking he was joshing Radaker, was, in fact, being joshed himself. I have no doubt that Radaker knew that Blackstone was "stretching the truth," but did not care since this was exactly the sort of material he was looking for. The more outrageous the lies, he knew, the more they would work to his advantage. To Blackstone, he may have appeared gratifyingly agog. Actually, I am sure that Radaker was mentally adding up the dollars to come even as he listened, openmouthed and "credulous," to Blackstone.

All unknowingly, therefore, thinking that he was only joking, Henry Blackstone began to build that structure of fictional absurdities upon which Clay was soon to climb to fame's precarious heights.

Let me be clear on this. Clay was as I have presented him; to all intents and purposes, fearless in a dangerous situation and, without a doubt, deadly with a six-shooter. He was not the Godlike figure all the stories make him out to be. No human being ever could be such a figure and Clay was human; very human.

The first articles in Radaker's magazine appeared that summer.

That dude, Radaker, was not joking when he said that he was going to write an article about me in his magazine.

Today, the stage brought in a copy of the magazine with the article in it. Radaker sent it to me. It is a caution sure enough.

Henry read it to me in the office this evening. I had already looked it over but the true foolishness of it was not apparent until Henry read it aloud.

"This Halser," he read, "has one of the handsomest physiques that I have ever had the pleasure to observe. His shoulders are incredibly broad and taper to a narrow waist at which hangs his brace of 'forty-fives,' ever ready for action."

I was trying to get some paperwork done and I told Henry to shut up. *Brace of forty-fives!* Radaker must have been blind not to see that I only wear one gun and it is a .41.

Henry would not shut up. "There is grace and dignity in his manly carriage," he read on. "His face is exceptionally well-fashioned by the Creator's art, his lips thin and artistically sensitive, his nose a strong, aquiline promontory, his eyes as gentle as . . ."

Henry snorted and almost fell off his chair, which was leaning against the wall. ". . . as a woman's!" he said.

I had to laugh. "*Will you shut up?*" I said.

He would not. There were tears rolling down his cheeks as he kept on reading. "One would not believe that these two gentle orbs have pointed the way to dusty death for scores of frontier miscreants. [That word really tied his tongue in a knot.] But, as they say on the border: When Halser shoots, it is to kill."

"Shut up!" I yelled and threw my hat at him. He fell off his chair and landed on the floor, kicking his legs he was laughing so hard.

I have thought about it all day and, I must say, it is not only amusement I feel. I suppose I can not blame Henry for telling

those whoppers to Radaker. He meant no harm and, even if he
had not told them, Radaker probably would have written the article any way.

Still, I am displeased. The article makes me sound foolish. I
may not be a Great Hero but I am not a fool. And I *have* done *some*
of the things he wrote of in the article. It is just that they are lost
in all those lies.

+━━◆━━━+

Two facts become apparent from this entry:

*One: Clay resented the exaggerations, being honest enough to rec-
ognize them for what they were.*

*Two: This resentment was equally directed at the fact that the ar-
ticle tended to obscure those of his achievements which were true.*

*In brief, he did not mind being placed in the limelight but wanted
facts to put him there, not fancies.*

*I speak from firsthand knowledge when I state that Clay was not
immune to the gratification of being celebrated. In the early days of
his newborn renown, he was not at all adverse to being famous, only
to being famous for the wrong reasons.*

*The possibility that this spurious acclaim might be a source of
danger did not occur to him.*

About that time, an old acquaintance returned to his life.

July 25, 1871

Got a nice surprise today. The Fenway Circus has come to Caldwell.

I was in the office when the wagons rolled by. I did not see
Hazel but I saw the name of the circus.

After having dinner, I took a stroll to the edge of town where
they were setting up the tent. Seeing my badge, Fenway thought
I was there to make problems but I told him that he was welcome
in Caldwell and asked him if Hazel and Carl were still with his show.

He said that they were but that Carl was now a ground worker and Hazel has another partner for the act.

He told me where to find her wagon and I went there. Carl was working, helping to set up the tent. I walked right by him but he did not recognize me. He looks terrible. He must be drinking more than ever.

I knocked on the door of the wagon and Hazel asked who it was.

"Clay Halser," I said.

She was silent long enough to tell me that she didn't remember my name. Then she said, "Clay!" and pulled open the door. She had been drinking some herself. Maybe that was why she didn't recall me.

I went inside and we kissed each other. She had only a thin robe on and the way she pressed against me I could feel every soft part of her.

She said that Carl would be working for hours and she bolted the door and took off her robe less than a minute after I got in the wagon.

I was worried about Carl but she said not to be as she took my clothes off. She said that even if he came in while we were "at it" he would not say a word. She takes care of him now, providing him with whiskey and a place to sleep. (Never her bed anymore.)

I had forgotten how good it was with her. Nancy and Myra at Mama Wilkie's place are not bad but nothing special. Hazel is special. I hope the circus stays here for a long time.

She is impressed that I am the City Marshal in Caldwell. She hinted that she is getting tired of circus life and of Carl and that a man "in my position" could use a "help mate."

I suppose that is true but I do not think that Hazel is the one. She is still married to Carl for one thing and, even if she was not, I do not think that I would care to make her Mrs. Halser. She is starting to look a little "worn at the seams" as they say and she is so willing to get into bed with me that I suspect she has gotten into bed with many other men too.

I wonder if it would make any sense to write to Mary Jane. I guess not. I am sure she is married already.

I would write to Anne if she had not betrayed me. I still have a warm place in my heart for her despite her treachery. Maybe treachery is too hard a word for what she did. What difference does it make? I will never see her again.

Any way, Hazel will save me the money I usually spend at Mama Wilkie's!

✦═══✦

At this point, I can break in personally, not only to comment on Clay's journal but to carry forward the story for a period of time.

In the summer of that year, I traveled to Caldwell to interview Clay. Having read Radaker's outlandish article, I recognized the unbelievable figure presented as being none other than the present day (exaggerated) version of the young soldier I had interviewed near the end of the War.

I persuaded my editor (I worked, at that time, for The Greenvale Review) *to let me travel West, speak to Clay and prepare a series of articles which, while no less fascinating, would be more factual and, therefore, more acceptable to the intelligent reader. Fortunately, I was able to convince him—because of personal experience—that Radaker's article was not completely false, only colored to a ludicrous extent. I assured my editor that a more realistic approach would prove even more popular; that, within the boundaries of truth, Clay had accomplished many things well worth recording.*

I was witness to such an occurrence one afternoon while talking to Clay in a saloon. A cowboy (later identified as the one who had pretended to be drunk on Clay's first night as Deputy Marshal) walked up behind Clay, drew out his revolver, and pressed it to the back of Clay's head.

"Now I got you, Mr. Marshal Big Time Halser," he said. "Let me see you get out of this tight."

While I observed in speechless dread, Clay replied, *"Now, Jim, that is not your way. You are not the kind to take a man's life without giving him a show."*

I do not know which aspect of the situation shocked me more—the sight of that cowboy with the muzzle of his revolver pressed against the back of Clay's head or Clay's incredibly calm voice. He might have been ordering dessert in a restaurant!

"We have no reason to be set against each other, Jim," he said. *"We both know it is Keller who wants me dead because I am trying to prevent him from cheating men like you in crooked card games. You and I have every reason to be friends so why not put up your gun and sit down to split a bottle of champagne with me?"*

I cannot put down every word Clay said because, in truth, I cannot remember them. The words above I wrote from memory that very evening. Even at that, I could not remember every word because there were too many of them—although the foregoing conveys the "gist" of their import. Clay kept telling the cowboy, over and over, that he was a person of honor who would not murder a defenseless man; that Keller was the one behind the situation and that there was no reason for the cowboy and Clay not to be the best of friends; finally, that Clay would be honored if the man would sit down with him and split a bottle of champagne. In the deathly silence of that saloon, Clay must have spoken without cease for a good twenty minutes before the cowboy pulled back his revolver and put it away.

At that, Clay moved for the first time, turning casually to the bartender and ordering a bottle of champagne. This was brought to the table where Clay poured some for me, the cowboy, and himself. What is more, I swear on the Bible that there was not so much as a tremor to his hand!

He toasted the cowboy (*"You are the right stripe of man, Jim."*), had a few glasses of champagne, exchanged several jokes, then left.

I followed him to his hotel room.

"Who is it?" he asked when I knocked on the door.

I told him and he unlocked the door to let me in.

He had just taken off his coat and vest and was in the process of removing his shirt. He might have just come in from standing in a rainstorm, it was so sopping wet.

"That was inspiring," I told him.

Clay smiled. "Perspiring," he said.

Notwithstanding, I was genuinely impressed and made haste to convey that feeling in the first of my projected series of articles for the The Greenvale Review.

When it appeared in the magazine a few months later, I was appalled by the changes made. It had been enlarged upon and, like the Radaker article, conveyed a general tone of grandiloquent hero worship. What I had intended to be an honest appraisal turned out to be merely another slice of lurid journalism.

Infuriated, I resigned my position with the magazine and vowed never to attempt such an article again. (Unfortunately, by then, I had already sent in two more which were, also, "doctored" beyond recognition.) I apologized to Clay, who accepted with grace. Again, however, I could see that, while amused by the article's excesses, he could not help but be affected by the fact that all those sumptuous words were about him.

◆━━◆

I remained in Caldwell for a number of months, working for the local paper, (The Caldwell Gazette) a position which Clay acquired for me.

It was not my intention to remain in Caldwell indefinitely but to stay there only long enough to collect an adequate amount of material regarding Clay, so that I might prepare a biography of his life. In this way, I hoped to be able to present, to the reading world, a more honest examination of his achievements.

It is to my shame that, to this day, no such biography has been written. (One reason, perhaps, I have prepared this volume.) Nonethe-

less, the period during which I lived in Caldwell did enable me to observe, at first hand, the rise of the Halser Legend.

After Radaker's article—and mine, I presume—had "started the wheels turning," an increasing number of magazines and newspapers sent representatives to Caldwell to interview Clay. He had "caught on" in the East as a symbol of Heroism. He was Hercules in boots, Samson with "a brace of pistols." (I never did know whether Clay's eventual practice of wearing two six-shooters was a matter of practicality or an unconscious desire to match the descriptions of himself which invariably referred to "a forty-five in each hand, spewing leaden death to all who opposed him.")

At any rate, Clay was plucked from the crowd by the hand of a thrill-loving populace and lifted to a height of dubious fame. Men everywhere began to envy him, women to dream romantically of him. He became an idol to the young.

Much to my uneasiness, I saw that he was starting to acquire a kind of helpless fascination toward the mounting flood of written matter concerning him. It was as if he read the articles and stories with a schism in his mind. For a time, he would be amused by the absurdities of what was written. Then, it seemed, it would rush across him that he was reading about himself; that all those words of praise and reverence were about him and no other—and he would react accordingly.

When the novels started to appear, his absorption became indelible. How many men, in their middle twenties, have novels written about them?—full-length books which refer to them by name, in which they are involved in one incredibly heroic exploit after another? Even discerning their flaws with a clear eye—which he never lost—he could not restrain an inward sense of pleasure. (Indeed, had he been able to do so, he really would have been a Super Being.)

Soon, a reaction began to manifest itself and he found himself becoming edgy and defensive. In essence, his rationale (though never actually voiced) might have been: "All right, the articles, and stories, and books are ridiculous exaggerations. Still they are not entirely made up. I have not exactly been sitting on my hands since leaving Pine Grove. Some of what they are writing is true.

"Quite a bit of it, in fact."

⊢══⊣

I have, deliberately, omitted, from this section of the story, the many journal entries which detail the day-by-day problems Clay faced as Marshal of Caldwell. I have done this primarily because they, largely, duplicate a later section of this book in which the elements of being Marshal in a "cow town" are more, graphically, covered.

Suffice to say that Clay's conflict with Keller continued unabated. Keller was never resigned to Clay's position as Marshal. Clay trod upon his toes on too many occasions, costing him money.

In addition to this conflict, there was, of course, the main body of Clay's duties which was to "keep the peace" (as well as he could) when the masses of cowboys descended on the town like locusts following their drives to the railhead. These periods were incredibly demanding. During them, he and Henry Blackstone were forced to be "on call" virtually twenty-four hours a day. Clay made some attempt to ease this situation; by swearing in additional deputies during these times but, almost always, they would quit when the "going" became too hard for them.

About this time, reactions to the laudatory articles about Clay began to occur periodically when cowboys, their courage fired by whiskey, would challenge Clay to gun fights.

On almost every one of these occassions, Clay used, to great advantage, his ability to "buffalo" his would-be opponents. Outdrawing them, he would knock them unconscious with the barrel of his revolver, toss them into jail, and release them the following morning, chastened and, almost always, grateful for his forbearance in not killing them.

On one occasion, however, when a cowboy tried, again, to "take him on" the next day, Clay was forced to shoot him. Fortunately, the cowboy's wound was not severe and, after a period of recuperation, he was able to return to the ranch on which he worked.

Clay ultimately solved the problem almost altogether by initiating a "no guns while in town" policy which, following some inevitable resistance, was generally accepted.

Finally, I have eliminated those entries which mention Clay's renewed dalliance with Hazel Thatcher.

During the time the circus was in Caldwell, he and she "took up" where they had left off in Morgan City. Their relationship was marked by a total lack of growth. Although Hazel suggested, more than once, the advantages she foresaw in a marriage between them, Clay never went along with her. Clearly, his moral standards would not permit him to associate with such a woman in marriage although he was perfectly willing to share her company and bed as long as she permitted it.

I might add that I am not able to appreciate how she could have been described, by Clay, as a "powerfully good-looking woman." Even allowing for the deterioration which attends "hard" living, I do not see how a truly "good-looking" woman could have lost so much in her appearance (between that time and the time they first had met in Morgan City), as to look the way Hazel Thatcher did when I knew her. "Coarse" is the only word which comes to mind.

In time, the circus left and there was a rather cool farewell between the two.

Soon after—as an unexpected dividend of his mounting fame—a relationship more meaningful in Clay's life was restored.

March 14, 1872

I am very excited and happy as I write this. I received a letter from Anne today!

I always hoped that I would hear from her again although I never really could believe that I would.

Now I have and I understand why she did not testify at my trial.

She explained that, after her father had run out (in the dead of night while she and her stepmother were asleep!) her stepmother had run off with another man and ended up, sick and destitute, hundreds of miles away. She had written to Anne for help and Anne had traveled to her side to remain with her for several months, nursing her back to health.

She had had every intention of testifying for me but her correspondent from Hickman—a Brady sympathizer she eventually discovered—had lied to her about the trial date. When she'd finally learned of my conviction, she had made immediate plans to return to Hickman despite her stepmother's illness.

Then she had been told about the Governor's amnesty and had assumed that I was safe and would wait for her despite the fact that I had failed to answer any of her letters. (I never received one of them and am convinced that they were destroyed before I could.)

Now she has read about me in the newspaper and "taken courage in hand" to write to me. She hopes that I remember her kindly and will come to visit her in Hickman some day.

I still love you very much is the final sentence of her letter.

My G———, I am happy! I have sent her a letter, telling her that I still love her too and want her to marry me and come back to Caldwell with me as my wife.

Things are slow now any way. I can make Henry temporary marshal while I travel to Hickman.

Anne!

┼━═━┼

Clay received a prompt, overjoyed answer from Anne and immediately prepared to entrain to Hickman.

Since I was planning to return to New York about that time, I arranged my schedule so that he and I could ride North together before going our separate ways.

A minor—yet telling—incident occurred our second day out.

Two young boys, discovering that Clay was on the train, approached him, saucer-eyed, to stare and listen reverently to his words.

Embarrassed by their gaping awe—especially with me sitting beside him and the other passengers observing—Clay resorted to the tall tale, spinning the boys a whopper in which fifty-seven Indians trapped him in a box canyon with his only weapon a knife.

"What happened?" *asked one of the boys.*

"I was killed," Clay answered.

His intent had, clearly, been to josh the boys out of their attitude of hero worship and give them a laugh. Instead, all he did was confuse them. I am sure that they believed that Clay had been telling them the gospel truth until his final words, at which point, for some unexplainable reason, he had chosen to avoid relating the gory details of how he had killed those fifty-seven savages with his knife.

As they returned to their mother, disappointed, Clay frowned and said he did not understand. It was the one time in all the years I knew him that I directed a remark at him which might have been interpreted as critical.

"You almost believe some of the stories yourself now," I said. "Is it any wonder that they believe them all?"

<hr />

Clay and Anne were reunited to discover that the fervor of their love was easily recaptured.

Clay remained in Hickman for a month, at the end of which time he and Anne were married in the community church and prepared to return to Caldwell.

Another telling incident occurred the day they went to leave Hickman.

May 2, 1872

I cleaned out an old sore today.

Anne and I were on our way to the train station when I caught sight of Sheriff Bollinger talking to some men across the street.

I stopped the carriage and told Anne that I would be right back. I crossed the street and walked up to Bollinger.

"There you are, you son of a b———," I said. "I have been wondering where you have been hiding while I was in town."

The man is a coward. I have always known that. All the blood in his face disappeared. He stared at me with the look of a man who knows he is about to die.

I did not try to change that look.

"You yellow b———," I said. "Maybe you would like to beat me now."

He raised his arms as though I had said, "Hands up." "I have no quarrel with you," he said.

"Well, I have a quarrel with you," I said. "And I am going to end it here and now. Go for your gun, you son of a b———."

"No," he said. "I have no quarrel with you."

"Either go for your gun or I will shoot you down like the dog you are," I told him.

"You would not shoot a man with his hands in the air, would you?" he asked.

"What makes you think you are a man?" I said. "You are a sneaking cur and a bully, nothing more."

Sweat was running down his face. He looked sick to his stomach.

"Are you going to fill your hand?" I asked. "Or must I murder you?"

"You would not," he said. "You would not."

I was getting tired of it by then. What glory is there in humbling such a specimen?

"Tell these men here that you are a coward and a G——— d———d son of a b———," I told him.

He said it right away as if he believed it.

"Now take off your gun belt and drop it in that water trough," I said.

He unbuckled his belt with shaking hands and dropped the works into the water.

"If I ever hear of you wearing a gun again," I said, "I will come back and kill you without mercy."

I turned on my heel and went back to Anne. I think that Bollinger will not be very popular in Hickman now.

━━━◆━━━

While Clay, perhaps, deserved some praise for his restraint in not ac-tually killing Bollinger, he failed to realize, I believe, that, to a large degree (if not entirely), Bollinger was cowed so pitifully by Halser the Legend rather than by Halser the man.

It is, of course, possible that Bollinger, being what he was, might have behaved in just as craven a manner had there not been any ar-ticles or stories recounting Clay's deadly skill with a gun.

I very much suspect, however, that the stories had affected Bollinger and that he believed himself to be confronted by some Super Being at whose dread hand he could expect no mercy.

May 9, 1872

This has been the roughest day I have spent in Caldwell since the day Lieutenant Gregory rode into town to kill me.

I have told Anne that it can not happen again but I do not think she believes me. It is too bad it had to take place the first day she arrived here.

Henry did not write to me while I was in Hickman but that did not disturb me. I assumed that he had things in hand.

I had a bad surprise in store when we reached the hotel. Anne and I had been stared at while we were walking from the train sta-tion but I figured that it was because they had heard I was getting married and were curious about my wife.

It turned out to be a different story altogether.

Claxton (*the desk clerk. F.L.*) was amazed to see me! He said that every one thought I had left Caldwell for good. I asked him how they could think that. Did they believe that I had made Henry the Marshal?

That brought on the second bad surprise. Henry left town two weeks ago, he told us! (To this moment, I do not know why.) The third bad surprise—a new Marshal had been sworn in by the Mayor!

I got Anne set up in a room and told her I would be back as soon as I had settled things. She seemed upset and I could not blame her. She must have thought that I had made up the whole thing about being Marshal of Caldwell! Now that I look back, she must have thought, for a while, that she had married a mad man!

I walked to the courthouse. For a change, Rayburn was not on the porch, sitting on his beloved rocking chair. I found him inside, in his office and asked him what the H——— was going on.

He looked surprised to see me too. He said that, like every one else, he had thought that I had left Caldwell for good—especially after Henry took out.

I asked him who had told him all this. I should have known.

Bob Keller.

Rayburn told me that the new Marshal was one of Keller's "toadies" just as Palmer had been.

"We will see about that," I said.

"I don't think that Keller is going to be glad to see you," Rayburn told me.

"I do not give a d——— whether he is glad or not," I said. "I am the Marshal and that is the way it is going to remain."

I was seeing red by then. I walked fast as I could to the *Bullhead* knowing that, whoever the new "Marshal" was, he would be there.

He was at that. I found him playing cards with a few of Keller's other boys. If I had not been so mad, I would have laughed. It was Nicholson! *(The other man Clay had put in jail his first night as Deputy Marshal. F.L.)*

He looked pretty d——d surprised to see me. I walked across the room to the table he was sitting at. He was about to take a drink of whiskey and the glass was frozen in the air between the table and his mouth. I knocked it out of his hand and grabbed him by the shirt front. Hauling him to his feet, I ripped the badge off his shirt and shoved him back into the chair.

"If you want it back," I told him, "you will have to take it from my dead fingers."

I waited for him to draw but was not surprised when he did not. He started to shake and put his hands on the table, palms down.

"Who in the H—— told you that you could be the Marshal?" I demanded.

"Mr. Keller," he replied. "He told me that you were gone for good. I swear I would not have put on the badge if I had known you were coming back."

I had to believe him because he was so scared.

Just then, Keller came down from upstairs and I walked over to him.

"If you ever try to pull a trick like that on me again," I told him, "I will bury you in Boot Hill."

He did not answer me but I could see, in his eyes, that he was close to the edge.

To make sure he could not back down, I told him that, from then on, I was going to hurrah him night and day. "I am going to make a set of rules for you alone," I said. "And if you break just one of them, I will toss you in the hoosegow and throw away the key."

I turned and started for the door, using the sides of my eyes to keep a watch on him in the wall mirror.

As I expected, I was almost to the door when he reached beneath his coat to draw the Derringer I knew was there.

Before he could fire, I dove to the left and took shelter behind the counter end as the shot roared and a ball tore wood away near my head.

Snatching out my gun, I reached above the counter and fired back at him. I heard chairs scraping back and men running for safety.

"Nicholson!" Keller shouted.

I thought he was asking Nicholson to assist him in killing me and I shouted, "Any man who helps Keller is a dead one!"

Another shot rang out and lead exploded through the wood close to me. I flung myself behind the counter and the bar tender took off. I did not realize, at that moment, that Keller had called to Nicholson to throw him his six-shooter.

Another shot roared and bottles were smashed above me, spilling whiskey on me. I looked up and saw a movement in the mirror. Keller was rushing toward the end of the counter to shoot at me.

I reared up fast. He was just passing by. I saw his head snap around, a look of shock on his face. Then I fired at point blank range and put two balls in his heart. He was flung away from the counter and landed, dead, on the floor, his vest on fire.

I looked around the room but all the others had gone. Keeping my Colt in hand just to be safe, I edged along the wall. I saw the bar tender peering out from the back room and told him to "put out" his boss.

I returned to the hotel. My clothes were dirty and wrinkled and there was a tear in the right knee of my trousers. Anne, who had heard the gun fire, was waiting on the porch of the hotel, looking terrified. I took her by the arm and led her back inside.

"Is this the way it *always* is?" she asked.

I had to chuckle at the sound of her voice. She sounded like a little girl.

"It will simmer down now," I told her.

✢━✦━✢

Simmer down it did. Keller disposed of, all organized attempts to weaken Clay's position ceased and, within the framework of

*what it was—a "wild and woolly" frontier cattle town—Caldwell as-
sumed almost a tranquil atmosphere. Clay had succeeded in "tam-
ing" it.*

*He had, also, succeeded in creating, for himself, a state of gilt-
edged boredom. Violence and tension, he discovered, are like drugs to
which a man of his temperament can become addicted.*

*The articles and stories and books continued, but the situations
which inspired them no longer occurred—or occurred in such minor
ways as to be without stimulation to him. As in Pine Grove, seven
years earlier, he started to become restless and discontented, yearning
for renewed excitement to "get his blood moving" again. (Clay's own
phrase.)*

*This situation was exaggerated by the problems inherent in the es-
tablishment of a marriage relationship with Anne. Always in the past,
Clay had sought out the company of women only when he needed to
assert his "male prerogative." He had never been required to make allowances for female tastes or desires. Now, he did, and it is probable
that these emotional demands on him caused him to yearn, all the more,
for some escape from marital responsibilities. It is even possible that
what he sought was an escape from marriage itself, using his desire for
action as an excuse to separate himself from the obligations of matrimony. With Henry gone (and unheard from) he did not even have a
"crony" to share his troubles with. Card games were out. Drinking was
out. Fighting was out. Accordingly, to Clay's way of thinking, enjoy-
ment of life was out.*

*When a letter arrived, from the City Council of Hays, Kansas,
offering him the job of peace officer, he was immediately eager to
accept. The deterrent was Anne. Despite the fact that the offer was,
financially, a better one, she was opposed to accepting it. With a baby
on the way, she wanted to live in a settled community. Caldwell might
not be "exciting" anymore but it was maturing sensibly. As a charter
citizen, Clay should be investing in its future, planning toward a quiet,
affluent retirement.*

It is my personal observation that Anne Halser never understood her husband's needs. A "typical" young woman, she desired a home, a family, and security. While, certainly, no criticism can be leveled at her for aspiring to these age-old desires, at the same time I believe that she should have realized that a marriage to Clay could not possibly bestow these things on her.

Her desire to remain in Caldwell and "live a quiet life" was, undoubtedly, more chilling a prospect to Clay than the prospect of facing those "fifty-seven Indians" with a knife would have been. His entries, during this period, consist, almost entirely, of reasons why the offered job was superior to his present one and why Anne should be able to "see" it.

Where his position in Caldwell brought in a salary of one hundred and twenty-five dollars per month, the new one guaranteed one hundred and fifty. Where the portion of fines he received in Caldwell was ten per cent, in Hays he would receive twenty-five. Where they had to live in the hotel in Caldwell (they could have moved into a house eventually, of course; Clay was "loading" the situation there), in Hays they would be given a house. If Anne was really concerned about the needs of their coming children, she should appreciate the value of the new job.

Anne's reply (unfortunately, for Clay, a devastatingly valid one) was that their main consideration should be the need of their children to see their father remain alive and not shot down in the street.

It took ten months for Clay to win the argument. After their baby—a girl which they named Melanie—was born and Anne could no longer use the argument that she did not want to travel while carrying the child, Clay renewed his attack, now almost threateningly, his boredom in Caldwell having reached a fever pitch by then.

Finally, Anne succumbed although convinced that Clay was making a terrible mistake. An entry made at this time is revealing.

Anne is in bed, upset. We have had another argument.

She said something that disturbs me. I can not believe it to be true and yet it bothers me.

I told her that I feel it is my responsibility to bring law and order to Hays as there are not many men who can.

"It isn't law and order you care about!" she cried. "You are just searching for excitement!"

She put her hand on my arm and asked, "Clay, do you *believe* all those stories about yourself? Do you feel that you have to *live up* to them?"

I scoffed at the idea but I am wondering, is it possible?

I do not know. All I know is that I can not go back to what I was. There is only one direction for me and that is forward.

My second book is filled.

BOOK THREE

(1873—1876)

Hays, Kansas, in the year of 1873, was one of the most tremendous "cow towns" on the frontier. Every season, in excess of half a million head of cattle were driven into its shipping yards and more than five thousand cowboys rampaged through its streets.

It was a brutal town, filled beyond capacity with every outcast type of male and female known in the West, all of whom "infested" the massive South Side area—a sprawling conglomerate of saloons, dance and gambling halls, brothels, and honky-tonks of all varieties.

It was this notorious zone which was to be Clay's responsibility.

April 4, 1873

Arrived in Hays this morning.

After leaving Anne in the house we are to live in, I was given a ride around the town by a man named Streeter, a member of the City Council.

He showed me the South Side first. It is like the South Main area in Caldwell but about five times as large.

I had to ask Streeter to be shown the North Side of Hays which is beyond the so-called "Dead-line." (The railroad tracks.) This is where all the "respectable" citizens live. I asked Streeter why the house they gave us is not on the North Side and he said that it was on the South Side so that I could be "closer to my work."

The way he said it made it clear that the real reason is that Anne and I are not considered good enough to live among the "gentry." I did not like his answer but did not make a point of it. I may, later.

As the buggy passed the Sheriff's office, I saw him at the window, glaring out at me. His name is Woodson.

"My rival?" I asked.

Streeter told me that I should not be concerned with Woodson.

"The ones to worry about are the ones who control Woodson," he said.

These are the Griffins who, he says, are nothing less than out and out criminals. Criminals, however, who have learned not only to remain within the "good graces" of the law but, actually, employ it for their own purposes.

They are very wealthy, Streeter told me. The bulk of their riches, he said, comes from cattle rustling and stage coach hold ups! No one has ever succeeded in getting the goods on them however. Any one who tries is soon put out of the way. The Griffin "empire," as Streeter called it, has been "well secured" by threats and violence.

In addition to the rustling and the hold ups, like The Circle Seven, the Griffins control all the usable water sources for miles around and require cattle drovers to pay dearly for its use. On top of that, any cows that happen to stray during these drives are quickly picked up, clumsily rebranded, and sold back to their original owners. The owners know that they are being "taken" royally but are in no position to object being far outnumbered by the Griffin forces.

As Streeter told me all those things, I could feel that long lost "tingle" returning. I welcomed it back as I would an old friend. I do not believe that this job is going to be more than I can handle but it promises to be one H——— of a hot one!

Later: After having lunch with Anne, I helped her to unpack.

She seemed a little more resolved to being here. The house is not bad. It is not as nice as her home in Hickman but it is a big improvement over the hotel in Caldwell.

After I had helped her, I took a stroll to the City Marshal's office. There, I met my Deputy, a man named Ben Pickett.

He is a small, quiet man in his forties (I guess) with a straggly mustache and a stocky build. He is not flashy in any way, looking more like a store clerk than a Deputy Marshal. He strikes me, however, as the sort of man who might be outdrawn and outshot but would "get his man" regardless. I took a liking to him and he seems to like me too.

He showed me this week's edition of the *Hays Gazette*. (The editor, he tells me, is another wheel in the Griffin machine.) The headline shocked me, I confess. It reads KILLER MARSHAL ARRIVING! The article goes on to state that "the well-known, cold-blooded pistol killer, Clay Halser, is arriving this week and all citizens of Hays can now look forward to a sanguinary reign of terror."

I must say that it is strange to read these words. While I certainly do not believe all the other kind of articles about me, I have gotten used to being praised. To see the opposite approach puts a fellow back on his heels.

Pickett told me that I should prepare myself for a good deal more of the same. Obviously, he said, the Griffins want me out of the way since I am the only possible fly in their ointment.

Pickett told me, next, about John Harris, a local gambler and saloon owner. Being strictly a "loner," Harris has always opposed the Griffin "regime" and has supported one peace officer after another. He allows them to use his saloon as their "hang out" and spare armory. While expecting no more than token leniency (since, Pickett says, he runs an honest establishment anyway), the value of having the city Marshal as an unofficial ally has been worth, to Harris, ten per cent of the saloon's earnings. Three per cent of this has, by custom, gone to the Deputy Marshal.

Pickett put this to me in a straightforward way and I replied that I was not against the idea if Harris and I got along. I knew that Anne would not object to the prospect of using that seven per cent to build a "nest egg" for the future.

Pickett took me over to the *Keno Saloon* and introduced me to Harris. He struck me right immediately and agreement was reached. He invited me to take a social drink with him and I said that I would.

When the bar keep brought the bottle to the table, I was delighted to discover that he was none other than Jim Clements!

Harris invited Jim to join us for a drink and we had a nice chat. Harris told me that he has been thinking of approaching various merchants with the idea of "co-sponsoring" a series of prize-fighting matches. Cow boys coming into Hays are always hungry for "diversions," he said. A special entertainment like that could make us all a good raise. He asked me if I would be interested in getting in on it. He said that I would not have to put up any money. My name alone would give the project "stature."

I told him that I would be happy to lend my name to such a venture if it would help. I had a few more drinks with them, then went home, feeling very good. Not only had I met two men who, I believe, promise to make fine friends, but have also gotten together again with Jim. Not to mention the sources of extra income I am finding here.

When I got home, I told Anne that, despite her fears, Hays is going to be the making of us. "We are going to like it here," I said.

As I spoke, there was a thundering of hooves outside and a body of men pulled up in front of the house. In my shirt sleeves, but wearing my Colt in plain sight, I stepped out onto the porch to see who it was.

It was the Griffin family out in force to take a look at Hays' new peace officer—and, I have no doubt, to try to rattle me from the start.

"Just rode in to see the famous Marshal Halser," said a toothless old man. He introduced himself as Roy Griffin, the head of the family. They all sat on their horses—"measuring me."

I thought that it would not hurt to get the jump on them so I said, "That is very kind of you. If you are planning to stay in town, however, you will have to check your weapons at the jail. It is the new rule."

Roy Griffin made a noise that was, I guess, amusement. "Is that right?" he said.

I did not reply but smiled to show him that I was not cowed by him or his sons and brothers.

"Seems as how the *former* Marshal tried to make that same rule," he said. "As long as we are in town, we might as well pay *him* a visit too. He is out on Boot Hill with the other Marshals."

"I intend to stay right here," I told him, trying to sound unconcerned.

"Bless me, sonny, so did they," he answered.

He pulled his horse around and the Griffins rode off in a cloud of dust. I watched them until they had ridden out of sight, then went back inside. Anne had been watching from the window. She did not have to speak. I knew the question in her mind.

We are going to like it here?

+>━━=+

Later: It is almost one o'clock in the morning. I have just gotten Anne to bed.

Relieving Pickett at six, I told him that, starting tomorrow, we would begin enforcing the "no guns while in town" policy. I asked him to go to a printer's shop in the morning and have some posters made.

He left and, after a while, I went out on my first rounds.

The South Side, at night, is like a city in H———, I think—all noise and smoke and flickering light. Partly, it excites the senses, partly it repels them.

I walked through it all as though I owned it. It is the only way to demonstrate authority. These kind of people do not recognize anything but a show of strength.

I gave them all the show they expected. I was wearing my best black suit, my best black hat and boots, a good white shirt with a string tie and my brocaded waistcoat; what they call "gambler's dress." I kept my coat unbuttoned so that they could see the butt of my Colt at all times. (I have decided, after some thought, to stick with a .45 even though it is harder to handle.) It has more "stopping" power.

Wherever I went, I knew that they were watching me. Looking for some sign of weakness. They never saw one. I did not exchange a word with anybody. I merely nodded at people, smiling a little as if the sight of them amused me. No one approached or addressed me.

Until, some hours later, when a gang of cow boys from the Griffin ranch rode in.

Although the "no guns" rule is not to take effect until tomorrow, I decided to "set the stage" by making an example of the Griffins.

I walked quickly to confront them as they were tying up in front of a saloon. I told them that the policy was to surrender their guns when in town and told them that I expected them to obey.

There were nine men in the group. One of them was one of Griffin's sons—I think his name is Jess. He looked at me with a scornful smile and asked if I intended to stand up against all of them.

"If that is what you want," I said.

They did some "tongue skirmishing" with me but I did not back down. Finally, they decided to take off their guns and went into the saloon, leaving their belts slung over a hitching post. As they went inside, they cursed and threatened me under their breath, but I did not object to that as it enabled them to "let out steam."

By that time a crowd had collected and I was glad they had as it gave them the opportunity to see me at work. I dispersed them and they went away.

One of them turned out to be John Harris. He came over and told me that he "admired" how I had handled the cow boys. He did not say so in as many words but I got the feeling that, if the cow boys had tried to resist, Harris would have given me back action.

This impresses me and makes me like him even more. We had a nice chat as he helped me carry the guns and rifles to the jail.

When I got home at midnight, my satisfaction turned to ashes. To my dismay, I found the house dark, its windows shot out and its siding pocked with holes.

I was about to run inside when Pickett came down the street from his house. He told me that Anne and Melanie were safe but that he and his wife had decided that it might be better for her to stay at their house until I had gotten back.

I asked him what had happened and he answered that a group of riders, leaving town, had opened fire on the house. I know d—— well it was Griffin's son and those cow boys.

I went to Pickett's house and got Anne. I told her that no such thing will happen again. She did not argue but I do not think she believes me. The incident really shocked her.

I will see to it that such a thing does *not* happen again. If war is what the Griffins want, I am prepared to give it to them.

✦━◆━✦

Standing back at a distance of time, it is possible to note a thread of what might be termed "over-assurance" running through Clay's entries during this period.

Although he was only one man, he seemed to possess a confidence

*in his ability which went beyond logic. His standing up to nine men
and demanding that they disarm is indicative of this overconfidence.*

*His writing that he was prepared to declare war on the vast Grif-
fin empire is, while, perhaps, courageous, also somewhat foolhardy.*

*There seems little doubt that Clay genuinely believed himself to
be the equal of any impending situation, however dangerous.*

The legend had begun to eclipse the man.

⊢━⋗━⋖⊣

The next edition of the Hays Gazette *described Clay's "brutal treatment" of a "defenseless" group of cowboys. That this group was from
the Griffin ranch was not mentioned. Neither was the riddling of
Clay's house with his wife and baby daughter inside.*

*Clay's wrath at this distorted account was not diminished by the
arrival, in town, of one well-shot-up, well-robbed stagecoach.*

April 13, 1873

I decided, this morning, that it was time to make a counter move
against the Griffins.

Pickett and I rode out to the Griffin ranch, timing our arrival so
that they would be at lunch.

Roy Griffin and his brothers and sons came out onto the porch
to see what I had to say. I saw their women watching at the windows.

I told them that, from now on, I intend to ride as guard on any
stage coach shipment of great value.

I also told them that, if any of them dares to shoot at my house
again, I will return the favor without asking permission of the City
Council—except that I will use shotguns loaded with scrap iron.

That done, Pickett and I backed our horses away from the
house—not from fear so much as a desire to show them how little we
thought of them—and rode back to town.

The next move is theirs.

Before he left the office tonight, Ben made the suggestion that I reload my revolver daily. He told me that an overnight temperature change, in cooling the gun, can gather moisture in the chambers and cause a misfire.

I have never given it much thought before but I will start to do as he suggests. He made the good point that, considering the hazards of our job, we can not afford the risk of a single bad shot.

I am going on my rounds now.

+◄═══►+

It is a coincidence that, after writing about the "hazards of our job," I went out and faced one.

Whether it was the "next move" by the Griffins, I do not know. It may have been.

While I was walking past an alley, some one took a shot at me. The lead bit off a corner of my hat brim but did not harm me.

I saw the man running away and started chasing him. After a brief pursuit, I cornered him in a blind alley and, drawing my Colt, ordered him to raise his arms.

I do not think it was bravery so much as panic that made him draw and try to kill me. I wanted to hit him in the leg but there was not time to aim and my instinctive firing took its toll. The man died instantly, a ball entering his body just below the heart.

It was one of Griffin's cow hands.

Another lying story in the *Gazette* today. This one tells how "Marshall Clay 'Heroic' Halser" shot down a poor, "un-armed" cowboy after "bullying him unmercifully."

I am trying not to let Bellingham (*the Gazette editor. F.L.*) make me lose my temper. Streeter said that I can not so much as threaten him. I am expected to prove, by "deed," that his words are lies.

I do not know how long I can go along with that. Anne is becoming very upset with the stories. The worst thing is that I am not sure whether she believes me when I tell her that every word is a lie. I guess it is hard to believe that something in print is completely false.

The sentence that bothers her most is: "It becomes more apparent, with each passing day, that Halser has come to believe all the extravagant myths about his Greatness and now regards himself as above the law."

We had some words about that.

"Do you believe it?" I asked.

"No. But . . ."

"But *what?*" I asked. "Either you believe it or you don't. Which is it?"

"I don't know," she said after a while. "I just don't know."

That got my wind up and I replied, "Well, let me know when you make up your mind."

I am feeling hot under the collar as I write this. I still love Anne but, I must say, she seems to think a good deal less of me than I do of her.

I do not believe she has any idea of what it is like to be in my position. On the one hand, I am swamped with printed lies that make me sound like the Second Coming Of The Lord. On the other hand, I am, now, being swamped with printed lies that make me sound like a cross between a rattlesnake, an Apache, and Emil Zandt!

Somewhere in between these two extremes I am trying to do my job as City Marshal of Hays . . . but it is not easy. If Anne knew how simple it would be for me to "throw my weight" around, she would be shocked. I could shoot down every man who stood in my way if I chose. I could horse whip that b——— Bellingham and shut him up too!

I am not doing any of these things. I think I am showing considerable patience and wish she could see it.

✦━━✦

Later: More trouble.

After I left the house, I went down to the bank and signed contracts which commit me to the prize fight exhibitions. John thinks that we should make a regular thing of them and I agree.

After signing the contracts, he and I went to the *Keno* for a drink.

We were standing at the counter, talking, when a cow boy came in and approached me.

"Halser," he said.

I looked at him. There was no doubt in my mind that he was there for blood.

"My name is Barrett," he said. "It was my friend you murdered."

"I am sorry about that," I said. "It was . . ."

". . . *murder,*" he interrupted me. "And I have come to right the wrong."

Here is a good example of what I was writing about before. If I had chosen, I could have drawn on him immediately. Instead I tried to talk Barrett out of it. As calmly as I could, I explained what had happened.

"What you read in the *Gazette* is a lie," I said. "I did not murder your friend. He tried to kill me from ambush and missed. I chased him through the alleys and, when I caught him, I told him to raise his hands. I was going to put him in jail but he drew his revolver and I had no choice but to defend myself. That is God's truth, Barrett, and I hope you will have the good sense to believe it."

I could do no more. As the Lord is my witness, I did the best I could but he would not accept it. He said that he wanted revenge and nothing else would satisfy him.

At last, I gave up trying and we went outside. By then, I had lost my temper and did not care any more. If the man would not back down from me, what was I supposed to do?

We faced each other on the street at a distance of approximately five yards.

"Your play," I told him.

Despite his air of confidence, he fumbled at the crucial moment. As in his friend's case, I would have liked to wound him. It was too late for that however. I can not control my reflexes that late in the game. I put a ball in his chest which passed directly through his heart. He was dead before he landed on the ground.

There is only one thing that disturbs me. (I do not feel guilty for having defended myself.) The man was very quick with his hand. (I learned, after, that he had won eight gun duels previously.) If he had not fumbled, it might have been a close thing.

Is it possible that his fear of my reputation won the battle for me?

✦━━✦

Two observations can be made about this entry.

One: Clay seems, for the first time, to be aware of the possibility that his eminence in Hays might not be based entirely on facts.

Two: One might question Clay's presentation of the incident with Barrett. If the two men were standing together at the counter, would it not have been possible for Clay to "buffalo" him and put him in jail, thus sparing his life? Of course, this may have been impractical. Barrett may not have been standing close enough. Further, Clay might have felt that, even if he did buffalo Barrett and put him in jail, it would only be forestalling the inevitable "moment of truth" between them.

At any rate, more conflict with Anne ensued because of the killing.

Despite Clay's efforts to convince her that he was justified, the incident drove yet another wedge between them.

Even John Harris coming to tell her what had actually happened did not diminish her reaction.

The situation was aggravated further by a special edition of the Gazette, *the headline of which shrieked WANTON MURDER!*

April 25, 1873

Jim has suggested that I tell Bellingham there will be genuine wanton murder if he does not stop printing lies about me.

I confess that I am giving his suggestion serious thought.

I have never been exposed to any thing like this. It is more than criticism. That d——d Bellingham is out to nail my hide to the wall! The Council told me again that I must not hurt him though.

They called me in this afternoon to let me know that my "image" is "assuming most unfavorable proportions." (A Rayburn remark if ever I heard one!)

"Is all this killing absolutely necessary?" Mayor Gibbs asked.

"No," I said. "It is not necessary at all. I could let them murder me."

That remark did not win any prizes but I did not care. The way things are in Hays, I figure that they need me a H—— of a lot more than I need them. Surviving Marshals do not grow on trees.

Any way, I told them that they could have my badge back if they wanted it because I did not plan to continue as peace officer if deprived of the basic right to keep myself alive.

They backed down as I knew they would. Streeter had to have the last word though.

"We *would* appreciate it," he said, "if you would, at least, *endeavor* to keep the peace with more decorum."

"I will certainly try," I answered. "The next time some one tries to kill me, I will slap their wrist and make them stand in the corner."

I left that meeting in a rage. I am beginning to see what a pawn I am in the game between the Council and the Griffins.

When Woodson stopped me in the street, I was just about ready for bear.

He told me that he might have to arrest me for the two shoot-
ings!

I looked at him as if he were a tarantula about to crawl up my
leg. "You do that," I said. "Any time at all." I unbuttoned my coat.
"Why not now?" I suggested.

He backed off, holding his hands away from his body. "There is
nothing personal in this, Marshal," he said.

"I would not bet on that hand either," I answered, walking off.

━╾═╼━

*An attempt, the following week, to rob the stagecoach of a valuable
gold bullion shipment failed as Clay and Ben Pickett rode as guards.*

*Clay's unexpected presence inside the coach proved to be the dif-
ference. His devastating rifle fire augmenting Pickett's routed the at-
tackers, killing four of them. All were known Griffin employees.*

Reprisal came the following night.

May 5, 1873

It is almost three o'clock in the morning. Anne has just fallen
asleep. I think that we are safe in Ben's house but I am not taking
any chances for a while and will stay awake.

It is fortunate that I am a light sleeper. I woke up about midnight and smelled smoke. Jumping out of bed, I found smoke filling the hall. I woke up Anne and got her and Melanie out the front
door before the blaze in the kitchen and hall had reached the
stairs.

Then I ran back upstairs and started throwing our clothes out
on the roof and then to the ground. Anne hurried to Ben's house
and he came down the block and helped me. We got almost all our
belongings out. The house could not be saved however. Ben rode
to get the volunteer fire fighters but the house was an inferno by
the time he rounded them up.

Ben has told us to stay here in their son's room until we find another place. He has been a lot of help tonight and Marion was very comforting to Anne.

After Melanie was asleep, Anne told me that she believes it was a terrible mistake for us to have come here.

"I think we should leave as soon as possible," she said. "We have Melanie's life to consider if not our own."

I tried to be patient with her and assure her that I would settle with the Griffins. (I know they were behind the fire.)

"That would do no good," she said. "There would just be some one else to settle with *you* then. Don't you see that this is more than you can handle?"

I did not care to hear her say that but I did not tell her so. I told her that I had two dependable Deputies (*Clay had persuaded Jim Clements to become his second Deputy. F.L.*) and could handle anything the Griffins chose to throw at me.

"Well, *I can't*," she answered. "I will not be able to sleep a wink now, fearing what they might do to us."

I tried to reassure her but there was no way of doing it. Finally, I had to remind her that I have signed a contract and am bound to respect it.

That made her cry. I put my arms around her and told her that things are not as bad as she imagined. We can find another house, I told her. I reminded her of the money we are going to make—not only from the higher salary and fine commissions but, also, from my percentage of the *Keno* earnings and my twenty per cent of the proceeds from the coming prize fight matches.

None of it helped. She kept crying and saying that Melanie was going to be killed. Finally, to quiet her, I told her that, if things do not settle down by the end of my year here, we will move back East, maybe to Pine Grove. That seemed to satisfy her although she still feels that something awful is going to happen if we do not leave right away.

I know one thing. I am not going back to Pine Grove unless it is in a Pine Box!

Well, we are off again.

Anne seemed to settle down a little after last night. Then she saw my journal on the bedroom table and read my last entry.

Now we are further apart than ever. I told her that I only meant that I hate Pine Grove. There are other places we can go, I said. But I think she knows that I do not want to go back East under any condition.

It is just as well she knows it now. She will simply have to learn to accept our life in Hays, that is all. I have a good setup here and am not going to be driven out by those d——d Griffins!

I am sitting on the balcony of the *Hays House* as I write this. I think I had better keep my Record Book in the office from now on.

Down on the stage, men are finishing up preparing the prize fight ring for tonight's match. John is down there with them, telling them what to do.

I have been reading that G——— d——d *Gazette*. Now Bellingham is serializing one of those stupid "novels" about me. He certainly went out of his way to pick the dumbest one he could find! He has added his own bright comments here and there. I do not know how much longer I intend to let him puff. If it were not for the City Council, I would–

⊨══⊨

Later: D———, d———, d———and double d———!

While I was writing before, Woodson came in with a summons to stop the match.

They have dug up some d——d city ordinance no body ever heard about which says that it is against the law to conduct "an athletic event" within the city limits. I do not know if it is a real ordinance or something they made up just for the occasion. Naturally, they waited until we had gone to all the trouble of getting things ready before making their move!

John and I are all for going ahead and saying to H—— with Woodson, the Griffins, and their d——d ordinance. But our "partners" have jelly in their spines and are afraid to tangle with the Griffins so they have run off like a pack of dogs.

The setback is a costly one, especially to John.

✦

Later: After midnight. I have just gotten back from duty.

Another killing. My luck is turning sour, it seems.

Not that I was the one who did the killing but that will not help.

It was after ten o'clock when I stopped at the *Keno* for a drink.

John was playing cards with some men. I had not spoken to him all day because he was in a black mood and I knew that he did not choose to talk. When I came in, he merely nodded his head at me.

As bad luck would have it, one of his opponents was a big cow boy named Ernie. Ernie kept peeking at the discards while they were playing. He was drunk and said that he always did that when he was playing.

John kept telling him again and again to stop monkeying with the dead wood and play cards but Ernie would not listen. He was obviously the kind of man who always goes his own way.

Except for tonight. John got sick of talking to him finally, threw down his cards, and raked in the pot (he and Ernie were the only ones left in the hand), telling Ernie to get out of his saloon.

Ernie got mad and demanded his money back. When John told him to go to H——, Ernie pulled a knife on him.

It all happened too fast for me to stop it. (I was across the room at the counter.) I have never seen John in action before. If he pulls a gun like he does a knife, I am certainly glad he is on my side. In a split second, he had thrown the blade into Ernie's chest.

We took Ernie to Doc Warner's place but he died a few minutes after we arrived.

This comes at a bad time. Still I do not see what else John

could have done. He was in the right about the game and in the
right about defending himself.

Still, knowing Bellingham, I suspect that John's association
with me will not be overlooked.

⊹═══⊹═══⊹

Clay's suspicion proved a sound one.

*What he did not foresee was that Bellingham, preferring Clay as
his main target, put as much blame on him as on Harris.*

*HALSER SUPPORTS MURDER! was the headline, the story go-
ing on to say that "with sneering defiance of lawful procedure" Clay
was permitting "one of his cronies, the notorious gambler-killer, John
Harris, to go scot free after having cold-bloodedly knifed to death an
un-armed, law-abiding" cowboy.*

*Clay's temper proved his master on this occasion—although its out-
come proved more confusing than satisfying to him.*

May 10, 1873

I went to see Bellingham before.

"Come to add me to your list of murders, have you?" was the first
thing he said to me. He said it almost before I had shut the door to
his office.

"I have not murdered any one and you know it," I said, taking
his words at face value.

"I do *not* know it," he replied. "On the contrary, I know that you
have committed murder and will doubtless do so again."

"If I do," I told him, "you are number one on the list."

"Good!" he cried. "That is my badge of honor!"

"You had better stop printing lies about me or you will be sorry,"
I said.

"That's it!" he said. "Threaten me! That is your way, isn't it?"

I swear to God I could not get through to him. I think he is loco. If he is afraid of me, he is certainly good at hiding it. I have a feeling that he *hopes* I will kill him!

I have never run across a man like him before. One thing is certain though. If he is not afraid of dying, threatening his life is a waste of time. Worse than a waste of time. The idea seems to thrill him!

I left the *Gazette* office in a stew. I am disgusted that it turned out that way. My only consolation is that Bellingham is crazy and the words of a crazy man are not as bothersome as those of a sane man.

While I was walking back to the office to see Jim, I met Streeter. He told me that the City Council wants me to break off with John.

I told him that, if there is ever a show down with the Griffins, there are only three men in this whole d——d town I can depend on and as one of these is John Harris, I intend to remain in contact with him.

I did not bother telling him that I like John and that John is my friend. He would not have understood.

+——————+

Later: That d——d crazy Bellingham has come out with a special one sheet edition of the *Gazette*, the whole thing devoted to a story about how I "bullied" my way into his office and threatened his "life and limb." "Nonetheless," writes courageous Mr. Bellingham, "so long as blood shall flow in my veins and breath in my lungs, I shall continue to espouse the cause of truth and justice though it may mean my very existence!"

I am sure now that he would love to be killed. I am also beginning to wonder if the Griffins really do pay him off. If they do, they are wasting their money. I think Bellingham would do it for nothing!

I guess I will have to learn to live with his *Gazette*.

I told Anne about my visit to Bellingham but I do not think she believes a word I say any more. Our life together has become nearly intolerable. I have not touched her for more than a month.

All she says to me these days is that she wants to leave Hays and that, if we don't leave right away, something terrible is going to happen.

+≻═≺+

Later: Past one o'clock in the morning.

Almost "cashed in" tonight.

While I was walking my rounds, eighteen cow hands from the Griffin Ranch galloped into town and started shooting up Main Street.

I was too far from the office to get there fast so I started for the *Keno* to pick up a shotgun.

I was running down the alley when three of the cow hands pulled up behind me and ordered me to stop.

I turned to face them. They had me dead to rights, all three of them pointing their revolvers at me.

"Why don't you draw, Marshal?" said one of them.

"Yeah, Marshal, why don't you draw?" said another. "You are so all-fired fast."

"Go ahead," said the third. "Fill your hand. You are the Great Marshal Halser, aren't you? You should be able to get the drop on us, you are so fast."

I knew that I would probably be killed but I was getting ready to take a crack at it when, fortunately, the play was turned. John heard the cow hands' voices through a window inside the *Keno*, grabbed a sawed off shotgun and crashed it through the window, pointing it at the three men.

"All right," he said. "Marshal Halser is ready now. Commence to firing."

Seeing him at the window with that shotgun pointing at them took the wind out of their sails. They dropped their irons and, while John marched them to jail, I took the shotgun and started after the other cow boys.

There is nothing like a few good blasts from a sawed off shotgun to clear a street. I did not even have to shoot any of them.

I owe my life to John now. And Streeter wants me to break off with him!

When I got home, Anne was still awake.

"So you are back," she said.

"What do you mean?" I asked.

"I heard the shooting," she said. "I thought they would be bringing your body home on a board."

"It was nothing," I told her.

I hope she does not hear what happened.

✦━━✦━━✦

Clay's hope was groundless. Not only did Anne learn what happened but other occurrences began to happen as well.

Clandestine attempts on his life—and, to a lesser degree, on the lives of Pickett, Clements, and Harris—picked up tempo steadily.

It was a rare night when, making his rounds, Clay failed to hear lead whistling by him in the darkness, followed by the sound of running feet and/or the hoofbeats of a galloping horse.

He began avoiding bright lights and dark alleys and took to walking in the middle of the street. He seriously considered Jim Clements's suggestion that he make his rounds on horseback in order to present a poorer target.

He entered buildings by shoving open doors with the barrel of the sawed off shotgun he always carried now, then sliding in quickly to place his back to the wall.

He began to wear a second .45 caliber Colt revolver at his right hip. He purchased a pair of derringers and carried them in his waistcoat pockets. He was a walking arsenal while on his rounds, prepared to deal with any and all emergencies. He was never again "caught short" as he had been outside the Keno Saloon *that night.*

Day by day, his state of tension mounted. While not actually afraid (his entries make this clear) he did become increasingly nervous until unexpected noises made him jump and minor irritations evoked responses far beyond their due. (His relationship with Anne reached its nadir during this period and several entries indicate that he began "taking up" with one of the dance hall girls.)

His appetite decreased and he began to lose weight. He had difficulty sleeping. His face became haggard and lined. All in all, he was a far cry from the lighthearted young man who had traveled West with such eagerness seven years earlier.

The legend had begun to take its toll.

August 20, 1873

This evening started bad and got worse.

While I was preparing to go on shift, Anne watched me in silence as I put the two reloaded Derringers into my waistcoat pockets and buckled on my pair of reloaded revolvers.

When I started reloading the sawed off shotgun, she exploded.

"Look at you!" she cried. "You are a one man Army! How long is this going to go on?"

I did not try to pacify her. I have given up on that. "I want to stay alive," was all I said.

"Then leave Hays!" she cried.

"I have a job," I said.

"Then *quit* the job!"

We went on like that for quite a while but nothing new was said.

Then, as I started walking her (and Melanie) down the block so she could pay a visit to Marion, a young fellow who had been waiting in the street blocked our way.

He could not have been more than sixteen, a skinny, mean-faced kid wearing a revolver. I almost knew what he was going to say before he opened his mouth.

"Are you Clay Halser?" he asked.

"Get out of the way," I told him.

"I hear that you are fast with a gun," he said.

My patience is not much to speak of these days. "*Get out of the way, I said,*" I told him. "Can't you see I have my wife and child with me?"

That got his back up.

"Are you hiding behind your wife's skirts?" he replied.

"For the last time," I told him, "*get out of the way.*"

"Not until I get my satisfaction," he said. "I have come a long way to meet you and will not be denied."

I had to restrain myself from killing him that instant.

"Go on ahead," I said to Anne.

"Clay," she began.

"Go on ahead," I interrupted her.

"Clay, don't do this," she begged.

"I said, go *on.*" I took her by the arm and started her off. She gasped at the grip of my hand, then, without another word, started for Ben's house, crying and not looking back.

Just then Ben came running down the plank walk with a shotgun in his hands.

"All right, drop your gun belt," he told the boy.

The boy smiled with contempt. "Well," he said to me, "no wonder you have lasted so long. You have so much help."

I was almost shaking with rage by then. The expression on his face finished it.

"Go back," I told Ben.

"Clay, let me put him in jail until he cools off," he said.

"*Go back!*" I yelled at him.

He started to say something more, then saw the look on my face and turned away. After he had walked some yards, I spoke to the boy.

"All right, you loud mouth, son of a b——," I said. "You want to try me, go ahead."

His face got tight. "Draw," he said.

"I don't have to draw," I told him. "I can wait. You haven't got a chance in H———."

He didn't either. He went for his revolver but never got it out. I have never been so fast. Before he could clear half his scabbard I had put two balls through his heart. He was dead before he started to fall.

I left him in the street and walked away. As I passed Ben's house I could see Anne looking at me.

I am sick and tired of that look! You would think I am a common murderer.

⊹═══⊹

While scarcely a common murderer, it does seem apparent that Clay had, by this time, reached the point where immediate killing was preferable to extended arguments. Completely confident in his ability to handle any armed opponent, he had lost the patience to deal with them in any other way than instant action. Like his guns, he was always "cocked and ready."

He no longer cared about the stories in the Gazette. *He paid no attention to the castigations of the City Council. He openly defied the Griffins to do their worst.*

Reports from other sources at this time confirm the fact that he had become almost brutal in his attitudes.

He was not surprised or even much disturbed when Anne decided to leave.

September 5, 1873

Anne is leaving.

She says that she can not go on living this way.

She says that she does not feel as though she knows me any more.

She says that I could have put that boy in jail if I had wanted to but that it was "easier" for me to kill him.

She says that she is going to Hickman to live with her aunt.

She says that she wants me to go with her but I think she is saying it because she feels it is the thing to do. When I reminded her that I have a contract to respect, she did not argue the point.

She says that she will expect me after my contract expires but I think she knows I will not be showing up.

My feelings about her leaving are mixed ones.

It does not do my "image" any good to have my wife "walk out" on me. I can tell people that she is leaving for some other reason but every one will know the real reason. That part I do not like.

At the same time, I feel as if a weight is being lifted off my back. I love Melanie and will miss her but my life with Anne has become a trial. There is nothing left between us. She does not respect me any more or believe in what I am doing.

It is just as well that she leaves.

+➤━━◄+

Following Anne's departure, Clay began to manifest, even more, the acid temperament which Marshal Hickok had vented on him years before.

He understood that temperament now. The strain of remaining alert for violence which could erupt at any moment of the day or night was wearing him thin.

He installed a bolt on the door of the hotel room into which he had moved.

He never went to sleep without placing crumpled newspaper pages at strategic places on the floor, most of them around the door and window despite the bolt and the fact that the window overlooked a drop of more than twenty feet.

He kept a weapon within easy reach at all times, sleeping with his gunbelt hung across the head board of the bed, a Derringer beneath the pillow.

He held a revolver in his hand when being shaved, concealing it beneath the barber's cloth, his eyes fixed on the wall mirror so that he could keep the doorway under constant observation.

He kept his right hand free at all times, even training himself to use a fork with his left.

He always sat with his back to the wall.

The need to remain ready for action, whether awake or asleep, drained him steadily. Jumpy and in constant need of rest, he began drinking more than usual.

An indication of his mental state is provided by the following entry.

October 27, 1873

Found out tonight exactly what those G—— d——d people on the North Side think of me.

A bunch of drunken cow boys started firing their guns as they were leaving town. That was all right with me. They do it all the time. It is a way for them to let off steam that hurts no body.

Then they rode into the North Side doing it and woke up the people. I rode after them and chased them out.

After they were gone, I saw the people at their windows and standing on their porches.

Not one of them addressed a word to me. They looked at me as if I was no better than the cow boys. No one asked me to chase after them but I did. Now these people looked at me as if I was a hound that had gotten out of the dog house. I almost fired my shotgun into the air to shake them up, they made me so mad. I didn't though. I touched the brim of my hat like a good Marshal should do and rode away.

B——s! I am their hired gun, no more! The strong right arm of the d——— merchants! They don't care about law and order! All they care about is making their "pound of flesh" in peace and quiet!

+⊨=⊨+

Clay's next problem came from an old source. F.L.

November 5, 1873

Henry Blackstone showed up today. He is staying at the hotel and tells me that he plans to pay me a "nice, long visit."

It is not bad to see him again but I do not have the same feeling about him I had before.

We are just not cut out of the same cloth. He is loyal to his friends, I suppose, but that is all he is loyal to. He had no reason to leave Hickman, it turns out. He had just gotten "bored" with me gone and had decided to "go find some excitement."

He is just not my sort as Jim and Ben and John are. He still looks the same too! It is unbelievable! When I look in the mirror, I see my years and more. But Henry does not look a day older. There is certainly something to be said for not taking anything seriously.

He still smiles all the time and my friends are taken with him. I do not imagine there is any reason to warn them about him. Since they are my friends, Henry will not do anything to harm them.

Still, I wish he was not here at this time. I have enough problems. He hinted that he would not mind being a Deputy and "helping me out" again but I told him that I had two Deputies and did not need any more. That is a lie. I could use *ten* good Deputies. *Good* Deputies though.

I am not sure, any more, that I could depend on Henry in a real tight.

I hope to G——— he behaves himself.

+⊨=⊨+

As the foregoing entry makes clear, Clay's attitude toward Blackstone had undergone almost a complete reversal.

Whether this was based on genuine awareness of Blackstone's potentially dangerous amorality or simply on resentment that time had treated his old friend so easily cannot be known. Probably, it was a combination of the two. Clay had been through many harrowing experiences since he had last seen Blackstone. He was simply not the same man Blackstone had known.

Since Blackstone (if we are to accept Clay's word) was exactly the same person as he had always been, there would, inevitably, have been no ground for a relationship between them anymore.

Several weeks passed during which Blackstone "behaved" himself. Clay began to feel a little more at ease with his old comrade although he never did manage to achieve the camaraderie they had once enjoyed together. He played cards and drank with Blackstone, spent considerable time with him, reminiscing.

Without mentioning, again, the idea of him being a Deputy, Henry made himself useful to Clay, Pickett, and Clements, relieving them off and on to give them more free time. In his almost childlike way, Blackstone was, perhaps, trying to "earn back" Clay's approval so that he could, once more, be Clay's Deputy.

Then, when Clay was actually considering the possibility, Blackstone altered everything.

November 21, 1873

Well, I am in the soup again with the Council, Bellingham, and every one who has heard what happened.

I have no excuse this time. I can not hold myself blameless because Henry is my friend.

I do not know what to do. I have Henry here in jail but, obviously, I can not keep him here because I owe him my life. Still, when I let him go, there has got to be an outcry heard from here to Texas.

It happened about an hour ago.

Henry was here with Ben, keeping him company. I was sleeping in my room.

Ben indicated his desire for a cup of coffee and Henry told him to go and get one. He said that he would "mind" the office while Ben was gone.

Since everything was peaceful, Ben accepted the offer and walked down the street to *Nell's Cafe.*

While he was having his coffee, a group of cow boys rode in. They had been on the trail a long time and were in no mood to "be trifled with," a witness later told me. (Ned Young from the feed store.)

Henry went outside with a shotgun and waved the cow boys over to the office where he told them that the policy was to leave their guns at the jail while they were in town.

The cow boys had never been to Hays before and did not cotton to the idea. One of them was particularly against it . . . and against Henry for suggesting it. Mistaking Henry's smile for weakness, he spoke more angrily by the moment.

He was in the middle of an insult when Henry (still smiling, Young said!) blasted him off his saddle with both barrels.

The noise woke me up and I ran to the window of my room. Seeing a crowd collecting outside the jail, I dressed as fast as I could and rushed down stairs.

By the time I got there, Ben was trying to calm the now disarmed cow boys who were in a lynching mood because of what Henry had done.

To quiet them down, I pretended to arrest Henry and put him in jail. That seemed to satisfy them and they rode away, although I have a feeling that the matter is not closed with them.

I put Henry in a cell, leaving the door open. He sat down on the cot and looked at me.

"For G——'s sake, Henry, why did you do it?" I asked.

Henry smiled.

"He was dirty talking me," he answered.

+►━━◄+

Later: Almost midnight.

Henry is gone.

I was making my rounds when the same group of cow boys rode into town and stopped in front of the office. I went over to talk to them and they told me that they were in for Henry's hide.

I told them that the law would take care of him and, after a while, they left. I knew they would be back after they had had a few drinks though and I moved Henry to my hotel room, using the back door of the jail to get him out.

Shortly after, the cow boys started gathering outside the jail again, this time with a rope in their hands. I knew that, sooner or later, they would find out that Henry was not in the jail so I got Henry's horse and brought it up behind the hotel. I went up and got him down a back staircase and saw him mounted.

"Thanks, old fellow," he said with a smile. "We are even now."

I am glad he realizes that and hope he does not come back any more. I shook his hand and wished him luck but I do not want to see his face again. He is pure trouble and I have enough of that already. I should have told him to stay out of Hays but I did not have the heart.

I just hope that I have seen the last of him.

+►━━◄+

Blackstone's departure, while relieving Clay of concern about his strange, young friend, did not, in any other way, diminish the tension of his demanding schedule.

Seven nights a week, from the hours of six o'clock to one in the morning, he stood duty as City Marshal.

He continued riding guard on all valuable stage shipments, thus completely cutting off this source of the Griffins' income.

He had to live with the mounting disfavor of the City Council and the North Side populace. Even the men and women of the South Side disapproved of his releasing Henry. (No one believed his story that Henry had "escaped," least of all Bellingham, who was in his glory with a florid account of "this new nadir of perfidy" committed by Clay.)

Finally, Clay had to continue living under the day-by-day, hour-by-hour, minute-by-minute strain of knowing that the Griffins wanted him dead and would continue "working" on that problem as long as he remained as peace officer.

About this time, another problem cropped up, Henry's disappearance strangely paralleled by the re-appearance of an old acquaintance.

December 2, 1873

I was having a drink in the *Keno* tonight when a man came dashing in and said that a cow boy had run amuck in *The Yellow Mandarin (one of Hays's largest brothels. F.L.)*, killed one of the girls, wounded two others, and barricaded himself in their room, threatening to kill any one who entered.

I hurried over to *The Yellow Mandarin* where a crowd was waiting downstairs. The room the cow boy was barricaded in was on the second floor in the rear. I went upstairs and started down the hall.

As soon as the cow boy heard my footsteps, he fired a shot through the thin door, shattering the wood. I jumped to one side and missed getting hit.

I removed my boots and edged along the wall, revolver in hand. I pressed myself against the wall outside the room and told the cow boy to come out with his hands up or he was a dead man.

"This is Marshal Halser," I told him, "and this is your last chance to come out alive."

"You will have to take me as a corpse!" he shouted.

"Are you going to let those two girls die as well?" I asked.

"I do not care about them!" he shouted. "They are just a couple of w——s!"

I asked him a few more times to surrender, then fired some shots through the door. He fired three shots back, then was quiet. I took the chance that he was reloading and kicked in the door.

That was almost my undoing. Only the shock of seeing me charging in kept him from killing me, I think. He had a Derringer in his hand but his arm jerked when I came in and he missed me by a hair, knocking off my hat. I answered his fire without thought and hit him in the chest, killing him almost instantly.

Then I put my revolver away and checked the girls. The first one I looked at had died from loss of blood.

The second one was not dead. She was not a girl either.

It was Mary McConnell, Anne's stepmother.

+>=+=+

Later: Mary McConnell is going to live, Doc Warner says. I have put her in a room at the hotel.

I do not know whether to involve myself with her or turn my back.

I do not owe her any thing but I feel that she needs a hand right now.

She looks terrible. She has lost a power of weight and has little left of the looks she had when I first met her in Hickman.

I do not know how long she has been here in Hays. She must have known that I was here. Maybe she figured that in a place as big as the South Side, our trails would never cross.

Now they have crossed though and I feel sorry for her. Even if she is only Anne's step mother, I feel as if there is a family tie. Anne went a good distance out of her way to help her once.

I suppose I can go a little way out of mine to do the same.

December 3, 1873

I spoke to Ben and Marion this afternoon and they told me that Mary McConnell is welcome to live in the small shed behind their house while she is recovering. It is nothing fancy but it is clean and Mary has no place else to stay. G—— knows *The Yellow Mandarin* does not want her and I can not afford to keep her at the hotel.

I will speak to Mary McConnell about it tomorrow morning when she wakes up.

⊹══⊰

As indicated earlier, the purpose of this volume is to convey, via choice selections from Clay Halser's journal, the unfolding of a phenomenon of these, our violent times: namely, the so-called gunfighter and/or lawman.

If one chose to deviate from this avowed intent, one could (as in the case of Clay's courtship of Anne McConnell) expend considerable space to the relationship between Mary McConnell and Jim Clements.

Indeed, an entire, tragic tale emerges from Clay's journal during this period. While not directly involved, he was close enough to the situation to view it with an acute eye and, while the bulk of his entries continued to concern themselves with his own problems as City Marshal of Hays, he did write many an extended paragraph on the McConnell-Clements liaison.

While Mary McConnell was recovering from the wound she had suffered at the hands of the cowboy in The Yellow Mandarin, *Ben and Marion Pickett behaved toward her with the very essence of that much abused word "Christianity."*

In the beginning, Mrs. Pickett brought meals to the shed and fed the injured woman by hand; bathed her, changed her bedclothes and her clothing. When Mary McConnell had recovered enough to care for herself, the Picketts invited her to share their meals in the main house.

It is, hopefully, not amiss at this point to comment briefly on the Picketts. Despite the more sensational aspects of Clay's life, and the lives of men like him, if we are to recognize the truth of the matter, it is people like the Picketts who are the true backbone of social development in the West. Undoubtedly, men like Clay Halser fulfill a definite need. Still, it is the strain of people represented by the Picketts which truly "tames" a town.

Excluding the fact that Ben Pickett was a Deputy Marshal—a somewhat exotic profession even for that time—his attitudes and those of his wife and their day-by-day behavior proved them to be the type which, in the long run, settles wildernesses and creates progress in barren lands.

It is also evident, by these facts, that Clay, despite his faults, had good taste in friends. Ben Pickett, as indicated, was a solid, stable individual. John Harris, despite his background and profession, was known to be an honest man with a straight-forward, dependable nature. Finally, Jim Clements, for all the rough-hewn simplicity of his moral standards, was fundamentally a kindhearted, generous person.

It was, perhaps, his kindness and generosity which led to his relationship with Mary McConnell. Then again, it may have been no more complicated than the loneliness of a man approaching his forties who feels the need of a permanent female companion.

Whatever the cause, when Clements—stopping by the Picketts' house for a visit one afternoon—was introduced to Mary McConnell, the "die was cast."

Before Clay learned of it, Clements was visiting the Pickett house regularly and developing a warm emotion for Mary McConnell who, in turn, was developing a warm emotion for him. On her part, it may well have been the first genuine feeling she had ever experienced. On

*the other hand, it may have been a move prompted by desperation
as, six years his senior and well on her way toward becoming one of
the "dregs" of society, she saw, in Clements, a last chance for regener-
ation.*

*When Clay discovered what was going on, he tried, without di-
vulging Mary McConnell's unseemly background, to discourage
Clements from considering her as more than a friend. This proved of
no avail. For the first time, there was friction between the two men
and, seeing that his friend was firm in his intention, Clay backed off,
not feeling justified in interfering beyond a certain point.*

*When Clements and Mary McConnell announced their wedding
plans, Clay could do no more than hope for the best. Using the
Griffins as an excuse, he tried to suggest, to Clements, that he and his
bride-to-be leave Hays and make a "fresh start" elsewhere. When this
did not work either, he gave up trying and, as his final entry before
the wedding states, "crossed my fingers hard."*

January 12, 1874

The wedding took place this afternoon, Mary is now Mrs. Clements
and I hope to G——— it works out for them. I have never seen Jim
so happy. He has always been a quiet, almost not-speaking kind of
man who, maybe, cracked a small grin once in a long while.

Today he was all smiles and like a different person.

Thank G———, I was able to keep him that way. After the cere-
mony, while Jim and Mary were accepting congratulations and well
wishes inside the church, I went out to get the buggy so they could
drive to their new house.

A couple of South Side men were riding by and stopped to watch
as the wedding guests came out. When the men saw Mary, one of
them said, "Holy C———, that is Mary from *The Yellow Mandarin!*"
He was drunk and I heard him say that he was going to ask her how
things were at the w——— house! He got off his horse to do so.

Just before Jim and Mary reached the buggy, I stepped behind the man, pulled a Derringer from beneath my coat and jammed it into his back.

"You say one word and it will be your last," I told him.

He turned into a statue and was as quiet as one as Jim and Mary got into the buggy. Whether or not Mary recognized him, I do not know. She did not seem to.

Any way, we all waved goodbye to them and they departed happily. After they were gone, I put the Derringer away. "If I hear about this any where," I told the man, "I will know who started the talk and come gunning for you."

The man swore on his mother's grave that he would never utter a word. I hope to G——— he does not. I really have got to get Jim and Mary out of Hays somehow. It is just too tight a situation. If Jim found out, I do not know what he would do.

✢═══✢

Later: After the party at Jim and Mary's house was over, I went back to the hotel to take a nap before going on duty.

As I neared my room, I saw a figure standing by the door and snatched out my gun.

"Don't shoot," the figure said in a weak voice.

It was Henry. He is very sick and may have pneumonia.

I could not very well turn him away so I helped him to take off his clothes and get into bed. I have never seen his body before. It is covered with scars of every sort, souvenirs from his many knife and gun fights in the past.

He seems quite unlike the Henry I have known. He tries to smile but can not do it too well. He has a terrible cough and can not speak too clearly. All I could make out of what he was saying was that no one saw him come into town and if I will only let him stay a while until he feels a little better, he will never bother me again. The only reason I got that was that he kept on saying it over and over until I understood.

I got Doc Warner and brought him to the room. He said that Henry probably had pneumonia. He gave Henry some medicine and said that he has to stay in bed and keep warm. He is coming back in the morning to check Henry.

I had to leave while I was on duty but I checked Henry every hour or so and he seemed to remain asleep. He must be exhausted. He does not look like a young man now. He looks like an old man with a young face. His skin is almost grey.

I guess I will have to sleep on the floor tonight. I do not want to leave him. Neither do I want to sleep in a room without a bolt on the door.

I am sitting in the chair, writing this. Henry is still asleep. I feel sorry for him. I have never seen him like this. I never realized how slight of build he is. He has lost considerable weight and, between that and that old-young face of his, he looks terrible lying on the bed.

How can such a pitiful looking creature be such a cold-blooded murderer? It is hard to understand. But then a lot of things are hard to understand. Life is not the simple thing I once believed it to be.

The thing which is most confusing of all to me is how I got to where I am. Was it all just an accident? A coincidence? As I look back, it seems that all the events of my life have combined to make me what I am.

Still, there are others like me who are as fast with a gun and have been Marshals. Why were articles and stories not written about them? Hickok is the only other man I know of who may be in the same position. *Why were we picked out?* Was it an accident? A coincidence?

I wish I knew.

✦⚊⚌⚊✦

Something about the marriage between Clements and Mary Mc-Connell plus his old comrade showing up so terribly ill seems to have

compelled Clay, for the first time, to try and understand the circum-
stances which had befallen him.

That this frame of mind remained with him for more than a
matter of hours is demonstrated by the following entry made six days
later.

January 18, 1874

Henry is feeling well enough to sit up. I have almost had to rope
him to the bed to keep him down. He keeps saying that he would
like to go out and have a drink and a game of cards.

Finally, I had to tell him straight out that he could not go out
under any circumstances because of what happened the last time
he was here.

"I am in enough trouble already," I told him. *"Don't make any*
more for me."

Henry smiled and I was shocked to see a trembling of his lips
when he did. "Sure, old fellow," he said. "I do not want to make
trouble for you. You are the only friend I have."

That made me feel like a low down skunk although I did not
know how to tell him so. I told him that I would bring a deck of
cards and some whiskey to the room later and we would have a
drink and a game.

＋＞＝＜＋

Later: It is almost three o'clock in the morning.

I should not have brought the whiskey, I suppose, although
Henry did seem to enjoy it despite the coughing. We both drank
too much.

He is asleep now. We had a game of cards and he seemed to
enjoy that too. He is so much like a child that it is strange to me.
I feel like his father now, in some ways. It is impossible for me to
believe that once we H——d it up along the border. It seems as if
it happened (if it happened at all!) a hundred years ago.

I think I got more good out of tonight than Henry did. After I had had too many drinks, I spent more time "unburdening" myself than playing cards. I do not know why I did it with Henry except that, really, he is the only one I *could* unburden myself to. Ben and John and Jim are all so strong. If I revealed what I felt to them, they would lose their respect for me.

Any way, the more I talked to Henry, the more loose my tongue got until I could not shut up. Henry listened patiently, nodding his head and smiling like he does. I do not know if he really understands what I feel but, at least, he gave me a good ear for the time I spoke.

I told him that, during the Brady-Courtwright War, I sometimes felt as though I was not a person but a part of a machine. I turned and moved but it was all within the confines of the "mechanism" that controlled me.

In Caldwell, I felt it even more.

Now, here in Hays, the feeling has reached its apex. It is as if the conflict between the Griffins and the Council is a chess game. In between the two forces is a pawn standing in the open, right in the middle and way out in front. That pawn is me and all I can do is wait for some Great Hand to move me to the next position where I may live or die.

"You are not a piece on a chess board," Henry told me when I was finished. "You are a man and can do what you want."

For a moment there, something "sparked" between us. Something that was deeper and stronger than any thing we had ever known in the old days. I do not know what it was and it did not last for more than a second or two.

Henry broke it when he smiled and said, "Don't let them ruffle you, old fellow. If they stand in your way, shoot them down."

+═══+

During Blackstone's period of recovery, Clay received a letter from Anne which multiplied, by many times, his darkened mental state.

She told him that Melanie had fallen down a flight of stairs and almost died. She had recovered but was in such a terribly weakened condition that Anne did not dare to leave her for a moment. Accordingly, she had been unable to look for work to help support the child. Since her aunt was not well off to begin with, what little savings she had possessed had gone to medical expenses for the child, and they were in consequent dire need of funds.

Clay sent whatever money he had on hand, which was not much since Anne had taken all their savings when she left. Newly ridden by a sense of guilt, Clay, in his journal entries, pondered endlessly on what to do. Harris was the only one he knew with any kind of money but he did not feel justified in asking him for a loan, the collapse of the prize fight venture having cost the gambler a large sum. Pickett and Clements were worse off financially than he was. Consequently, all he could do was send whatever portion of his earnings he did not actually need to live on and hope that it was sufficient.

It was not. Anne wrote him constantly, making it clear that the amounts he was sending were not enough to cover her modest cost of living plus the continuing medical expenses for Melanie. There was even the possibility, she wrote, that the child might have to be placed in a hospital for extensive surgery. This, added to Clay's other problems, proved a harrowing blow to his frame of mind.

He was at a peak of inner turmoil when Henry, well and restless, turned the situation into total nightmare.

February 16, 1874

Sweet G———, is there no end to it? Henry has done it *again*!

While I was sleeping this morning, he "got bored" (says his note) and, in spite of everything I have told him, left the room and went to the *Maverick Saloon* for a "drink or two and a quiet game of cards."

With Henry there is no such thing as a quiet anything. I do not know if Galwell was as bad as some say. The few times I have come across him he seemed a little arrogant but no more than a lot of young men whose fathers have money.

I do not know. Maybe he was like Menlo but I doubt it. All I know for certain is that, when he started losing money to Henry, he got mad and made a few remarks.

Shortly after, he paid for that mistake with a bullet in his brain. Henry has fled. I do not know where he is and care less. I *told* him not to leave the room! "Sure, old fellow. I do not want to make trouble for you. You are the only friend I have." *Sure!*

Galwell's father has offered a reward of a thousand dollars for Henry's capture. Right now, I think I would collect it if I could. I am in the dog house with every body. Henry was recognized as the one who "escaped" from jail that other time. Now every one thinks I let him "escape" again. I can look forward to a blast from Bellingham, several from the City Council, and a lot of trouble from the South Siders.

D—— Henry! Why did he have to do it? *What is the matter with him any way?*

+⊨——⊨+

Later: I have just heard from Henry.

He sent a note to me by a Mexican sheep herder. He is hiding in the Mexican's shack a few miles out of town and needs a horse. He wants me to bring him one and says that he will never bother me again after today.

+⊨——⊨+

Later: it is almost ten o'clock.

I have put Henry in jail.

I never saw such a startled look in my life as that on his face when I pulled my gun and told him he was under arrest. He thought that I was joshing him at first. When he saw that I was not, he never said another word.

He is going to have to stand trial for murder. I can not back him up any more. I paid off my debt to him and we are even. I just can not let him go. He is a cold-blooded killer and must be punished.

I am sending the reward money to Anne to use for Melanie. I suppose that, now, every one will accuse me of "selling" my friend for money. Let them think it if they choose. I am the City Marshal and Henry has broken the law. There is no question about it at all. It was out and out murder.

Galwell was not even armed.

+—=—+

The trial of Henry Blackstone was a brief one. The jury found him guilty of murder and he was sentenced to be hanged.

March 5, 1874

I am writing this in the office. I do not know if I have done the right thing or not. I feel that I have but I am not sure. Is there any way to be sure?

It happened about an hour ago.

It is a cold, rainy day so I brought Henry a good, hot meal from *Nell's Cafe*—soup, and steak, and bread, and pie, and coffee.

When I brought it to the cell and opened the door, Henry smiled.

"Will you sit and jaw with me while I eat?" he asked.

I did not see any harm in it. He seemed calm to me. As he ate, he spoke of different things, mostly his family.

"I hope you will write my Mother," he said to me. "I hate that she should learn I met my end this way but I want her to know. Tell her all that happened. Do not leave out anything."

He talked and talked as he ate. He said he was resigned to his fate and hoped that all the bad talk about him would cease when he had paid his debt and was hanging by a rope, his "soul flung to eternity."

"There has got to be a law," he said. "I see that now. The world would be barbaric if every young fellow lived like me. Now, as the gallows stares me in the face, I recognize what a poor wretch of a person I really am."

I never suspected a thing until, in the middle of a word, he smashed me suddenly across the head with his tray and lunged from the cell.

Dazed, I struggled to my feet and staggered after him. Henry ran outside and started down the plank walk.

If it had not been raining so hard, he might have made it. He started to run across the street to grab a horse that was tied in front of the General Store. He was half way across when he slipped and sprained his leg.

By the time he had limped to the horse and gotten on, I had reached him. I grabbed him by the leg and pulled him off. He fought me like a wildcat but has not recovered from his illness yet and was too weak to beat me. Finally, I got his left arm twisted up behind his back and stuck a gun against his ribs.

It is the only time I ever saw Henry lose control.

"What are you doing?" he cried. "Why don't you let me go?"

I did not answer him which only got him more excited.

"I understand about the reward money!" he cried. "I know you needed it for your baby! But you have *sent* it now! They can not take it back! And no one can blame you if I escape by force!"

I did not answer him. I was still dizzy but also angry that he had pulled such a mean trick on me.

"Clay, I could have killed you if I had wanted to!" he cried. "Don't you see that? *I could have killed you if I had wanted to!*"

He kept saying that over and over as I locked him into his cell. He could not seem to understand why I had not let him escape.

I do not understand it myself.

What made me chase him like that? It would have been simple to let him escape. There would have been an outcry but, soon enough, it would have passed.

Why didn't I let him go then? I know he is a criminal and a murderer and it is my job to keep him under lock and key until he is punished for his crime.

Still, he is *Henry*.

I can see why he does not understand me.

I do not understand myself.

March 9, 1874

This morning came, a desolate one.

Days of rain had ended but the sky was dark and there was a heaviness in the air.

Henry was sitting in his cell, smoking a cigar, when Ben and I went to get him. He had eaten every scrap of the breakfast we had brought to him—steak, and eggs, and coffee, and apple pie.

"I have been listening, for days, to the work men building that contraption out there," he told us with a smile. "I sure have wondered what it looks like. I am glad I am going to see before I die of curiosity."

I could barely speak. I had been up all night and had nothing in my stomach because I felt sick.

"I am sorry," I said, holding up the shackles and chain. "We have to put this on you."

"Oh, that is all right," Henry said.

Ben stood guard with a shotgun while I went into the cell and put the manacles on Henry's wrists and ankles. He puffed on his cigar and hummed as I did.

Then we took him outside where Jim was waiting, also armed with a shotgun.

"Think you boys can handle me?" Henry asked, smiling.

There was a crowd of people present to witness the hanging. Henry walked through them as if he were taking a stroll, still puffing on his cigar. He looked at the scaffold and said, "That is good work. I had an uncle who was a carpenter. I used to help him some times and I know good work when I see it."

I took him up the steps and read the death warrant to the crowd. As I did, I saw Jess Griffin, grinning as if he were at a circus. I guess it was a circus to him.

I finished reading the warrant and turned to Henry to ask if there was any thing he wanted to say.

"No, I think that I have said enough for one life time," he replied.

He threw away the cigar and got on his knees to pray. I thought I was going to vomit as I watched him. Henry was smiling while he prayed.

Then he got up and raised his manacled hands in the air. "Goodbye all!" he cried.

The hang man put the black hood over his head. I felt my heart starting to beat faster and faster. I began to feel dizzy and had to hold on to a scaffold post.

"Draw it tighter," Henry told the hang man. I pressed my teeth together praying that I would not get sick in front of every body.

Then, just before the hang man sprang the trap, Henry cried out again, this time in terror, his voice like that of a frightened boy.

"D——— you, Clay!" he cried. "*You didn't have to do it!*"

I felt as though all the blood in me was rushing out of my legs and into the scaffold as the trap door opened and Henry fell. I heard his neck crack and the sound was like a knife blade plunging straight into my heart.

My God! Henry! *I have killed you!*

⊷⊶

Later: Every thing is finished now. I do not care.

I can not remember how I got down the scaffold steps after Henry was hanged. I think that Jim came up to help me but I am not sure. I know that he looked at me strangely. Later on, when I saw my face in a mirror, I knew why. I was as pale as a ghost.

Ben told me to come to his house but I pulled away from him. I walked over to Henry and put my hand on his chest. I could not believe that he was dead. I told Ben that I felt a heart beat and whispered to him that we had to get Henry to Doc Warner before it was too late.

He told me that I was imagining it because Henry was dead.

I turned away and walked to the first saloon I could find. I went inside and bought a bottle of rye and sat at a corner table to drink. I was cold and shaking and the first drink tasted like fire.

I intended to drink until I was unconscious. That was not to be. While I was sitting there, Jess Griffin and several of his friends came in. They stood at the counter and I heard them whispering. Griffin looked at me in the mirror and grinned.

It was all the push I needed. I got up and walked across the room where I started to bait him without mercy, wanting more than anything in the world to kill him. I called him a "mouth fighter" and a "yellow livered son of a b———."

He tried to back down with a joke because he was afraid. I would not let him. I insulted his father and mother and every person in his family. I told him that his mother and his sisters were all w———s. Still, he would not fight. I slapped his face and told him that I would murder him where he stood if he did not have the guts to defend himself.

He started to cry so I could not do it. I took what little pleasure there was in slapping him a few more times, then threw him out of the saloon and went back to my table.

About an hour later, when I went outside and started to cross the street, he tried to ride me down, shooting as he came. He almost knocked me over with his horse. I barely managed to avoid getting hit by leaping to the side and landing in the mud.

He wheeled his horse to gallop back and finish me. Pushing to my feet, I rested the barrel of my Colt across my left arm and, ignoring the hail of lead, brought him down with a single ball through the head.

Jim was the first to approach me after the shooting. He checked Griffin's body, then walked over to me.

"It is war to the knife now, Clay," he said.

"Good," I answered. *"Let it come."*

March 10, 1874

Ben came into the office.

"They are riding in," he said.

"How many?" I asked.

"I count eleven," he replied.

I nodded and looked toward Jim who was buckling on his gun belt. It was just past breakfast, maybe nine o'clock.

We did not exchange words as we armed ourselves. I had told them it was not their fight but they had paid no attention to me. It was their job to help keep the peace, they said. If the Griffins rode into Hays with iron on and my life as their intention, it was their duty to assist me. I should have argued but I could not. I needed them. Three of us together had some kind of chance. Alone, I was a dead man.

We finished getting ready and went outside onto the plank walk. It was a brisk morning with a little wind.

Roy Griffin and his three remaining sons plus his two brothers and five of his hands stopped in the street, looking toward Ben, Jim, and me.

The area was deserted, every one indoors. In the silence, there was a sound of footsteps on the walk and John appeared, carrying a sawed off shotgun. He took a position behind some crates in front of the mercantile store.

"Are you in on this?" Roy Griffin asked him.

"I am," John answered.

"Then get out from behind those crates and fight like a man," Griffin said.

"What is the matter? The odds not good enough for you now?" John asked in a mocking voice.

For a split second, Roy Griffin seemed to hesitate.

"Maybe you would rather back down," I told him.

He stiffened. "You murdered my boy," he said.

"He tried to ride me down and I shot him in self-defense," I replied.

"Well, you will never shoot any one else," Griffin said.

For a moment, it seemed as though he was going to draw. Then he glanced at John and smiled. "We will be waiting for you at Kelly's Stable," he said. He pulled his horse around and they all rode down the street.

John came over to us.

"This is not your battle," I told him.

"I am a civilian," he said. "I can join if I want."

The four of us walked down the street to Kelly's Stable. Outside, dismounted, were the Griffins and their cow hands. The eleven of them stood in a line and we stopped to face them at a distance of approximately six yards.

"Surrender your weapons or face arrest," I told them.

"Die, you b——!" Griffin cried, clawing for his gun.

The next instant, the air exploded with a thunder of gun fire. The next, every one of us was obscured by a fog of powder smoke.

It was a scene from H——. The deafening roar of rifles, shot-guns, and six-shooters. The fiery muzzle blasts lighting up twisted faces. The screams of wounded and dying men. The gushing sprays of blood. The bodies falling to the muddy ground.

I do not remember how I felt. I acted like a machine. I fired my shotgun, then dropped it, and drew a revolver. I emptied the revolver, drawing the second as I fired. I dropped the first and tossed the second into my right hand to continue firing without halt. I drew one of my Derringers as I fired. When the second Colt was empty, I dropped it and continued firing with the Derringer, drawing out the second Derringer as I did. I did not aim but fired quickly at the figures across from us. They kept falling. Lead whistled all around and the air was filled with the smell of burning powder.

It seemed to go on forever but, I am told, it lasted less than a minute. I lost all sense of what was real. A pistol ball knocked off my hat. Another grazed my right cheek. Several others tore at my clothes.

Otherwise, I was unhurt. John was shot dead beside me. Jim was hit in the chest and fell to the ground. Ben took lead in his shoulder and fell to one knee. Only I was standing, unharmed. As in a dream, I chased the three remaining Griffin cowhands down an alley, all of us reloading as we went.

I caught up with them behind the General Store and we exchanged fire. Not one of their shots came near me but I killed them all.

Then I heard footsteps running up behind me and I spun and fired without thought, killing Ben with a ball through his heart. He had been running to help me.

I could not comprehend what I had done. I knelt beside Ben and felt for his heart beat the way I did with Henry. I could not believe it was real. I was positive that I was going to wake up in my bed and find it all a dream.

I left Ben and went back to the stable yard. Townspeople were beginning to appear. They gaped at all the corpses. I helped Jim to his feet and led him to Doc Warner's office. He was bleeding badly.

When I came out of Doc Warner's, Streeter was there. His face was white. "You are no better than the Griffins," he said.

I walked past him. My legs felt like wood. I went to where John was lying dead, his body riddled with lead. His eyes were open and I closed them. I stood up. The street wavered around me. I thought I was going to faint. I walked down the alley. I was amazed to see that Ben was still there. I started to cry because I knew it was not a dream.

I picked up Ben and carried him to the undertaker's. I put him on a table and sat beside him, holding his hand and crying. I do not know how long I was there. Marion appeared and sat beside me. I felt as if the insides of my head were going to explode. She sat beside me, holding my hand and crying with me and I was the one who had killed her husband. Eleven men against us and he had survived only to be killed by me.

I am sitting in my room. I still feel dazed. My hands and feet are like wood. My head is numb. I still hope it is a dream. I know it is not.

John is dead because of me. I could have made him leave. I was selfish. I wanted him by my side because I needed him. Now he is dead.

Jim is badly hurt. Doc Warner says that he does not know if he will live.

Ben is dead. I killed him. Eleven men against us. Dozens of rifle and revolver balls fired at us yet he was only slightly hurt. And I killed him. *I killed him.* Without a thought. Spinning like a machine. Firing like a machine. Killing the best man I ever knew except for Mr. Courtwright. Ben Pickett was as true as steel and I killed him. In an instant. Ben is dead because of me. Because of *me*, not the Griffins. I can not believe it. It has to be a dream.

✦══✦══✦

It was not a dream despite the fact that Clay rewrote that sentence sixteen times.

He had just taken part in the most real, *most bloody encounter ever to take place in the West which, later, became known as "Carnage At Kelly's Stable."*

This was the high-water mark of Clay's career as a gunfighter. Never again was he to achieve such a summit of deadly efficiency with the six-shooter.

While making allowances for erratic observation, eye witness accounts indicate that, of the eleven men killed in the Griffin force, Clay killed a minimum of seven.

John Harris was killed almost immediately although it is logical to assume that, armed, as he was, with a shotgun, he took at least one of the Griffin men with him when he died.

By his own statement, Jim Clements killed two others, one of them Roy Griffin himself, before a severe chest wound knocked him to the ground.

Which leaves one life, accountable, no doubt, to Ben Pickett.

As Clay indicated in his journal, it must, indeed, have been a scene from H——, fifteen men exchanging shots as rapidly as possible, using shotguns, rifles, six-shooters, and Derringers. At that close range, violent mortality must have come with extreme quickness. Estimates of the true length of the battle run as low as twenty-five seconds, which sounds perfectly feasible.

The incredible factor—here, we must openly admit, it seems more legendary than real—was that Clay did not receive a single wound more serious than a scratch across his right cheek. How this could have happened when, clearly, he would have been the principal target of the Griffin force, is difficult to understand.

Nonetheless, it did happen precisely in this manner. Perhaps it was because Clay knew instinctively which of his opponents was more likely to hit him and aimed for them first. Certainly, he was at the absolute zenith of his prowess in this battle, a veritable colossus of death, emptying and dropping one weapon after another, so rapidly that his fire never ceased for a fraction of a second until his ammunition was exhausted.

Whether the total fury of this encounter was what changed him will never be known. Surely, it had its affect on him. Whatever he had been involved in before, no battle could have matched, in brutal intensity, the Carnage at Kelly's Stable.

More than this, however, it was, doubtless, the loss of two of his closest friends that ultimately drove the spirit from him. Having just been the instrument of execution for Henry Blackstone, to now have been indirectly responsible for John Harris's death and directly responsible for Ben Pickett's must have been an emotional blow of severe force. Clay's entry, following the battle, seems to have been made by a man almost literally struck dumb by horrified disbelief.

He was never the same again.

March 15, 1874

The Council called me in today.

They told me I was a murderer. A shame to my profession. They said they were not going to renew my contract.

I did not say a word to them. While Mayor Gibbs was ranting, I took off my badge and threw it on his desk. They do not need me now because the Griffins are dead. The pawn has done his job.

On my way back to the hotel, Bellingham approached me. He did not know that the Council was not renewing my contract or that I had quit. He told me that he had "searched his soul" and decided that I represented "true law and order" in Hays and had decided to "switch his hat" and come out in my favor.

If I could have laughed, I would have. After everything he has written about me, to tell me that. I guess he needs another "friend" now that the Griffins are dead.

I felt too tired to hit him so I just walked by him without a word. The way I feel, I could not harm a man if he stood in front of me with a gun in his hand and said that he was going to kill me.

I am tired. I am going to rest. I will get out of Hays as soon as I feel strong enough.

To H—— with this journal. To H—— with every thing. I am

going to finish this bottle of whiskey. Then I am going to finish another bottle of whiskey. I am going to drink until I pass out.

I have not told Marion. I am the only one who knows that I killed him. I can not tell her. It would be too awful. I will carry the secret to my grave.

✦━✦

I might add, at this point, that Mrs. Pickett died less than a year after her husband. Accordingly, as far as she is concerned, Clay has carried his secret to the grave.

Following the above, a month went by without another entry. What reports are available indicate that Clay sank into a state of almost total vegetation, sleeping and drinking and never leaving his room except to visit Marion Pickett and Jim Clements and bring fresh flowers to Ben Pickett's grave.

Clements started to recover from his wound in late April, and Clay decided to leave Hays and return to Hickman, hopefully to reconcile with Anne.

The day he left Hays, he lost his final friend.

April 29, 1874

I am sitting on the train as I write this. Hays is many miles behind me. I will never return to it. There is nothing there for me any more.

I was packing my bag when a man came running upstairs and knocked on my door. He told me that Jim had murdered his wife and a seventeen-year-old boy who worked in the General Store.

I rode out to Jim's house. There were some people standing in the street. One of them told me that I had better not go near the house or the "crazy man" inside would kill me.

I walked on to the porch and tried to open the door. It was locked.

"Get away from there," Jim said, inside.

"Jim, it is Clay," I told him.

He was silent for a while. Then he said, "You do not want to see this, Clay."

"Let me in," I replied.

He was silent again. Then I heard his footsteps and he unlocked the door. He was wearing his night shirt and an old robe. His hair was out of place. His eyes looked old.

"She is over there," he said, pointing.

I walked in to the parlor. There was a blood soaked blanket over two bodies. I drew it back and saw Mary's white face staring up at me. Beside her was a young boy. Both of them were unclothed.

Jim came up beside me and looked down at his dead wife.

"She thought I was asleep upstairs," he said. "I found them in here. Mary screamed at me. She said that, since I could not 'service' her, she had a right to find some body else. My rifle was above the mantel. I took it down and shot them both."

He started to shiver and I put an arm around him.

"Listen," I said. "I understand. Get dressed, mount up and leave town."

"I have to be punished," he replied.

"You have been punished enough," I told him. "Get dressed and leave. Start over somewhere else."

He looked at me and, after a while, he smiled sadly and put his hand on my shoulder. "You have been a good friend, Clay," he said.

"Go up and dress," I said. "You can take my horse. It is already saddled. I will not need it anymore."

He nodded. "All right," he said.

I put the blanket over the bodies after he had left the parlor. I knew that I was helping him to break the law but I did not care. He was the only friend I had left. I was never going to tell him about Mary either.

The shot rang out as I was leaving the parlor. I ran upstairs.

Jim was lying on the bed, dead by his own hand. His Derringer had fallen to the floor. There was a hole in his chest and blood was running across his body.

I almost fell. My legs shook and I could not stop them. I sat on a chair and looked at Jim. After a long time, I got up and left the house. I returned to the hotel and finished packing. Then I went to the railroad station and sat there for two hours, waiting for the train to come.

I have been reading, in the *Gazette*, what really happened at Kelly's Stable. It is strange that I did not notice at the time.

It seems that a group of "hard working cow boys" riding into town for a little "well earned relaxation" were set upon by a "brutal police force in an unprovoked attack." Now the "head murderer" (me) is fleeing town and, under Sheriff Woodson's "upright aegis," law and order will, at long last, return to Hays.

Bellingham does not know it but he is beating a dead horse.

Some people nearby have recognized me. Word of my presence is moving through the car. I do not want to raise my head and see them staring at me. I will just keep writing.

Jim. Ben. John. Henry.

Me.

✦━✦

A week passed without an entry. Then, in Hickman . . .

May 6, 1874

I knew that I was fooling myself.

Anne is not interested in me any more. I think she was just hoping I had some money to give her.

She has received an offer of marriage from the man who owns the lumber yard in Hickman. She is going to accept, she said. She has already gone to a lawyer to get a divorce from me.

Melanie is better. She did not remember me.

Oh, why bother writing about it?

Why bother writing about anything?

⊹——⊱—⊰

Now Clay's last, close human contact had been severed and he was truly alone.

Again, a month passed without an entry. What Clay was doing during that time is any man's guess. In keeping with his past behavior, it is to be assumed that he spent the bulk of his time drinking, gambling, and consorting with the lower grade of female so common to the West.

Whatever he was doing, while he was doing it, the legend was increasing.

In contrast to the Hays Gazette, *the stories about Clay in the Eastern magazines and newspapers continued in an adulatory vein. (Sans my assistance, I am proud to state.)*

The headline for one of the stories recounting the now famous battle at Kelly's Stable reads: SINGLE-HANDED, KILLS SEVENTEEN MEN!

Despite the depths to which his will for life had fallen, his fame was at its peak.

It was a fame completely artificial now. No one in the East had any concept of him as a man. To them, he was untouchable. If there was blood in his veins, it was the blood of gods. Standing on the summit of some frontier Mount Olympus, he looked down, with august superiority, on lesser mortals.

No one realized that he had been thrust upon that mountaintop, condemned to stand alone.

So began the final phase of his life—wherein the legend ruled the man.

In dire need of funds, Clay agreed to appear in a play which was to have its "tryout" in Albany, tour the state and surrounding areas, opening, at last, in New York City.

The play, Hero of The Plains, *was the epitome of all the ludicrous tales about him.* Nonetheless, the offer from its producer was a handsome one and Clay accepted it rather than accept the various positions of City Marshal being submitted to him.

June 18, 1874

I am sitting in my hotel room. I have just finished reading *Hero of The Plains.* It is as stupid as any story about me. It is worse.

When I picked up the manuscript at the theatre, the man who hired me shook my hand and said that this play is going to make me more famous than ever.

His name is Budrys and he has produced plays for some years, he told me.

I took the manuscript to my hotel room, took off my coat and boots, and stretched out on the bed to read it.

I was in a low state of mind, but, in spite of that, the play was so ridiculous it made me smile. I began to chuckle as I turned the pages, reading on. Finally, I had to laugh. There is nothing real in the play. I kill hundreds of Indians, and save wagon trains and towns, and shoot down dozens of outlaws and renegades.

Finally, I started laughing so hard, I could not read any more. I started writhing on the mattress, kicking my legs. Tears rolled down my cheeks. I dropped the manuscript on the floor. I was as hysterical as a woman. I pounded on the bed and howled with glee.

Then I realized that I had lost control. I was not laughing any more. I was crying and hitting the bed in fury. I was losing my mind, and I stopped myself.

For the first time in my life, I know what fear is.

Too bad Frank will never know it. But no one will read these words. It is the way I want it. I would not write them otherwise.

┼══╫

Rehearsals of Hero of The Plains *were degrading.*

Clay's entries make it clear how sickened by himself he was.

Standing on a Western street, facing an armed opponent, he had been the very image of steel-nerved deadliness.

Standing on a stage, attempting to mouth the pompous dialogue of the play, he was absurd.

Embarrassed by the words and how he spoke them as well as by the staring actors, he stumbled and stammered. His movements were clumsy and inept. The director, in an agony of prescience, foresaw complete disaster and did not care who knew about it.

Clay foresaw it too but had to continue. A contract had been signed and money paid and he was still a man who honored his obligations.

What neither of them realized was that people would be attending the play for one thing only and that was to see the man who was a myth—the legendary Clay Halser. Whether he was actually portraying himself in a "True Account Of His Death-Defying Adventures" was beside the point. That he moved and spoke with awkward blundering was not important.

That it was him—*Clay Halser, in the flesh—was all that mattered.*

July 23, 1874

"First Night" as they say!

Sitting in my room. Drunk as a hoot owl. Don't give God d——— about it!

Could not face the audience sober. Drank all day. Came to the theatre half booze blind. They did not know. I can hold it. Stand up. My breath maybe. Who cares? To H——— with them!

Could not remember lines. Kept missing them. Every body laughed. Did not care. To H——— with every body! Whole play falling apart.

Saloon Scene. Supposed to tell my "comrades" about an adventure. Shot down twenty-seven outlaws "six guns spewing leaden death!" *That* again! S——!

Bar tender in play hands me a drink. Thought it *was* a drink. Every one on stage cried, *"Tell us the story, Marshal Halser!"*

Took a swallow of the drink. Spat it all over the stage, on half the actors.

"Who the H—— put cold tea in a whiskey bottle?" I roared.

Audience loved it. Roared back with laughter. Made me grin. Forgot the God d——d play! Said, "I don't tell stories 'til I get some *real* whiskey!"

Thought I was fooling. Was not. Bar tender poured another glass of tea. I poured it on his head. Audience roared. *"Real* whiskey!" I cried. Audience loved it. "Get him whiskey!" they shouted. They began to chant. "Whiskey, whiskey, whiskey!" as I pounded on the bar.

Some one brought a bottle of rye. Audience cheered. I grabbed the bottle and pulled out the cork with my teeth. Spat out the cork. Audience loved it. Laughed and clapped. Took a swig of the whiskey. *Real stuff.* I made believe it was *hot.* Stamped my foot and howled like a coyote. Audience loved it. Laughed loud. Applauded. Hit of the evening!

I forgot the play. Who needs the play? Dumb thing. Started to tell about Henry and Cullen Baker and us in the trench house. I understand though. Not tell the truth. That is not what they want. They want lies. Made it *two hundred* Indians! Made us only five men! Killed the last fifty Indians with knives and hatchets! Blood up to our knees!

I expected laughter. Gales of laughter. No. They cheered! J—— C——. They cheered! Stood on their feet, applauding. "Standing ovation," they call it. Cheering! *Bravo! Bravo!*

Stared at them like a dumb man. Can not understand. I lied to them! Stupid, dumb, crazy lies! And they believed every G—— d——d word!

To H—— with people!

＋══＋

Whether Clay ever truly understood that the legend had enveloped him is hard to ascertain. ·

His confusion in this entry seems complete. True, he was drunk when he wrote it, but it is my conviction that he never was truly aware of how he had been victimized by the myth—no, not even to the end. Being a man with a straightforward, logical turn of mind, he seemed, always, to attempt to locate some connection between himself and the legend which surrounded him.

He never seemed to comprehend the obvious fact that there was no such connection; that Clay Halser, the man, and Clay Halser, the legend, were two entirely separate entities.

This is, in essence (perhaps), the gist of the phenomenon which destroyed him.

＋══＋

Having succeeded in captivating an audience without adhering to the manuscript of Hero of The Plains, *Clay continued doing so, achieving a kind of freewheeling (and half-drunken) style somewhere in between the play and his own heavy-handed sense of drama—and humor.*

Accordingly, the play became workable and the company began to tour New York and its adjacent states.

Off stage, Clay continued to be a "loner," unable to make friends with anyone in the company. In general, they either regarded him with fearful awe or, in the majority of cases, with superior contempt, believing him to be a poseur and a fraud, a belief no doubt justified in light of his behavior on stage which, of course, was all they knew of him.

Occasionally, he spent some time with various of the actresses in the company but received no comfort from them and no sense of communication.

In addition, the preponderance of "deviates" among the male actors put him off completely and he was compelled, on several occasions, to let it be known that any such approaches toward him would be met with violent hostility.

As a result of all this, he was pretty much left to himself by the other members of the cast and his days and nights were lonely ones, the long, empty hours made palatable by heavy drinking.

The first result of this intemperance occurred in early September.

September 10, 1874

I am locked in my room. I am afraid to go out. I am afraid to drink and I am afraid to not drink. I am shaking so bad that I can hardly write.

There is the scene in Act Two. A "shootout" between "Black Bart" and me. I always win.

Tonight, I heard him walking up behind me on the street set and I turned.

It was Ben.

I stared at him in horror. "Ben?" I said.

He looked at me. His face was white and streaked with mud and there was blood flowing from his chest.

I screamed and ran from the stage and theatre. I ran all the way to the hotel and to my room. I am sitting here now. I have put a chair against the door and it is locked.

But locked doors can not keep away the dead.

It was the whiskey. I know it was the whiskey. I must not drink so much. I swear I will stop before it is too late.

Ben. Oh, God. Ben looking at me with those sweet, grave eyes. The man I loved and killed. Ben.

Oh, God! I *saw* him!

⊱━━━⊰

Firmly believing that whiskey alone caused him to suffer his hallucination, Clay attempted to cut down on his consumption.

An added impetus to this resolve was the fact that the tour was soon to take him near Pine Grove. Despite apprehensions, he hoped that a visit to his hometown would provide him with a needed boost.

It did exactly the reverse.

To his utter disheartenment, he discovered that he had even lost his identity with his own family who, in spite of knowing him all his life, tended to regard him as the super man of violence portrayed in all the articles and stories and not as the young man they remembered.

Mary Jane Silo (Mary Jane Meecham for many years by then) was remote and uncomfortable in his presence. Whatever relationship they had had was entirely a thing of the past and, it seemed to Clay, that past was irrevocably dead.

Indeed, it was as if Clay Halser, the man, was also dead while pretending to be him was this frightening impostor who looked and sounded like him but was, quite obviously, without his soul.

It was in Pine Grove that Clay suffered his second hallucination, one far more terrifying than the first.

October 23, 1874

I have to stop drinking or I am going to lose my mind. I *know* it.

It is four o'clock in the morning. I am still cold from what happened.

I was supposed to be in Fort Wayne last night. The "Hero of The Plains" was not there, however. He was here in Pine Grove, drinking.

I should never have come here. I was a fool to think that it would work out. No one knows me for what I am. They have all read the stories and I am unreal to them. Even my Mother does not know me! It was like being with a stranger. My brothers. My sisters. All strangers to me. I thought that Ralph, at least, would see me as I am. All he did was ask about Indians and how many I had killed bare handed. I could not get away from the house fast enough.

I went to the *Black Horse Tavern*. It looked different to me. Smaller, more dingy. I sat at the same table where I had played cards with Menlo. I sat in the chair that I had used. It gave me a strange feeling. Did it all start that night? Was it the beginning?

Some local men came in and gathered around. I tried to be friendly with them but they held back. I was desperate to get a laugh out of them. I thought if I could make myself foolish in their eyes, they would know that I was really just a man after all.

I told them the wildest story I could make up. I told them that I held back a lynch mob of three hundred and fifty people armed only with a rusty, unloaded revolver. I waited for their laughter but it did not come. They wanted to hear the rest of the story! I lost my temper and told them to get away from me.

They scattered like sheep. They were afraid of me. They hated me too. I saw the way they whispered about me. Men always hate what they fear.

I drank by myself. I sat there drinking rye and trying to think what I should do. I could not make up my mind. I do not like it here in the East but I do not want to go back West either. At least men do not challenge me here. There are no boys with pimples on their faces traveling distances to "try" me.

I do not know how long I drank before my brain got muddled. I thought I would rest and I laid my head on my arms on the table. It was late. There was only one other man in the saloon beside myself and that was the bar tender. I guess he wanted to close the saloon but did not dare to tell me to leave.

It is all so clear. I do not see how it could have been unreal. It was so *clear*.

I heard a voice say, "Howdy, Clay."

I lifted my head from the table and looked around. The room seemed to ripple like colorless jelly.

I saw Henry standing in the doorway.

My God, I swear that he was real! I stared at him, a hundred thoughts tumbling through my head. Ben had been wrong! I *had* felt a heartbeat and someone had rescued Henry and saved his life. It was *him*. He had followed me back East.

Then he moved outside and I jumped to my feet. I was dizzy and almost fell. I staggered to the door, calling out his name. The bar tender looked at me but did not say a word.

I pushed through the bat wing doors. "Henry!" I cried. I looked around the dark street but I could not see him.

Fear chilled me. Was he hiding in the shadows, waiting to kill me for what I had done to him?

I threw myself to the ground and looked around. The street ran like water before my eyes. "All right, go ahead!" I told him. "Shoot!"

There was no shot. I looked around. "Henry!" I shouted.

"Here!" he said.

I saw him down the street, standing near a store front.

I pushed to my feet and ran after him. I did not care if he was there to kill me. I deserved to be killed.

When I reached the place he had been standing, he was gone.

I looked around. "Henry, don't hide!" I told him. "If you want to kill me, *do* it! Just let me see your face!"

"Here I am!" he said.

I whirled and saw him standing in an alley. I ran after him. He turned and went away. I ran around a corner. He was standing twenty feet away from me, near a hitching post.

"All right, if you won't draw, I will!" I cried. I snatched out my revolver and fired.

Henry ducked away. I ran to where he had been standing. "Don't do this to me, Henry!" I shouted. "Face me like a man!"

"Clay!" he cried.

He was standing down the street.

I ran after him but he was gone. He was across the street from me. I chased him there and he went into another alley. I cursed and fired at him until my gun was empty. Lights went on in windows. People looked out at me.

I chased him all the way to the graveyard. He stood on a grave and laughed at me. "You will never catch me, old fellow!" he said.

Then he vanished and I fell on the ground, crying. "Henry, please come back," I begged. "Let me see your face."

He can not come back. He is dead. He was not in the doorway or the street or in the alleys. I know that now. He was a vision in my mind. The whiskey again.

Yet it was so clear! I remember what my Gran said when I was a boy. "The dead do walk at times," she said. "When they have need."

Sweet God, *do* the dead walk?

If so—*how many will walk with me?*

<hr>

After that night, Clay was never to see his hometown again.

Returning to the company, he continued touring with Hero of The Plains.

Approximately one month later, the play opened in New York City.

It was a huge success, not only the "masses" turning out in force but all of "high society" as well.

Clay, just drunk enough not to give a d—— (although, because of fear, he had tapered off his alcoholic consumption), performed with bombastic theatricality and the cheering and applause—albeit partially satirical, I feel—was deafening.

At the time, I was in Kentucky and unable to attend. To this day, I am not sure if I regret it or am grateful. Although it would have been good to see Clay again, I think it would have saddened me to see him making sport of himself.

That night, following the show, he was taken to dinner by Miles Radaker. On this occasion, Clay revealed that underneath the veneer of foolishness he had assumed, there still remained part of a man of ice-grained substance.

November 27, 1874

Went out tonight with Miles Radaker, the man who wrote that first article about me more than three years ago.

I gather he has made a tidy fortune exploiting what he called "The Halser Chronicle." In gratitude, he and his current mistress (he told me that when she had left the table) took me out to dinner.

I should not have gone. It is the first time in my life that I have been in such a "posh" restaurant. I made a fool of myself, not knowing which piece of silver to use, not knowing how to eat with delicacy, and not knowing how to conduct the "chit chat of the elite" as Radaker called it.

His mistress—Claudine—is a beautiful young woman. I think she liked me or was attracted to me any way. Or to the legend, I do not know. What I do know is that it became clear very soon that they were having fun at my expense, pretending to be interested in what I had to say but snickering in such a manner that I knew they took me for a perfect fool. I believe that Radaker truly thought me a country bumpkin who believed all the stories.

I held my temper as long as I could. When they started to make remarks about my clothes and hair, though, I decided to turn the table. I took my Derringer out of my inside coat pocket and laid it on the table between Radaker and myself.

"Here is a game we used to play," I told him. I cocked the Derringer and drew back my hand. "We put our hands on our laps and count to three. The one who grabs the Derringer first gets to live."

Radaker smiled. He seemed amused. "What are you talking about?" he asked.

"A game," I said. I put my hands on my lap. "Put your hands on your lap," I told him. "I will count to three."

"What are you talking about?" he asked. There was a quaver in his voice.

"One," I said.

"Wait a second," he told me. I saw a dew of sweat breaking out on his forehead. "What is this, a joke?" he asked.

"No," I said. "It is a game we played to discover which of us was the real fighter and which could only fight with his mouth."

"All right, all right," Radaker laughed nervously. "Very funny, Mr. Halser. Now put that thing away before it goes off."

"It *will* go off," I said. "In the hand of the first of us to grab it."

"This is not amusing to me any more," he said. There was quite a bit of sweat on his forehead by then.

"It is not supposed to be amusing," I said. "It is a game of life and death. Put your hands on your lap."

"I will do no such thing," he said. His voice shook badly.

"Then I will have to do it by myself," I said. "One."

"Stop this," Radaker said.

"Two," I said.

"For God's sake, are you *mad?*" he asked.

"You had better get ready to grab for it," I said. "Or you are going to die."

"What are you *talking* about?" he asked.

"You are very good with your mouth," I said. "Let us see how good you are with your hand."

"All right, I apologize," he said. "You are very clever."

"One," I said.

"Stop it, stop it," he said. He was sweating hard now and his face was white.

"I will start the count again," I said.

"For God's sake," Radaker began.

"One," I said.

"Halser, if it's money . . ."

"Two," I said.

He pushed back from the table with a whimper.

"Three!" I said. I snatched up the Derringer so fast that he could not even blink before I had it in my hand. I pulled the trigger and the hammer clicked against the empty chamber. Radaker lurched back in his chair and fell to the floor with a cry.

I put the Derringer in my pocket and stood up.

"Good night, Mr. Radaker," I said. "I have enjoyed the dinner. Thank you very much."

I left the restaurant. It was the first time I have felt any pleasure in a long time.

The pleasure is gone now. I am tired of the people back here. I may go back out West after all. Despite the perils, it is, at least, a place where I can breathe my own kind of air.

+➤━◄+

Four days later, following a night's heavy drinking, Clay's "career" as a stage actor terminated abruptly.

December 1, 1874

I am leaving the show. Tomorrow morning, I am going to catch an early train and start back West.

We had a matinee performance today. There were a lot of children present. I had a headache from the drinking I did last night.

In between each scene, I told the stage manager to tell the spotlight man not to shine it in my eyes because it made my headache worse. He never did it and I got angrier by the minute.

During the first act intermission, I got my Derringer from my dressing room and loaded it.

When the next act started and the spotlight hit my eyes again, I pulled out the Derringer and shot it out.

Then something took me by the hand and walked me to the footlights. I looked out over all the faces in the audience. I saw the children looking at me, and suddenly I could not bear the idea that they thought they were seeing truth on that stage.

I do not remember exactly what I said to them but it was something like this.

"You have been watching nonsense, do you know that? Not a word spoken up here has been a truthful one.

"You have come to see me, Clay Halser, the Great Western Hero.

"Do you want to know what it was really like out there? The truth and not the nonsense you have all been looking at?

"I will tell you.

"There was nothing pretty about it. There was nothing brave and gallant.

"I had a wife and a child but my wife left me because she could not stand facing each day, wondering if I would be coming back for supper on my own two feet or stretched out dead on a board. I was not a *Hero of The Plains* to her.

"I had five good friends but now they all are dead. They did not die like characters in this play. The blood they spilled was real.

"I had a friend named Mr. Courtwright you probably have read about. He was murdered by three hired renegades. I followed those men and when I found them, I did not say, 'Draw, you varmint,' or anything like that. I did not behave like the *Hero of The Plains*. I walked over to the table they were sitting at and shot them down in cold blood because they had murdered my friend.

"I had a friend named John Harris. You probably have read about him. He was a good, honest man. He was shot down by my side and died without a word. There was nothing 'thrilling' about his death. He was just filled with lead. He was not a *Hero of The Plains*.

"I had a friend named Jim Clements. He was brave and honest.

He was wounded helping me at Kelly's Stable. He married a woman who had almost been murdered in a w——— house where she worked. While she was recovering, Jim fell in love with her.

"I never told him she had been a prostitute. But, while he was recovering from his wounds, she began consorting with a seventeen-year-old boy. Jim found them together in the parlor and he shot them both dead with his rifle. Then he went upstairs and killed himself with a Derringer."

There was a murmur of shocked voices by then. I saw mothers and fathers rushing their children up the aisles but I kept on.

"I had a friend named Ben Pickett. You probably have read about him. He was a good, brave man and the best Deputy a City Marshal ever had. Do you know how he died? Not at the hands of the Griffins at all. No. *I* shot him. *Me.* I was so worked up by the fight at Kelly's Stable that, when he ran up behind me to help me, I spun around without thinking and shot him dead. I killed my own friend. I was not much of a hero when I did that.

"I had a friend named Henry Blackstone. You probably have read about him. He was a strange, young fellow but a friend of mine. I sold him for money. He could have escaped but I would not let him. I wanted the thousand dollars reward money offered for him. He could have killed me and escaped but he didn't want to hurt me. So they hanged him. He was my friend and I was the one who put the noose around his neck. Do you know what a neck sounds like when it breaks? Like a piece of wood being snapped in two. I did that to my friend, Henry. Then I goaded Jess Griffin into a fight even though he was afraid of me. I did it even though I knew his family would have to seek revenge after I had killed him. And they did and John Harris and Ben Pickett were killed. Because of me.

"That is just a small part of what it was like in the West. I know it is not as exciting as *Hero of The Plains* but that is the way it was and I can not change the facts."

There were a few people who applauded when I left the stage

but mostly there was bedlam. People do not like a legend to have flesh and blood.

Budrys said that, if I leave, he will get even with me, somehow. I told him to go to H———.

+══◄►══+

Later: Budrys really meant what he said, the son of a b———.

I have just finished washing off the blood and am sitting in my room, a power of cuts and bruises.

I feel great!

I was down in the hotel saloon, having a drink, when these three big galoots came in. I was standing at the corner and they stood beside me, two on one side, one on the other. We were the only customers.

"Howdy, Buffalo Bill," the one on my left said.

I did not look at him.

"I said *howdy*, Buffalo Bill," he repeated.

I looked at him.

"Are you talking to me?" I asked.

"I ain't talking to your brother," he said.

"I did not think you were," I replied, "since my brother is not Buffalo Bill, either."

"You *are* Buffalo Bill," he said.

"You are wrong," I told him.

"And you are a dirty, stinking liar who eats s———," he came back. "What do you think of that?"

That was when I realized that Budrys had hired them to take his anger out of my skin.

"Permit me," I said. I finished my drink and put down the glass. I sighed with contentment. Then I knocked that big, ugly b——— halfway across the room with a blow to the jaw that had my fullest cooperation.

The other two lunged at me. I gave one the whiskey bottle right across the face. The other one, I gave a knee in the b———s and a fist in the eye.

By then the first man was back at me and the "battle was joined" as the *Hero of The Plains* used to tell his "comrades."

I do not say it was an easy fight. Those fellows were strong enough and they did put their heart and soul to it. But they were dudes. I mean, a man who has not learned to fight "western style" has not learned to fight.

I used every trick I knew (all dirty) and gave it to them knuckle and skull. By the time I had done with them, those three, poor fellows were stretched out cold and bloody on the floor.

I poured myself a drink and threw it down. It tasted like the nectar of the gods. It was good to win a fight again. I have lost so many in the past year.

"Send the repair bill to Mr. Budrys at the Lyceum Theatre," I told the bar keep. "He will be glad to pay for all damages."

I gave him a smile and left.

Lord, one of my teeth just fell out!

✛━━✛

No entries of interest occur for more than a month and a half following the above.

Clay returned to the frontier and began to follow old paths, gambling, drinking, and spending occasional time with the lesser females of the towns he frequented.

As further indication that the legend had, by then, so surpassed the man as to make him literally unrecognizable, the following entry is displayed. Clay was, at the time, in Dawes in the Indian Nations.

January 25, 1875

I was sitting in a saloon this morning when it happened. I was reading the local newspaper. The story of prime interest to me was headlined CLAY HALSER IN TOWN! It told how the "nationally, nay, internationally" famous Marshal-Gun Fighter is "passing through" on his way to "who knows what incredible adventures." I know what. *None.*

Any way, I was reading when there was a sound of gunfire next door. I mean *lots* of gunfire.

I did not intend to find out what had caused it. How ever, a cry went up which, I admit, somewhat stirred my curiosity.

"Clay Halser has been killed!" was the cry.

Every one ran out of the saloon. I got up to follow.

"My God, to view those storied remains," an old man said as I went outside.

"It will be a thrill," I said.

He and I walked to the next door saloon and pushed in through the bat wing doors. There was quite a crowd.

I was lying on the floor, dead.

As a matter of truthful fact, the man did somewhat resemble me. He was dressed in gambler's black and was about the same height and build. There were two pearl-handled revolvers clutched in his hands however. A little too fancy for me.

It must have been one H——— of a shootout. There were an awful lot of holes in that man. I counted five, at first. Blood and people hid the rest from view.

One of the customers was telling how it happened.

"Just came in, mean drunk," he said. "Picked a fight with Bobby there and, by God, Bobby won."

I looked at Bobby. He must have been all of eighteen years of age. He looked like a kid at Christmas, flushed and over joyed.

I moved closer to take a good look at myself. There were seven bullet holes in me. Bobby had taken no chances.

"Should have thought that one would be enough," I said.

The old man was standing next to me. "Against *Halser?*" he demanded. "Are you *insane?*"

I did not argue the point. I left the saloon and went back to the hotel. I think I had better move on. Sooner or later, someone will discover that that body is not quite me. Then Bobby will feel obliged to find the real me and repeat his triumph. Except that he will end up in a pine box. And I am in no mood to start killing again.

I wonder if it would be a good idea to change my name and appearance. I could grow a mustache like Ben's and call myself . . .

Blackstone! that is what I will do.

Henry will live again.

+‒✕‒+

Despite his resolve—which seems to have been a wise one—Clay did not change his name. He grew the mustache but went no further than this in the attempt to prevent others from recognizing him.

Whether this was a result of apathy or ego it is hard to determine. He might have decided not to bother. He might have tried, then given it up. When one spends his lifetime writing and speaking his true name, it is difficult to remember to write and speak a false one however strong the intention to do so.

On the other hand, it may have been ego; a reluctance to remove himself entirely from the myth. It is possible that man and legend had become so inextricably bound by then that he was unable to separate them anymore.

An uneventful month passed by, Clay continuing his life as a gambler. While never a truly accomplished card player, he was good enough to win if his opponents were not of the highest caliber. Remembering past experiences, he saw to it that he never played with members of the professional "circuit." Accordingly, his winnings always exceeded his losses by enough of a margin to support him.

The next noteworthy entry occurred when Clay was in Topeka, Kansas.

February 28, 1875

Maybe I can get by with my "gift of gab" as they say. After accusing others of being "mouth fighters" all these years, it turns out I am not too bad a one myself.

I was having a game of Faro in the *Cimarron Saloon* this afternoon when a gaunt, whey-faced gent came walking to the table on
legs as stiff as logs. Oh, God, here it comes, I thought.

"Halser?" he said.

I looked up at him. His face was so white, it could have been
dipped in biscuit batter. His hands were shaking. Still, I knew that
he had "made up his mind" to face me.

"Before you say another word," I told him, "let me tell you what
will happen to you if you do not turn around and walk away from
here. First of all, you can not win. You are shaking like a wheat
stalk in a wind storm. You will probably drop your gun, assuming
you get it out of your scabbard at all.

"On the other hand, I have been a gunfighter for ten years now.
(We mouth fighters like to stretch the facts.) I am so fast that you
will have three bullets in your body before you can fire one. They
will hurt like H———. I can not promise you a quick death either.
You might drag on two or three days in utter agony before you die.
Is is worth it? You do not look as though you want to die. So just
turn around and leave. I will not hold it against you. I will admire
you for your ripe good sense."

That poor fellow turned and moved out of the *Cimarron* like a
sleepwalker. After he had left, a great laugh went up from all. "Shall
we continue with our game now?" I said.

Those idiots applauded me! For a moment, I thought I was
back on the d——— stage, doing *Hero of The Plains*.

<hr />

Later: I am in a strange mood. Part of me is happy and part of me
is afraid. The two feelings are mixed and I can not seem to separate them.

Maybe if I write down how they came about, it will grow clear
to me why I can not get them apart in my mind.

I went to the theatre after supper tonight. They were performing a comedy called *The Dude Finds Out*.

I bought myself a box near the stage because I felt like sitting alone. I brought a bottle of rye with me and had a drink or two as the play went on.

I had not bothered looking at the program so the first I knew of it was in the second act when a character entered who was referred to as "bawdy Aunt Alice."

To my surprise and pleasure it turned out to be Hazel Thatcher.

I was close to the stage (being in the box) but, when she saw me the first time, I do not think she recognized me, probably because of the mustache. Then, during a scene in which she had to listen to a long speech by "Ned the Dude," she peered at me in curiosity. I raised my hand and smiled at her. "Clay," I said with my lips.

She looked delighted and the next few lines she had came out badly.

I confess to being so absorbed in the welcome sight of her that I never noticed what was going on. If I had been a quarter so careless in Caldwell or Hays, they would have buried me ten times over.

The first I knew of it was Hazel looking across my shoulder in dread and breaking the scene by shouting, "Look *out* Clay!"

Before her words were out, I threw myself to the right grabbing at my revolver. A shot rang out close by, almost deafening me. Rolling over as fast as I could, I shot up at the figure in the shadows. He screamed and doubled over dropping his gun.

I stood and put my Colt away, moving to the man who was sitting on the floor of the box, hands pressed across his bleeding stomach, groaning with pain. It was the fellow I had talked out of fighting me this afternoon! I guess the laughter which greeted his departure had been more than he could stand.

Two men came and carried him away, and I said, "Please continue," to the cast and bowed to them. There was applause and the play went on.

I was not as blithe as I sounded. My hands were shaking and

there was a cold knot in my stomach I could not untie. Later, I had to step out to relieve my b——s.

I am glad that I survived, of course. I am grateful to Hazel for having saved my life.

But I am shaken that I would have been killed if it had not been for her. I am shaken that I shot the man where I did. In the past, my shots, however rushed, almost never failed to kill men instantly, most often through the heart.

The man will die, of course. He will die exactly as I told him he would—in two or three days, in utter agony. But I told him that to frighten him. I did not really believe it.

Now it is *so*. And I am shaken. Have I lost my skill? How is it possible that he was able to sneak up behind me like that without me hearing a sound? Is it the whiskey again?

I am afraid, but I do not know how to deal with the fear. I feel anxious, and my heart is beating strangely, and my breath is hard to control.

What a thing to happen just as I find Hazel again. For that is what is making me happy. I am going to pick her up after she has changed her clothes. We will have a late supper and, I hope, spend the night together. Maybe I will sleep without the dreams tonight. *(The first reference Clay ever makes to (doubtless bad) dreams. F.L.)*

After the show, I went backstage and we held on to each other for a long time, kissing as though we were hungry for each other. "To have you back," she murmured. "To have you back."

I might have spoken the same words. To have her back. Someone to be with. Someone I know. It makes me very happy.

If only I was not afraid as well.

‡—⊶—‡

To rediscover Hazel Thatcher at this point in his life was clearly a moving experience to Clay. So moving, in fact, that his eyes and ears endowed Hazel with a charm she no longer possessed—if, indeed, she had ever possessed it at all.

Time had not been kind to her. The desolate life she had led made her look far older than her thirty-nine years.

Clay never knew it but, some months prior to this meeting, I had run across her in Wichita.

She had come up to my hotel room and tried to get some money from me, telling me that she was Clay's "old friend" and that she had heard "so much about me" from Clay and wished that she knew me better "because I was his friend." Could I loan her ten dollars for a few days? The poor woman even offered, obliquely, to sell her "favors" to me for the amount.

I wish I could describe the sense of utter corruption she conveyed to me. She may have been a "handsome" woman at one time; Clay seems to have thought so, at any rate. But that night, every second of her dissipated life showed in her pale, somewhat bloated face, especially in her green eyes and in the downward cast of her over-painted mouth.

That Clay was moved to see her again can only demonstrate the measure of his loneliness.

She was more than just a woman to him then. His entries make this clear. She represented, to him, the happy past which he longed to recapture.

As for her, Hazel Thatcher was, doubtless, fully as delighted to see him. Her path had been a downward one since they had last met. Carl was dead, a victim of alcohol poisoning. She drank heavily herself. No longer able to attract men of any taste whatever, she had been forced to be content, for the indulgence of her physical desires, with men of less and less degree, stable hands and the like.

To have Clay reappear so unexpectedly must have been, to her, like Manna from Heaven. Consequently she, no doubt, displayed every last iota of allurement she could manage, not realizing that it was not necessary; that Clay, alone and dispirited, would not have left her for anything.

So, each of them needing the other desperately—neither seeing the other with an eye the least bit objective—they fell into groping resumption of their old affair. Shortly after, Clay became convinced that, this time, it was genuine love and, when Hazel mentioned marriage, he could not resist.

Disenchantment set in quickly.

March 17, 1875

I never knew Hazel had such a sharp tongue. I never saw evidence of it before.

March 21, 1875

Another fight today. Hazel thinks I should take a job as City Marshal somewhere. I told her no.

April 3, 1875

How could I have thought she was beautiful?

Now I know why she prefers to ———— in the dark.

April 9, 1875

I am beginning to think that Hazel is stupid.

April 28, 1875

Hazel said I look like an old man. She said she should have married the stories instead of me.

Another battle. She insists I take a peace officer job. I told her that it will be snowing in H——— before I do that.

I am making enough on my gambling to keep going. Of course, when the acting company leaves, Hazel will be without a job.

Unless she goes with them.

I am so tired of squabbling with her. I cannot sleep late anymore. She wakes me up each morning with a new complaint. She wants to have children and a home now!

A H——— of a Mother she would make!

"Get a job as a peace officer in a *peaceful* town then!" she yelled.

"You stupid b———!" I told her. "Any town that is peaceful does not *need* a peace officer!"

I thought it was going to be so nice with Hazel. It is a nightmare.

She wants me to go back on the stage!

"Cash in on yourself, for C———'s sake!" she said.

She has some bright idea about us getting people to give us money so we can start a publishing house. Then *I* will write stories *about myself* and "we will be rich!"

She is such a stupid woman.

June 17, 1875

She called me a "three-toed b———" and I hit her.

June 23, 1875

I told her I might do some mining.

"And in the meantime, what?" she said. "Sleep late every morning? Spend your afternoons and nights gambling while I work?"

She says she is going to quit her job with the play. Let her. There are always w——— houses.

July 4, 1875

Independence Day.

I wish I was independent of Hazel.

July 12, 1875

She read my journal today and laughed at me. I hit her and she scratched my neck until the blood ran.

Then she cried and begged me to take a job as City Marshal. She said that she is getting old and wants a family of her own. She pleaded with me to help her. When I said I would not, she scratched my neck again.

July 19, 1875

I am thinking of leaving Hazel and doing some mining. A man can make a fortune in the gold or silver lodes.

+━━+

I can not bear to touch her. She does not wash.

I am drunk. I am sick of Hazel. I wish I had not married her. We fight all the time. She curses and throws things at me. She hates me because I will not "be a man" and take a City Marshal job somewhere and let her have a home and family.

I do not hate her. I feel sorry for her. I feel sorry for myself. There is nothing in the past. The past is dead. John and Ben are lucky. Jim and Henry are lucky. Mr. Courtwright is lucky. They died in their time.

I have gone beyond mine. I am useless.

+╼══╾+

What would it have been like to marry Mary Jane and be a farmer in Pine Grove?

+╼══╾+

So it went from day to day. The marriage was doomed and both of them knew it. Still, they attempted to keep it alive.

With Clay, it was—his entries make apparent—mostly from a sense of loyalty because Hazel had saved his life and was a meaningful part of it.

With Hazel it was—I feel certain—pure and simple desperation. She recognized that, despite their differences, Clay was still her only chance. If they separated, she would go, forthwith, to the bottom, ending up in some trail town brothel. (A fate she has, I fear, suffered by this time.)

The weeks and months dragged by, Clay sleeping until afternoons, then gambling and drinking until the early morning hours; Hazel working in the theatre, then, when the theatre company left Topeka, taking a job as a saloon "girl."

Their life together was increasingly empty and dissatisfying. Both of them drank to excess, their conflicts taking on the aspect of drunken brawls replete with mutual physical violence, the details of which I will not exhibit.

Clay began suffering regularly from nightmares, often waking up, screaming. Several times he experienced further hallucinations, on one occasion becoming so convinced that Henry Blackstone's vengeance-seeking corpse was waiting for him in their hotel room that he would not return there for two days.

Money became a larger problem all the time, Clay's win-loss balance shifting to the debit side more often than not. He sold his horse and saddle, his shotgun, his second Colt, finally his Derringers, keeping one revolver for self-defense which, fortunately, he was not called upon to use during this period. If he had been, it is doubtful whether he would have survived because of his inordinate drinking.

Withal, restless, discontented and unhappy, he continued to maintain his marriage to Hazel, wondering, almost longingly, when it was going to end.

The one interesting entry during this time has to do with his meeting of a man who was his equal in fame if not in skill.

September 23, 1875

I was sitting in the *Colorado House* playing poker when a cheer went up behind me and I looked around.

A tall man dressed in black had entered the saloon. His hair was long and light-colored and his mustache drooping. It was Hickok.

I returned to my game but knew, from that instant on, that some one would bring us together, hopefully toward some violent incident. I made up my mind that—as in Morgan City—I would defer to him in all things. I was not afraid of him. I still am not. I simply did not care to face anyone in a life and death contest. I hope I never have to face a man in that fashion again.

My apprehension proved groundless. Hickok had no more desire to clash heads with me than I had to do the same with him. We were brought together (as I knew we would be) and sat with each other, drinking and chatting. I suppose it was a thrill for all those in the saloon to see two "legends" sitting in the corner.

Hickok is no more a legend than I am. In truth, he has gone through much of what I have. I feel that he has managed to live with it better than I have but his existence has been no bed of roses, either.

The first thing I asked him after we were together was whether he remembered hurrahing me in Morgan City.

He smiled a little. "No, sir, I do not," he said. "However, I dare say that you understand, now, why I acted as I did."

"I do," I said. "Being a cow town Marshal is not the most relaxing job in the world."

He chuckled at that. "No, it is not," he agreed.

It was a pleasant evening, I must say. I think that he enjoyed it too. Who, more than me, could understand what he has experienced—just as who, more than he, could appreciate what I have been through? I will not say that we "poured out" our hearts exactly. Neither of us are the kind to do so.

Still, we did chat, at length, about our experiences. It is interesting to note the similarities.

Both of us were born in the Middle West and grew up in like ways.

Both of us fought in The War Between the States on the Union side.

Both of us have "tamed" towns only to outlive our usefulness to those towns.

Both of us have achieved national if not world-wide "fame" for the identical reason—an ability to draw a revolver quickly and kill with it.

Both of us have appeared in the theatre in "self-exalting" plays, as he called them. We enjoyed discussing this particularly, laughing at the foolish things to which we were exposed. Our laughter, however, was not untinged with bitterness.

Inevitably, our conversation grew more solemn.

I discovered, to my surprise, that he believes in "life after death," and feels convinced that he has seen the ghosts of several of the men he has killed. His saying that disturbed me and I wonder now if what I have seen was really due to whiskey after all.

He suggested that I acquire and read a book on the subject of Spiritualism. I told him that I would, but I think I would rather not know if these things are true.

He also said that there is a woman here in Topeka who can "communicate" with the dead. That thought really chilled my blood and I changed the subject as soon as I could.

I told him about the man I had seen shot in Dawes. I said that seeing that body riddled with lead had made me aware, for the first time, of the fear and hatred with which I must be regarded.

Hickok nodded. He knew the feeling well, he said. I recall his exact words.

"We are victims of our notoriety," he said. "No longer men but figments of imagination. Journalists have endowed us with qualities which no man could possibly possess. Yet men hate us for these very nonexistent qualities."

His smile was sad.

"Our time is written on the sands, Mr. Halser," he said. "We are living dead men."

I believe that he is right. All this time, I have been telling myself that the skills I have to offer continue to be of value.

Now I wonder if this is so. It may be that the day of the so-called "gunfighter" is on the wane; that, soon, it will be little more than the memory of a brief period in time when masters of the handgun ruled the frontier.

A living dead man. That is what I have been for some time now.

✦━━✦━━✦

The following night, Clay's marriage ended.

I wonder if fate had anything to do with what happened tonight. The facts seem to support the notion. More and more, I have this feeling that my life has been worked out by some one other than myself.

It is the first time I have ever eaten in *Waltham's Restaurant.*

It is the first time I have ever eaten lobster.

It is the first time I have had a belly ache in such a long time that I can not recall the last.

All these things combined to bringing me back to the hotel room hours earlier than usual.

I found Hazel in bed with some cow boy, both of them drunk.

"*Oh, my God,*" Hazel said when I unlocked the door and came into the room.

The cowboy stared at me in shock.

Then, I guess, he thought that I was going to kill him on the spot because he lunged from the bed and ran across the room, stark naked, going for his gun belt.

I did not shoot him. I kicked over the chair on which his gun belt hung. Then I hit him two or three times with the barrel of my revolver and threw him into the hallway the way he was. His clothes I threw out the window.

Hazel started crying and begging me to forgive her. She said that she was "lonely" with me gone all the time and needed a little "companionship."

I paid no attention to what she was saying. I got my bag from the closet and put my few belongings in. I felt grateful to her. She had made it easy for me to leave.

Not that she wanted me to leave. She kept hanging on to my arm, and crying, and begging me to forgive her, and stay.

Finally, when she saw that I was going to leave any way, she started cursing me and calling me a "no good, three-toed son of a b———" who had lost his "guts." She told me that she has been sleeping with "dozens" of cow boys while I was out gambling. She started to describe to me what she did with them. I had to hit her to shut her up. It was either that or kill her.

I am staying at the *Richmond Hotel* tonight. Tomorrow, I am going to leave Topeka and head West. I hope I never see Hazel again. I have accepted the fact that I am to be alone until the end, however soon or late that may come.

+⇒══⇐+

The following day, Clay entrained from Topeka and began his final "tour" of the West, if such a random peregrination can be called a tour.

He was like a man without a country now, incessantly on the move.

Everywhere he went, the result followed one of two patterns.

One: the town was "rough and ready" and, challenged, Clay was forced to talk or shoot his way out of trouble. Twice, he managed the former, once was compelled to perform the latter. On this occasion, he killed his opponent.

Two: the town was so domesticated that he felt uneasy and out of place. Here, the pressures against his life were replaced by pressures even harder to adjust to—the pressures of civilization crowding him out, making him extinct before his time.

He kept moving West.

One town he visited listed him as a vagrant and ordered him to leave within twenty-four hours. Enraged, he tore the notice off its board but, in a day, departed as requested.

In another town, suffering the effects of drink, he had to be hospitalized for two weeks.

In yet another town (Red Hill, Nebraska) he actually committed himself to the job of local peace officer, then, after making his "rounds" for one night, became so terrorized by a rise of deep-seated dread within himself that he drank himself unconscious and, following a week-long bout of drinking, fled the town in ignominious defeat, thus ending, before he started it, his resolve to "get back into living."

Finally, eschewing towns altogether, he spent the rest of the winter "grub lining," riding from ranch to ranch and living off them, a welcome guest because he brought, with him, news of the "outside" world. During this time, reverting to an earlier notion, he introduced himself as Mr. Blackstone. Except in one case, no one ever recognized him.

In February, he began to experience eye trouble and, after ignoring it as long as he could, went to see a doctor in Julesberg, Colorado. There, he discovered that he had contracted a venereal infection (probably from Hazel) and was in a median stage of gonorrheal ophthalmia. The doctor did what he could for Clay but told him that, in course of time, blindness was inevitable.

Clay remained in Julesberg for a week, uncertain as to his plans, then, on a sudden impulse, decided to try some mining and left for Silver Gulch.

I will comment no further. The rest of the tale speaks for itself.

April 18, 1876

I have arrived in Silver Gulch. If my eyes hold out, I am in hopes of raising enough money to pay for Melanie's education. I will have it placed in a bank in Hickman in her name. I will make sure that the money can not be used for anything except her education. It is something I will do for her.

This town is certainly a crude place. There is only one, narrow street filled with stumps, boulders, and logs. Dozens of small, ugly saloons line the street, all made of raw pine, as are the gambling halls and w——— houses. The street itself is thick with wagons, houses, mules, and ox teams. There seems never a moment when there is not a haze of dust in the air.

I have taken a room at the one hotel here—*The Silver Lode*—a ramshackle building built of cheap, cracking wood. I have cleaned and shaved off my mustache. I look younger but not much.

I am sitting on the bed, making this entry. I am very tired. It has been a long trip and I am bone weary. My old wound is giving me "action" again and feels like a toothache in my right leg. Also, the foot hurts some. It is strange that I can *still* feel those missing toes once in a while when I am really tired!

I am going to take a nap now. Later, I will go out and have some supper and, perhaps, a game of cards.

⊹⊱━━⊰⊹

Later: Back from supper. It is almost nine o'clock. I was going to play some cards but have lost the desire. I am tired and have no energy. I do not see how I can do any mining the way I feel.

What fool idea made me get all dressed, I wonder? My white, ruffled shirt and flowered waistcoat, my black string tie, black trousers, black cutaway, black sombrero, and dark calf skin boots. Why here, in this God-forsaken place?

Why do I pretend? I shaved off the mustache and got all dressed up so that I would be recognized. I wrote "Clay Halser" on the hotel register and not Mr. Blackstone. It seems I can not live without recognition. I hate it but, like whiskey, it has become a weakness. Even knowing the pain it brings, I can not stay away from it.

It worked, of course. The hotel clerk had, undoubtedly, told everyone I was in town. When I came down he said, "Good evening, Mr. Halser." People in the street looked at me and some of them said, "Good evening, Mr. Halser." Many were surprised to see that I am still alive. They thought that I had died during the time I was grub lining.

And "he" was pleased. Poor Clay Halser in his gambler's dress, pleased to see that they knew him. Because there is nothing else left for him.

There is less than nothing left. Before I had finished supper, whatever pleasure I felt was taken from me.

Some local merchants approached with an offer of the City Marshal job. I told them I would think it over for a few days. I do not have to think it over for a second. I knew, before they were finished speaking, that I could not take the position. I have no will left any more. What happened in Red Hill is fresh in mind and humbles me. My City Marshal days are over despite my need for money.

Worse than that, my days for courage seem to be at an end too. After eating, I went to a saloon for a drink and a card game. I was told, by the bar tender, that a group of six men (three of them former employees of the Griffin Ranch) are threatening to kill me, saying that I am a murdering dog and back shooter.

I pretended to be amused. Soon afterward, however, I left and came back to the hotel room like a dog with my tail between my legs. I am afraid to meet them. After all the years of . . .

No, by God . . . !

＋＝＞＝＜＝＋

Later: Victory that is not victory.

I am back in my room again. While making the earlier entry, I suddenly became enraged and vowed that I would rather die in a "blaze of glory" than hide in my room like a coward.

I put on my gun and went to the saloon I had been in. I asked the bar tender where the six men were and he told me that they had been hanging out in *Number 9 Saloon:* I left and started down the street followed by some people. At the time, I did not care. I was so mad. Now I know that they were following the *Hero of The Plains,* not a living man.

I went into *Number 9* and placed my back to the wall, unbuttoning my coat.

The six men were standing at the counter. I recognized two of them from the Griffin Ranch. My heart was pounding, but I managed to keep my voice clear because I was angry.

"I hear that you have been making threatening remarks against me and I have come to give you your chance to kill me," I said.

The six men stared at me.

"Well?" I said. "Are you going to start shooting or shall I?"

They did not stir.

"If you are really brave and not just a pack of sneaking curs, you will give me a show right now!" I said.

They were statues.

"*Well?*" I shouted. "Go *on!*" I told them. I have not felt such fury since the night I badgered Jess Griffin. The strange thing is that I do not even know if it was really the six men I was angry at.

"Draw, you b——s!" I told them. I wanted them to fight me more than any thing I have ever wanted. I think I wanted them to kill me.

They would not draw.

"All right," I said. "Unbuckle your gun belts and hand them over."

They did it without a word. I picked them up with my left hand, keeping my revolver in my right.

"In the future," I said, "I suggest you wear skirts instead of guns."

With that I left the saloon amid the cheers of many. I dropped their guns into the first horse trough I came to and went back to the hotel. My moment of "glory."

I am sitting here, cold and shaking. What if they decided to come and get me? I could not hope to win. They would kill me in seconds.

I am just not up to these things any more. I have lost my nerve. There is nothing left inside me. I am empty.

⊹═⊱⊰═⊹

Later: It is almost four o'clock in the morning.

I guess they are not going to come for me.

I know I can not sleep however.

I dozed off for a little while before and had another dream. A man without a face was drawing on me. My arm and head were like lead and I could scarcely move it. I woke up as death struck.

My mind is a turmoil of thoughts.

I have been thinking about Anne and Melanie. I have been thinking about Mr. Courtwright and those days in Hickman long ago. I have been thinking about Pine Grove and my family and Mary Jane. I have been thinking about Caldwell and Mayor Rayburn and Keller. I have been thinking about Henry and our days together. I have been thinking about Ben, and John, and Jim.

I have been thinking about all these things but I can not believe that any of them really happened. It is not that I can not believe that Henry, and Ben, and John, and Jim, and Mr. Courtwright are dead.

I can not believe that they ever lived.

I feel very odd. Out in the street, it is noisy. I hear some one singing. I hear a man curse. I hear a horse walking by. There is a snapping noise which I can not identify. I sit in this ugly room and think about myself. *Who am I?* I look at my body but it seems to be another man's. I look at my hand as it writes these words, but the hand seems to write by itself. Is it my hand? Are the words my words?

No memory is real. I try to catch one in my mind. They run like water. I can not hold a single, true remembrance. I do not think they ever existed. I can not believe in any thing but this room because it is all I can see. I do not think there is a Hickman, or that there is an Anne, or a Melanie. There is no Hays. No one ever lived or died there. I did not kill Ben because there never was a Ben. I did not hang Henry because no one named Henry ever lived.

I run on without purpose. The words I write are the words of a fool. Who am I to say that nothing is real? Every thing is real.

I am the one who is unreal.

It is after noon. I have slept too late. The pains in my leg and foot are bothering me. My back is stiff. The air is very damp.

I am going to get dressed and have some breakfast. Then I will find out about getting started with the mining. A lot of men are making a good raise here. The hills are full of silver. There is no reason why I can not get some for myself.

What a folly if I hit it rich and become a wealthy man!

It looks as though it may rain before the day is over.

More later.

The Memoirs of
WILD BILL
HICKOK

I dedicate this book
with much gratitude
to all those who helped me
in my writing career:

William Peden, Anthony Boucher, J. Francis McComas,
H. L. Gold, Harry Altshuler, Ray Bradbury, Robert Bloch,
Howard Browne, Al Manuel, Albert Zugsmith, Alan Williams,
Malcolm Stuart, Rick Ray, Sam Adams, Lee Rosenberg,
Rod Serling, Buck Houghton, Jules Schermer, Jim Nicholson,
Sam Arkoff, Roger Corman, Anthony Hinds, Dan Curtis,
Larry Turman, Steven Spielberg, Allen Epstein, Jim Green,
Stan Shpetner, Stephen Deutsch, Jeannot Szwarc,
David Kirschner, Jeff Conner, David Greenblatt,
Gary Goldstein, Bob Gleason, Greg Cox

and, especially, Don Congdon.

AUTHOR'S NOTE

Since I am best known as a writer of fantasy, it is appropriate, I feel, to state at the outset that this novel may well be a fantasy. While there is evidence supporting much of what I fictionally contend, at the same time I do not wish to offend historical purists who believe that Wild Bill Hickok was an authentic frontier hero. In any case, I did not write the book to demean Hickok in any way and, regardless of my take on his character, his reputation will continue to endure.

The Memoirs of
Wild Bill Hickok

To the Reader

⊷⫘◉⫘⊶

You may recall that, some years back, I was witness to the violent demise of famous gunfighter–lawman Clay Halser.

Following that tragic incident, I was requested by the management of the hotel at which Halser was staying to inspect what meager goods he possessed with the intent of returning them to his family in Indiana. This request was made of me because I had known Halser since we first met during The War Between the States.

In the course of examining his goods, I ran across a stack of record books in which Halser had kept a journal from the latter part of the war until the very morning of his death.

This journal was prepared and edited by me and published in May 1877 to some measure of success.

⊶⫘⫘⊷

I mention this as introduction to the incident that occurred in September of that year in the town of Deadwood, the Dakota Territory.

As you may know, this was the town in which James Butler Hickok—known by the sobriquet of Wild Bill—was murdered by a drifter named Jack McCall, whose assassination of Hickok will doubtless be the single notable event of his life. McCall was hanged for the crime on March 1 of that year.

By coincidence, I happened to be present in Deadwood on

assignment from *The Greenvale Review,* preparing an article on the aftermath of Hickok's murder: its effect upon the community, their reaction to McCall's hanging, their recollections of Hickok as a man and a celebrity.

I intended to incorporate, within these facts, some comment as to the perilous mortality of men like Hickok, who had not yet reached the age of forty when he was killed. Halser had, as a matter of fact, died even younger, at the startling age of thirty-one.

✛━✚

I was staying at the Grand Central Hotel, compiling the disparate elements of my article, when someone knocked on the door of my room.

I rose from my work and moved across the floor to see who it was.

A woman stood in the corridor; short, comely, with glowing red hair. She was wearing a dark brown dress with a white lace collar and a small brooch fastened to it. On her head was a brown bonnet with green ribbons. She wore dark gloves on her hands in which she carried a wooden box approximately twelve by ten inches in dimension, four inches thick.

"Mr. Leslie?" she asked.

"Yes." I nodded.

"My name is Agnes Lake Thatcher Hickok," she said.

I felt a tremor of astonishment at her words. How incredibly synchronous, I thought, that Hickok's widow should be knocking at my door at that very moment.

"I'm delighted to meet you," I told her. "Did you know that I am in Deadwood preparing an article about your late husband?"

Was that a flicker of uncertainty across her face? She seemed, for an instant, to be on the verge of drawing back.

"Nothing captious or lurid, I assure you." I told her hastily, "Only a generalized appraisal of the community's reaction to your husband's . . . death." I had almost said "murder," then withheld myself from the word, fearing that it might prove disturbing to her.

"I see," was all she responded.

I stepped back and gestured toward the room. "Will you come in?" I invited.

A natural hesitation on her part; she was a lady, after all, and not about to enter a strange man's room unquestioningly.

I was about to suggest that we retire to the dining room when she murmured, "Thank you," and came in. Later on, I arrived at the conclusion that she had not wanted to be seen in public saying what she had come to say lest it be overheard and misconstrued.

Quickly, I removed some books from the one chair in the room and set them on the room's one table. I gestured toward the chair and, with a "Thank you" spoken so indistinctly that I could barely hear it, she sat down, placing the box on her lap.

"*Well,*" I said. I hesitated before sitting on the bed, thinking that it might make her uncomfortable, then decided that my standing would make her even more ill at ease and quickly settled on the mattress edge.

I forced a polite smile to my lips. "What can I do for you, Mrs. Hickok?" I asked.

She gazed at me with a restive appraisal for what must have been at least thirty seconds. Then she swallowed—the sound of it so dry that I considered asking her if she would like a drink of water—and clearly came, once more, to the decision that had brought her to my room in the first place.

"I have read your . . . presentation of the journal written by Mr. Halser," she began.

I nodded. "Yes?"

Another lengthy hesitation on her part. I heard her swallow dryly once again and, this time, did inquire as to whether she would care to have a drink of water.

She responded that she would, and I stood at once, moving to the table where I kept a carafe of water and two glasses. I poured some water into one of them and handed it to her. She thanked me with a bow of her head and took a sip from the glass.

She then placed the glass on top of the table and looked at me again.

"I have come to Deadwood to visit my husband's grave," she said. "I am traveling with Mr. and Mrs. Charles Dalton and Mr. George Carson."

I nodded, wondering why she told me this. I said nothing, however. Clearly, she was discomposed, so I sat in quiet, allowing her to proceed at whatever pace was necessary for her.

"We have all decided," she went on, "that the grave should remain undisturbed."

I nodded; still waiting.

"Accordingly," she said, "we have agreed that arrangements will be made to erect a fenced monument to my husband's memory."

"Of course," I said, nodding once more. "A splendid idea."

She drew in a long, somewhat tremulant breath and fell silent again. I had to wait further, sensing that, were I to press the situation, she might depart, her mission unstated. And I was beginning to sense—with a tingle of expectation—what that mission might be.

"I have, in this box," she said at last, "a journal written—*no*," she broke off suddenly, "not a journal," she amended. "My husband *did* keep a journal, but that was burned."

Burned! The shock of hearing that obscured her continuing statement. *My God*, I thought; it was *true* then, the protracted rumor that Hickok had composed a journal. And it had been *burned*? I could not adjust to the revelation, it was so confounding to me.

"I'm sorry," I was forced to say. "I didn't hear that last remark."

She hesitated as though questioning my reliability.

Then she said—repeated, I assumed, "What my husband *did* leave behind was an account of his life based upon memory."

She patted the box. "I have it here," she said.

I tried not to reveal the eagerness I felt at what she'd told me. She had brought this manuscript to *me*? I was overwhelmed.

"I . . ." She swallowed again and required some moments to reach for the glass again and take another sip of water. I sat in rest-less silence, attempting with great difficulty to keep my fervor from showing. I doubt if I entirely succeeded.

"I presume—" she said, then drew in wavering breath, "that . . . the magazine you represent is willing to . . ."

She gestured feebly.

I don't know why I felt such a rush of terrible embarrassment for her. There was no reason whatsoever that such an astounding find should not be compensated. If she had mentioned this imme-diately, in a matter-of-fact manner, I would have merely nodded in agreement, thinking nothing of it.

Not that I felt any less that Hickok's reminiscences should be paid for. It was her awkward broaching of the subject that made me feel a sense of great discomfort for her.

She needed money; that was clearly the situation. She had every right to it and yet the obvious tribulation of her need for it was un-settling to me. *I* swallowed dryly now.

"Well, of course—" I began and had to clear my throat in order to continue, "I am certain that the magazine will be more than pleased to remunerate you for the manuscript."

I felt an inward groan assailing me. It was apparent that, no matter what I said or how discreetly I said it, it was going to come out wrong; which, of course, it had. Mrs. Hickok could not contain a blush of disconcertion and, from the warmth I felt on my cheeks, neither could I.

"You . . . feel they would be . . . interested then," she said.

"Oh, definitely. *Definitely*," I replied, acutely aware that I spoke too loudly, too excessively.

Her smile was—I can use no more apt description—heart-wrenching.

"I never intended for the book to be seen by the public," she explained. "I thought of burning it as my husband had burned his journal. To keep it from the world, to . . . protect his reputation. However . . ."

I could only stare at her in mute distress. What could there be in the memoirs that she thought might harm her husband's reputation? For several moments, I felt an urge to tell her to leave immediately and take the manuscript along with her. I had a specific image of Hickok. Did I want to risk it?

What was there in the man's account that might conceivably undo that image?

⊬⊨⊧

Without telling them why I was asking, I approached a number of people who knew Hickok personally, seeking in their recollections some verification for the memoirs he wrote.

For a time, I convinced myself that the manuscript was fraudulent; that I had been the victim of a hoax.

That soon abated. The memory of Mrs. Hickok's unquestionable pain made it clear beyond a doubt that her words were sincerely motivated.

So, with due emphasis on this point, I present to you the memoirs of Wild Bill Hickok.

I have done a minimum of editing on them. Unlike Clay Halser's journal, this is not a day-by-day account, with the inevitable excesses of such a manuscript.

There is a minimum of repetition or irrelevant commentary in Hickok's memoirs. It is, instead, a remarkably clear-eyed appraisal of the events of his life, written with the intent of describing it exactly as it was.

The contents may surprise you.

Frank Leslie
July 19, 1878

My Intention,
Wise or Otherwise

I, James Butler Hickok, being of chafed mind and dilapidated body, hereby declare what I intend to accomplish by the writing of this account.

In brief, a presentation of the truth; the details of my life as they occurred, not as so many think they did.

For more than fifteen years, commencing after the war, I maintained a daily journal of my activities. It was, sad to relate, more than somewhat self-justifying if not self-aggrandizing. I reread it awhile back and found it to be a generous heap of cow chips. Sensibly, I put a match to it.

I am thirty-eight years old now, and it is time to set the record straight about my life. Despite my scarcely venerable age, I have a lingering impression that I am near the end of my trail. It is, accordingly, now or never.

If what I disclose offends or dismays those legions who have, over the years, shaped me in their minds as some manner of icon, a two-gun god set up on a pedestal—well, sorry; my regrets. But truth is truth and facts are facts and I cannot change that anymore, although I tried to do it once.

To begin with, then, step back in time to my childhood.

Growing Up
(as Much as Possible)

⭒⇌◉⇋⭒

I was, as you may know, the youngest of four brothers. Oliver, born in 1830; Lorenzo in 1832 (another Lorenzo, born in 1831, died soon after birth); and Horace in 1834. In 1836, the family moved to Homer, Illinois, where I was born the following year. My two sisters, Celinda and Lydia, were born in 1839 and 1842.

Herewith, a brief quotation from a description—not mine, I rush to clarify—of my early life.

"The deadliest killer of men the West has ever known, James Butler Hickok was born in a tiny log cabin in Troy Grove, Illinois, on June 27, 1837."

It was a small house in Homer, Illinois, on May 27, 1837. The inaccuracies began immediately, you see.

"As a boy, Young Hickok [as a boy I could hardly be called Old Hickok] was enthralled by tales of the wild frontier, poring avidly over many a volume that recounted, in hair-raising detail, sagas of adventure in that barbarous land."

I see myself, about the age of twelve, a wispy, blond, extremely doe-eyed boy, sitting cross-legged by the fireplace, a book of true adventures on my lap.

Concealed inside it was a torn-out catalog page on which were illustrated ladies' corsets.

"In this, he was encouraged by his father, a kindly, tolerant man."

Visualize Young Hickok emitting squeals of utmost pain as his father hauled him to his feet by one ear.

Moments later, picture in your mind Young Hickok stretched across his father's lap, reddening buttocks being walloped with a belt. Young Hickok's blubbering has no effect on Elder Hickok, whose features, in moments of such stress, bore all the animation of a statue's.

"A Hickok is a gentleman," he told me, alternating blows with that reminder. "A Hickok is a gentleman." *Whop!* "A Hickok is a gentleman." *Whop!* "A Hickok—"

You get the idea, I think. All of this observed by my mother, watching in subservient distress, unable to prevent her favorite son from getting his bottom belabored.

Afterward (it was a regular occurrence, I assure you), my mother would apply—with tender, loving touch—goose grease to my fiery, stinging backside as I lay on my stomach on her bed, her tone of voice as loving as her soothing application.

"You must always be a gentleman, James," she would tell me gently. "Remember that. It is your birthright. You are descended from the Hiccock family of Stratford-Upon-Avon, Warwickshire, England. A noble line, James."

To which I snuffled pitifully, eyes bubbling tears, and murmured, "Yes, Mother."

⊢═══⊣

Oliver and Horace and Lorenzo were tall, strong boys, my father was tall as well and constructed like a tree.

I, on the other hand, was a stripling, slender and graceful in appearance (if I do say so myself). Hardly a likely prospect to become "the deadliest killer of men the West has ever known"; but more on that anon.

I believe that my facial features were inherited from my father, a man of distinguished appearance, with dark hair, high cheekbones, and a Roman nose.

My disposition (I am glad to say) came from my mother, a warm-hearted, seraphic woman whom I loved intensely.

That my disposition came from her, I did not overly relish in my youth. The other boys in Homer treated me—what is the proper word?—*abominably?* Yes, that will do. They called me Girlboy, inviting (actually goading) me to wrath and fisticuffs.

Said invitation was rarely accepted by me unless their physical and verbal tormenting grew so extreme that I saw red and responded with sudden, mindless violence that for a moment or two, sufficed to startle them into retreat. My fury vanished quickly, however—almost instantaneously—at which point they would, once more, charge and chase and cuff me to the point of tears.

I wept a good deal as a boy. My father hated that, so I attempted to conceal it from him as well as I was able—which, too often, proved impossible. My mother, bless her saintly heart, understood and sympathized with all that I was going through. Without that loving sympathy, I wonder now and then if I would have survived my childhood.

⊹═⊰⊱═⊹

When I was twelve or thirteen, I cannot recall for certain, my father tried to teach me how to fire a revolver. I emphasize the word *tried*, for I was just about as far from being a candidate for "the deadliest killer of men," etc., as the Earth is from the stars.

See Young Hickok standing there, a look of calcified intent on his girlboy face as he aims a huge (to him) revolver at a distant target.

"At an age when other boys knew naught of such pursuits, Hickok was already mastering the art of pistol firing . . ."

Closing his eyes, a grimace of total apprehension on his face, Young Hickok pulls the trigger, the violent recoil of the pistol flinging him into his (prevalently tenderized) backside, the revolver jumping from the grip of his delicate hand.

". . . aided always by the patient ministrations of his beloved sire."

Patient and beloved sire drags Young Hickok to his feet by his (also tenderized) ear and leads him to the fallen revolver. *"Again,"* he says through clenched teeth.

Young Hickok picks up the revolver gingerly. He aims, grimaces, shuts his eyes, and pulls the trigger once again. A repetition of the same, Young Hickok flung down forcefully onto his sensitized haunches, the revolver flying, the target as safe as a babe in church.

How many times did this go on? I believe the proper word is *interminably*. Until Young Hickok's face was smudged from the black powder smoke, his hand and arm and shoulder aching from the pistol's sharp recoil, and his behind on its way, once more, to peaks of throbbing pain.

Grimace, eyes shut, pulling of trigger, exploding percussion, Young Hickok thrown flat on his arse, beloved sire hauling him up by the ear, intoning, in the same sepulchral tone of voice, *"Again."* Until Young Hickok, injured and despairing, breaks into a fit of weeping, at which patient sire twists his son's ear and instructs him that "a gentleman does not cry."

If the blubbering did not cease forthwith, off came the belt, Young Hickok's trousers were lowered to half-mast, and another buttock drubbing ensued.

Followed, as the custom was, by my mother applying further layers of goose grease to my battered backside, comforting me, and reminding me in her loving way of my heritage.

I recall the day she opened up a family chest and drew forth from its aromatic depths a copy of the Hickok family tree.

Our family can be traced back (she informed me) to one Edward Hiccox, Esquire, of Stratford, England. A relative named John Hiccocks was a Master of the High Court of Chancery from 1703 to 1709.

A William Hitchcock sailed to America in 1635, settling down in Connecticut.

A hero in the Revolutionary War was Aaron Hickok; he was, it is believed, present at the Battle of Bunker Hill.

"You see, son," said my mother on that occasion and many others, "you are descended from a fine and noble line."

I found that somewhat comforting and there were times aplenty when I needed that comfort to assuage the aching in my heart (and bottom).

I Become a Bibliolator

❖⟾◦⟽❖

If you have read this far, perhaps you wonder at my command of
language.

My mother constantly encouraged me to read in order that I
might educate myself. This I did, keeping the habit as much a secret as possible from my P.A.B.S. (patient and beloved sire) since
he felt that such a custom was a waste of time, a man's attention to
be concentrated exclusively on the higher values of life such as
commerce, farming, politics, and (I took it as a given) shooting
pistols at targets so as to perfect the shooting of them at men. I
find it beyond ironic that I ended up so deeply entrenched in this
latter "manly" pursuit.

I have been, by necessity (I believed that it was necessary, anyway) obliged to conceal my reading and education from the general public, feeling that, in their eyes, it besmirched my image as
the deadliest killer of blah ad infinitum. I have gone so far as to
deliberately misspell words and misuse grammatical construction
in order to maintain that image as a rough-and-ready pistoleer.
Well, bah to that. The truth emerges now.

I have read—naturally—the novels of James Fenimore Cooper
such as *The Last of the Mohicans, The Leatherstocking Tales, The
Pathfinder,* and *The Deerslayer.* I tried to read *Santanstoe* but found
it less interesting than his other works and did not complete it.

I have also enjoyed a number of works by the well-known English author Charles Dickens, most notably *The Pickwick Papers* (which I found delightful), *Oliver Twist,* and *David Copperfield.* I tried to read *American Notes* but found a good deal of it quite offensive in its criticism of our way of life and broke off the reading.

I read (with many a shiver, I confess) Mary Shelley's novel *Frankenstein,* the idea for which (I read elsewhere) was derived from the witness of a certain alchemist who claimed to have created a tiny human being in a bottle; *homunculus,* I believe it was called. I also read much of Carlyle's *History of the French Revolution* and found it to be of much interest.

I have read some of Edgar Allan Poe's works but, in general, thought them oppressively dark in tone although his poetry is singularly powerful, particularly "The Bells" and "The Raven."

I have also read, throughout the years, *The Count of Monte Cristo* by Dumas, *Don Quixote* by Cervantes, *Gargantua and Pantagruel* by Rabelais, *Gulliver's Travels* by Swift, *The Memoirs of Casanova* (I sensed a kindred spirit there), *Pilgrim's Progress* by Bunyan, *Robinson Crusoe* by Defoe (I, too, have known that sense of utter isolation felt by Crusoe), *Tom Jones* by Fielding, *Ivanhoe* by Scott, and even *Uncle Tom's Cabin* by Stowe (of whom Lincoln, I recall reading, upon meeting her, said something like, "Well, here is the little lady who started the war").

All this in addition to a regular perusal of as many newspapers as I was able to lay my hands on.

Why do I mention this? As indicated, to square my account. I intend to tell the truth regardless of its consequences. My Wild Bill image may be tarnished by the facts, but let that be. I wish it so.

I might add, since it is not a fact generally known, that my mother also introduced me to the subject of Spiritualism, telling me about it when I was a boy. Naturally, as in so many other areas of my life at that time, I did not (dared not) mention this to P.A.B.S.

Nor did my mother tell any of my brothers about it; I was the only one she trusted with such information. I confess that, to this day, I am not certain how I feel about the subject. God knows I have been exposed to death in many ways, but as to its penultimate significance, I am not sure. Naturally, I would like to believe in a continuation of existence, although I do confess that the vision of men I have killed remaining about as lingering shades does nothing but chill my blood.

Birds, Bees, and Pistology

⋆⟶◉⟵⋆

"Young Hickok spent many an hour in manly pursuits, his endless quest for bold, exciting enterprises leading him into more than one tight squeeze."

One of these manly pursuits was Hannah Robbins, who I lured into a haystack on a sunny afternoon, urged on by the mounting juices in my lower realm.

Unfortunately, P.A.B.S. happened to be passing by and found us there.

I recall his features—stonelike as always—as he hauled me upward, trouserless and jutting in a most unseemly way, and escorted me across the field (by ear, of course) while naked fourteen-year-old Hannah scrambled from the stack, snatched up her clothes, and ran for home.

Inside our barn, a typical posterior-hiding took place, my body (ungarbed below) stretched across my father's legs as he wore his belt down farther on my burning buttocks.

"A Hickok is a gentleman," he told me sternly. "Repeat."

"A Hi-Hi-Hi-Hi—" was all I could manage.

I cried out as another blow resounded leatherly across my bottom.

"Hickok isagen'l'man!" I blurted.

"Correct," my father said.

Another belt delivery to my hapless rump.

"Repeat," my father said.

"Oooh," I replied.

Another blow. *"Repeat,"* my father said.

"A Hickokisagen'l'man!" moaned I.

"Correct," he said. Another blow. *"Repeat."*

Another limping, weeping visit to my mother's consoling presence. Another gentle application of goose grease to my harrowed haunches. Another kind reminder of my legacy.

"You must always be a gentleman, James," she said. "It is expected of you."

"I *know,* I *know,*" I muttered dismally.

But it *did* sink in. I *am* a gentleman. Whatever else I have failed to be, I have always been a gentleman.

Has it served me well?

I wouldn't bet my stash on it.

━━━

Fourteen years of age: my father trying, once again, to teach me pistology.

"With constant practice, Young Hickok soon perfected that deadly eye, which was to serve him with such potency in days to come."

I aimed, I fired, keeping my eyes open at any rate and managing to stay on my feet, albeit staggering noticeably.

The target—a bottle standing on a boulder top—remained untouched, the ball whistling off into the distance.

"Again," my father said, features ossifying in their usual fashion.

I aimed and fired, tottering.

The bottle remained safe and sound.

"Again," my father said.

Not much point in putting down the further details. P.A.B.S. watching me with monolithic detachment, mute save for the one repeated word. Young Hickok contorting his greenhorn visage into a gargoyle mask of concentration as he aims, fires, teeters, misses.

With each new miss, my father took me by the ear and moved me closer to the target. I kept on aiming, firing, stumbling, missing. With each new miss, my father's incredulity at my ineptitude with the revolver mounted until his eyes were bulging so with his determination not to lose his temper that it would not have surprised me at all had they popped from their sockets. Soon, his "Again's" were delivered behind tightly clenched teeth.

On one occasion, at a distance of some fifteen feet, I managed to hit the boulder, the ricocheting ball knocking off my father's hat and causing him, from startlement, to topple, crashing to the ground.

Seeing that, a woebegone expression on his face, Young Hickok began to undo his trousers as his P.A.B.S. rose to his feet and began removing his belt.

I leaned against a tree as my father laid said belt (with special vigor) across my much harried fundaments.

"A gentleman is skilled in the use of weapons," he instructed me.

"A gentleman—" I began.

A wallop on my rump concluded my remark.

"You were not instructed to repeat," my father said.

I do not recall my exact response, but I feel confident that it was something in the neighborhood of "Oooh!"

<hr />

Of course, in time, I actually learned to shoot, first with a Pennsylvania long flintlock, then a better rifle (a percussion-lock Remington). I did this minus my sire's patient and benign presence and learned much faster.

I have always preferred the rifle as a weapon. If I had been permitted to conduct all street confrontations with a rifle instead of a revolver, I would have faced these moments with far more equanimity than, in fact, I did. But I suppose it would be less dramatic for two opponents to face each other with rifles sticking out of their holsters.

During that period, Oliver traveled to California, where he found a profession (teamster) and lost an arm. Horace and Lorenzo worked on the farm, leaving me to spend the greater part of my time shooting squirrels, rabbits, deer, and prairie chickens to augment the family larder. I became quite good at that.

But then none of those critters were armed.

Egress and Egest

"Thus was Young Hickok admirably equipped to master any peril he might face—which soon proved necessary as he was exposed to the sound of hostile gunfire and the near proximity of death when he assisted his father in delivering runaway slaves from one station to the next of the so-called 'underground railroad.'"

I remember one occasion when I was fifteen, an evening on the road outside of Homer, my father driving a small hay-filled wagon, underneath said hay an assortment of fear-ridden slaves who had escaped from the South.

We had just turned a curve in the road when we caught sight of three mounted men ahead, waiting for us.

"Bounty hunters, I'll wager," my father said.

His words petrified my limbs. Bounty hunters made their living capturing runaway slaves and returning them to their owners—at gunpoint, needless to say.

I made, I fear, a feeble sound of apprehension.

"A gentleman does not show panic when in danger," said my father.

"Yes, but—" I began.

"Repeat," my father told me.

I answered through my teeth, which I was gritting to prevent their chattering. "A gentleman does not show panic when in danger," I repeated.

"Correct; repeat." Despite my dread, I knew, at that moment, what a brave man my father was.

The words had a tendency to vibrate in my throat as I repeated them.

"Correct; repeat," my father said. We were almost to the three men now.

"A gentleman does not—"

My voice choked off as my father shouted at the horses suddenly and cracked his whip above their heads. The bounty hunters began to draw their pistols, then were forced to yank aside their mounts to avoid getting run down as the team and wagon hurtled by them.

Behind, the bounty hunters opened fire and pistol balls began to buzz around us like infuriated bees. I sat on the seat, eyes wide and unblinking, utterly benumbed with fear, mumbling to myself, making an endless litany of my father's family maxim, "A gentleman does not show panic when in danger a gentleman does not show panic when in danger a gentleman does not—" And so on.

How long that chase continued is lost in congealed recollection. All I do remember is emerging from a blinding stupor of dread to discover that my father had steered the team and wagon behind a great clump of bushes, eluding the bounty hunters who were galloping by.

After they had disappeared, my father turned to me.

"You behaved well," he told me.

"Thank you, sir." Was that my voice I heard? It could have been that of a frightened girl.

P.A.B.S. patted me on the back. "You see. It *can* be done."

"Yes, sir," replied Young Hickok, hoping to God above that P.A.B.S. did not notice the spreading puddle by his feet.

I plucked discreetly at my soggy trousers.

"Now you are a Hickok," said my father.

Somewhere Between Boyhood
and (Hoped for) Adulthood

A brief enumeration of the passing years and my varying occupations.

1853: Canal mule driver.

1854: Homesteader.

1855: Stable tender.

1856: Bull whacker.

1857: Freight wagon driver.

1858: Stagecoach driver.

This last employment, for three men named Russell, Majors, and Waddell, went on for several years and was, if you are not aware, a giant pain (literally) in the a———. Roads were little better than rutted tracks stocked with rocks and hidden stumps; only the open prairie and mesa country were accessible without danger of spinal havoc. The spring-steel brackets were of little assistance when the going was extreme, not to mention the clouds of dust that billowed around the coach as it rocked along, threatening to smother driver and passengers alike.

Toward the end of 1858, I fell in love with a young woman named Mary Owens and came close to marrying her and taking up a life of farming.

Lorenzo traveled to Kansas and convinced me that it was a

mistake. I think of that often, not certain why I let him talk me out of it; could it possibly have been only because she was part Indian? I can scarcely believe that now, yet I did not marry her. I also think often that, had I married her, I might have lived a peaceful existence on that farm. It would, God knows, have been a simpler life.

+═══+

As heretofore indicated, I did become as proficient with the pistol as the rifle.

Had I known what roads that skill would lead me along, I would have dropped the ability as quickly as I would have dropped a red-hot branding iron. But, of course, I didn't know. Accordingly, I disappeared into the woods at every opportunity to hone the edge of my revolver skill. Indeed, in time I derived undue pleasure in astonishing all and sundry with my mastery of the handgun.

But that is simple; don't you see. Time and practice, nothing more. Shooting an apple from a tree and putting a second ball in it before it hits the ground? No great achievement. An apple doesn't shoot back.

+═══+

I had begun to read any periodicals that came my way by 1858 and was aware of myriad things occurring outside of my personal life.

For instance, Senate candidate Abraham Lincoln declaring that "the Union cannot permanently endure half slave and half free." Little did we know where those words would lead us.

That summer, the first Pony Express mail delivery traveled from St. Louis to the west coast in twenty-three days; an incredible feat.

The Seven-Year War with the Seminole Indians had concluded; cost: ten million dollars and the lives of fifteen hundred men. Does mankind ever come out in the black from a war?

On August 5, 1858, two steamers began to lay cable across the bottom of the Atlantic Ocean. Upon completion, England telegraphed our government: "Europe and America are united by telegraph.

Glory to God on the highest; on Earth peace, good will toward men."

In September, the cable's insulation ruptured and the service discontinued.

✦━━✦

By 1860, I was still a stage and wagon driver; not much progress there.

Homer's name was changed to Troy Grove since there was another Homer (larger) in Illinois.

Abraham Lincoln won his party's nomination for President of the United States (his progress had considerably outstripped mine). His vice presidential candidate was a man named Hannibal Hamlin. Where is he today?

In autumn of that year, none of the four presidential candidates obtained a majority vote, and Lincoln was elected with a plurality of half a million votes more than Stephen Douglas.

In December 1860, Congress debated and President Buchanan hesitated and the North stood by in hapless silence while the South made ready to redress their grievances with a plan to secede from the Union.

By January 1861, the South's secession was rolling along steadily: first Mississippi, then Florida, Alabama, Georgia, Louisiana, and, by February, Texas. The other states were soon to follow.

In Lincoln's inaugural address, he stated that he had no intention, directly or indirectly, to interfere with slavery wherever it might exist. I could not help but wonder—along with many others—what had happened to his conviction that the Union could not permanently endure half slave and half free. I presume that when politicians actually assume office, their convictions, of necessity, become more flexible.

In the spring of 1861, to my amazement (along with others), I read that the Confederacy actually hoped to establish its independence by means of peaceful negotiation. This was, to say the very least, substantially naive, considering that the United States government regarded supporters of Secession as traitors to the Union.

It is interesting to speculate, in retrospect, how different the war would have been if the man who was offered the command of the Union Army had accepted instead of resigning his commission and offering his services to his native state of Virginia, which, naturally, accepted this offer by Robert E. Lee.

Why do I go on about these things? Perhaps to avoid the beginning of it all: my appearance to the public eye, my notoriety and increasingly demanding residence in an outsize hornet's nest. But, heaven help me, it is time to tell the tawdry tale.

By July of 1861, I was about to secede from anonymity.

The Straight Goods

"Hickok's first manhood brush with violent death occurred on Friday, July 12, 1861, when he became involved in the horrendous incident that first revealed his lethal prowess as a slayer of men and brought to life the Hickok legend: *the Battle of Rock Creek Station.*"

Rock Creek Station was a stagecoach station six miles out from Fairbury, Nebraska.

I was there recuperating from some injuries I had incurred when a wagon I was driving ran over a bear, overturned, and pitched me to the ground. On the afternoon of July 12 (my imaginative biographer, Colonel George Ward Nichols, got the date right, anyway) I was in the sleeping quarters of the station, not, I must confess, sleeping but—well, let it be said—dallying with a most attractive young woman by the name of Sarah Shull. Both of us were on my cot, as the French would have it, au naturel.

I was lying on my back while Sarah spoke to me, alternating words and phrases with a rain of kisses on my face, my neck, my shoulders, chest, and—to be decorous—et al.

"Hickok was alone when it happened," Nichols wrote, fully on the mark, as usual.

"You ain't really going to leave your job here, are you, darling?" Sarah asked.

"Soon enough," I answered.

"Why?" she asked.

"A gentleman does not drive wagons and coaches for a living," I replied. If that sounds egregiously pretentious to you, you're correct. I had a manner of behavior then that, in recollection, makes me alternately smile and cringe. Some might say that I was full of myself. Actually, I was full of manure.

"What *does* a gentleman do?" asked Sarah.

"Something appropriate," responded I.

"Something *what?*" inquired Sarah.

I frowned at her in lordly disdain. "Ap*prop*riate," I pronounced the word again. "Something *fitting.*"

"Like what?" asked Sarah.

"I'm not quite certain yet," I let her know. "I'll find out, though."

"Marry me and take me with you," she pleaded.

After she allowed my lips their freedom once again, I looked at her, not so much in scorn but in surprise that she could even conceive of such an occurrence.

"You?" I said.

She stopped her kissing frenzy and looked sulky. "Why not?" she demanded.

I gazed into my (unpromising at the time) future and replied, "Because the woman I *marry* will have to be a *lady.*"

"Oh!" cried Sarah, angrily.

She glared at me for many moments, then once more pressed herself against me, snuggling close.

"If only you weren't so gorgeous," she said.

"No man is gorgeous, Sarah," I chided. But of course she was right. I *was* gorgeous then. What can I say? I looked in the mirror and there it was. No feather in my cap, of course; I know that now. Heredity; my father was a handsome man. My looks were not remarkable at all, but at the time I certainly made the most of them.

So when she countered, "You are," I did not contest the point. *Why argue with the unarguable?* I probably thought.

Idiot.

+⊷⊶+

At that point, both of us looked toward the window as we heard the sound of approaching horses. Sarah gasped.

"I thought you said no one was coming here today," she said.

"I didn't think they were," I replied. I didn't either, or I wouldn't have arranged our assignation.

Sarah jumped up hastily and hurried to the window as I rose and pulled up my long johns over my (rapidly decreasing, let me tell you) equipment.

At the window looking out, Sarah caught her breath in such obvious shock that the sound made me twitch, lose balance, and topple to the floor from where I looked up at her with a combination of vexation and alarm.

"What's wrong?" I demanded.

"It's Dave," she said.

"Dave who?"

"McCanles."

"So?" I responded, struggling to my feet, rubbing my bruised elbow.

"He looks mad," Sarah replied uneasily.

I felt myself beginning to tense as I limped to the window and looked outside.

Some fifty yards away, dismounting by the corral, were three men, Dave McCanles, James Woods, and James Gordon (the identities of the last two of the trio I discovered later).

McCanles was looking toward the station with an expression that more than confirmed Sarah's observation. He looked, in point of fact, on the verge of spitting fire.

"What's he mad about?" I asked.

I looked at her inquiringly as she failed to respond.

"Well?" I asked.

Her smile was wan. "Us?" she said.

"Us!"

"Well . . . yes," she admitted. "I'm his . . . sort of . . . well, I'm sort of his mistress."

"You never told me that!" I cried, aghast.

Her face curled up. "You never asked," she offered feebly.

I looked back at McCanles, looked at Sarah, looked back at McCanles, and felt my breath cut off. I believed I leaned toward the window, my mouth as widely open as the window was.

McCanles was drawing a shotgun from its saddle sheath.

"That's not a shotgun," I actually heard myself say, my tone of voice incredulous and weak.

"Yes, it is," Sarah verified.

I saw McCanles say something to Woods and Gordon, the two men nodding grimly.

Then he started toward the station.

I gaped at Sarah, pointing toward McCanles. I attempted speech but failed to produce more than a succession of inchoate sounds, which fluttered in my throat.

Then I blew.

"Good Lord, girl!" I exploded.

She began to bawl. "I'm sorry!"

"Sorry!" I repeated at a higher, angrier pitch. "Don't you realize—?"

I pointed at McCanles with a trembling finger.

"—that man is going to get hurt?" I wheezed.

I grabbed her arm and pulled her to the bed, picked up her shift, and flung it at her.

"Put it on," I ordered, swallowed, pointed. "Then go out and tell him he's a dead man if he comes in here. You understand?"

She stared at me.

"You understand?" I repeated.

Sarah, whimpering and snuffling, nodded as she drew the shift over her head and down across her body. I shoved her toward the doorway.

"Go!" I cried.

She stumbled through the doorway.

"Tell him I'm a deadly shot!" I ordered. "*Tell* him!"

I felt the gases in my stomach taking flight, an involuntary belch escaping me. Turning toward the window, I assumed a stiff expression on my face.

"The man's a fool," I mumbled.

I belched again, eyes bulging as a wave of nausea plowed through my stomach. I looked outside.

McCanles was almost to the station. As he moved, he was loading his shotgun.

"Don't *do* that," I remember saying in a faint, offended tone.

I turned and strutted about the room in aimless patterns, lower lip thrust forward, a look of dignified affront on my face. It was an expression I had cultivated through the years—if not the knowledge of when it was appropriate.

With an abrupt descent, I plopped down on the cot and with casual albeit palsied movement, pulled on my right boot. I looked toward the window, drawing in a deep, quavering breath, then looked toward the doorway.

Hastily, I stood and snatched my trousers off the chair back they were lying across. I tried to push my right foot through its proper leg but could not because I'd donned my boot first.

Nonetheless, I strained to shove the boot through. "D———n it, man," I muttered sternly.

With a stifled cry, I lost my balance and crashed down on my side.

"*D———n* it, I say!" I cried, pathetically, I fear. I tried to pull the boot free now, could not, and reaching down with quivering hands, yanked off boot and trousers both, almost pulling down my long johns.

I hurled away the boot and trousers, looking toward the doorway suddenly as Sarah's voice was heard outside.

"No, Dave!" she cried. That was not exactly reassuring.

I stumbled to my feet and lurched toward the bedside table, tripping over the right leg of my long johns, which I had partially removed with the boot. Flailing for balance, I banged against the table, knocking down the oval, gold-framed photograph of my mother. Setting it back up quickly, I pulled out the table drawer and jerked out my Colt Navy .36 revolver, whirling to face the doorway, gun extended.

"I warn you, sir!" I said. I'm sure McCanles never heard a word of it, so gargly was my voice.

With my left hand, I pulled up at my sagging long johns, listening to the voices of Sarah and McCanles outside as she tried— obviously in vain—to dissuade him from his purpose.

I received a sudden demented inspiration and tossed the Colt on the cot. I posed as nobly as I could, arms crossed, shoulders back, head high.

"Sir, I am unarmed, as you can see," I practiced. "Let us settle this like gentlemen, not—"

"Hickok!" roared McCanles.

I swallowed what felt like a large stone in my throat.

"A gentleman does not show panic when—" I started in a hurried whisper.

"Prepare to meet your maker!" cried McCanles.

So much for nobility. My stomach doing flip-flops, I lunged for my pistol, juggling it for several moments, then got a grip on it. I looked around for some location of advantage, seeing none. I heard the stomp of McCanles's boots as he entered the station, and I found it difficult to breathe. I mumbled to myself, "Have courage, Hickok." I did not convince myself.

Then, on impulse, I strode quickly to a pair of hanging blankets that served as a closet divider. Pushing in between the blankets, I turned and pressed my back against the wall, the Colt clasped to my chest. I forced my lips together, face a mask of willful and terror-stricken resolution. The approaching footsteps came closer and closer, entering the room. They stopped.

"Hickok!" shouted McCanles.

I was immobile save for my gaze, which dropped to a pair of boots set side by side against the blanket.

Carefully, I reached out one bare foot and nudged them forward.

McCanles obviously saw the boot tips sliding out beneath the blanket edge for he clumped across the room and, with a glare of triumph (I have no doubt) raised the shotgun, firing both barrels simultaneously at where he thought I stood.

I would like to say that my returned fire was deliberate, but the truth is otherwise. Jolting back in dazed shock as the double shot-gun blast tore apart the blanket, I fired my pistol more by reflex than design. I heard McCanles cry out.

After a passage of moments, when nothing more occurred, I peeked around the tattered blanket edge, reacting to a vision in its pall of smoke.

McCanles stood motionless, a hole in his chest.

He inched his head around and stared at me.

I stared back, speechless.

Then he spoke, at best a wheezy, bubbly sound.

"You . . . dirty . . . cheating . . ." He gathered gurgling breath to complete his insult. ". . . luck-out son of a b———h, you."

I drew myself erect and answered, with distaste. "That is not a proper remark, sir. You insult my mother's good name."

I contemplated firing a second shot but found it needless as McCanles toppled backward like a fallen tree and stretched out on the floor, entirely motionless.

⇥⊱⊰⇤

I had little time to savor my escape as I heard the sound of run-ning boots outside and rushed back to the window.

Gordon and Woods were racing toward the station, pistols in hand, Gordon in the lead.

I stiffened with resentful dread. "But that's not *fair*," I said, as if it mattered.

Another eructation puffed my cheeks and passed my lips as I looked from side to side, searching, once more, for advantage.

My harried gaze fixed on the fallen shotgun and I tossed the Colt onto the mattress of my cot. Lunging for the shotgun, I bent over, snatched it up, and posed dramatically, feet set apart, weapon pointed toward the doorway.

Several Argus-eyed moments ticked by before a disconcerting observation struck me.

"Hold on," I remember saying to myself.

Breaking open the shotgun, I winced at the sight of spent shells. With a sound of impending (if not already fully present) panic, I dropped to my knees beside McCanles's body, hissing at the pain it caused on my knees. With trembling fingers, I began to search the dead man's pockets, ransacking for additional shells. *Dear God!* The thought appalled me. *He had more, didn't he?*

He didn't, I discovered, stupefied by mounting dread, tossing coins, strings, keys, and a red bandanna in all directions, whines vibrating in my throat.

Boots pounded on the floorboards at the station entrance. Staggering to my feet, I bolted for the nearest window, trying hard to open it, in vain, of course. The whine increased in pitch and volume and I grabbed a chair to smash the window from its frame.

The thumping footsteps entered the room. I whirled, my cry of shock unheard beneath the shot's explosion. The ball chopped off a chair leg and, unthinkingly, I slung the chair at Gordon.

How I managed to hit him, I have no idea. Nonetheless, the chair slammed into him and drove him, staggering, back.

Diving for my cot, I grabbed the Colt and snapped off two shots, both of them missing Gordon as he dropped to the floor. Scrambling to his knees, he started firing back. I flung myself behind the cot, balls whizzing by me, powder smoke beginning to obscure the room.

From behind the cot, I had a view of Gordon's legs and, lunging underneath its frame, I fired upward twice, returning Gordon's rapid fire. One of the balls found its mark and Gordon made a grunting sound, began to stumble back and, clumsily, collided with Woods who was, just at that moment, running hard into the room. The two fell in a mutual heap, one alive, one, I discovered consequently, dead.

Rearing up behind the cot, a dread avenging angel, I aimed my Colt at Woods and pulled the trigger, greeted by the clicking of my pistol's hammer on an empty chamber. I palm-slapped back the hammer, pulled the trigger once again, then tried once more. Clicking, only clicking.

"Aw, no," I believe I mumbled.

Helpless and aghast, I watched Woods standing with a languid movement, a grin of vengeful satisfaction on his fat lips. Extending his arm, he pointed his revolver at me. I had read about ghouls but had never really seen one until that moment; Woods's leering visage qualified in spades.

Still on my knees, I think I said, "That isn't gentlemanly, Woods." Perhaps I only thought it; memory fails. I know the notion did occur to me however I expressed it, in my mind or with my mouth.

Woods's finger must have actually been squeezing at the trigger of his gun when Sarah rushed into the room, a grubbing hoe clutched in her hands, and smacked him potently across the back of his head. Woods staggered forward with a startled cry and dropped his pistol.

I watched with an open mouth as Sarah walloped Woods a second time. Reeling to his feet, bleeding profusely, he stumbled from the room, Sarah in pursuit.

Starting toward the doorway, overwhelmed by Sarah's unexpected action, I failed to notice the shotgun on the floor and stubbed my toe on its stock. Hissing with pain, I almost fell, cursing as I flailed about, then finally regained my balance and began to limp from the room, my hobble a conspicuous one.

At the station entrance I was forced by a wave of dizziness to lean against the door frame for support.

Far out on the station grounds, I witnessed Sarah, hoe brandished, chasing Woods away.

Reaction set in then; immediately, I was sick to my stomach and felt my cheeks puff out as I resisted losing the unstable contents in my stomach.

I went rigid as a pair of horses galloped hard around the station, reined in by their riders. They were, thank the Lord, two locals with no interest in McCanles's vengeful jealousy.

"What happened?" cried one. "We heard shots!"

I gestured with grandiloquence. That I was good at.

"Nothing in particular," I actually said.

I stepped aside and waved the two men by as they jumped from their mounts and rushed inside to investigate.

As soon as they were out of sight, I staggered from the doorway and moved away from the station, trying to effect a casual stride despite the loose-limbed state of my legs.

Reaching the well, I dipped both hands into a bucket of water and washed off my face. I cupped my right palm and took a drink, belched stentoriously, then hiccupped. Leaning on the rim of the well, I began to belch and hiccup alternately, trying—not with great success—to look assured despite the detonating, honking noises I kept making one by one.

Citizen Hickok
Makes a Gesture

"Self-Defense Verdict on Rock Creek Shootout!" howled the headline of the *Brownville Advertiser*. "Stage Driver J. B. Hickok Exonerated."

"Yay, J. B.!" exulted a patron of the Fairbury House saloon.

I stood at the counter, corraled by a horde of red-faced tipplers who pumped my aching hand, pounded my smarting back, and eyed me with respectful awe. It had begun, you see.

Jefferson once wrote, "He who permits himself to tell a lie once, finds it much easier to do it a second time." Not to mention a third and fourth and fifth time and beyond.

In other words, I did not refute their adulation but accepted it with regal deference. How easy it was.

"Here's to Jim Hickok!" cried one of them, his glass raised high in a toast.

Cheers. Applause. Further drinking. J. B. was near believing it had all occurred as they believed.

"Tell us how you did it, Jim!" a man's voice rose above the rest.

There was a sudden, eagerly respectful silence. Later, someone referred to it as a hush of awe.

I gestured modestly; I had perfected that display by then.

"There's really not that much to tell," said I.

Fervent protests ensued.

"Sure, there is!"

"Aw, *come* on, Jim!"

"Tell us, J. B., *tell* us!"

I conceded with that simple grandeur I had mastered. "Three men came to kill me. Three men died. That's all."

A rippling of veneration for my humble understatement.

Then a man said with a smirk, "By God, I just can't *wait* to see what happens when the rest of that McCanles clan shows up!"

The room was filled with sounds of happy expectation. "Yeah!" they bellowed. *"Yeah!"*

My stomach was filled with bubbles of curdling whiskey.

"They'll be gunning for you sure as hell!" some other follower elated, cackling loudly.

I maintained a frozen smile, although my eyes were glassy, I have no doubt.

"How many *are* there, Jeb?" another man inquired of the follower.

Jeb replied, exhilarated, "No more than *seven*! Mean as *sin* though." Another cackle. *"That'll* be a showdown! Yippee! I can hardly wait!"

Someone with a heavy hand slapped me hard across the back. "What do *you* say, Jim?" he asked.

Everyone regarded me with eager anticipation. I managed an approximation of the modest gesture. Thankfully, my voice held steady as I spoke.

"If it comes, it comes," I told them.

Maddened cheering. I raised a glass of whiskey to my lips and downed its contents in a swallow. The liquor hit my stomach like a burst of sour flame. My cheeks inflated, and I barely managed to repress a belch. At that moment, I decided it would be a grand idea to get blind drunk, so I poured myself another glassful, quickly swallowing it.

+=—=+

Some hours afterward, I had handily achieved my goal. The saloon floor tilted back and forth with gentle, rocking motions, my head and fingertips had lost all physical sensation, and my plight had satisfactorily been numbed away.

Near sundown, my comrades and I exited the Fairbury House, two of them supporting me like weaving bookends. Everyone was talking at the same time, laughing, snorting, singing, belching. I could not step back and view my face, but I believe it was a mask of absolute inebriation, eyes unblinking, staring, my expression one of hapless stupor. As the saying goes, I could not have hit the floor with my dropped hat.

Politely, I crimped the brim of said hat to a passing lady, discovering in the act that the hat was nowhere near my head, its location unknown. A belch escaped my lips involuntarily, and the lady frowned. I could not find it in my heart to blame her for that.

The two men now attempted to elevate me to the back of my horse. A flicker of awareness made passing contact with my brain and, offended, I armed my two assistants back away.

Assuming an expression of dignified aplomb on my torpid features, I raised my left boot toward the stirrup, missed it totally, and lost my footing, saved from falling only by my grip on the saddle horn.

"Hey, Jim, let me help you," said my first assistant, the words, you may be sure, not at all as clear as I have written them, something more like, "Heyjimle'mehel'ya."

I flung aside my right arm, barely hanging by my left. "Stand back!" I cried. "Stanba'!" I probably garbled.

Features set with stiffened resolution, I raised my left leg once again, located the stirrup, and stood on my right leg, swaying back and forth with the movement of my horse and of the ground itself.

I braced myself, clenching my teeth, and, inchingly, rose up to throw my right leg over the saddle. In doing so, I threw the weighted balance of my body too far to the horse's right and toppled to the ground with a hollow cry of disappointment. Fortunately, my left boot did not remain in the stirrup or my situation would have been inopportune.

My two assistants, mumbling words of consolation, pulled me to my feet again and helped me board the horse's saddle. There I wavered for a number of moments, on the verge of falling off again. I gripped the saddle horn with both hands. "D———n you, sir," I muttered, to whom I cannot say because I do not know.

"Yay, Jim!" my second assistant crowed. "You did it!"

They mounted their own two horses and we three started down the street.

"Jim can do anything," my first assistant claimed. "Jim is hell incarnate!" At the time I didn't have a clue what that connoted, but then I'm sure he didn't either.

"D———n right," I said, agreeing nonetheless.

"Those poor McCanles b———s," said my second assistant. "They won't know what hit them."

"Right," I mumbled.

"Jim'll get 'em, get 'em good." my first assistant added.

"Right," I mumbled.

"Jim'll blow their a———s off, that's what he'll do!"

"D———n right," I mumbled.

My friend cackled wildly. "I can't hardly wait!"

I attempted to maintain a look of unruffled determination but was close to spewing up my entire evening's consumption of both fluid and solid. Nausea swelled my stomach like the contents of a volcano about to erupt.

That is when I saw the sign—and my salvation—nailed to the wall of a building we were passing.

The Union Needs You! it huzzahed. Help to Fight the War Back East! Enlist and Leave Today!

The last two words struck fire in my soggy brain. Citizen Hickok, answering the crisis of his nation, decided to enlist.

Heroics: Pea Ridge
and Wilson's Creek

I joined the Eighth Missouri State Militia and was off to war.

Talk in Washington that first of July (1861) was of a ninety-day limit to hostilities. A somewhat imprecise estimation, shall I say?

I believed it, though, and went to join the fray, if not with over-joyed anticipation, at least with some degree of assurance that my tour of duty would be brief.

For a while, I was spared the ferocity of man-to-man combat by an assignment to be a sharpshooter. It was the first time I felt grate-ful to my P.A.B.S. for starting me on the path toward marksmanship. I confess I did not relish shooting down men from a distance but, at least, they *were* our enemies (or so we were told) and, at most, I didn't have to confront them face-to-face.

At the battle of Pea Ridge in Arkansas I even managed to ac-quire some reputation (as though I wanted it) without endanger-ing myself when my commanding officer ordered me to find an advantageous spot overlooking Cross Timber Hollow, if I recall the name correctly, and pick off (lovely euphemism for *exterminate*) as many of the Rebels as I could.

I was there for several hours, virtually unseen, and what an irony it is that on that single afternoon, I killed more men than I ever did again. And from a distance, let me emphasize. Heroic? Doubtful. That was Pea Ridge.

I cringe to cite details of the afternoon near Wilson's Creek.

+≡≡+

"Ever the loyal patriot, eager to serve his country in her hour of need, Young Hickok [getting older fast] joined the Union forces in the War Between the States during which his next audacious exploit took place: the ambuscade at Wilson's Creek!"

Our wagon train moved sluggishly along a dusty road, soldiers in the wagons, marching, or on horseback. Steep hills bordered both sides of the road.

I was driving one of the wagons (not too much advancement there) my uniform splattered with caked mud and layered with dust. We didn't know it, but a detachment of Rebel guerrillas was lying above us, crouching or standing behind boulders, bushes, logs, and trees.

We learned about it when an officer in charge of them leaped up and shouted, *"Fire!"*

Four cannons—two on each side—and a slew of rifles and pistols roared and crackled. Explosions started blasting all around us. Men cried out in shock as they were hit by balls and shrapnel.

I struggled to control my pitching, panicked team as with savage Rebel cries, the guerrillas started charging down the slopes, firing weapons, and converging on the wagon train. Union soldiers fired back and bodies toppled everywhere.

An explosion roared beside my wagon, the concussion throwing it aside. With a startled cry, I started over with its toppling, then leaped clear, landing at a dead run, the velocity of which I had to sustain in order not to fall.

This caused me to collide, head-on, with a hurtling Rebel, the violent impact knocking both of us backward, each emitting grunts of startlement. Dazedly, we gaped at one another. Then, hastily, I fumbled for my Colt.

The collison had caused it to slip below my waistband and I had to reach down clutchingly inside my trousers as the Rebel staggered to his feet and raised his rifle dizzily to fire at me. With teeth clenched, I jerked upward at my pistol, thumbed the hammer desperately, and blew a hole directly through the crotch of my trousers, yelping as the enclosed percussion burned my privates.

The Rebel crashed down, dying, as I lurched to my feet, whining with pain while I attempted, still in vain, to pull my pistol free despite its tangling in my long johns. Something hit and caused my hat to fly; making me hitch around so sharply that I lost my balance and went thudding down onto my left side.

The sound of galloping hooves nearby made me scramble around to gape at what I saw: a riderless horse bearing down on me at high speed.

I lunged up to avoid getting trampled and, leaping, managed to grab the horse around its neck. I was yanked precipitously from my feet and strained to pull myself aboard the horse's back, my boot heels alternately flying in the air and gouging at the earth.

My fourth attempt succeeded, carrying me across the horse's back and straight across its other side where I dangled anew, legs flapping uselessly, boots dragged or running along the ground.

I tried again and, finally, was successful, managing to throw my left leg over, not the horse's back, but its neck.

How long I would have stayed there is beyond my knowing. As it happened, the requirement was brief, as an explosion on the road ahead made the horse rear wildly, in so doing flinging me directly onto its back, unhappily straight down on the saddle horn, which stressed my privates even more.

With a heavy groan, I shifted backward quietly as the horse turned right and started charging up the slope. I hunched forward as a bullet skimmed through my hair, straightened up, then ducked abruptly once again as the horse charged underneath a low-hanging branch.

I glanced back in startled relief, then turned back, facing front again and cried out in shock as the horse ran underneath another tree branch lower than the first.

I had no choice but to clutch at it and remain behind, legs dangling, as the horse raced on. A buzzing rifle ball ricocheted off the branch, making me gasp and twitch. Hastily, I pulled myself onto the branch, yelping as a fiery fragment of shrapnel creased the seat of my trousers. Further pistol balls whizzed by me as I looked up the slope.

A Rebel officer was riding down directly toward me, firing his revolver. I ducked and bobbed in desperation, trying to elude his aim. He jolted on the saddle suddenly as someone shot him; then he toppled off the horse.

I saw my opportunity and scrabbled around, not noticing that I'd caught my boot in a crook of the branch.

As the horse galloped by below, I made a dive for it, was caught, and wound up swinging upside down by one leg, hot lead flying all around me. It seemed as though my finish was inevitable until my pinned foot slipped free of its boot and I landed on my head below the tree.

Staggering up, I started hobbling up the slope, right foot shorter than the left by the height of one missing boot heel, causing me to lurch from side to side in clumsy rhythm. As I lumbered upward, I kept trying to remove the pistol from my trousers so as to use it without shooting off my groin. I kept tripping, sprawling, slipping, sliding, and flinching at the cannon's roar as I escaped the ambuscade below.

Reaching the top of the slope, I plunged into a clump of bushes and immediately began a headlong tumble toward the creek below.

I hit the water, rolling, swallowed more than some, broke surface, spluttering, then started thrashing toward the opposite bank, choking and gagging as I went, soaking wet and bruised from head to toe.

"Thus with an intrepid skill that bordered upon the uncanny did J. B. Hickok, two guns spitting fusillades of death, make good his escape from the Rebel entrapment!"

The Unsolicited Birth
of Wild Bill Hickok

⋯⟫⟨⋯

Following my military triumph at the Wilson's Creek engagement, I found an unoccupied Confederate mule grazing in a field and commandeered it as a prize of war. Mounting same, my feet, one booted, one without, both close to dragging on the ground, uniform a filthy, rumpled miscellany of hanging threads, shreds, and tatters, I rode into the nearest town, the war on forced deferment for the moment, my need for a strong drink outweighing all martial interests.

I came upon a mob of grumbling men assembled in the street in front of the saloon. Dismounting, I began to shoulder through them, whiskey bound.

A man took firm hold of my arm and held me back. "I wouldn't go no farther, soldier," he informed me in a voice so deeply rumbling that it seemed to issue from his bowels.

I glared at him, in no mood to be hindered from the gratification of my thirst. "Why?" I demanded.

"Because a bad 'un's holed up in there," he said. "Had a shooting fracas with a couple of our local boys, killed one, near killed the other. We're just fixing now to lynch him."

I needed no additional information, my thirst restraining of its own accord. "Is there another saloon around here?" I inquired.

"Right down the street," he answered, pointing.

"That will do," I said with a nod. I turned away, moving past a couple in their sixties or seventies.

"You can't just lynch a man without a trial!" the old woman was protesting.

"You just watch us, Maude," the old man, who I assumed was her husband, replied.

"You're animals!" cried Maude. "Wild animals! Isn't there a man among you?"

Some of the men made angry noises at her as I pushed through their assembly and started down the street, eyeing the saloon some thirty yards away; a satisfactory distance from the unpleasantness, I estimated.

I started, gasping, as a man came staggering from the alley between the saloon and a dry goods store. Wounded in the shoulder, he could barely stand and flopped against me, causing me to grab him without thinking.

"For God's sake, mister!" he begged, "get me to my horse!"

I didn't even have the time to think of a reply when someone in the mob caught sight of us and shouted, "There he is!"

I looked around in shock to see the mob surge in my direction, one of them brandishing a rope above his head.

I could only gape at them until the wounded man began to draw his pistol. Then I had to move.

"Wait a second," I muttered, wrestling him for possession of the revolver, at the same time trying to observe the approaching mob from the corners of my eyes. Let me say, they were an ominous vision as they stalked the wounded man and, for all I knew, me as well.

The man and I continued grappling for the pistol. "Wait, I said!" I told him frantically.

Suddenly, the man collapsed and, in abrupt possession of the pistol, my trigger finger jerked by accident and I fired.

The mob recoiled like a wounded beast as a man in its front rank was shot in the leg and flopped to the ground.

I stared at them and, in that moment, knew them for what they were: a company of craven cowards.

Smelling victory, I took the opportunity to vent my aggravation concerning every rotten thing that had occurred that day.

"All right, that's enough!" I yelled.

The mob—now a disorganized crowd—stared at me in silence.

With lordly mien, I instructed them to return to their homes.

No one stirred. I scowled at their slow-wittedness and fired over their heads, hearing a distant window shatter.

"I said return to your homes!" I shouted. *"Now!"*

The mob began dispersing hastily.

"And send your constable to hold this man for trial!" I added.

The old woman, Maude, raised her fisted right hand in a gesture of triumph.

"Good for you, Wild Bill!" she cried.

I was going to correct her, then decided that it wasn't worth the effort.

The story in the local newspaper the following week referred to me as Wild Bill Hiccock.

It was not the last time I would be misrepresented by the press.

Some Further History

⊷⇌⊂⊷

In July 1862, President Lincoln called for three hundred thousand more volunteers. The ninety-day limit to hostilities had already been dead and buried nine months.

By the autumn of 1862, the national debt, enhanced by the war, reached the staggering amount of $500 million, an increase of $436 million in the past two years, a sum too vast to even imagine at that time.

As an interesting side note, in the summer of 1863, two French scientists discovered little rod-shaped bodies in the blood of animals infected with anthrax. They named them, logically enough, little rods, or bacteria. This could result in interesting health developments someday, I believe.

Back to the war: in October 1864, submersible boats were being utilized by the Confederates. The first of these, despite sinking five times in succession, was recovered each time and finally succeeded in exploding a torpedo underneath the Union ship *Housatonic*, which promptly sank. The submersible also sank again, this time permanently, drowning its entire crew.

At last, in April 1865, General Lee surrendered to General Grant at the Appomattox Courthouse.

It turned out that the Union Army had lost three hundred and eighty-five thousand men in the war, the Confederate Army ninety-four thousand men.

The cost of the war was—I still cannot fathom the amount—$8 billion!

It was, of course, stated that the Union had won the war but, in my opinion, no one won it and no one ever will win a war considering the cost and agony involved.

But enough of serious matters. Back to my life.

Until the end of the war, I served in various capacities: scout, wagon master, courier, sharpshooter, spy, and policeman. I was not, as claimed, a member of the Red Legs or the Buckskin Scouts.

After Appomattox, like most other veterans, I was without employment, which carries my chronicle to Springfield, Missouri, in July of 1865 and my next step up—or is it down?—toward nationwide acclaim.

Destiny and Springfield

At the risk of being repetitious, I must disclose that the incident began inside a hotel room with me in the company of an unclad young woman named Susannah Moore. I, too (need it be said?), was devoid of clothing.

The two of us were reclining on the bed while, with princely care, I trimmed my new mustache, scissors in right hand, mirror in left.

Susannah was pressed against me, playing with my hair, which I had now allowed to grow down almost to shoulder level.

"I just *love* your hair, Bill," she remarked. "It's so soft and shiny." It was that because, when I resided in a town or city, I washed it regularly.

You notice that she called me Bill. Mistake or not, I had gone along with the old lady's miscall and permitted the name to prevail.

Frowning at her careless touch, I put down the mirror and removed her hand from my hair. "Easy, girl," I told her, "you're snarling it."

Contrite, she began to stroke my hair more carefully as I returned to mustache snipping. "Sorry, Bill," she said. "I just lose all control when I'm around you."

"Try not to," I responded with a distracted tone. I really *was* that way. The memory makes me squirm.

I appraised the reflected trimming job and made a sound of satisfaction. "Not bad," I said.

Susannah flung an arm across my chest and pressed her cheek to my shoulder as I performed a few last snips of lip hair surgery. *"Watch it,"* I cautioned.

"Oh, Bill," she said, "why won't you marry me?"

I didn't even feel the need to answer that.

"I know you think I'm just not good enough for you because I'm not a lady," she went on, bearing out my lack of response. "But I could change, Bill. I could *make* myself a lady."

Did I really reply with such pretentious self-importance? I'm afraid I did.

"A lady is *born,* Susannah," I informed her. "The same as a gentleman is." My Lord in heaven above, how arrogant could a young man be? Susannah bristled, hurt. Who could blame her? "Well, I don't know what *you're* acting so high and mighty about!" she pouted. "You're just a no-count wagon driver!"

I gave her one of my self-engendered wintry looks, which caused instant repentance on her part.

"I'm sorry, Bill," she apologized. "I know you're only driving for a while. I know you're headed for bigger things. I'm sorry."

I nodded curtly. "Don't let it happen again," I said. Oh, if I could only step back through the corridor of time to give that fatuous idiot a hearty boot on the rump!

Susannah writhed against me, groaning. "Do me, Bill," she begged. "Don't make me wait no more." She reached down to hasten my readiness for same.

I was concentrating on the final stages of my mustache pruning. "Take it easy, girl," I said, "I'll get to it."

She rubbed against me more insistently. "Do me *now,* Bill," she pleaded, the pitch of her voice rising at least an octave. "*Do* me." She worked at my utensil with increasing vigor. "Oh, *Bill,*" she said.

"Oh, *h———l,*" I responded.

Laying aside the scissors and mirror, I turned to face her on the bed and we began to kiss determinedly.

"Do me," Susannah muttered between osculations. "*Do* me, *do* me."

"All right, all right," I told her. "Just stop yanking at me, will you?" I yelped as she wrenched my appointment. "D———n it, girl!" I stormed.

"I love you, Bill!" she cried as we commenced. "I love you, love you! I could be a lady!"

"No chance," I gasped, at work now.

"You're the only man I'll ever love!" she moaned. "Ain't never going to see Dave Tutt no more!"

In the heat of the encounter, it took several moments for the words to register on my otherwise-occupied brain. But suddenly they did, and I grabbed her by the shoulders, jerking her devouring mouth from mine.

"*What was that?*" I demanded.

"What was what?" she inquired, breathless.

"You said Dave Tutt," I prompted her.

She tried to get at my lips again. "He don't matter none to me," she said. "You're the only one, Bill."

A cloud of gloom had drifted in above my head by then. "You're Dave Tutt's girl," I said.

She smiled at me adoringly. "Not anymore I'm not," she reassured me.

With that, she wriggled from my faltering grip and climbed all over me, kissing my face, my lips, my chest, my stomach, and prime points south.

"I'm *your* girl, Bill," she gasped between attentions, "*Wild Bill.* The strongest . . . toughest . . . *biggest* man in all the—!"

She broke off in dispirited perplexity. "*Bill,*" she said, "it's gone all *diddly.*"

The following selection is derived from an account of the Dave Tutt incident as described by a man who was self-named Captain Honest and notated by (who other?) Colonel Nichols, a double dose of bona fide accuracy.

The account, of course, had to do with Dave Tutt taking my pocket watch.

"This made Bill shooting mad, so he got up and looked Dave in the eyes and said to him: 'I don't want to make a row in this house. It's a decent house and I don't want ter injure the keeper. You'd better put that watch back on the table.'

"But Dave grinned at Bill and walked off with the watch. At which I saw that Bill was fixing ter get into a fight with Dave. 'It's not the first time I have been in a fight,' he said. 'You don't want me ter give up my honor, do yer?' He added that Dave Tutt wouldn't pack that watch across the square unless dead men could walk."

Well, first of all, if I'd ever spoken like that, I would have holed up in a cave with a book on English grammar until I learned how to speak correctly.

Second of all, it never happened that way.

Third of all, you know I'm going to tell you how it really took place.

Fourth of all, read on.

The incident occurred in a room in the old Southern Hotel on July 20, 1865.

I was playing poker with three gentlemen of my acquaintance, one of them the aforementioned Captain Honest. I remember wearing my one good article of clothing, a shabby Sunday-go-to-meeting coat. My watch, as was my custom, had been placed on the table so that I could keep track of the time as well as use it as an excuse to depart ("An early rising hour, I fear, gentlemen") in case I was losing too heavily.

I had already achieved some measure of social standing by virtue of the incident at Rock Creek and my reported heroics during the war, and one of the men, a Mr. Cosgrove as I recall, was using it to make conversation as we played.

"Mr. Hickok," he said.

"The same," I answered.

Chuckles from the trio.

"I have wondered," said Cosgrove, "in light of your increasing reputation as a man of cool nerve and action, whether you have ever given thought to the possibility of becoming an officer of the law—a constable perhaps, a U.S. marshal, or a county sheriff."

"As a matter of fact, I have," I said offhandedly, although the thought had never crossed my mind for an instant.

"Splendid," said Cosgrove. "When may we anticipate your entry into this select endeavor?"

Now, I knew the English language passing well, but I confess to several moments of brain blankness before I got the gist of that inquiry.

"One of these days, for certain, Mr. Cosgrove," I declared then. "One of these days for certain," I repeated to emphasize my resolution on the matter.

"I sincerely hope so, Mr. Hickok," Cosgrove replied. "Since the war's conclusion, our frontier has become infected with scofflaw men of violence. We need your kind of stalwart to put them in their place."

"I observe that fact, sir," I began, completely in the mood of it by then. "And I assure you—"

I broke off speaking with a twitch of startlement as the door to the room was flung open so violently that it crashed against the wall. I jerked around so sharply that my chair was toppled.

Standing in the doorway was Dave Tutt, a man of frighteningly malignant countenance, an authentic nightmare of a man who contained his dread temper at the cost of straining breath and a voice that cracked at regular intervals.

"It was in the summer of 1867 [Nichols's flawless accuracy with facts again], in Springfield, Missouri, that Hickok's next man-to-man encounter took place: the justly celebrated gun duel between himself and gambler Dave Tutt. The cause: a card game difference of opinion."

As though nothing had occurred, I turned back to the table, set my chair back in place, and reseated myself.

"Shall we continue, gentlemen?" I said, hoping that my voice did not sound as hollow to them as it did to me.

The game resumed, albeit somewhat tentatively. I succeeded in maintaining visible composure (at least, I think I did) as Tutt clumped over measuredly and stood behind my chair, his voice as tight as the walls of my stomach as he muttered, "*Evenin'*, Mr. Hickok."

"Evening, Mr. Tutt," I replied.

I continued playing cards, teeth set on edge, the three men acting as though nothing out of the ordinary was taking place—not an award-caliber performance by any means.

They caught their breath as one man—fortunately obscuring my gasp—when Tutt raked out a spare chair from beneath the table and sat down heavily on it. I swallowed and began to add some money to the pot.

"Talking to Susannah Moore a while ago," Tutt said.

The money made a clinking noise as I dropped it prematurely on the table. "Who?" I asked, my voice not dissimilar to that of a jittery owl.

"Susannah Moore," he said, then added through clenched teeth, "My *woman*."

"Oh. Yes," I said, trying my utmost to keep my voice steady. "I believe I've met her."

"I *know* you've met her," Tutt responded.

I grunted, feigning full absorption in the game. Breathing hard, Tutt stared at me for several minutes before speaking again, at which time he said, "You owe me twenty-five dollars, *Mr. Hickok.*"

"What?" I asked. I heard but didn't know how to respond.

"You *do* recall our card game last week, don't you?" Tutt inquired.

"Oh. Yes," I said, reaching for my money.

"I believe the sum was twenty dollars, Mr. Hickok," said Cosgrove. I stared at him blankly. "I was in that game, if you recall," Cosgrove reminded me.

Idiot, I thought. But I was forced to agree. "Yes, I recall," I said. "It was twenty."

I picked up money from my pile and counted, "Ten . . . fifteen . . . twenty, Mr. Tutt. I believe that squares us." I held it out to him.

He made no move to accept it, so I laid it on the table in front of him. "There you are," I said.

"The sum was twenty-*five*, Mr. Hickok," he said.

I was painfully aware of the three men eyeing me with keyed-up expectation, and I sensed that I was trapped. I had conceded one point to the man. Another could be ruinous to my reputation. I lowered my head to conceal the movement of my bobbing gullet, then looked up at Tutt, praying to the skies that he noticed I was unarmed.

I guess he did, because he whined with repressed frustration as I continued playing cards. I suppose there is the possibility that my notoriety—as modest as it was—had some effect on him.

At least until, some moments later, he reached out suddenly and took my watch off the table, stood, and slipped the watch into his vest pocket. Then he spoke, again through clenched teeth (not too easy, try it sometime).

"This cheap, five dollar watch will make up the difference," he announced.

I didn't want to shudder, but I did. I hoped nobody noticed it or, if they did, mistook it for a shudder of rage.

"I'll be walking in the square tomorrow morning with this watch inside my pocket," Tutt informed me.

He glared at me in outright challenge, which I chose not to accept. Then he turned and left the room, slamming the door so hard that a picture fell from the wall, its glass front shattering, making all of us wince.

The three men stared at me. I cleared my throat, tried to speak, could not, cleared my throat again and managed, then, to speak. "Shall we continue, gentlemen?" I asked.

The game went on, but I could feel dissatisfaction hovering in the air. I knew a statement was expected, so I made it.

"He will not be walking on the square with my watch in his pocket," I said, then added, with portentous melodrama, "unless dead men can walk."

A collective sigh escaped the lips of the three men; they were fulfilled.

As I continued playing cards, I felt my stomach moving and my cheeks puffed out in the repression of a belch.

<hr />

I did not sleep that night.

How did I get into this insanity? I asked myself. *Because you haven't got the brains to keep your God d———ed trousers on!* I answered, furious with myself. First Sarah Shull, now Susannah Moore. Why was I so God d———ed handsome? (Yes, I really *thought* that, poor beleaguered fool that I was.) I actually felt sorry for myself for my appearance. Shake your head if you like. I am shaking mine as I write this.

What made me say what I did? *Unless dead men can walk.* It didn't even make sense; of course dead men couldn't walk! Stupid; idiotic. Pride goeth before a fall; no doubt of that. I had no inclination whatsoever to face Dave Tutt. He was a deadly shot and, unlike me, was accustomed to having men shoot back at him, one to one. He wasn't a falling apple, a fence post, or a bottle on a stump. The man intended to kill me, for God's sake!

For hours, I lay on my hotel bed, propped up by pillows and a bottle of rye whiskey. I felt ill and apprehensive. *Deadly killer of men?* The phrase would have been uproarious if it hadn't been unnerving.

Much of the time, I stared at the small framed photograph of my mother, which stood on the bedside table. In my mind, I heard her speak again those certain words, particularly unsettling at that moment.

"You must always be a gentleman, James. It is expected of you."

"Yes, Mother," I murmured, which finally brought about the notion.

◆━━◆

At six o'clock the following morning, I packed my carpetbag and left my room. There was no one at the lobby desk. I'd send them the amount I owed them later on; I wasn't going to wake them up.

It pleased me to observe that the street was deeply misted and, as far as I could hear, unpopulated. I walked along the plank walk with unhurried strides, telling myself that I was not, in any manner, pressed for time.

Soon I stepped down from the walk and started across the square toward the livery stable, where the one sound in the world I didn't want to hear, I heard: Dave Tutt's voice.

"*Morning*, Mr. Hickok," he said. How could he have possibly known that I was getting up so early?

I opened my mouth, ostensibly to answer him, but nothing audible emerged.

"Up mighty early, aren't you?" he said. *D———n his bones, he'd been waiting for me!*

I stared at his form, barely visible in the mist.

"Going somewhere?" he asked. I knew that he was ready to explode by the cracking of his voice. I tried to estimate how far from me he was. I guessed it was fifty feet or so.

Clearing my throat as softly as I could, I told him, "Yes, as a matter of fact, I am."

"And where might that be, Mr. Hickok?" he inquired, his voice still breaking—not with fear, I was certain, but with blinding rage.

I answered gravely. "To visit my mother, if it's any of your business, Mr. Tutt."

He whined with held-in fury, voice continuing to crack as he responded. "My business, Mr. Hickok, is to meet you in the square this morning."

"I am aware of that," I replied, amazed by the unperturbed sound of my voice. "However, my mother's health takes precedence—"

"And what about *your* health, Mr. Hickok?" he interrupted.

I knew in that instant that I could not avoid this confrontation. Hastily, I tried to summon up (in his mind anyway) the exaggerated image that the newspapers and journals had created.

"Worry about your own, Mr. Tutt," I warned him.

Was it conceivable that he would back down from the act of facing Wild Bill Hickok? Lose courage and avoid the moment? For several, glorious moments, I actually thought that he might.

Then I saw that, indeed, he *had* reacted nervously to my image and was, now, incensed at himself for doing so. Intent on recapturing the frenzy of his rage toward me, he grabbed for his pistol.

His first shot knocked the carpetbag clear out of my hand. Catching my breath, I clutched for my pistol, which was thrust beneath the waistband of my trousers.

Tutt's second shot knocked off my hat and sent it sailing. Stumbling backward in startlement, I opened fire blindly.

We blasted away at each other across the square. The dark,

swirling powder smoke added to the mist and made visibility close to zero. I shot at him till my gun was empty and, in the sudden, heavy silence, squinted hard to see through the smoky mist.

When it had cleared enough, it revealed the sight of Dave Tutt, unharmed, grimacing fiercely as he reloaded his pistol.

"Sweet Jesus," I murmured.

I looked around abruptly for my carpetbag. Catching sight of it, I lunged to where it was and dropped to my knees beside it. Tearing it open, glancing constantly toward Tutt, I fumbled in the bag for my box of pistol balls.

I could not locate them right away and started yanking out shirts and socks and long johns, tossing them in all directions, muttering. *"Good God,"* through gritted teeth.

I gasped as Tutt began to fire again and flung myself onto my chest as lead balls whined and spattered around me. All shots missed, and I looked up again.

Tutt was, once more, invisible behind the black smoke and white mist.

Scrambling to my knees, I started searching in my carpetbag again, still unable to locate the box of pistol balls and, with a scowl of demented fear, I upended the carpetbag and spilled its contents onto the ground. "Come *on,*" I mumbled. "Come *on.*"

Seeing the box, I opened it so hastily that balls spilled all across the ground. Shaking, dropping half of them in haste, I started to reload, glancing up and hissing with alarm.

Dave Tutt was advancing through the smoke and mist, pistol extended. As stunned as I was, I could not help noticing that, indeed, he did seem afraid of me, his graven features set in an expression of frightened determination.

That didn't help my nerves from threatening to shred as I continued struggling to reload.

Tutt opened fire again, and I grunted as a burning sensation tore a furrow through my right side. Pitching onto my chest again,

I finished loading and began to fire back, holding my revolver with both hands, elbows braced on the ground. By the time I'd fired six times, Tutt was hidden in the smoky mist again.

Struggling to my knees once more, wincing at the pain in my side, I started to reload.

By then there were sounds around me: doors opening and closing, boots running, people shouting, "Hey, what's going on?" and "God above, what's happening?" and a woman's shrill voice, "Don't you dare go out there, Beauregard!"

As I reloaded, I kept glancing anxiously into the clearing mist and smoke.

Then, I stopped reloading and, pushing up shakily, moved across the square and stopped by Dave Tutt's sprawled and motionless body.

His eyes were open, his berserk grimace of fear and hatred still frozen hard on his features.

I stared at him; then, after several moments, reached down and tugged at the fob hanging from his vest pocket, pulling out the watch.

A ball had mangled it.

"Aw, s——t," I muttered.

I began to gather my belongings and stuff them into the carpetbag. Then I started back toward the hotel, limping as I walked. I could feel blood trickling on my right side and down my leg.

I do not recall the trip across the square and down the street to the hotel. I recall only moving through the lobby and starting up the stairs with slow, stiff movements, aware of the awed, admiring gazes of several guests.

As I moved woodenly along the upper corridor, a sock fell from my carpetbag and fluttered to the floor. A man, peering out from his room, stepped forward, picked it up, and held it out to me, mouth opening as though he meant to speak of it. My stonelike expression kept him still. I continued down the hallway like a trudging statue.

A pair of long johns now dropped to the floor, but I did not essay to pick them up. Reaching my room, I unlocked the door (thank God I'd forgotten to leave the key on the lobby desk) and went inside. Closing the door, I relocked it, dropping the carpetbag as I did. Then, straightening up, I felt my eyeballs rolling back and toppled over in a dead faint.

Thus the "justly celebrated gun duel" between Dave Tutt and myself.

Enter the Lord of Liars

‹‑═◎═‑›

They indicted me for murder and I had to face a trial. The indict-
ment was against one William Haycock for the death of David
Tutt. I attempted to correct the spelling of my name and it was
promptly amended to James Hickcock (one of many spellings of
my name I have been saddled with). I gave up trying to achieve
the proper spelling and the trial took place. The jury found me innocent, although public sentiment did not appreciate the judgment
entirely, believing that it might not have been a case of self-defense
but one of deliberately fomented murder or, at the very least
manslaughter.

In great discomfort from my wound, I purchased opium from a
local druggist. In tandem with a jug of frontier corn whiskey, I
remained in a state of semiconscious numbness.

I remained in that condition throughout the remainder of August and nearly half of September, at which time it was my lot (I
will not say my good fortune) to meet that prince among prevari-
cators, that lord of liars, that emperor of exaggeration, Colonel
George Ward Nichols.

‹‑═‑›

I was lying on my bed reading the *Missouri Weekly Patriot* when
there was a sudden pounding at the door. The newspaper flew
from my hands and I lunged for the bedside table, knocking it

over. Diving off the bed, hissing at the pain in my side, I snatched up my revolver and rolled into a rigid crouch, teeth clenched, eyes slitted, expecting members of the Tutt clan to come bursting in, guns firing.

When there was nothing, I asked (the epitome of manly calm), "Yes?"

"Have I the honor of addressing Mr. James B. Hickok?" asked a man's voice.

I rose, picking up the bedside table. "Who are you?" I asked.

"Colonel George Ward Nichols, sir!" the man responded.

"Who?" I asked, suspiciously.

"Colonel George Ward Nichols, Mr. Hickok!" he replied. "Assigned by *Harper's Magazine* to interview you!"

"Interview me?" I mumbled in confusion.

"May I come in, sir?" inquired the voice.

"Are you alone?" I asked.

"Alone, yes!" cried the voice, so loudly that it made me twitch. "Empty-handed, no! For I carry with me, sir, an all-consuming admiration for your bravery and courage!"

"Huh?" I muttered.

"The world awaits your story, Mr. Hickok!" cried the voice. "May I enter to seek it out?"

I hesitated before moving to the door. There, to be on the safe side—I was still gun-shy from my battle with Tutt—I unlocked it, then stood with my back to the wall, pistol at the ready.

"Come in," I said.

Colonel George Ward Nichols burst in eagerly, a heavyset, florid-faced, overdressed man in his fifties. Seeing no one, his mouth fell open in astonishment. Then he whirled. "Ah-ha!" he cried delightedly. I flinched a little at the volume of his voice. "Always on the qui vive, sir! Argus-eyed! Prepared for bloody confrontation at a moment's notice! *Wild Bill!* Alert and vigilant! *Semper paratus!* My *dear* Mr. Hickok!"

I must have gaped at him. Right from the start, he seemed un-hinged to me.

He snatched his card from a vest pocket and proffered it grandly.

"Colonel George Ward Nichols, sir!" he proclaimed himself. "Former aide-de-camp to General Sherman on his heroic March to the Sea! [I swear I heard capital letters in his voice.] Your obe-dient servant, sir! As one gentleman to another—"

He caught me in that moment; that was my Achilles' heel, all right.

"—may I express to you my heartfelt approbation and respect! You are a giant, sir! A *giant!*"

+‑‑+‑‑+

What is it that narrators always comment in those Gothic novels?

Had I but known . . .

How apropos to the occasion. Had I but known the perilous by-ways Nichols's articles would route me through, I would have flung him through the doorway of my room—perhaps even the window. He is the author of the role I have been cast in, the legend I have been imprisoned by. D———n his bloodshot, twinkly eyes for do-ing that!

Still, he was just a reaper, not a sower. I can see that now, al-though I certainly didn't at that time. I thought myself a victim then. That I had given full cooperation to the deed was not a part of my awareness. My conceit and deluded arrogance would not allow me to admit the truth. So who am I to blame this blustering equiv-ocater, this frontier Munchausen? I gave him the raw materials; he only manufactured them to sell his articles. Did it ever occur to him for an instant that his grandiose depiction of me was not only blown completely out of proportion but that, in fact, it would, in addition to aggrandizing me, put my life at considerable and mounting risk? I'm sure he didn't. How could he? *I* didn't even consider it.

For instance, how could I allow myself to swallow, much less digest, the following?

"This verbatim dialogue took place between us. 'I say, Bill, or Mr. Hickok, how many white men have you killed to your certain knowledge?' After a little deliberation, he replied, 'I would be willing to take my oath on the Bible that I have killed over a hundred.' 'What made you kill all those men? Did you kill them without cause or provocation?' 'No, by heaven! I never killed one man without good cause!'"

And the following, me as "quoted" by Nichols:

"Just then McKandlas [McCanles] poked his head inside the doorway, but jumped back when he saw me with a rifle in my hand.

"'Come in here, you cowardly dog!' I shouted. 'Come in here and fight me!'

"McKandlas was no coward, even if he was a bully. He jumped inside the room with his gun leveled to shoot; but he was not quick enough. My rifle ball went through his heart. He fell back outside the house, where he was found afterward holding tight to his rifle, which had fallen over his head.

"His disappearance was followed by a yell from his gang and then there was a dead silence. I put down the rifle and took the revolver and said to myself, *Only six* shots and nine men to kill. Save your powder, Bill, for *the death-hug's a-comin'*."

And this:

"'I hardly know where to begin. Pretty near all these stories are true; I was at it all during the war.'"

And, of course, the following, straight from the mouth of Captain Honest to Colonel Nichols's ear and pen:

"The instant Bill fired, without waiting ter see if he had hit Tutt, he wheeled on his heels and pointed his pistol at Tutt's friends, who had already drawn their weapons.

"'Aren't you satisfied, gentlemen?' cried Bill, as cool as an alligator. 'Put up your shootin' irons or there'll be more dead men here.' And they put 'em up and said it was a fair fight."

When Nichols first began to question me, I made no attempt to conceal my knowledge of the English language. As I spoke, however, it became apparent that he expected, even probably yearned for, a more rough-hewn manner of speech, so I began to drop the bandbox image and feed him more the lingo he was looking for; thus my use of the vernacular in describing the Rock Creek incident (the fanciful building of the facts was Nichols's).

Does it go without saying that I have mulled interminably over my decision to wear the blinds where it came to factuality about the more sensational events of my life? I do not know whether it does, so I will state clearly that yes, I have gone over it as many times as you could possibly imagine.

Not that I was capable of facing pure and simple truth when Nichols, Henry M. Stanley (of Africa fame in finding Dr. Livingston), and the others wrote and published their inflated accounts of my stout-hearted feats of valor. No—*Tell the truth now; Hickok*—I could not resist the journalistic blandishments enough to say them nay. Consider: I was twenty-eight years old. I should have known better, there is no denying, but I simply didn't. I *enjoyed* it, basking in the sunlight of the public's reverence for my accomplishments. I was just a farm boy after all, no city-bred sophisticate. How could I resist? I ask you. *How?*

Anyway, I didn't. Oh, I knew that they were stretching the blanket out of shape but, when I considered it, I told myself that those distorted articles were nothing but a lark, something to chuckle over in private but not be overly concerned about.

My mistake.

In time, while never noticing the day-by-day construction, I built a wall in my mind that separated facts from fancies, truth from lies.

Guess which side of the wall I chose to live on?

Into the Law
and Out of It

Very few know of this, but I was briefly—oh, so briefly—a constable in Morgan City, Kansas, in July and August 1866. I was not, as some have stated, a marshal. I was an underpaid and overwrought constable. Because of my "triumphs" at Rock Creek and during the war and in Springfield, I allowed myself to be coerced (my own failure to differentiate fact from fable) into taking the job where, for several months, I was an agitated misfit of a man, snapping pettishly at everyone, despite the fact that it was a relatively well-behaved community, and in short order, getting the blazes out and returning to safer employment.

Fort Riley

Despite my mounting glory as a man of action, I continued to be a wagon driver to support myself.

Picture me, inside a wagon in a wagon camp, sprawled against the tailgate, wearing filthy work clothes, a week's growth of beard on my cheeks, a layer of grime on my skin, hair a greasy mat across my shoulders, as I read by candlelight the premiere article by Colonel Nichols in *Harper's Magazine*. I could not, of course, have seen my face, but I would wager its expression was akin to that of my twelve-year-old self, open-mouthed and vacantly enthralled, as I pored over the torn-out catalog page on which were illustrated women's corsets.

"His is a quiet, manly face," the article read, "so gentle in its expression as to utterly belie the history of its owner. Yet it is not a face to be trifled with—[I narrowed my eyes] the lips thin and sensitive [I pursed my lip], the jaw not too square [I shifted my jaw], the cheekbones slightly prominent [I attempted in vain to move my cheekbones], a mass of fine, dark hair [I frowned at that. "Dark?" I muttered] falling to well below his shoulders ["Below my shoulders?" I said], the eyes as gentle as a woman's. [*"What?"* I snapped.] In truth, the woman nature seems prominent throughout."

"God ——n!" I slapped down the magazine and glared at it. But I could not ignore it very long and picked it up again.

"You would not believe that you were looking into eyes that have pointed the way to death ['All right,' I grumbled] to hundreds of men."

My mouth fell open; it was the first I'd heard of that.

"Yes, Wild Bill, with his own hands, has killed hundreds of men; of that I have no doubt. As they say on the border, 'He shoots to kill.'"

I stared at the article with undecided detachment. At least I had the moral decency to feel dubious about it in the beginning.

Footsteps sounded outside, and I quietly hid the magazine behind a wooden crate.

It was the wagon train leader. "Bill?" he said.

I cleared my throat (thickened by emotion because of what I'd read? Who knows?). "Yes?" I answered.

"You signing on for the drive back to Fort Riley?" he asked.

"What's the pay?" I countered.

"Still fifty a month. You in?"

I replied without enthusiasm. "I suppose."

"I'll put you on the list then," he responded.

After he'd walked away, I thought, *He obviously hasn't seen the article.* Was fifty a month for wagon driving the best I could do?

A man of my stature?

◆—◆—◆

Fort Riley was aswirl with dust and din as I steered my wagon into the quadrangle. Braking it to a halt, I stepped down, slapping dust from my clothes as I crossed to the nearest water barrel. I detested being dirty!

Removing the barrel top, I lifted up a dipperful of water and flung it into my face. Blowing out spray, I removed my hat and dumped another scoop of water over my head, then another. I poured some water into my mouth, worked it around, and spat it to the ground. Then I stood immobile, hair plastered down, face dripping wet, feeling thoroughly disgruntled. "Son of a b———h," I remember muttering. "I have got to find a better way." *You deserve more than this,* I told myself, slapping a cloud of dust from my shirt.

Did the cosmos answer me? You be the judge.

I turned as the wagon leader ambled up to me, speaking my name. Well, not my real name of course, the one that old lady had christened me with.

"What?" I asked.

"Captain Owens asked to see you."

"Who?" I asked.

"Captain Owens, Post Quartermaster."

"Why?" I asked.

"No idea. He just wants to see you."

"Where?" I asked.

"His office." The wagon leader pointed. "Over there."

"When?" I asked, covering the journalist's Five W's in record time.

"Now," the wagon leader said with not a little aggravation.

I walked over to the building pointed out to me and knocked on the door.

"Come in," said a voice. It might have been that of a prepubescent boy.

I went inside to face a pudgy, pink-faced balding man in his early forties. He looked like a prepubescent boy as well, playing soldier in somebody else's cut-down uniform.

I walked up to his desk, exuding dust, and stopped in front of him. "You asked to see me." I told him not too genially, I fear. I was truly disgusted with my lot.

Captain Owens pointed at me, clearly thrilled. "You awe *Wiwd Biw Hickok?*" he inquired.

I blinked. The man lisped terribly in a voice pitched as high as that of a choirboy. This was not to be an easy interview, I saw.

"Yes?" I said.

He sprang to his feet, pink, pudgy hand extended. "My honow, siw! We have heawd much good about you! *Much* good!"

He pumped my hand relentlessly. I was speechless, which was just as well, as he plunged on, his tone abruptly grim. That I kept a straight face is a tribute to my acting skill.

"May I discuss with you a cewtain vexing pwobwem which confwonts us hewe in Fowt Wiwey?" he inquired.

"Uh . . . *sure,*" I managed. *God, don't laugh,* I thought; *he is a captain.*

He replied with reverent appreciation. Obviously he'd read the article in *Harper's.*

"*Thank* you, Mr. Hickok" (I cannot convey what he did with the word *Mister*). "Thank you vewy much." His expression altered to one of deep gravity. "As you may ow may not be awawe, Fowt Wiwey is the home station fow the undewpaid, undewfed, dissatisfied, and bwawwing subdivision of the United States Awmy. Mowawe is at wock bottom." (That almost got me, I confess.) "We awe suwwounded by undesiwabwe wecwuits who have enwisted onwy fow the puwpose of being twanspowted west at ouw expense, Mr. Hickok, at *ouw expense!*"

I hung on his every word now, hoping that by concentrating intensely on the meaning of his words, I would not be toppled by the sound of them.

"Many of these wecwuits" (that word again; it pummeled at my will to keep from collapsing into laughter) "desewt soon aftew awwiving at the fowt," he continued, unaware of my intense struggle to remain of serious mien. "Consequentwy, thew is uttew *chaos,* don't you see. Open hostiwity between scouts and twoopers." (Twoopers! God in heaven!) "On the scouts' side awe the teamstews and the wabowews" (that one I almost didn't get at all until I realized that what he was trying to say was *laborers*), "on the othew side are what the teamstews cwudewy wefew to as *bwue bewwies.*"

"I beg your pardon?" I said; I missed that entirely.

"Bwue bewwies, bwue bewwies," he repeated testily. *Why should the teamsters refer crudely to blueberries?* I wondered, then realized, as he went on, that he meant to say *blue bellies.*

"Thewe awe not, you see, enough twoops to fowm a weguwar peace patwol."

Oh, Jesus, wind it up before I crack, I thought, face straining to remain composed.

"That is why we need you, Mr. Hickok."

Fortunately, curiosity replaced my resisted urge to guffaw in the man's pink, pudgy face. "Me?" I said.

Again, he pointed at me as though identifying me to a crowd that wasn't there.

"*You,* siw, and no othew. Thewe is a big job to be done hewe at Fowt Wiwey. It calls fow a big man. You awe that man, Mr. Hickok. Bwave. Intwepid. A dauntwess, pistow mastew." Despite my curiosity, I almost snapped at that.

"Wiw you," challenged Captain Owens, "accept the position of United States marshaw, siw?"

I was stunned. "United States—" I began, then couldn't finish.

"Youw sawawy" (salary, I gathered) "wouwd be one hundwed dowwaus a month."

"A *hundred,*" I murmured, forgetting how he spoke in the shock of the moment.

"Can we count on you, Mr. Hickok?" Owens pleaded. "Wiw you wend us youw gweatness in this houw of need?"

He gazed at me dramatically. *Just don't say anything to destroy this moment,* I thought.

"No one else can fiw the biw, sir. Onwy you awe big enough to meet this chawwenge; onwy you awe wedoubtabwe enough to cast this gauntwet with wespwendent twiumph!"

I had to settle for a fit of coughing, which I told him was caused by dust in my lungs.

Duding Up for Doom

❖═◉═❖

Obviously, I did not consider the matter too deeply, thinking only that I'd double my income and be able to bathe regularly; not exactly an exhaustive appraisal of the job of U.S. marshal. I was in the way of being desperate, though. I hated wagon driving, hated being dirty, felt underpaid, and, more to the point I'm afraid, underappreciated for my burgeoning prestige. I was already pushing aside any memories of Morgan City.

So I accepted Owens's offer, although I vowed to converse with him as little as possible. After bathing to a fare-thee-well (the ablutions extending to more than an hour) and burning all my clothes except for those I had to wear to the post store, I went there to prepare for my new position of importance with an outfit of appropriate distinction.

First of all, I purchased new undergarments, new buckskin trousers, boots, and a fine white shirt with a ruffled front.

Then I got down to serious dressing.

The clerk began it all by carrying an ornate buckskin jacket to where I was standing in front of a full-length mirror, putting the trouser legs over the boots for appearance's sake.

"Try this one on, marshal," said the clerk. Smart man, he, to address me as such even though I didn't have my badge yet.

"Right," I said.

I put the jacket on and started to button it but stopped, not caring for the effect. I removed the jacket and handed it back to the clerk. "Have you nothing larger?" I asked.

"Yes, we do," the clerk said, beaming.

"Fetch it then," I told him.

"Yes, *sir*," he said, moving off from me on dancing legs.

While he was gone, I eyed myself in the mirror, leaning in to fiddle with my mustache; I was not quite satisfied with it even then. I nodded, approving of my general handsomeness. I squirm to say it, but a picture of that younger me is necessary to explain the pitfalls I so persistently allowed myself to fall into.

The clerk returned on the run, carrying a longer, far more elaborately decorated buckskin jacket, so pale it was almost white.

"I think you'll like this better, Mr. Hickok," he said.

He was right. I liked it on sight. I slipped it on and regarded my reflection, an expression of carefully calculating assessment printed on my face.

"It's a beauty," said the clerk.

It was. Nonetheless, I sustained the questioning look. "I don't know," I said. "I just don't know."

At which point, I did *not* know. This was a significant moment in my life; I sensed that strongly. I did not want to make a mistake. I liked the jacket and knew that I'd be happy with it. Still . . .

"Have you nothing . . . larger?" I inquired.

"Well . . . *yes*, sir," said the clerk as I removed the jacket. "There *is one* but . . ." He hesitated.

"What?" I asked.

"Well . . ." he said. He took back the jacket I'd removed. ". . . it's . . . awful expensive, marshal."

Did he know that he would twang a nerve in my self-regard when he said that? Probably; he was a *sales* clerk after all, not a philosopher.

Whatever the case, the nerve was twanged, and I responded grandly, "Fetch it, my good fellow!"

"*Yes*—sir, Mr. Hickok!" he responded, fairly leaping off to do so.

I turned to examine myself in profile, drew in my stomach tightly, crossed my arms, and raised my chin, a positively noble expression on my face. What an ass I was! But then, I must look back with greater charity on that deluded young fool. He knew no better.

The clerk came running back, a little breathless now. In his arms was the most ludicrous jacket ever styled by man. It had a fur collar, double fur ringlet at the wrists, a double fur trim with heavy buckskin fringing at its bottom, and buckskin fringe on each arm.

It was perfect.

Slipping it on, I gazed at myself in the mirror, trying hard to look uncertain and wary again but hard put not to reveal that it was love at first sight. I plucked at the jacket, stirring it around my knees; that's how long it hung. "Hmm," I said. Then, finally, unable to restrain my feelings anymore, "This is more like it."

"It looks *wonderful*, Mr. Hickok," said the clerk, all choked up, no doubt from calculating the total sale receipts.

"Yes," I agreed, regarding my reflection with intense satisfaction. Then I nodded. "Now a sash," I said.

The sales clerk's face went suddenly devoid of all expression. "A—?" he started.

"Scarlet," I instructed.

"You—?" he started.

"Want a sash," I said. "A *scarlet* one."

"I see," he replied.

My gaze shifted to his reflection in the mirror. "You *have* one, don't you?" I asked, a trifle testily. Who was he to question my fashion acuity?

"Oh . . . *yes*, sir, Mr. Hickok!" he replied, scuttling backward like a threatened crab.

As he turned away, I buttoned up the coat, trying to repress a smile but too pleased to manage it.

I forced the smile away as the clerk dashed back with a broad, scarlet sash in his hands. "It's a little wide, Mr. Hickok," he apologized.

That didn't bother me. "Is it your *best*?" I demanded; that was more important.

"Oh, *yes*, sir, Mr. Hickok," vowed the clerk. "Absolutely. Made in Boston."

I grunted and began to tie the sash around my waist.

The clerk and I appraised my reflection.

"What do you think?" I asked. I'd already made up my mind but wanted verification.

"It looks," he said, straining for the proper word, "—*lovely*."

"What?" I growled.

"I mean—tremendous, marshal! *Tremendous!*" cried the clerk.

I looked at his nerve-wracked reflection for several moments, then, clearing my throat, reached out and took my Colt Navy from a nearby table and slipped it under the sash.

It looked drab against the sash and jacket.

I said so.

"Mr. Hickok?" inquired the clerk.

"*Drab*, I said."

"Oh," he responded. "Yes." He had no idea of what I was saying.

"I saw some over there with ivory handles," I said.

"*Yes*, sir!" he cried in total delight, bouncing off.

"The .36 caliber Colt Navy, mind!" I called after him. It was, of course, my favorite weapon. The 1851 model with the seven and a half inch barrel; very accurate and hard-hitting, always the most popular of Colt's percussion revolvers.

In the clerk's absence, I returned to mirror-gazing, tossing back my hair, which I'd decided to grow longer yet in keeping with my new image.

The panting clerk rushed back to me, carrying one of the revolvers. Taking it from him, I slipped it underneath the sash on my right side, butt to the rear as was my custom.

I stared at my reflection, pleased. The ivory handle looked very smart indeed.

"I thought—" the clerk began.

"Yes?" I asked.

"Well," he said, "I thought you carried *two* revolvers, sir."

"What?" I looked at him, confused.

"That's what Colonel Nichols wrote in his article," the clerk explained. "'Mr. Hickok always wears a brace of pistols at his waist.'" *My God,* I thought, *the man can quote from the blasted article!*

I cleared my throat again. "Well . . . yes, usually I do," I lied. "Sometimes one needs a deuce of weapons in a pinch." I gestured regally. "So bring me another," I told him.

"*Yes, sir!*" he exploded, disappearing in a flash of movement, returning quickly with the second ivory-handled Colt. I took it from his hand and thrust it underneath the sash on my left side.

"Do you think that, perhaps—" the clerk began to say.

He broke off, both of us wincing as the sash was pulled loose by the weight of the two pistols. I tried to grab at them but missed, and both clattered to the floor. The sash I managed to catch.

The clerk and I regarded each other. I attempted to cover my embarrassment with a look of aggravation. "*That* is why I only use one pistol with a sash," I said.

"Yes, sir," said the clerk, picking up the pistols and handing them back to me. "I—I wonder," he faltered, "if a—a—a *belt* might be more . . . you know, Mr. Hickok, more . . . *practical?*"

"For *two* guns, *yes,* of *course,*" I scoffed. "Very well—" I gestured with impatience. "A *belt* then."

"*Yes,* sir," said the clerk and ran off.

I hefted the two revolvers. Awfully heavy, I thought. I tried to twirl them both and about dropped them, glancing quickly toward the clerk to make certain he hadn't seen.

He was occupied in searching for a belt.

I turned back to the mirror and posed abruptly, both revolvers pointed at the mirror, my eyes narrowed, an ominous expression on my face.

"As they say on the border, 'He shoots to kill,'" I mumbled. *Oh, Hickok, Hickok.*

I lowered the pistols as the clerk returned on the run, carrying a belt, gasping for breath as he handed it to me, "Here you are, marshal," he wheezed.

I looked for a place to set down the pistols while I put on the belt. Finally, I handed them to the clerk and fastened the belt around my waist; it was a little snug. I had to suck in my gut to fasten the buckle. "The revolv—" I stopped; my voice was wheezy now. I drew in a deep breath. "The revolvers, if you please," I requested.

The clerk handed them to me and I managed with some effort to force them under the belt on each side. Unfortunately, my arms would not hang normally now. I frowned, not knowing what to do, then sighed and reversed the pistol butts.

"Prefer the cavalry draw," I told the clerk.

"Yes, sir. That's what Colonel Nichols wrote," he said.

"Oh, yes," I responded.

"You'll also need a knife though, won't you?" he inquired.

I stared at him.

"Colonel Nichols said that in the battle of Rock Creek Station you used a knife against those ten men."

"Oh. *Yes.*" I nodded. "A *knife.*"

"I'll get it right away, sir," said the clerk, running off, shoes thumping on the floor.

I made a face, uncomfortable because the belt was so tight. I tried to loosen it but couldn't without removing it entirely. I belched as softly as I could, then forced back a look of majestic composure as the clerk rushed over, carrying a knife so huge it would have made Jim Bowie pale. "I brought the biggest one we have!" he said unnecessarily.

"Good," I said. I nodded. *"Good."* Idiots, both of us.

I took the knife away from him and slid it gingerly beneath the belt, hissing as it slid across my stomach. I shifted it to the left.

"Oh, *Marshal Hickok,*" said the clerk in awe.

"You don't think it's . . . a bit much?" I tested; I already knew it was.

"Oh, *no,* sir, marshal, *no,* sir! You look *wonderful!*"

I nodded again. *I don't look bad,* I thought.

"You should get a photograph taken!" enthused the clerk.

Good idea, I told myself. "Well," I responded gravely. "Perhaps, for my mother."

"Yes, sir!" cried the clerk.

Some of you may have seen that photograph. It has been reprinted many times.

If you do happen to see it, remember how it came about.

And remember the young man who had no conception of the billy hell he was about to raise.

If My Brains Were Dynamite

⊷⟹⟸⊷

The saying goes: If his brains were dynamite, there wouldn't be enough to blow his nose. Another states: He was so ignorant that he couldn't drive nails in the snow. Either applied to me in those days.

Within a day of my assumption of office and formal pinning on of my badge by Captain Owens ("It is my gweat pweasuwe, Mawshew Hickok, to pwace this on youw manwy bweast"), my first emergency broke out: a full-scale brawl between the teamsters and the soldiers.

I watched it from around the corner of a building, dressed in all my finery, my stomach gurgling.

Across the quadrangle, I saw Owens waddling from his office, looking agitated; heard him dispatching soldiers in all directions to "find Mawshew Hickok!"

I looked back at the brawl, my nausea increasing. I then looked back at Owens and felt my body stiffening as though with instant rigor mortis.

He'd caught sight of me by the building and was staring, half expectant, half dismayed.

I had no choice. More loathe to face a sudden loss of image than to face this challenge to my office, I lurched forward as though I was just arriving to notice the brawl, forcing a look of stern disapproval to my face as I strode toward the battle like an offended king. I was considering, as a matter of fact, that if it came to it, I'd rather be involved in a fistfight than a gunfight. It wasn't likely that one could die from a fistfight.

Reaching the fringes of the brawl, I stood there royally and haplessly unnoticed for several moments before raising my voice.

"All right, uh . . . *here,*" I said. "That's quite enough of this."

The battle raged on as though I had achieved not only inaudibility but invisibility as well. I was, to say the least, nonplussed. I glanced at Owens, who was watching me with uneasy curiosity. I had to do something and do it fast.

Without thought, I drew both Colts from beneath my belt and fired them into the air.

The explosions made everyone stop fighting simultaneously and look at me. I swallowed hard.

"The name—!" I stopped, forced to clear my clogged throat as hastily and quietly as I could.

"The name is Hickok!" I said then, my voice, thank the Lord, now booming over the quadrangle. Not wishing to take any chances, I added, very loudly, *"Wild—Bill—Hickok!"*

To my relief and utmost gratification an immediate buzzing of impressed, excited conversation began. I let it spread a bit, then fired two more shots into the air. Instant silence ensued.

"I have been appointed as the U.S. marshal at this fort!" I said. "*As* such—" I had to clear my throat again. "*As* such," I repeated, "I intend to see that brawls like this do not take place!"

I drew in a deep (and shuddering, that part fortunately unnoticed) breath and completed my declaration.

"Now, return to your work!"

Crucial moments passed as all the gathered men observed me standing there, the picture of unruffled vigilance. *For God's sake, go, I was thinking.*

Then (bless the man) one of them said, loud enough for most to hear, "Hell, let's not screw around with *him.*"

I did my all to repress a smile of relief, managing to do so by elevating my chin and willing back the look of watchful self-possession; slightly undone, I'm afraid, by a puffing of my cheeks as I stifled escaping stomach gas.

◄═══►

"In the weeks that followed [more drivel from Nichols], Hickok proved beyond a shadow of a doubt that his reputation was no journalistic fancy but a hard, cold fact of life."

I kept the door to my office locked as often as I could.

"The office where he quartered soon became the center of control and retribution at the fort."

Even if anyone had managed to enter the office, they would most likely have found it empty.

"All problems of misdeed and discipline forthwith ceased to exist."

My real center of control was out behind the office.

"Each day, Hickok gained in stature and authority, his will unquestioned, his dominion firm."

If such is possible with trousers down, head slumped against the door, bent over, groaning, in the outhouse.

I kept a bottle of whiskey there with me from which I would take periodic belts, grimace, cough, hiss, and belch.

More than once, a nearby horse's neigh or someone shouting or (God forbid) calling my name as I drank would cause my hand to twitch so sharply that I threw whiskey on my clothes or in my face, and I was forced to dry myself with a torn page from the current mail-order catalog.

I pondered, more than once, over what President Lincoln had said (when he was still alive). "What kills a skunk," he'd said, "is the publicity it gives itself." Not that I believed I was a skunk, but I feared the publicity I was getting just might end up killing me.

Once (I forget the year) I made the mistake of revealing the truth to a journalist. "I'm not ashamed to say," I told him, "that I have been so frightened that it appeared as if all the strength had gone out of my body and my face was as white as chalk."

I regretted saying that to him, as I regretted far more deeply making a similar confession years later; but I will speak of that presently.

Not, in the long run, that it mattered in the least what I said to that journalist or any other journalist for that matter. As time went by, they all ignored me as a human being anyway, so intent were they in making me a legend.

There were moments when, despite the puffing pride I felt at what they wrote about me, I yearned to run across a skeptic. When the tales became too tall for even me to overlook, I, of course, continued my attempt to feel amusement at the exaggerations and downright lies; but it grew increasingly difficult, especially as each new grandiose account put my life a little more in jeopardy.

Not that everyone adulated me. There were a number of my contemporaries who regarded me (and said so) as a bully, a braggart, a cheat, and a rogue.

There was even such an article written about me in *The Kansas Daily Commonwealth* in 1873. I carry it in my wallet.

"It is disgusting to see the eastern papers crowding in everything they can get hold of about 'Wild Bill.' If they only knew the real character of the man they so want to worship, we doubt if his name would ever appear again. 'Wild Bill' is nothing more than a drunken, reckless, murderous coward who is treated with contempt by true border men and who should have been hung years ago for the murder of innocent men."

A little overstated surely, but at least it was counterbalance for the exasperating mountains of horse turds piled up by the fabricating worshipers.

One day, while sitting in my second office, I heard someone call my name.

I was going to remain silent, then decided that there was no point to that; they'd locate me sooner or later, anyway.

"What?" I called back, wincing as my stomach juices bubbled.

"Captain Owens would like to see you, sir!" the man replied; a soldier, I discovered consequently.

"All right!" I said, "I'll be there in a while!"

What now? I wondered. Had I deluded myself into believing that Owens—albeit a fool—had failed to notice my complete ineptitude at marshaling?

My stomach growled and bubbled. I drained the bottle of whiskey, dropped it into the pit, and bent over once again, groaning, leaning my head against the door.

Twenty minutes later, calm and dignified as always (my public self), I entered Captain Owens's office.

"You wished to see me?" I inquired.

"It is my pwiviwege, Mawshew Hickok," he declared, "to intwoduce you to Genewaw Wiwwiam Tecumseh Shewman."

I started, looking around. I hadn't noticed the man standing by the window who turned to regard me. He was tall and strong faced, barely bearded, with receding hair and probing eyes.

"I'm honored, general," I said.

"Marshal," Sherman replied in a noncommittal voice.

"Genewaw Shewman has just awwived at Fowt Wiwey," Owens said, "showtwy to commence an inspection touw of the awea. Accowdingwy, despite awe need fow youw sewvices, I am appointing you majowdomo fow him."

I thought I'd gotten it, but I wasn't quite certain. "Major—?"

"Domo, domo," Owens repeated. "I want you to wun his wagon twain."

"Oh," I said. Now his lisping was a wonderful sound to my ears. He *hadn't* found me out. I felt like laughing aloud.

I masked my face with dignity, however.

"It will be my honor, General Sherman," I told him.

I was thinking: *Hallelujah! I'm reprieved!*

Buttons and Bows

-*≒◎⋐*-

As we moved from the fort, Sherman and I at the head of a column of men and wagons, I looked back to throw a farewell glance at my problems.

I saw a soldier and teamster circling one another with drawn knives, a group of men observing.

Hastily, I turned back to the front lest anyone think I'd seen what I had. I cleared my throat portentously.

"I understand we have a mutual acquaintance, general," I said.

He glowered at me. *"What?"* he snapped.

"I understand that we know the same man." I revised my words.

"I doubt it. *Who?*" he replied.

"Your former aide-de-camp, Colonel George Ward Nichols."

Sherman made a snorting noise. "Aide-de-camp, my a———!" he snarled. "He ran some wagons for me, just like you're doing. And he was no more a colonel than my horse!"

I must confess to being blanked out by his harsh response. I stared at him, speechless. Then, at length, I cleared my throat again, this time not portentously in any way.

"Well," I said, "time to go check the wagons."

"Do that," Sherman told me.

I pulled my mount around and rode along the train, feeling properly chastened. I'd known that Colonel (hell, I wouldn't call him *that* anymore!) Nichols was a man fully skilled in stretching the truth like taffy, but I hadn't known that the stretch included his title as well.

After riding back three wagons or so, I turned my horse and rode along beside one of them. I'd leave Sherman to himself, I decided, do my work, and expect no more. Curse Nichols's dissembling bones anyway!

Lost in depressed thought, I had not noticed the small girl of eight or so sitting on the front seat of the wagon by her father. It took a while before I grew cognizant of her coquettish glances. I looked over at her, and immediately she averted her eyes. I had to smile. She was an absolute darling of a girl.

When I looked away, she looked back at me again. I looked back at her; she looked away. I had to chuckle now as we commenced a duel of sidelong glances and eye evasions. Finally, after some time, I contrived to catch her eye and winked at her. Instantly she was reduced to hand-stifled giggles.

"What are you doing?" her father asked.

"Being a delightful young lady, sir," I told him and nudged my horse forward.

As I rode beside the next wagon up, I smiled to myself, considerably cheered.

"All right, stay together now!" I ordered. "Don't start lagging! We've got a long way to go!"

I felt good now; away from that hateful fort and out on the plains again. And all because of the innocent flirting of a little girl. *How marvelous,* I thought.

+➤═◄+

I may forget or simply not get around to revealing my admiration for the charm of children.

I have always found myself at ease with them, able to enter, as it were, their world in place of my own, become a child along with them, and enjoy their pleasures as my own. Few know this of me. Accordingly, I feel it not amiss to comment on it now.

I must add that children have always warmed to me and liked my company, whether it was to play their childlike games along with them, spend a carefree afternoon fishing with them, or take part in serious discussions with them about their dogs or cats or dreams. To sit with a child or with children and chomp on an apple or candy while conversing on any subject that appealed to them was more than just a pleasure to me, it allowed me to forget whatever cares were besetting me and escape to a relaxing, peaceful period of time.

I remember, in particular, when the wagon train stopped at Marysville, Kansas, how I spent an enchanting afternoon with the young daughter of a certain Dr. Finlaw, scrambling along a riverbank and consequently getting horrendously muddy, me laughing until tears ran down my cheeks, the small girl bursting with peals of hysterical amusement while we tried to catch bullfrogs, totally in vain I must add.

Custered

A particularly ironic quote from Nichols's account of my activities at that time: "Some months later, General Sherman's tour of inspection having been concluded, Hickok happily returned to his duties at Fort Riley."

Ironic, did I say? I should have termed it crackbrained; farcical. I felt devoured by gloom as the wagon train moved toward the distant fort, my future there a dismal prospect as I saw it.

But then, as I rode in apprehensively, I reacted in great surprise to what I saw.

Everything was spit and polish, total order, total discipline. *What had happened while I was gone?* I wondered. *Had Owens gone insane and turned from a hapless lisper to a hard-edged disciplinarian?* I found that difficult to believe. Yet something had to explain this wondrous transformation: soldiers drilling smartly; teamsters working hard, with much efficiency; everything in view running like a well-oiled clock.

I had, I confess, been keeping my marshal's badge in my pocket, planning to avoid the pinning of it to my shirt as long as possible. Seeing this miracle taking place before me, I removed the badge from my pocket and pinned it back in place, thinking, *How?*

The answer was not long in coming: Custer.

I was taken to Custer's office, and instantly I took notice of his appearance. As a handsome man myself (remember, I speak now as I thought then) I appreciated his flamboyant grace; thick, blond hair hanging as long as mine, full, drooping mustache and goatee, flashing eyes and teeth, dressed in an immaculately tailored uniform. Is it retrospective imagination that causes me to remember an atmosphere of threatening, even impending mania about him? Perhaps memory errs. Still, why do I recall this if it wasn't so?

Seeing me, he thrust his hand out with the swiftness of a sword thrust. "Colonel George Armstrong Custer—*at* your service, Mr. Hickok," he said.

I shook his hand, trying not to wince at the strength of his grip. "Honored to meet you, sir," I responded.

There was another man in the room, a cruel-faced, glowering man. I will always think of him as such.

"This is my brother, Captain Thomas Custer," the colonel told me.

I extended my hand. "My pleasure, captain," I said.

He did not take hold of my hand immediately but made me wait for the gesture, running his gaze over my face and outfit with an attitude of contemptuous amusement.

Then he took my hand and squeezed it even harder than his brother had. *"Marshal,"* he said. Somehow, he made it sound like an obscene word. I didn't know what to make of the man. Clearly, he looked down on me; why, I had no conception. Still, in those opening moments, I seemed to understand that Captain Thomas Custer was going to be a large burr underneath my saddle.

I turned back to the colonel as he spoke.

"As you have doubtless observed, Marshal Hickok," he said, "the discipline problem at Fort Riley has been duly solved."

"Uh . . . no," I said; unconvincingly, I think. "I hadn't noticed, having just come in."

Custer had continued speaking over me, as though he had no time for either listening or reacting. "Accordingly," he said, "I must request that you relinquish your assignment as United States mar-shal, the necessity for your services no longer existing."

God's in his heaven, it occurred to me; *all's bright in the world.* I pressed down any facial expression that might reveal my thoughts and said, "Of course. I would have suggested it myself as soon as I'd noticed . . ."

My voice trailed off and, as the Custers watched, Tom with a scornful smile (How could he dislike me so soon? It usually took awhile.), I unpinned the badge, tossed it on the desk edge where it fell to the floor, bent over, picked it up, and set it back on the desk.

"Thank you, Mr. Hickok," Custer said.

I smiled and nodded and began to turn away.

"And now, perhaps, you'll sign on as a scout with us," said Custer.

I turned back, unable, I'm afraid, to conceal my surprise. I saw Tom Custer's look of scorn return and deepen. "Uh . . . well, I—" I began.

"We need you, sir," said Custer, overriding me again. "Need you badly." He smiled that toothy smile for which he was so well known. "I've been counting on your help."

Once more, as on so many other dark occasions, I was cor-nered. "Oh," I said, "well, naturally I—"

I flinched as Custer clapped me on the shoulder; heartily, I sup-pose it would be called; painfully, is how it should be described.

"Splendid, Mr. Hickok!" he said, enthused. "As our British cousins say: *Good show!*"

He smiled and pointed at me, looking every inch the potential lunatic he was. No, memory does not err. It was all there in his face: a madman's glee.

"I understand your hesitation, however, I assure you," he said.

I felt myself tensing. *He did?*

"Fear not, however," he assured me, "I can promise you that life with us will not be dull."

"I—" was all I managed to utter before he rolled on across me, a grinning juggernaut, his eyes gone glittery.

"Orders have come through from Washington," he said. "To wit: 'Settle with the Red Man at any cost.'"

I felt my smile—polite as always—ossifying.

"I am therefore," Custer went on (I am tempted to write "raved on" but his voice was not that rabid even if his brain was), "launching an immediate and mass campaign against the Sioux, the Cheyenne, and the Kiowa Nations."

He smote the air elatedly. "Much excitement lies ahead, Mr. Hickok!" he cried. "I'm *delighted* you'll be with us all the way!"

Snatching up a piece of paper from his desk, he slammed it down in front of me, grabbed a pen, and jabbed it into his inkwell with the stab of a deranged picador, then held it out to me, white teeth flashing in a dazzling smile.

"Your contract, sir!" he cried.

I stared at him, the polite smile still frozen on my lips.

I then took hold of the pen and leaned over to sign. As I did, I saw, from the corners of my eyes, the Custer brothers exchange a look, Custer's one of satisfaction, his brother's one of continuing scorn. To his credit, Custer, at least, frowned at his brother.

I wish he could have done more to control him.

Scouting Days

Henry M. Stanley was, for a time, a special correspondent for the *Weekly Missouri Democrat*. It was for that publication that he penned the following: "Riding about in the late field of operations, he was seen by a group of red men who immediately gave chase. Too soon they found whom they were pursuing and then commenced to retrace their steps but not before two of them fell dead before the weapons of Wild Bill. A horse was also killed and one wounded, after which Wild Bill rode unconcernedly on his way to camp."

I interpolate in Stanley's account of the same event to show you how it really happened.

Visualize me, if you will, galloping at high speed across the prairie.

"Among the white scouts in Custer's Seventh Cavalry were numbered some of the most noted in their class. Nonetheless, the most prominent of these was 'Wild Bill' Hickok."

The reason I was galloping at high speed was that three Indians were chasing me, shooting arrows at my back.

After a while, I steered my horse into a canyon, looking back across my shoulder, relieved to see that the trio of Indians was not in sight at the moment.

"He was a plainsman in every sense of the word, ever watchful and alert."

The three Indians came charging from a side canyon ahead, catching me completely by surprise. I had to yank my horse around and gallop in the opposite direction.

Soon I faced a slope and drove my mount up the boulder-filled incline. The Indians were out of sight again. Lifting myself in the stirrups to twist around and get a better view, I lost balance and toppled from the saddle, tumbling to the ground.

"Whether on horseback or on foot . . ."

I staggered to my feet and hobbled dizzily after my horse.

". . . he was one of the most perfect examples of physical manhood the West has ever known."

I dived for my horse's tail and managed to grab hold of its tip. I tried to run but tripped over a rock and was dragged by the horse for several yards before letting go. I somersaulted over, then sat up on the hot ground, panicky and furious at the same time. "S———t!" I cried.

"Of his courage, there can be no question."

Moments later, face bloodless, eyes slitted, teeth clenched, features tight with apprehension, I crouched in the center of a boulder formation. At the bottom of the slope, the three Indians were riding past, searching for me.

As they rode out of sight, I stood and backed off slowly, a pistol in each hand.

I cried out, startled, as I backed into a cactus, flinging up my arms, and dropping my revolvers, one of them bouncing off my head. Dazed, I glanced back groggily, saw the cactus, and scowled.

Abruptly, I looked up the slope. The Indians had doubled back and were now above me. Grabbing my pistols, I began to run and leap down the slope, glancing across my shoulder. The Indians came riding quickly down the slope, shooting arrows again (thank God they had no rifles). I opened fire as I fled.

"His skill in the use of the revolver was unerring."

My pistol balls knocked dust into the air everywhere but near the Indians.

Racing down the slope, I skidded, slipped, and rode the seat of my pants down the rock-strewn incline, teeth set against the fierce abrading of my bottom. I hit a boulder, feet first, reared up, and flew across it, headfirst.

Landing hard, I struggled to my knees, very dizzy now, and looked across the boulder. (Unless I imagined it, the seat of my pants was smoking.)

The three Indians still charged down the slope on their ponies, shooting arrows.

Raising my pistols, I pulled the triggers, looking at the guns in shock; they were empty.

Suddenly, I cried out as an arrow flew into my right hip, causing me to topple over. Laboring up, convinced that I was finished, I looked up at the Indians to see, with astonishment, that they had dragged their mounts around and were charging up the slope in flight.

I watched them dumbly, totally perplexed.

Then I heard the thundering of hooves and looked around. A cavalry patrol was galloping toward me with—of all people—Tom Custer in command.

I stood slowly, grimacing with pain, looking rather awkward with an arrow jutting from my hip. The cavalrymen galloped by on each side of the boulder, pursuing the Indians; Tom Custer reined up to talk to me. Despite the agonizing pain, I tried to look blasé; I gestured casually.

"His department was entirely free of bluster and bravado; always well controlled."

I collapsed and fainted dead away.

When I came to some minutes later, still lying on the ground, it was to see a sadistically smiling Tom Custer heating a knife blade in a fire, troopers watching.

"Even when severely wounded, as he often was, Hickok bore his pain with Spartan resolution . . ."

Custer kneeled beside me and, before I could speak, began to gouge the red-hot knife tip into my hip, digging for the arrowhead.

". . . never uttering, at any time, so much as a murmur of complaint."

If there truly is a God in heaven, I believe he had no difficulty whatsoever hearing my squall that afternoon echoing and reechoing across the terrain.

Elizabeth

❖⟶⟺◉⟺⟵❖

Since I do not anticipate that this manuscript will ever be published—or, if it is, that it will not be published for many years—I feel it is appropriate—well, no, that is not the word for it; say, rather, it is in the name of truth—that I add the following. Not that I intend to spell it out in lurid detail; far from it. I have too much deep respect for the person involved. Well, call it ego then; perhaps I have not matured quite as much as I would like to believe and it makes me feel a sense of personal pride to say this.

I believe that Elizabeth Custer was in love with me.

I hasten to add that, beyond a host of exchanged looks (some of them definitely fervent) and a single, passionate kiss, there was never anything untoward in our relationship. I respected her marriage as well as the lady herself and would never have compromised or sullied her name in any way. If this sounds hypocritical in light of what I have already indicated about Sarah Shull and Susannah Moore (and others I have not mentioned) remember that Elizabeth Custer was a genuine lady and I respected that.

I met her, of course, while I was a scout for Colonel Custer at Fort Riley, and during the period of my recuperation from the arrow wound, I got to know her well.

We discovered that we had a mutual interest in the subject of Spiritualism. She let me read several books she owned on the

subject and we discussed their contents at length. Her husband—
and brother-in-law, thank the Lord—were in the field most of the
time, so we had uninterrupted hours together. I wondered more
than once whether anyone who saw me entering her quarters suspected the worst. If they did, they were in error and, at least, nobody chose to speak of it to either Custer or his brother.

Elizabeth was a truly lovely person. I thought on occasion that
she was too good for her posturing spouse, but she maintained
a steadfast loyalty to him that I am certain will endure long after
Custer's unfortunate death.

What drew us to one another may have been as simple as a
physical attraction between two handsome people. (I *was* good-
looking; then at least.) But I feel it was more, in fact. She seemed
impressed by my family background, as I was with hers. We were
both fundamentally genteel (I know this sounds bizarre considering my reputation, but it's true) and soft-spoken. And, as I have already indicated, we shared an interest in Spiritualism and enjoyed
long conversations on the topic.

The looks we exchanged, the sudden drawing in of breath by
her at times, and, of course, the one kiss during which we clung to
one another tightly—all these verify, in recollection, my belief that
she cared for me.

One more piece of evidence does the same.

I carry, in my billfold, a page she wrote. She said that she had
planned to use it in a book about her life with Custer but decided
against it as it might disturb her husband. I was truly honored that
she trusted me to keep it in my possession.

Herewith: "Physically, Wild Bill [I have always been sorry I did
not ask her to call me James] is a delight to look upon. He walks
as if every muscle is perfection and the careless swing of his body
as he moves seems perfectly in keeping with the man. I do not
know of anything finer in the way of physical perfection than Wild
Bill when he swings himself lightly from his saddle and, with

graceful, swaying step, squarely set shoulders, and well-poised head, approaches. I will not discuss his features, but the frank, manly expression of his fearless eyes and his courteous manner give one a feeling of confidence in his word and in his undaunted courage."

Not the words, I submit, of a disinterested woman.

Home

⊱⋅ ───── ⋅⊰

Two things made me leave the fort when the condition of my wound had improved. One was, as indicated, to leave behind any temptation that might exist between Elizabeth Custer and me. The other was more in keeping with my general desire to avoid danger.

My wound was getting close enough to healing to present me with the likelihood of Custer asking me to scout for him again, so I decided that it was a most propitious time to visit my mother.

Accordingly, I purchased a dress from the fort post, announced my plan, and packed my carpetbag.

The day I left, I limped to my horse with the aid of a cane and tied the bag and cane behind the saddle.

As I did, I saw Tom Custer walking across the quadrangle, heading in my direction.

"B——d," I muttered under my breath. "Don't know which of them is crazier."

I lifted myself onto the horse, wincing at the pain in my hip.

"*Leaving*, Hickok?" Tom Custer asked.

"Yes, sir," I replied, sounding as genial as I could. "Going home to Illinois to visit my aging mother."

"So I heard," said Custer, almost interrupting me. "You *will* return though."

"Oh, yes. Definitely," I replied.

Touching the brim of my hat, I turned my horse away, murmuring to myself, "The day hell freezes over."

+➤━━◄+

My mother was overjoyed to see me, though my family made it clear that bringing a dress and a few other trinkets was scarcely adequate when she really needed contributions toward her welfare; that I had never made such contributions annoyed them mightily. Since I was now, in their eyes, a celebrated personage, they assumed that I was rolling in money. Why they would think that I have no idea, but I was too proud or angry to let them know that my income for the past few years could be described with one word: *sparse.*

While I was home, my wound began to suppurate and a doctor had to come to lance the wound and scrape the bone.

Nichols's version:

"The doctor made four cuts outward from the wound, making a perfect cross. Then he drew the flesh back and began to scrape the bone. I [my sister Lydia] was holding the lamp and felt herself getting faint. 'Here, give it to me,' said Bill. He took the lamp and held it while the doctor scraped away, never flinching once."

The truth:

As soon as the doctor made the first cut, I fainted dead away and was out cold through the entire operation.

+➤━━◄+

The year 1868 was rather strange.

Mount Vesuvius erupted in Italy.

Mount Etna did the same.

Earthquakes troubled England.

A cyclone hit the island of Mauritius, making fifty thousand people homeless.

The Hawaiian Islands were swamped by a tidal wave sixty feet high, and Mauna Loa erupted.

Gibraltar was struck by an earthquake.

Peru and Ecuador suffered enormous earthquakes. Mountains collapsed and immense tidal waves swept towns away and carried huge ships far inland.

Gigantic waves hit California, Japan, and New Zealand.

An earthquake hit San Francisco.

With such things taking place, even Nichols was hard put to find anything exciting to write about me.

<hr />

After conducting a short-lived freighting business with a man named Colorado Charlie, I traveled from town to town, looking for a place to settle down, a place where everything was peaceful.

The pattern of my stops at any given community was similar.

I would seek out some old-timer sitting in front of the general store, usually with his chair tipped back. Approaching him, I would crimp the brim of my hat and say good afternoon. He usually responded, "Howdy."

"Nice community you have here," I would comment, testing the waters.

In one place, the old man spat and said, "Like h———l it is."

I gazed at him reflectively, recrimped the brim of my hat, and wished him a good day. Then, remounting my horse, I rode back out of town.

In another town, I reined my horse up near another old man sitting in another chair in front of another general store. I touched the brim of my hat, said good afternoon, and commented on what a nice community he had.

"That's what you think, bub," said the geezer, spitting.

Without another word, I tapped the brim of my hat, steered my horse away, and started out of town.

I have lost count of the number of communities I briefly visited this way.

"Ever on the search for new adventure," Nichols wrote, "Hickok rode into Hays City, Kansas, in the summer of 1868."

I reined my horse up by yet another general store porch on which yet another old-timer leaned back in his chair and, yet another time, crimped the brim of my hat; it was thinning from the surplus of crimping it had experienced.

"Nice community you've got here," I said.

The old man spat. "We like it," he said.

I leaned in toward him.

"Good marshal?" I said.

"Nope," he answered.

I straightened up with a frown. "You don't have one?" I asked.

"No, sir," said the old man. He gathered spit. "Sheriff," he explained, then spat. "Tom Gannon."

"*Ah,*" I said, leaning forward again. "Good man, eh?"

The old man looked around and gestured with his aged head. "Judge for yourself," he told me.

I looked around to see Tom Gannon lumbering along the plank walk, an enormous, ominous-looking man with a handlebar mustache and a derby hat, a shotgun tucked beneath his right arm.

The sight of him warmed the cockles of my heart.

"Yes, sir," I observed. "A nice community."

+〉━•━〈+

Hays was, of course, far more than a community. It was the terminus of the railroad, so the roundhouse, the turntable, and all the other buildings that go to make a railroad town were located there.

North and South Main Streets were built on either side of the railroad tracks.

On them were such establishments as the Capless and Ryan Outfitting store, the Leavenworth Restaurant, the Hound Saloon and Faro House, Howard Kelly's Saloon, Ed Goddard's Saloon and Dance Hall, Tommy Drums Saloon, Kate Coffee's Saloon, Mose Water's Saloon, Paddy Welsh's Saloon, and so on. You may observe that drinking was a major feature of the social life in Hays.

The others were gambling and prostitution.

Someone wrote the following about this final occupation. I have carried it with me all these years, thinking that I might make use of it.

"Streets blazed with the reflection from saloons and a glance within showed floors crowded with dancers, the gaily dressed women striving to hide, with ribbons and paint, the terrible lines that the grim artist Dissipation loves to draw upon such faces. With a heartless humor, he daubs the noses of the sterner sex a cherry red but paints under the once bright eyes of women a shade as dark as the night in the cave of despair."

Where did all these women come from? Every European nationality was represented and, occasionally, the Far East. They came in every shape and size. Some were pretty, many were not. Some were mean and vicious, carrying knives or pistols. Age was no barrier, but those older than thirty were the exception. Most of the girls were in their teens, and once I met a fourteen-year-old.

Many entered the profession unwittingly, answering advertisements for domestic servants only to discover on arrival their dreadful mistake.

A few escaped their fate but, for the rest, there was only constant degradation and the threat of disease. Some died naturally, but more took their own lives, laudanum the preferred method.

I had not intended to convert this tale into a tract. Perhaps I do it from guilt, for I was no abstainer from these women who were "horizontally employed" as it is said.

Leave it to us men to denigrate these poor soiled doves with such mocking sobriquets as *ceiling expert, nymph du prairie, frail denizen,* and *crib girl.*

Excuse me for this bleak diversion but it is my story and I'll tell it as I choose, especially since no one is likely to read it, anyway.

I have wondered, now and then, if my descent into drunken

and libidinous pursuits in 1868 could have been the result of my bitter disappointment that I could never possess Elizabeth Custer.

But then, perhaps that is no better than a foolishly romantic excuse for what I did. God knows I was no stranger to the artist Dissipation at that time, a more than willing companion to his every carnal blandishment.

✛━━◄━━✛

Because a book was published at that time *(Wild Bill Hickok—King of Pistoleers* or was it *Hero of the Plains?* I forget) purporting to be a true account of my adventures, the descriptions of my character were so adulatory that they made me feel guilt about the unseemly life I was leading. Accordingly, I tapered off my profligacy and attempted to resemble more closely those glorifying words; probably the only time that lies improved the truth. Certainly, it was the only time one of those toadying accounts served to help me rather than hinder.

At any rate, I no longer cut the wolf loose. I caroused less with the ladies of the night and played my cards closer to the vest. Accordingly, my health, my energy, and my income were all enhanced and I began enjoying life again.

Until that afternoon.

Served Up Brown, Twice

I was playing poker in Tommy Drums Saloon, my fellow gamblers a trio of local men, all well respected, as I certainly was by then. A gathering of male and female admirers watched the game, drinking in my every word and gesture.

I tossed down my hand. "Well," I said, "the cards are certainly not cooperating with me today." Not a particularly witty observation, even by the most lenient of standards. If anyone else had said it—or if I had said it in a world (blessedly) free of Nichols and his hyperbolizing ilk—not a glimmer of appreciation would have ensued.

As it was, a wave of intense amusement ran through the assemblage. I picked up my dwindling pile of chips and made a face at its diminutive size. More laudatory chuckles from the Wild Bill Congregation. I tossed down the chips in disgust. Crinkled eyes and delighted laughter. "Perhaps I should have stayed in bed," I said.

An old man slapped his thigh and cackled as though my remark was the funniest thing he'd ever heard in his life. The others joined him in merry mirth; by God, this Hickok fellow belonged on the stage.

The next hand was dealt.

One of the players inquired of me, "Do you think you'd become our sheriff, Mr. Hickok, if Tom Gannon wasn't here in Hays?"

"Oh . . . I suppose I might," I responded offhandedly.

"Wouldn't *that* be something," said another of the players.

A thrilled murmur flowed through the room. "Yeah!" "Wouldn't it though!" "I sure would like to see *that* day arrive!" et cetera, ad nauseam.

I examined my cards, continuing grandly. "However," I declared, "Ellis County *does* have a sheriff. And a d———ned fine one, we must admit," I added generously.

"Oh, well, sure, of course," another man begrudged.

"You'd be better, Wild Bill," player number three observed.

"Ay-men!" a woman cried.

I nodded, smiling graciously. (These moments I could not resist. Could you?) "Well," I drawled, "I guess I'd get the job done somehow."

"*Somehow?*" "S———t, man!" "Huh!" Incredulous sounds from all and sundry.

"We'd *never* have a problem if *you* were sheriff!" Player number two was positively effervescing.

I gestured with princely restraint. I was really good at it by then; my gestures could not have been improved upon. "I appreciate your confidence, gentlemen," I told them self-effacingly, "and truly hope that, one of these days, I can repay it with deeds instead of words."

I looked askance at my cards.

"I also hope that, one of these days, I'll be dealt a decent hand."

Much gladsome risibility. I was a hit. Basking in their wide-eyed admiration, I began to speak again, saying, "Well, now—" when I had to break off as the batwing doors were flung ajar and a young man pounded over to us. His name (Do I remember that because he was the bearer of ill tidings?) was Bob Cooney and he was panting, wheezing, sweating. "Bad news, boys!" he cried.

"What?" "What is it, Bob?" "What happened?" All queries, virtually simultaneous.

"Sheriff Gannon's been shot from ambush!" he told us.

I recall a nerve twitching in my cheek.

"Is he *dead?*" someone demanded.

"Deader than a mackerel!" cried Bob Cooney.

An awed sound rippled through the group. Then, almost as one person, everyone turned their eyes toward me, trying not too successfully to restrain their enthusiasm so soon after learning of Gannon's murder. I felt my cheeks puff as my stomach made its presence known.

"Well, now," I said, hoping that my voice was not quite as faint as it sounded to me.

⊷═⊶

Walking back to my hotel, still limping slightly, I tried to pretend that I didn't notice everyone's anticipating looks.

"Hey, Jeb, you heard about Gannon?" someone shouted from across the street, making me start.

"Yeah!" said Jeb; he was walking behind me. *"Wonder who they're going to get to take his place!"*

"Yeah! I *wonder!*" shouted back the man across the street.

I tried to freeze my face as though absorbed in momentous thought. Two women (ladies, I presume) passed me on the walk, casting sidelong glances; I was so distracted I forgot to touch my hat brim, much less respond to their glances.

I passed an older man who smiled at me broadly. "Afternoon, Mr. Hickok," he said.

My returned smile was closer to a momentary wince, I think.

"Heard about Sheriff Gannon?" the older man inquired.

I pretended not to have heard the question, increasing the length and speed of my stride. Gaze fixed straight ahead, I limped by a group of men who murmured eagerly among themselves, looking toward me with equal eagerness.

"*Now* we'll see some action," I heard one of them say as I left them behind.

"Boy, *will* we!" vociferated another.

I clenched my teeth and walked faster yet, even though it made my hip ache.

I entered the lobby of my hotel and, crossing to the stairs, ascended them. Happily, no one present there had heard the news, and all I had to deal with was the usual goggle-eyed veneration.

Reaching my room, I unlocked the door and went inside, closing and relocking the door, then taking off my hat and slinging it onto the bed. Moving to the bureau, I picked up the bottle of whiskey there and poured myself a glassful; the neck of the bottle rattled on the rim of the glass. Putting down the bottle, I emptied the glass's contents in a single swallow and stared morosely at my reflection in the mirror.

My stomach let go and I exploded with a deafening belch.

"Good . . . *God,* sir!" I addressed the white-faced craven in the mirror. "You *offend* me!"

<hr />

It was almost dark now; night was coming as it always did despite man's fear of it. Correction: despite *my* fear of it.

Boots off, I was sitting on the bed, staring glumly toward the window, more than just a little drunk.

Reaching out, I picked the bottle off the bedside table and poured the last of its contents into my glass. I held the bottle upside down for near a minute so the final drops would not be lost.

I then drank the glass empty, sighed, and hiccupped. I was waiting for what I knew was coming. I asked myself why I was doing so, why I wasn't getting out before it came. I had no answer; I sat waiting helplessly. The edges were numbed by liquor, but the core still pulsed with that apprehension I'd experienced so often in the past.

I looked now toward the door as footsteps approached my room. I felt paralyzed. Would I be able to react at all to what was now about to happen? I had no idea whatever.

The footsteps stopped. I felt myself begin to tighten with involuntary prescience.

Then I flinched, legs jerking, as someone knocked on the door.

For an instant, I visualized Death in his black, cowled robe standing outside, skeletal hand poised to knock again.

He did, and I flinched again. I stared mutely at the door.

"Mr. Hickok?" said the voice.

Absurdly, I thought, *It couldn't be Death, he wouldn't call me mister.* I drew in a trembling breath.

"Mr. Hickok?" the voice repeated.

I was tempted not to answer; I wasn't there, I'd gone out for the evening, I was riding, I was sleeping, I was dead.

The temptation affronted me. I raised my chin, assuming, even in the semidarkness, my most imperious expression. "Yes?" I asked.

"This is Mayor Motz," he told me. "May I enter?"

I swallowed with effort. That I couldn't handle. "I'm not dressed," I told him.

"Ah, well . . . in that case." I heard him clear his throat. "As you have no doubt heard by now," he continued, "Sheriff Gannon has been killed in the performance of his duty, and as mayor of Hays, it is, therefore, incumbent upon me to appoint a temporary sheriff until a new election can be held."

Stop babbling and get on with it, I thought.

He did. "I would be pleased and highly reassured if you would be that man, Mr. Hickok," he said.

I gazed at the door with lifeless eyes.

"Your salary," he babbled on, "would be one hundred and twenty-five dollars per month plus fifty cents for each unlicensed dog you shoot. However, after the election—which I *know* you'd win hands down—those figures can, I guarantee you, be improved upon."

I opened my mouth to speak, then closed it without making a sound.

"What do you say, Mr. Hickok?" asked the mayor. "Does that sound agreeable? Can we count on you?"

I drew in a very long, very shaky breath and braced myself.

"I'll think about it," I told him.

The silence in the hall was like a knife blade sinking slowly into my heart.

"I'm *supposed* to be reporting back to Fort Riley after my hip is better," I explained unconvincingly.

It was a lie I could not maintain. I tensed with aggravation, resenting Motz for putting me in this position.

"I'll let you know in the morning," I told him stiffly.

"Fair enough, sir!" Motz responded cheerily. "In the morning then. But please—don't let the salary affect your decision, for, as I say, it can definitely be improved upon."

He paused, then said, "Until tomorrow then," and left.

I slumped back weakly on my pillow. "Sure," I muttered, "it's the salary that will affect my decision."

Approximately twenty minutes later, I retrieved my carpetbag from the closet and began to pack it with my few belongings. *Time to move on once again,* I thought.

I looked at my mother's framed portrait for a while before putting it into the bag, trying not to think of what her reaction would be to this, much less—I shuddered at the image—my father's.

It is hard to believe that an illustration from a magazine altered the direction of my life.

Still, as I began to put it in my bag, I stopped and found myself staring at the well-worn copy of *Harper's Magazine,* the article about me and illustration of me prominent.

It was how I looked in that illustration that struck me so hard. Grand and noble. A gentleman par excellence.

It reminded me of how I looked when I first read that article; dirty, lying in filthy attire in the back of a wagon, a drifter and a derelict par excellence.

Was I to take the risk of sliding back to that?

I could not. Whatever the risks (and, of course, I downplayed them in my mind, believing that my reputation would enable me to once more triumph over any situation), I would not permit myself to retreat. I was here, I was wanted and admired, and Hays had not, in recollection, been all that woolly a place since I'd arrived.

Revealingly, the first thing I removed from my bag was the framed portrait of my mother, which I set back up on the bedside table. Sitting down, I gazed at it, remembering how she told me that I had descended from a long and noble line.

"I will not dishonor it," I promised her.

✦━━✦━━✦

At the Hays City Tailor Shop I did my best to bring that illustration to reality. Once more my personal self was imitating my created one; very strange behavior, I can see now more than I did then.

When I finally stepped forth onto the street, sheriff's badge displayed for all to see, I was the very model of sartorial splendor in my pleated shirt of finest white linen, my flowered waistcoat cut low to reveal my silk cravat, my Prince Albert frock coat with silk collar, my black salt-and-pepper trousers tucked into custom-stitched boots with two-inch heels, a scarlet silk sash fastened snugly at my waist, my two new pearl-handled revolvers under it (Colt Navy .36, of course), and my low-brimmed black hat. I was a true-life version of the *Harper's* illustration except, I feel compelled to add, even grander. I had achieved, at least as far as my clothing was concerned, my greatest dream. I was a living fashion plate.

Strutting along the plank walk, I paused by the window of a store to admire my reflection, and it seemed as though I saw in the glass my mother's smiling face as she reminded me to always be a gentleman.

"I *am*, mother," I assured her.

I stepped down from the walk to cross the street, impressing everyone who saw me, who then stepped aside with fearful reverence to let me pass. Horses, mules, and wagons stopped. Dogs paused to wonder and adore. (All right, that's a Nichols's worth of bologna.)

"Thus," he really did write of that afternoon, "did this Beau Brummel of the frontier bring his glory and magnificence to the job of sheriff of Ellis County, Kansas, in the United States of our America!"

A slight exaggeration granted but, on that occasion, I believed it to be the only time the foolish man had put down God's unvarnished truth.

The Peace Pipe
Goes Out

⋯⋙◉⋘⋯

Six weeks passed by in blessed and unexpected tranquillity, convincing me that I had made the right decision.

I practiced regularly with my pistols and must say that my increasing skill with same was virtually akin to awesome. I could center hit a two-foot circle at a hundred yards, hit two telegraph poles seventy feet apart by firing from a point midway between, and drive a cork through the neck of a whiskey bottle without breaking the neck. I even developed a dazzling quick draw, my speed "as quick as thought." Guess who wrote that?

Still (as I have indicated) to draw with speed and fire accurately, hitting dimes and a top fence rail is meaningless, because the dimes do not lug sidearms and they never wished me malice.

That was not the case with Bill Mulvey on that August afternoon in 1869.

⋯⋙⋘⋯

I was in Kate Coffee's establishment, standing at the counter, having a drink, my right boot propped on the brass rail. Ralph, the barkeep, and I were alone in the saloon. I raised my glass in a toast to him, my comportment that of a man imbued with confidence, which, at the moment, I was.

"Your health, sir," I wished him loftily.

"Thank you, sheriff," Ralph replied.

I drank down half the glassful and sighed with satisfaction. Ralph and I exchanged a smile, mine eminent, his reverent.

"Things have sure been mighty quiet since you took over, Mr. Hickok," Ralph observed.

"Which is the way we like it, Ralph. That is the way we like it," I responded, my tone of voice indicating that it was, of course, a joke. I winked at him and downed the remainder of the glass's contents, Ralph chuckling with appreciation at my subtle jollity.

"Seriously, though," he said then, "you must be bored stiff after a month and a half of absolutely *nothing* going on."

"Well," I said, admitting it, "a *little* action might not be too disagreeable." I held up the thumb and index finger of my right hand to indicate how much.

I chuckled amiably as Ralph poured me another drink, chuckling in response. Then he glanced toward the front entrance.

"After marshaling and scouting at Fort Riley," I began, "this *is* a bit—"

Ralph interrupted, muttering, "Uh-oh."

My hand twitched just enough to spill some whiskey on the bar. Ralph didn't notice, leaning toward me to murmur, "Looks like you might be getting that action right now, sheriff."

With his head, he gestured slightly toward the entrance. I looked in that direction, tensing at what I saw: a nasty-looking young man glaring over the batwing doors, eyeing me with hostility.

"I haven't seen *him* before," I said, turning back to Ralph.

Ralph was gone. I turned my head to see him heading quickly for the back room. I began to speak to him, then realized that there was nothing to say, and gave it up. I saw him shut the back room door. "Son of a b———h," I murmured. He'd certainly retreated fast.

I turned my head so quickly that my neck bones crackled as I heard the swinging doors creak open. The young man started toward me, boots clumping on the wood floor. I took my right foot off the brass rail and replaced it with my left so I could face him.

He stopped before me. "Hickok?" he said. Not mister nor sheriff; I was in for it, I saw. His eyes were wild, his expression bordered on mania; a veritable Dave Tutt, Jr.

"The name is Mulvey," he informed me.

"Well, I'm—" I began.

"*Bill* Mulvey," he cut me off.

"Well, I'm—" I tried again.

"*Wild* Bill Mulvey," he interrupted me again. "What do you think of *that?*"

The breaking of his voice told me what to think; he was afraid of me.

"Pleased to meet you, Mr. Mulvey," I greeted him coolly.

The tremulous snicker in his throat reinforced my conclusion as did his lamentable attempt to sound mocking as he repeated, "Please t'*meet*cha Mistuh Mulvey."

He tried to laugh, did not succeed, and stopped, face stiffening with anger.

"Well, *I* ain't glad to meet *you,* Hickok," he declared, his voice breaking again. My confidence increased.

"Mr. Mulvey, I suggest—" I started.

He broke in, features twitching, obviously terrified. "And I suggest your father was a chicken and your mother was a pig!" he ranted.

I smiled at him, amused.

"I believe that you're confusing your parentage with mine," I said.

His eyes bulged. He sensed that he was being defamed but couldn't quite comprehend how. He leaned forward, lower jaw jutting out. "*Say that again,*" he ordered.

I had only to threaten him with death now; that was obvious.

"Go home, Mr. Mulvey," I told him. "This is more than you can—"

I stopped, went rigid, as he stepped back quickly, right hand poised to draw.

"I told you to say it again," he said, "You yellow, long-haired, leaky-mouthed, no-souled, egg-sucking dandy!"

I might have taken pleasure in his vivid, creative epithet had I not, at that instant, come to the stunned realization that, despite his terror-stricken state, he was determined to go through with this. It was a new variety of plight for me. My mind went blank.

Then, inspired, I looked abruptly toward the entrance.

"Don't shoot, boys!" I ordered.

Mulvey jerked around, deceived. I grabbed for one of my pistols, moving so precipitately that my boot slipped off the brass rail and I crashed down to the floor as Mulvey whirled back, drew, and fired at the spot where I had been.

Sprawled, I fired upward, hitting him square in the gut; not a fatal shot but one that gave him such a shock, his brain was paralyzed. He stumbled backward, trying to raise his arm to fire a second time. My second pistol ball, more accurately aimed, entered his heart and killed him, causing him to topple over clumsily.

I stared at him, heart pounding, then glanced around as Ralph's muffled voice emitted from behind the back room door. "Is it over, Mr. Hickok?" he inquired.

I scrambled to my feet, replaced the Colt beneath my sash, and brushed my clothes off hastily. Straightening up, I swallowed hard.

"Yes, it's over," I responded sonorously.

The back door opened and Ralph peered out uneasily.

Seeing me on my feet, stately and composed, he emerged and looked across the counter, eyes widening as he caught sight of Mulvey's body lying motionless nearby.

"Holy . . . jumping . . ." he mumbled.

"Best fetch the undertaker, Ralph," I instructed calmly. "I'm afraid our friend here just cashed in his chips."

Turning, I strode toward the doorway, wincing as I felt my legs begin to quiver. I fought it off as two men rushed in, causing me to twitch in startlement.

"What happened, sheriff?" one of them asked in an excited voice.

I gestured airily. "Ralph will explain," I told him.

They watched me, openmouthed, as I departed.

A good thing for me they weren't watching minutes later when I lost my lunch and part of my breakfast.

⊹══⊰⊹

Several points that no one seems to know about.

In all the elaborations on my skill in the use of my pistols, never once have I read a single word about my constant efforts in maintaining them; as though the blasted things functioned perfectly with no attention paid to them whatever.

Far from it, let me tell you.

Almost every day, I took the trouble of refurbishing my Colts.

Living in this h———lish climate filled with ever-present sand and dust, using salt-laden black powder, which attracted moisture like a drunken man, my revolvers would have, very early on, ceased to perform as needed if not constantly kept intact.

First I would empty them and meticulously clean out the chambers, pushing a pin or needle through the nipples until, by holding the cylinder at eye level, I could see daylight through the rear of each chamber.

I would then carefully load each chamber with powder, ram home the lead balls (five, of course, the hammer left on the empty chamber; "five peas in the wheel," as they say). Finally, I would inspect each copper cap—filled with fulminate of mercury—before placing it on the nipple.

In that wise, I made certain that my guns were never damp in any way.

I already had enough problems using my pistols in defense of my life.

My second point has to do with my use of the English language.

It began to be more and more apparent to me that to present myself as an educated gentleman might have a tendency to vitiate the image I'd acquired in the past eight years as a tough and rugged man of action, someone to be feared and respected.

Accordingly, I began consciously to write with more deliberate care, taking the time to misspell words and twist the rules of grammar out of shape, for example, "you would laugh to see me now Just got in Will go a way again to morrow Will write in the morning but god nowse when It will start," and so on.

Easy enough to do. *Wright* instead of *write*. *Noncence* instead of *nonsense*. *Marryed* instead of *married*. *Agoing onn* in place of *going on*. *Achres* in place of *acres*. *Pririe* instead of *prairie*. You get the idea.

Actually, I think I overdid it and hope, with this account, to correct the misapprehension that I have been and am an uneducated clod with little to recommend me in the intellect department. Of course, would it have really mattered if I had let it be known that I had full use of the English language? Who can tell?

Smitten to the Core

❖━━◯━━❖

It was a peaceful, sunny afternoon in the spring of 1870.

Life in Hays had been remarkably placid, except for a brief incident the previous September when I was forced to shoot a man named Sam Strawhun, who was behaving in a threatening manner in John Bitter's saloon. To maintain my verity, I feel compelled to mention that the threatening gesture he was making toward me was with a beer stein, not a pistol, when I shot him through the head. The jury found the homicide justifiable, "being in self-defense."

Oh, there had been a brief confusion in October when the governor of Kansas—one James M. Harvey—had approved the refusal made by a certain Colonel Gibson to honor a warrant for arrest I had tendered him, claiming that he didn't recognize me as the sheriff of the county. But that was of little consequence in my life since no exchanged pistol fire was involved.

Indeed, the *Daily Commonwealth,* in December of that year, remarked that "Hays City, under the guardian care of 'Wild Bill,' is quiet and doing well."

That afternoon I ambled slowly along the plank walk, a monarch strolling through his kingdom, touching the brim of his hat as he passed various women, nodding (once) with regal recognition as he passed various men, patting (benignly) the heads of children as he passed them. All regarded me with the mien of worshipers, murmuring, "Afternoon, sheriff," or "Good afternoon, Mr. Hickok," or "Good afternoon, sir." Oh, let me tell you, I was truly into it by then, playing the role to the very hilt, not allowing to myself for a second the faintest glimmer of recognition that it was a role and nothing more.

I remember stopping on the walk and standing there, stroking the index finger of my right hand underneath my mustache as I gazed across my domain.

Then I heard a distant sound I did not recognize at first. Only after a number of perplexed moments did I recognize the sound as being that of a calliope. I stepped out into the street to get a better look. The calliope music grew louder, coming closer. The monarch smiled.

Approaching down Main Street was a traveling circus: animals in cages, elephants, costumed midgets, clowns, and performers walking and on horseback or in wagons, acrobats performing cartwheels along the dusty thoroughfare; all to the shrill accompaniment of the calliope. Printed on the wagon's sides I saw the name: Lake's Hippo-Olympiad and Mammoth Circus.

I watched with a kindly smile. The king was pleased.

As the circus continued moving along the street, more and more citizens emerged from their stores and offices to watch in grinning delight. It was not often that the torpid tempo of the community (which I, of course, found very much to my taste) was broken in such a captivating way.

Along with the citizens, I watched with high good spirits.

Then I caught sight of something—some*one* I should say—who abruptly galvanized me to the bone.

It was a mounted woman wearing red tights. A silk cloth on her horse's back bore the stitched name Madame Agnes Lake.

I ran an awed, admiring gaze along her shapely legs, up to her voluptuous, tightly bound figure, then farther up to her lush, red-haired beauty. Since this entry will, as likely as not, never be seen by the prurient eyes of man, I can reveal these things that ordinarily, as a gentleman, I would not deign to mention. I can add as well (I know it now, I didn't then) that Agnes Lake's appearance was greatly similar to that of my beloved mother.

At any rate, she smiled at the people as she rode by, nodding and gesturing gracefully. I find it amazing now to realize that she was forty-three years old at the time; I would have bet my stack that she was in the lower portion of her thirties, that at most.

I think I gaped at her, eyes unblinking, mouth (I hope not, but I fear) hanging partly open.

In fantasy, I saw her floating by me in a glowing, pink cloud, the shrillness of the calliope music somehow muted to my ears, even sweetened now.

I was, in brief, struck dumb by amour, let there be no doubt about that.

I was positively stupefied by Madame Agnes Lake.

And when, as she passed me by and saw me standing there, she extended me not only a dazzling smile but a gestured flirtatious greeting, I was an instant victim of calico fever. I had always believed that I would eschew all thoughts of matrimony until cows climbed trees, yet here I was, seconds after viewing her for the first time, already contemplating a quick jump over the broomstick.

⊷⊶

Shortly thereafter, I strode across the circus grounds on a search for her.

I found her giving orders to some tent hands. "Now remember, boys, we have to set up quickly, here," she said, her voice (as I'd hoped and was enraptured to hear) was as melodious as her looks were ravishing.

"Madame Lake?" I said in as deep a baritone as I could summon.

"Yes, what is it?" she asked, turning to face me.

The word "it" popped like a soap bubble in her mouth when

she saw me and I knew with instant felicity that she found me as attractive as I did her. Actually, with the ego that nurtured me so resolutely in those days, I most likely would have been stunned if she hadn't been attracted to me.

However, I could tell by her smile and the sudden way in which she started fussing with her thick red hair that she did find me attractive.

"I am Sheriff Hickok," I told her. "If there is anything at all that I can do to assist you . . ."

Her eyes had widened at my words. "Wild Bill Hickok?" she asked in awe.

I was hard put to restrain my heart's delirium.

"I have been called that on occasion, yes," I responded.

She pressed the fingers of her left hand to her (copious, shall I describe it?) bosom, gasping prettily.

"Oh, my," she murmured.

Thus did we stand there, dumbstruck by each other's beauty and position.

◆──═──◆

That evening, I attended the premiere performance of Lake's Hippo-Olympiad and Mammoth Circus.

Not that I paid much heed to the bulk of it. I was too intrigued by Agnes Lake. I stared, spellbound, as, costumed in her blue figure-hugging tights, she rode around the ring, upright on her cantering horse. I know that there was music being played by a band as she performed, but I don't remember hearing it, bewitched as I was by her appearance and her supple movements.

Each time she passed the stand in which I sat and turned her head to look at me, a delicately sensuous smile on her lips . . . well, I was a resident of Paradise, a feeble sound of ardor quivering in my throat.

My ecstasy soared completely when, later, she performed a high-wire act, a yellow, even more close-fitting outfit on her eye-filling form. High above, she smiled down at me more than once and I was certain (perhaps it was no more than self-delusion at that particular moment) that I saw invitation in her eyes. Looking up at her, I felt my Adam's apple bob with laborious effort.

Later still—it was nearly too much for my stricken heart—adorned by yet another skintight costume, this one green, she entered a cage with two lions and a tiger and made them sit on boxes, cracking her whip above their heads, then raising both her ivory arms in triumph. I was overwhelmed. My hands grew red from pounding them together. Fortunately for me, I didn't have to draw a pistol that night; I could never have done it successfully.

Even from the cage, she looked at me and I could not help but dream that she, like I, had romance in mind; I returned her looks with total fervor.

⊹⇒⊷⇐⊹

After the performance, following a chat with several citizens (me pretending to be casual about the circus and its owner), I strolled (instead of running, which I yearned to do) to the wagon in which Agnes Lake resided while her show was traveling, and knocked on its door.

"Who's there?" I heard the voice that thrilled my body to its marrow.

"Sheriff Hickok," I replied.

A rustling sound. "One moment, sheriff," she responded musically. Breath faltered in me as I visualized her drawing a robe over her provocative figure. I stood on the doorstep, feeling as though time had stopped completely and would not resume its movement until I had her in my gaze again.

She opened the door and I saw that my imagination had been on the mark, the silk robe clinging to her obviously unclad curves and valleys. I could not recall the way in which I breathed, all movement ceasing in my chest.

It did not cease in hers. A deep breath swelled it out with maddening inflation. "Yes?" she inquired.

I want to get in bed with you and let my bodily derangement satiate itself.

Of course, I didn't say that; couldn't. "May I offer you a late supper at the Leavenworth?" I invited.

"The Leavenworth?" she asked.

"Our finest restaurant," I told her.

"Ah," she responded, hesitating momentarily. Was it possible that she would not go? It was, after all, late in the evening and she could—understandably—be weary from the performance.

But no—my heart danced at the sight—she smiled and said, "That would be lovely, Mr. Hickok. If you'll wait, I'll put some clothes on."

Don't; just take the robe off and we'll dive into a pool of heavenly passion!

"Of course," I said, "I'll wait outside."

✦━━✦

We sat in the restaurant long after every other patron had departed, our only company a lone waiter who stood yawning by the kitchen door. It was an occasion (one of many, actually) where my status in the city kept the owner from requesting that we leave, that it was late, he had to lock the doors and go to bed. Instead, he waited patiently by the front door, sitting and reading a newspaper, smoking a cigar as he did.

I will not put down our conversation, even if I could remember every word of it, because it went on for hours. I will only say that we spoke of many things as we drank champagne and ate, our eyes gazing intently at one another.

You already know about me so it is not necessary that I repeat my side of the exchange. It is enough to encapsulate her recital, which I drew from her with rapt attention.

Her birthday is August 24, the year unrevealed, nor did I intimate that I wanted it revealed; it is, of course, a lady's prerogative to keep that information to herself, a gentleman's duty to make no effort to uncover the information.

She did reveal to me—an honor, I felt that she trusted me so—that although she tells everyone that she was born in Cincinnati, she was in fact, born in Alsace, Germany, and her last name was Mersmann. Her parents had immigrated to this country when she was three, settling in Cincinnati, where she grew up.

At the age of sixteen, she met a circus clown named William Lake Thatcher and ran away with him to join the circus. After her husband spent a winter in Mexico with the Rich Circus, leaving her in New Orleans, he barely escaped with his life as *americanos* were not popular at the time. The war between Mexico and the United States was shortly to break out. Completely devoid of funds, the couple returned to Cincinnati, where her parents were not exactly overjoyed to see them.

For a while, the couple struggled with their careers, working in various theatrical companies, then joining the reorganized Rich Circus, where they remained for two years before joining the Spaulding and Rogers Floating Palace. They stayed with this show for eleven seasons, during which period Agnes bore a daughter, Emma, who I would later meet, a charming and highly versatile fourteen-year-old.

The couple and their child rejoined the show Lake had been attached to when Agnes had first met him. When this show did poorly, the Lakes, by now very experienced in the circus business, formed their own show, which succeeded in great part because of Agnes's skill as an equestrienne, lion-tamer, and queen of the high wire.

Their success was marred by tragedy when a patron ejected from the show by Lake returned later and shot him dead.

Her husband's murder was an enormous shock to Agnes, which

she was compelled to bear since she was now the sole owner and operator of the circus.

Under her management, the circus prospered, its current tour bringing her to Hays, where she entered my life.

⊣⊨━⊨⊢

Even though I truly do expect that this account will merely languish on a dusty shelf or, at the very most, receive a limited publication many years after I have taken up residence in the bone orchard, I find most difficult the prospect of revealing the more intimate details of those days with Agnes.

We took drives in the daytime, Agnes with her parasol protecting her face from the blazing rays of the sun.

Sometimes, we would only go for a ride. At other times, we would find a peaceful glade on a stream where we would share a picnic lunch, which either she had packed in a basket hamper or I would have the Leavenworth prepare for us.

There, in the glade, we would converse, hold hands, then, later, share a gentle kiss, a clement embrace.

I went to each and every performance of the circus, naturally, pleased yet somewhat embarrassed when Agnes blew me a kiss as she galloped by, standing on her horse.

More and more, I would come to her wagon at the conclusion of the performance, there to hold her hands, then, later, embrace and kiss her with increasing passion.

We shared candlelight dinners in her wagon, gazing at one another with undisguised infatuation.

Finally, with candles extinguished, we consummated our relationship; I find myself able to say no more; she is, after all, a lady.

All was progressing splendidly, or so I thought. But, then, I have always had a flawless gift for counting my eggs before I even had a chicken.

My Horns Sawed Off Again

✦═◑⚊◐═✦

I was sitting in my office, whistling cheerily as I opened official mail, when the front door opened.

Looking up, I saw a small, timid-looking man standing in the doorway.

"Mr. Hickok?" he said inquiringly.

"Yes?" I answered.

I saw his Adam's apple bob as he swallowed. "Don't you remember me?" he asked.

I regarded him for a moment or two, then replied, "Can't say I do."

"Charlie Gross, Mr. Hickok," he said. "We knew each other in Homer years ago."

"Ah, of course," I rejoined with not a scintilla of recollection. "How are you, Mr. Gross?"

"I'm fine, Mr. Hickok. Fine," he said. I think he knew that I didn't remember him.

We stared at each other in silence.

"Well," I said.

"I'm a bookkeeper now," he told me. "In Abilene."

"Are you?" I said, politely.

"Yes, sir. I work for Mayor McCoy."

"Ah-ha," I said.

"When I told him that I knew you, he sent me here directly to ask if you'd be our city marshal."

Sure, I thought. *When pigs can fly and robins oink.*

"Your salary would be one hundred and fifty dollars per month plus one quarter of all collected fines; if that would be agreeable."

I smiled, amused.

"That would be entirely agreeable," I began to reply.

"Then may I—?" Charlie Gross broke eagerly into my answer.

"—*if* I were looking for a new position," I interrupted his interruption.

He opened his mouth to interject, but I continued.

"I am not, however," I informed him. "I am quite content in Hays and fully expect to remain here for the remainder of my life." (Complacency, thy name was Hickok.)

I should have known that my state of affairs was about as lasting as corral dust.

✢═══✢

We were lying in my hotel bed, unclad, cuddled close together. That much I'll reveal.

I was feeling petulant.

"I surely wish that you could cancel at least *some* of your engagements, Agnes," I said.

She stroked my hair soothingly, but I wasn't soothed. "I do, too, love," she replied. "You *know* I do. But there are contracts. I'm required to appear with my circus, just as you are under contract to be the brave, wonderful sheriff that you are."

"Oh, I suppose," I answered, grudgingly. As you can see, I still held myself in very high esteem.

"It won't be long, Bill," she assured me. "I'll be back in less than two months, put the circus up for sale, and settle down with you and Emma."

She kissed me tenderly. "And I *will* be Mrs. Wild Bill Hickok before I leave Hays," she said.

I nodded, sighing. "Two months, though," I said.

"I'll write you every day, Bill," she promised. "Every single day in the week. And maybe you can take some time off from your important duties to come and visit me. Or maybe I can take some time off and see you here—or, meet you someplace."

I sighed again. She kissed me again.

"It won't be bad, my love, my precious Bill," she said. "In two short months, we'll be together permanently—Mr. and Mrs. Wild Bill Hickok. We'll buy some property, build a home, settle in for good, maybe even have another child."

She hugged me enthusiastically, face radiant with anticipation.

"Oh, it's going to work out, Bill!" she almost cried aloud. "You'll see! I'll make it work! For my Bill, my Wild Bill."

I remember clearing my throat, wondering whether to say it, then deciding that I must. "You, uh, *know* . . . that my real name is James," I told her, wanting her to see me more as myself than as the dime novel hero.

"*Is* it, love?" said Agnes languidly.

"Yes," I continued. "James Butler Hickok. Of the Warwickshire Hiccocks in England." I cleared my throat again. "A noble line," I said.

"Oh, I'm sure it is, Bill," she replied. She laughed, amused by her unwitting mistake. "I'm afraid you'll always be Bill to me," she said. She sighed with happiness. "My Wild Bill Hickok."

I felt myself withdraw inside. *Not the right time yet*, I thought.

"I've read that you've killed hundreds of men," Agnes said, startling me. She shuddered with excitement, I could tell. "That isn't true, is it?" she asked in a tone that told me she hoped I would say it was true.

"Well," I answered, awkwardly, not really knowing what to say. "That may be cutting it a little fat."

"How many were there?" she inquired timorously.

What to say? I wondered. *Lie? Tell the truth?*

"Let's just say I've lost count," I told her. Even as I spoke, I winced within.

"My God, what a man you are," said Agnes. "What a *man*."

Stimulated, flushed, she turned to face me, kissing me passionately.

"Oh, Bill," she said, breathing with effort. "Bill. *Lover*."

"Yes," was all I could manage.

"I *love* you, Bill!" she said. "I worship you! I'll make you so happy! I will, I *will*!"

"Agnes," I responded, barely able to speak. I did love her something powerful. I hated having to spread the mustard with her, but I didn't want to disillusion her, either.

We pressed together in passionate liaison.

Abruptly, then, we twitched and looked around in startlement as gunfire erupted somewhere down in the street; the drunken hoot and raucous laughter of a man, the shattering of glass.

"My God, what's *that*?" gasped Agnes.

I didn't reply, staring uncomfortably toward the window.

Agnes rose and moved in that direction. "Be careful," I told her. "Best not . . ." my voice trailed into silence as she continued to the window.

Outside, the shooting, hoots, shouts of laughter, and shattering of glass continued.

"There's a man on Main Street," Agnes told me.

I heard another shot and the crash of breaking glass.

"He's shooting out store windows," she told me.

"Oh?" I said.

Another shot, another crash of glass.

"And a lamppost," Agnes described.

A shot. A yelp.

"And a dog," she said.

She turned back and moved to the bedside, looking down expectantly.

"Well," I said, feigning a tone of mild exasperation, "I guess I'd better take a look."

She smiled at me with adoration.

"They're so lucky to have you for the sheriff here," she said. "Someone could get hurt."

I felt certain that my smile was somber. "I know," I agreed.

As slowly as I could without being transparent in my reluctance, I dressed and left the room with Agnes's plea to "Be careful, Bill" in my ear as I descended the stairs to the lobby. By then, silence had fallen.

Three guests plus the desk clerk were down there, peering outside. As they turned to face me, I yawned extravagantly. "Did I hear gunfire?" I asked.

They stared at me as though to say, in mutual incredulity, "You did unless you're stone deaf."

"What's been going on?" I inquired casually.

The desk clerk answered me, "A soldier's been burning powder," he said. "Shot out nine store windows, broke six streetlights, wounded two dogs, one cat, and a midget."

That made me blink. "A *midget?*" I said.

"From the circus," the desk clerk explained. "Took a slug right in his tiny butt."

"Interesting," I said. "Curious I slept through all that."

The repressed grin of the desk clerk suggested to me that he didn't find my physical exhaustion curious at all; I had tried to get Agnes to my room in such a manner as to preserve her reputation but did not always succeed. I pretended not to notice his smirk but moved to the doorway and peered outside. "Soldier gone now, is he?" I asked, trying to disguise my hopefulness.

"No, sir," said the clerk. "He's in Kate Coffee's place. Claims he's going to shoot the whole damn town up, make a fool of you."

"Oh?" I said; I felt my stomach walls begin to close in on my dinner. I cleared my throat to hide my swallow. "Well, we'd better see about that."

I felt a tremor of excited expectation from the desk clerk and the three hotel guests.

I stepped outside and started along the plank walk, moving against my will toward Kate Coffee's Saloon. I drew in a deep breath, pulled back my shoulders, and strode as erectly as I could, looking straight ahead. *He's just a soldier,* I consoled myself. *When he sees who he's up against, he'll quail and back off fast.*

Notwithstanding, I paused outside Kate Coffee's batwing doors to peer inside.

A number of men were clustered at the counter, talking in excited murmurs. Ralph caught sight of me and smiled with great relief, gesturing hurriedly for me to enter.

Bracing myself, I pushed open the swinging doors and went inside. The men at the bar descended on me like a pack of vultures sighting dead meat.

"Thank God you're here, sheriff!" said one of them, as quietly as he could, considering his mad exhilaration.

"We been looking for you everywhere!" another said, equally deranged by eagerness.

"Well, I was—" I began.

"He's in the back room, Mr. Hickok," said Ralph, flapping in to join his fellow vultures. "Dead drunk. Mean as hell. Says he's going to—"

"Yes, I heard, I heard," I said, cutting off his melodrama.

I looked toward the back room. Everyone looked at me, contemplating gunfire. I planned to disappoint them on that score, boogering the soldier into frightened submission. I started away from them.

"Better not kill him, sheriff!" said one of the men. "He's a captain in the cavalry!"

"I'll try not to," I responded, hoping that they didn't hear the disparagement in my voice. I started forward again.

Ralph whispered after me, "Says he's Custer's brother!"

I froze in midstep; stood there like a statue on a town square: Sheriff Hickok Above His Head.

"Sheriff?" said Ralph.

No answer from yours truly.

"Mr. Hickok?"

When I didn't stir—paralyzed by indecision—Ralph moved up behind me and tapped me on the shoulder. I had never in my life before taken leave of my skin, but I very nearly did at that instant, jerking out both pistols in the fastest draw of my life, and whirling in the quickest spin.

Ralph recoiled with a stricken gasp, and the men scuttled backward like a startled multiform crab.

"Don't . . . *do* that!" I whispered fiercely to Ralph.

"Sorry, Mr. Hickok," he apologized, backing off to join the men. I glared at all of them; for the moment, they represented, to me, the major source of my troubles.

"Stand back!" I ordered them in a hoarse whisper. "Just . . . *stand back.*"

"Yes, sir," they said as one man, retreating, again, as one crab.

I made an angry, hissing sound and turned back toward The Room of Peril, staring at it gloomily.

I forced myself to edge forward then, pistols extended. I could almost feel the beady-eyed stares of the men on my back as they hoped for the best (for them), an eruption of exchanged gunshots, a body (preferably dead) sprawled on the floor, an eyewitness thrill of watching Wild Bill in bloody action.

I hesitated, looking down now at my Colts. I could not allow it to appear that I was taking unfair advantage over Tom Custer; that was alien to my prestige. Reluctantly, I pushed them loosely back beneath the waistband of my trousers; I'd had no time to don my sash. My face twitched as I struggled to repress a stomach eructation.

Reaching the bead curtains that separated the main saloon

from its back room, I peered inside, reacting to what I saw—and instantly suppressing that reaction.

Tom Custer had passed out cold on a chair, his upper body sprawled across a table.

I shut my eyes, releasing a cheek-puffing exhalation of relief.

I was about to turn and tell the men when, suddenly, a thought occurred to me. I didn't like it but could not dissuade myself from it. I turned, face adamantine, and flicked the wrist of my right hand in a signal for the men to step back. They did so, eyes widening, breath bated. Life and death was on the line; they knew it, they loved it.

After they had completed their backward movement, I turned and, standing tall, pushed through the bead curtains, wincing at the slight rattling noise they made, bracing myself in the event that the noise awakened Custer.

It didn't. Bracing myself further, I said, in a loud, ringing voice, "I'll have that pistol, captain!"

I mimicked a drunkenly rumbling reply, "Like h———l you will."

"I'd just as soon not pull down on you, captain!" I emoted as myself again. "I respect the uniform you're wearing but I don't—"

I broke off, stunned, as Custer stirred and began to sit up.

Jerking out one of my pistols, I laid its barrel across his skull and he collapsed back onto the table.

"Sorry—!" I gurgled. I cleared my throat as quickly and softly as I could. "Sorry I had to do that, captain!" I cried out, nobly.

Then I swallowed hard and had to gulp down several times in order to regain my breath. I belched softly and hiccupped seven times before controlling my system at last and turning back toward the main room of the saloon.

I came out, an expression of sovereign command on my face; I could still do that to a fare-thee-well.

"Will two of you boys carry the captain down to the jail for me?" I asked.

I moved toward the exit as the men came galloping to see what had occurred to Captain Custer.

I knew they would be disappointed at the lack of blood.

━┝━━┥━

Tom Custer's fingers gripped the cell bars so tightly that they were white, drained of blood. There was a purplish lump on his forehead where I had clouted him. His face was a living testament to homicidal rage.

"I'm telling you, Hickok," he muttered, "you better clear out of Hays right now, because when my brother gets me out today, I'm going to curl you up, you hear me? I'm going to *kill you dead.*"

I stood before the cell, regarding him in silence.

"You *hear* me?" Custer shouted.

I turned away, then stopped as he continued ranting.

"You may have everybody else bamboozled, but you don't have me!" he said. "Because I know what you really are! A *coward,* Hickok!"

His voice became a slow, grinding, knife-twisting sneer as he continued, "A yellow-bellied, white-livered, spineless, two-bit, no-good, big-talking s———t of a coward!"

My heart was pounding as I looked down at my right hand.

It was clutched around the stock of a half-drawn pistol.

Appalled to find myself in this revealing state, I shoved the pistol back beneath my sash and moved abruptly toward the doorway to my office, ignoring Custer's further words.

I shut the door to the cellblock, locked it, and pulled the key loose, trembling, shaken to the core by what I had been—without thinking—on the verge of doing.

A gentleman about to commit murder?

Moving to my desk, I sat down heavily behind it and opened a lower cabinet, removing from it a glass and a bottle of whiskey. Pouring myself a large drink, I downed it hurriedly, then sat there gazing into troubled thoughts.

Approximately twenty minutes later, I exited the office and

locked the front door, dropping the key ring into my coat pocket as I started down the street.

When I arrived at the circus grounds, Agnes was rehearsing Emma for her specialty horseback act.

Seeing me, she ran over and we came together in a fiery embrace and kiss. I did not usually care to display my passion in front of others, but there was no time for niceties at that moment.

"I heard what you did last night," she said.

"It was nothing," I replied, distractedly.

"Nothing!" she cried. "My *God*, what a man!"

I held her tightly, dreading that it was the last time I would ever see her.

Then I said, "Agnes?"

"Yes, love?" she responded, drawing away to smile at me.

I hesitated, then got it out. "I'm leaving Hays today," I told her. She caught her breath. *"Today?"* she said. Then, "Why, Bill? Why?"

I tried not to swallow but couldn't help it.

"Well, you see," I explained, "I've been offered the position of city marshal in Abilene—at a considerable raise in salary."

"Well . . . yes, I understand," she said, obviously trying to do so. "But . . . why do you have to leave today? So suddenly?"

"Well, you see," I responded, "they have no marshal at the moment, and they're in dreadful need of one."

"I see," she murmured. Was she convinced? I doubt it, because she quickly added, "But what about our marriage? Can't you delay your departure a day or so for *that?*"

"Well—" Lord, I sounded unconvincing! "I rather promised them, you see. Signed a contract."

"I see," she murmured. "I just wonder . . . why you didn't tell me before."

"I had no chance," I lied. "Their message just arrived today."

"Mm-hmm," she said.

Heavy silence weighed us down. I was terribly uncomfortable

at her expression: one of disappointment mingled with a palpable suspicion that I was running out on her.

She tensed as I put my arms around her.

"We'll write each other every day," I said. "And your circus *is* scheduled for Abilene, isn't it?"

"Not for quite a while," she answered.

"Well, I'll be waiting for you there," I said as reassuringly as possible. "All right?"

She did not respond.

"All right, Agnes?" I asked.

She tried to smile; it was extremely forced. "All right," she said, "if you have to go."

"I really do," I said in my expansive tone. "They're rather in a muddle there, it seems. Need a firm grip on the city reins," I finished with my famous crooked smile.

She nodded again, her smile even more strained. I kissed her, held her close.

"Don't fret now, Agnes," I told her. "Everything is going to be all right."

It was not a hand I would have bet on.

Fording a stream a few miles out of town, I reined in, took the ring of keys from my pocket, and tossed it into the water, then rode on.

"And so, his work well done," Nichols later wrote, "Hays City now a peaceful, law-abiding township, Hickok rode on to his next appointment with historic destiny: Abilene."

Out of the Frying Pan

✦━◉⊂━✦

Of Abilene it was written: "There is no law and no restraint in this seething caldron of vice and depravity."

A perfect place for me to be the city marshal. Fortunately—or unfortunately depending on one's point of view—I didn't know how bad the place was when I went there. If I had, I doubt if I would have gone. Where I would have traveled is anyone's guess. Back into the wilderness, perhaps. At least it would have been safer than in what we naively label civilization.

Now that it is all concluded, I can quote extensively without my hair turning white as it well might have done had I been aware of these quotations prior to my journey to Abilene.

"It is a place where men shoot off their mouths and guns both day and night."

"Money and whiskey flow like water downhill."

"Youth and beauty and womanhood and manhood are wrecked and d———ed in that valley of perdition."

"Plenty of rotten whiskey and everything to excite the passions are freely indulged in."

"Here you may see young girls not over sixteen drinking whiskey, smoking cigars, cursing and swearing, until one almost loses respect for the weaker sex."

Pure heaven on earth for a gentleman descended from the noble line of Hiccocks of Warwickshire, England.

Thank God I had no idea what was in store for me. Or, were I inclined to profaning: d———m God for keeping it a secret from me.

The darkest irony of said secret being that the year I was there was the concluding year of Abilene's supremacy as a cow town.

⊹≻━━≺⊹

Named after the biblical city, the Tetrards of Abilene, the city was, a mere four years before my arrival, no more than a frontier village. If only, for my sake, it had remained one—although, of course, in that event, they would not have needed a city marshal in the first place.

Then Joseph McCoy, searching for a location that would serve as a shipping point for cattle, found Abilene, which, as he described it, was "a very small, dead place consisting of about one dozen log huts." It was, however, situated in the middle of grassland and water. Therefore, it was but a matter of time before he had seen to the construction of a barn, a livery stable, an office, a hotel, a bank and, most important, a thousand-head-capacity shipping yard. Negotiations with the Union Pacific Railway Company followed.

Within a year, the log hut settlement had become a city to which cattle herds were driven in constantly increasing numbers.

By the time I arrived, hundreds of drovers (some called them cowboys or cowpokes or cowprodders or cowpunchers, etcetera) were nursing tens of thousands of cattle to Abilene in preparation for their long train ride to Chicago stockyards. These drovers, after spending months on the trail, wished only to "let her rip."

⊹≻━━≺⊹

Riding into Abilene in April 1871, I took a look around what was to be my new domain. I was not, in any way, expecting the peaceful time I had in Hays.

Running east and west and parallel to the railroad tracks was

Texas Street. Its main intersecting thoroughfare was Cedar Street, off that street the smaller one named A Street, at the end of which was Drovers Cottage (no cottage but a three-story hotel) and the Shane and Henry Real Estate office.

North of the railroad were the dance halls and the brothels. These, too, would be of concern to me since drovers were, as always, a natural prey for gamblers, pimps, and prostitutes as well as rotgut whiskey and, on occasion, lead poisoning.

+===+

In Mayor McCoy's office, the worthy gentleman pinned the city marshal's badge on my vest and declared, "With the authority vested in me as mayor of Abilene, I now appoint you city marshal."

I shook hands with him and with my deputy, Mike Williams.

"Congratulations, Mr. Hickok!" the mayor said, "or should I say Marshal Hickok!" He laughed. "We're delighted that you changed your mind!"

He leaned in close to confide in me: "As for myself," he told me, "I feel that I can finally draw an easy breath now that you are in charge. Hays City's misfortune in losing you is Abilene's good luck."

"Thank you, mayor," I responded in my accredited florid wont. "I shall certainly do everything in my power to earn your praise."

"I'm sure you will, marshal," the mayor replied elatedly.

"Congratulations, marshal!" Williams said.

"Thank you," I responded. "And now, if I could see my office."

"Yes, sir, marshal!" Williams cried; he had a minimum of teeth, I noticed. "Right away!"

Leaving the mayor's office, we walked down Texas Street to the jailhouse, a fortlike structure built of stone.

"First building in the whole d———n town made entirely of stone!" Williams informed me; I noticed as well, that he invariably shouted rather than spoke. I suspect that he was on his way to deafness, though he never mentioned such a failing.

"Why stone?" I asked him as we went inside.

"Used to have a wooden one!" he answered. "Drovers used to pull it down with ropes!"

He chortled merrily. "Those Texans, they're like wild gorillas when they come in off the trail!"

I glanced around the interior with its beat-up, rolltop desk, an oil lamp on its top along with some obviously never-used law volumes. A chair sat in front of the desk, a spittoon on the floor, an old rifle and a plethora of wanted posters hanging on the walls. Versailles it was not.

"Yes, sir!" Williams continued, "them Texans are a bunch of maddened creatures, they are! In April, the city population is five hundred! By June, it's up to seven thousand with the drovers! Sleep everywhere, they do! In houses, hotels, tents, or in blankets on the ground! D———n, they're loco! Yelling like Comanches! They'll do anything! *Anything!* So tough they'd fight a rattlesnake and give it two bites to start! Just wait! You'll see!"

"How interesting," I told him, the old stomach walls contracting once again.

"Old Tom Smith kept them all in line, though!" Williams said.

"My predecessor?" I observed.

"Your *what?*" asked Williams.

"The man who was marshal before me," I said.

"*Yes,* sir! *Yes,* sir!" Williams said. "That was him! Old Tom Smith! Never even used his pistols either! Did it with his *bare hands,* with his *fists!*"

Smart man, I thought.

"Sure glad they got *you* to replace him, Mr. Hickok, *Marshal* Hickok! Ain't no one else I know of who could handle Abilene! No, sir! This place is like a crazy house come shipping season!" He cackled wildly. "It'll take a man like you to fill old Tom Smith's shoes and that's a fact!"

"What made him leave?" I asked.

"Didn't leave! Never left!" said Williams. "Got hisself all chopped up by an ax, he did!" He grunted grimly at the memory. "Almost took the head right off his shoulders!"

I stared at him in silence. *Thanks for telling me,* I thought.

Several minutes later, I was walking numbly down the plank walk, staring straight ahead. I didn't see the woman's face as I was passing her.

"Bill!" she cried.

My twitch was so violent as I jerked around with a gasp, clutching for one of my pistols, that the woman flinched and backed off sharply, gaping at me; at which point I recognized her.

"*Susannah,*" I said.

"Bill Hickok. Of all people." She was smiling now. "What are you doing in Abilene?"

I shuddered.

"I'm the city marshal," I told her.

"Well, isn't that exciting!" she said. She stroked my arm. "I've missed you since Springfield," she murmured. "I hope I see you again."

I swallowed, my throat as dry as desert dust.

"I'm sure you will," I lied.

⊶═⊷

I sat in my hotel room, writing a letter to Agnes.

"Well, I have arrived in Abilene and everything looks fine."

I'd like to tell her the truth, I thought, but, of course, that was impossible.

"Although my task as city marshal promises to be a stiff one, I foresee no problems." All I *did* foresee were problems.

"I have handled worser situations in my day and I expect—"

I stopped writing. *Worser situations?* I thought. *What brought that on?* Was I trying to coarsen my image to her as well? If so, it was a stupid effort.

I stood up from the table and walked to the window. My room was on the third floor of the Cottage and from its vantage point, I could see across Abilene, out to the plains. I gazed toward the south, visualizing the cloud of dust that would give evidence of the first cattle drive approaching from Texas. The vision chilled me. In my mind, I heard Mike Williams chirruping, *"Just wait! You'll see!"*

I shivered convulsively. *"This place is like a crazy house come shipping season!"* I heard, in memory, Mike Williams's crazed remark. *"A crazy house!"* My stomach made a noise. It was preparing for the onslaught.

━┝━━┥━

It is truly indescribable, the Entry of the Drovers. (I think of it as some insanely operatic scene.)

First, as noted, comes the cloud of dust. Then the drum and rumble of hoofbeats, which come closer and closer.

Then, at last, the horde of wild-eyed drovers gallop into town, screaming and whooping, hurling their hats, and shooting their pistols into the air, as they charge down Texas Street, rein up death defyingly, leap down, and charge into saloons, dance halls, and brothels, intent on abandon of every sort and vice of all varieties.

This was now my world.

It was my first night on the job. All establishments devoted to depravity were filled to capacity and beyond. The air was alive with shouts and laughter, singing and tinkling pianos, shots and sounds of breaking glass.

I was sitting in the jailhouse with all lights extinguished. Coat off, unarmed, drinking steadily, shaking so much that the bottle neck rattled on the lip of my glass as I poured, whiskey spilling on the desk. I felt a face tic jumping on my right cheek at particularly alarming noises on the street.

I tensed as someone came running along the walk and tried to open the door, which I had locked some hours earlier.

"Marshal!" I heard Mike Williams call.

I flinched as he knocked on the door. "Marshal Hickok?" he

asked. "You in there?" He was silent, then said, "J——s C——t, where *is* he?"

I started as he shouted to someone, "Hey, Sam, you seen the marshal?"

"Ain't he in his office?" Sam shouted back.

"No, he ain't!" cried Mike.

"What about the Cottage?"

"Ain't there, either!" Mike responded. "Nor any other place I looked! God d——n it! He's supposed to do the night patrols, not me! Oh . . . *hell!*"

I heard his running footsteps move away. *Thank God he doesn't have a duplicate key for the door,* was all I could think.

I poured myself another drink and downed it in a swallow, coughing at the fiery flare in my throat.

Then I froze as two men started talking just outside the door. *Oh, God,* I wondered, *had they heard me cough?*

"Hey, Bob, you seen the marshal?" one of them asked; it sounded like Sam.

"No. Why?" Bob asked. "What's up?"

"He's supposed to be patrolling," Sam responded. "Just talking now with Mike Williams. Says he can't find Hickok anywhere."

"That's odd," said Bob. "Don't sound like Hickok. 'Less he's with a girl or something."

"Or he's *scared,*" replied Sam.

"Hickok *scared?*" said Bob. "You crazy? Man, he's not afraid of *anything!* You know that, Sam!"

"Well . . ." Sam faltered. "Where is he then?"

Nothing more was said and their footsteps moved away. Standing, I began to pace, then after a while, caught sight of myself in a wall mirror and, stopping, gazed at my shadowy reflection. I felt something rising in me, something dark and filled with corrosive bile.

"A gentleman does not show panic when in danger," I muttered to myself, my tone a caustic one.

My breath shook suddenly and I began to punch the wall at every repetition of the word *gentleman.*

"A *gentleman* does not show panic when in danger. A *gentleman* does not show panic when in danger." My voice was now savage. "A *gentleman* does not—!"

I broke off with a sob of pain and clutched at my right hand, trembling strengthlessly, staring at my dark reflection in the mirror.

"*Coward,*" I snarled.

The word impacted on me violently, acting as a purgative, and, whirling, I staggered to the trash basket where I lost the contents of my stomach in gagging spasms, doubled over like a man just gut shot.

At last, I straightened up and lit the oil lamp. Moving to the table by the wall, I poured some water into the pan and washed off my face, rinsing out my mouth.

I dried myself, then walked to the wall rack, took down my coat and donned it, putting on my hat then, watching myself in the mirror as I adjusted my tie, my features ashen, like the face of an unfamiliar statue.

I moved to the desk and picked up my brace of Colts, thrusting them beneath my sash. I poured myself an inch of whiskey, took a swallow of it, then put down the glass and turned for the door.

Unlocking it, I came out and shut the door again, relocking it. I turned my gaze toward Texas Street, that suburb of Dante's Inferno.

Drawing in a long and cheek-expanding breath of air, I started to walk along the plank walk, only semiconscious of where or who I was, knowing only one thing: that I had to make that walk or die.

Reaching the first saloon, I moved aside and stopped, gazing with apparent apathy at the festivities before me. The din decreased and I became aware of murmuring voices, of reactions. "It's *Hickok!*" "It's *Wild Bill!*" "It's the *marshal!*"

The saloon did not grow deathly still, but the contrast between its babel as I'd entered and its present sound was extreme; so much so that I thought I heard my stomach gurgling. Turning, I left.

Outside, I continued down the walk, moving with a passing semblance of calm, and went into the next saloon, stopping, once more, just inside the entrance, evincing the same reaction, the ratio of noise to silence altering noticeably. Once again, the voices, murmuring, "It's Marshal Hickok!" "Wild Bill!" "It's *Hickok*!" Once again I stood in silence, moving an arctic gaze across the room, focusing on no one. Then I left.

My first patrol was—albeit only partially aware—an unqualified success.

My reputation had preceded me well. That plus my stiffly ominous appearance, caused to a large extent by petrifyingly suppressed terror, brought me deference wherever I went.

As my patrol progressed, I walked more and more erectly and with mounting poise, my stride that of a king en route to his coronation, its pace no doubt in rhythm with some regal pomp.

Later, I returned to my room at the Cottage, locked the door and, in silence, removed my hat, coat, pistols, sash, and vest, my face still set in the imperious expression I effected on my patrol.

I unbuttoned my shirt and removed it. Face unchanging, I began to wring it out; it was so soaked with sweat, it might have just been washed. I listened to the dripping perspiration on the floor, trying to avoid considering what I would have done had anyone challenged me.

"Thus," wrote Nichols consequently, "did Hickok—quickly and irrevocably—establish his omnipotence in Abilene."

+➤━◆

"Never did a man confronted by such overwhelming odds behave with such composure and authority."

I kept two bottles of whiskey in my desk in case one of them ran

out unexpectedly. Before going out on patrol, I drank enough to os-
sify my nerves. What the townspeople took for granite sovereignty
was, in fact, paralysis by liquor.

"Each night, he patrolled on Texas Street, his dominion absolute."

Stiff-faced with inebriation, I strode the walks, unchallenged.
(Well, almost.) I suppose it was my pistols and my assumed willingness to utilize them should the need arise that kept Abilene
more or less under control that summer, which was its greatest and
its last season as the cattle shipping center of the nation.

I had, some time before, come to the realization that my long,
drooping mustaches and shoulder-length hair looked absurdly
affected but, by then, I also realized that they were part of my imposing persona and I was stuck with them, not wanting to take any
risk of weakening that image in any way. Too bad. I would have enjoyed an extended visit to the nearest barber shop.

So, long-haired and fully mustached, fortified with stomach
pills and whiskey, I walked abroad on Abilene's h———lish streets,
maintaining as menacing a posture as I could with my stomach
rumbling like Vesuvius.

I said *almost* unchallenged for, on a number of occasions,
attempts were made to bushwhack me. Fortunately, the aim of your
average drover leaves a lot to be desired, and the pistol balls aimed
at putting a window in my skull usually whistled by my head or
slammed into a nearby wall, causing me to take a startled header
and hide behind whatever might be handy, whether it was a hay
bale, a water barrel, or horse trough.

"Never did a man endure such daily peril with such utter equanimity."

I shaved in my room, not trusting a barber shop with its chair
backs to the entrance, nor my reaction time, should I note an attack
reflected in the mirror. Even in my room, I angled my mirror to re-
flect the locked door, my pistols close at hand, my hand at times so
palsied that I nicked my skin more than once.

"Never flustered, never disconcerted, Hickok faced his day-by-day duties with that calm sobriety of purpose for which he is so justly famous."

I had begun to supplement my artillery with a pair of Remington derringers, which I kept in my vest pockets, one on each side, concealed beneath my frock coat. The two Colts I maintained as always underneath my sash and, as always, I maintained in my system two glasses of whiskey before essaying out each evening.

"Night after night did this man of steel discharge his obligations with unswerving zeal."

My face congealed by alcoholism, I paced the plank walks of Texas Street, no longer entering alleys, having come close to being shot in those dark passages.

Even when I stayed on the *main drag*, as the drovers called it, a badly aimed shot might shatter a nearby window, causing me to fling myself plankward, panicked eyes searching for the source of the shot and never finding it.

"Week after week did Hickok display his courage and unyielding stamina."

By August, when I shaved, my cheeks and throat were festooned with fragments of blood-soaked paper. More often than not, I would sling aside my razor in a fury of frustration, yearning to lean back in a barber chair and have a barber's steady hand slice off my whiskers, not—as I was doing—shards of my epidermis.

I was, by then, so far into foreboding that I wore my sash on my long johns, one of my Colts beneath it for immediate use, if needed.

I had, in addition, purchased a shotgun and hacksaw, cutting the double barrel short. This I carried slung across my left shoulder, still packing the pair of derringers in my vest pockets and my two Colt revolvers under my sash.

I could feel my body sag with each new arsenal addition. One afternoon, draining an oversize glass of whiskey, I tilted back so far that I lost balance and crashed to the floor, spilling whiskey on myself.

"Texas Street became the unchallenged kingdom of this Prince of Pistoleers, the all-encompassing domain of this gun master of the border, whose name shall always be emblazoned in the annals of the West: Wild Bill Hickok!"

Thus I trod the boards of my domain, if the overweighted, drunken hobble I managed to achieve can be considered walking. I skulked from shadow to shadow, moving hastily past doors, windows, and alley entrances.

It was an evening in early September that, stepping off the walk to cross the street, I lost my balance and tumbled to the ground. Pushing to my feet, infuriated and, of course, embarrassed, I muttered to myself as follows:

"To h——l with this patrolling s——t! Let toothless do it! From now on, I stay inside!"

I groaned and whispered fiercely, "J——s C——t and twelve disciples, I must weigh a *ton* with all this s——t on!"

I hobbled on, stumbled on a street rut, almost fell again. "J——s C——t!" I snarled, not even caring anymore who saw or heard me.

Nichols, you're an idiot!

The End of the World

⟡

From that day forth, the location of my office changed to the Alamo Saloon, which was more in keeping with my taste and disposition; they even had an orchestra, by God, playing forenoons, afternoons, and evenings. Just the place for yours truly, J. B. Hickok of the Warwickshire Hiccocks.

There I spent the bulk of my time playing poker, my back to the wall (a habit I had taken up out of self-preservation), a bottle of whiskey and a pistol at close hand on the table.

I even had the time to read an interesting book about one of my favorite subjects: cards.

I learned that, from a fifty-two card deck, it is possible to deal 2,598,960 different five-card hands. Of those hands, 1,088,240 will contain a pair, 123,000 will contain two pairs, 54,912 will contain three of a kind, 10,200 will contain straights, 5,108 will contain flushes, 3,744 will contain full houses, 624 will contain four of a kind, 36 will contain straight flushes, and (no wonder I've never drawn one) 4 will contain royal flushes.

I was interested to learn that playing cards were derived from the tarot fortune-telling deck, cups, wands, coins, and swords becoming hearts, clubs, diamonds, and spades, kings and queens remaining, but knights becoming jacks.

During the French Revolution, kings, queens, and jacks were

removed from the card deck (too Royalist) and replaced by nature, liberty, and virtue; hearts, clubs, spades, and diamonds becoming peace, war, art, and commerce. I suspect it made betting somewhat complicated.

I also suspect that I am taking up space to avoid continuing with my story—and the worst experience of my life.

┼══┤

"The first major challenge to the iron Rule of Abilene's marshal occurred one day in the fall of 1871. Hickok was, as customary, working in his office when it began."

I pushed several chips across the table. "See you twenty and raise you ten," I said, deeply involved in marshaling duties.

I glanced toward one of the doorways as Mike Williams came in. The deputy's attitude toward me had changed somewhat since I had converted my patrols to poker games; not exactly disrespectful, but not as impressed anymore. I had decided I could live with that, the key word being *live.*

He came up to the table. "Marshal?" he said.

"I'm here," I answered, peering closely at my cards; I was seeing them a tad more blurrily those days.

"Could I talk to you?" he asked.

"I'm right here; talk," I told him curtly.

"In private?" he asked.

I started to flare, then held it back. Standing, I picked up my Colt and slid it underneath my sash as we moved into an empty corner.

"Well?" I asked.

"Town council has laid down the law. Faro tables in the Bull's Head Tavern can't stay in the back room anymore; too many complaints about cheating."

I stared at him, considering whether to object to the order. Then, seeing that I couldn't, I scowled and turned toward the street.

As we walked along the plank walk, Williams said, "Mayor also said the 'no guns while in town' rule isn't being strictly enforced."

I shook my head, affecting irritation. "That's ridiculous," I said. "Any man who wears a gun might have to face me in a showdown. In light of that, how many men are wearing guns in town?"

"A lot," said Mike.

He winced as I glared at him.

"It's what the mayor says, not me," he told me.

"Well . . ." I grumped, "the mayor's wrong."

Mike sighed. "If you say so," he responded. I tried to ignore the obvious disappointment in his voice and manner.

We turned in at the Bull's Head Tavern. One of the owners, Ben Thompson, gave me pause; I'd heard about him, nothing good.

But we were there, and I couldn't very well back down. *Time to play the role again,* the thought occurred; *the Prince of Pistoleers in action once more.*

The other owner of the Bull's Head, Phil Coe, was taller than me, better-looking than me, stronger-looking than me; I hadn't counted on any of this. When I informed him of the mayor's wish, he only glared at me.

I didn't really want to, but I turned to his partner, Ben Thompson, a square-jawed, burly, black-haired, blue-eyed, inky walrus-mustached Englishman.

"I beg your pardon?" he inquired coldly.

I was, of course, aware of their hostility but, at the same time, I was now possessed of the numbing self-delusion that, whatever the situation, no one would stand up, face-to-face, with Wild Bill Hickok, since no one ever had since I arrived in Abilene. At that moment, I'm afraid the legend was propelling the man.

"The faro tables have to come out from the back room," I repeated, knowing that he'd heard me perfectly well.

"Do they, now?" he said in the iciest voice I'd ever heard.

"They do," I said, starting for the back room.

I knew the sound behind me and froze; it was that of a pistol pulled from its holster. Clearly, I could not defend myself and could only hope that whoever had drawn the pistol wasn't the sort to shoot a man in the back.

Very slowly, I turned back. It was Thompson, his revolver pointed at my chest.

"What are you doing?" I asked as though I didn't know.

"What does it look like I'm doing?" Thompson answered with a question.

The oddest thing about the moment was that I really couldn't believe he was opposing me.

"Put the gun away," I said, fully expecting compliance.

I twitched as Thompson stepped forward and jabbed the end of his pistol barrel into my stomach.

"You don't seem to catch my meaning, *marshal*," he said and—oddly again—I was very much aware of the refinement of his English accent. The thought flitted across my mind of telling him that my family line went back to Warwickshire.

"The faro tables stay in back," he informed me.

He jabbed the barrel end into my stomach even harder.

"What's more," he said, "if I see you on the streets at any time from this day forth, I shall take the extreme pleasure of blowing out your guts."

Another jab; it hurt. "You *understand?*" he demanded.

I was riven to the spot, my expression—I'm sure—as indecipherable as my thoughts. For a while, I couldn't seem to determine whether to stand or retreat.

Then the soft but audible gurgle of impending nausea in me revealed to them—and worse, much worse, to me—that the self-delusion had been shattered.

I saw Coe smiling with contempt. I noted my deputy staring at me unbelievingly, the remainder of his respect fading fast. I stood immobile for several moments longer, returning Thompson's ominous gaze.

Then I said, in a hoarse and unconvincing murmur, "This isn't over," and, trying to summon (and failing) a look of dignified aplomb, I turned and headed for the front door.

The sound of Coe beginning to chuckle came close to making me whirl and draw, the agony it gave me so severe as to wipe away all sense of fear. The moment ended quickly, evidenced by little more than a tensing of my body as I continued across the room. I did not fully realize it at that moment, but my world had just collapsed.

Tarantula Juice Interval

◄─►═◄◐►═◄─►

In the event the reader of this chronicle (if, in fact, there are any) fails to comprehend the title of this section, let me pass along the following piece of information.

Booze has a multiplicity of names.

It seems to be a characteristic of man that, where it comes to his most profound weaknesses, he cannot help but create endless words for same. Why this is so, I cannot say. Perhaps men's fascinations need many means of depiction because men speak of them so often that they must have varied ways of accomplishing it lest boredom set in. Perhaps they are compelled to derive an infinite number of ways to describe them because they are obsessed with them. Or perhaps, fearing their compulsions, they devise endless ways of portraying them in order to dilute inner fear with outer words.

Whatever the reason, man certainly does have multiple descriptions for killing, sex, and liquor. Being a gentleman, I will not essay to enumerate the many sobriquets for sexual parts and congress; the reader can supply these from immediate memory.

Killing people (men primarily) has, of course, its ready lexicon of terms such as: bed him down, curl him up, down him, kick him into a funeral procession, make wolf meat of him, serve him up brown, wipe him out, put him in the wooden overcoat, and such.

For liquor: brave maker, bug juice, coffin varnish, dynamite, gut warmer, leopard sweat, pop skull, prairie dew, snake poison, sudden death, tonsil paint, and, as already noted, tarantula juice.

I had no use whatever for all the words comprising death descriptions. I confined myself to the two remaining areas of man's ruling passions. In brief, in the following weeks, I drank without cease and remained in bed the better part of each day and night in the company of any soiled dove I could purchase or lure to my room.

+⟩━⟨+

The shade was drawn, the room in shadows. I had come to eschew the sunlight in any way I could.

I was abed with Susannah Moore, who I had not seen in my early days in Abilene, wishing to remain as faithful as I could to Agnes.

Now she was back in my life, one of many I craved to provide physical and mental surcease from unending depression.

I must have looked a tragic sight: red-eyed, unshaven, unbathed, uncombed, and generally disreputable in appearance. Even Susannah, not exactly a paragon of judgment, seemed to recognize my wanting state.

"Bill, you can't stay up here *all* the time," she told me, "Everybody's talking, saying you're afraid of Thompson. Phil Coe's telling everybody you're a coward."

"Shut up," was all I said; slurred and barely understandable.

"You're not afraid of Thompson, are you?" asked Susannah. "Are you? After all the men you've killed?"

"Shut *up*," I repeated.

"You've killed hundreds of men," she told me. "How can one man—"

I stopped her lips with mine, kissing her with brutal force. She struggled in my grip and finally managed to wrest herself free. "You're hurting me!" she complained.

I grabbed her again; she twisted loose.

"You're *hurting* me, God d⸺n it!" she cried.

I shoved her away as hard as I could. "Then leave!" I ordered as she went flying off the mattress, landing on the floor with a loud thump.

She bounded to her feet, infuriated.

"D⸺n it, who the h⸺l do you think you are?" she raged.

"Get out!" I yelled.

"You no-good b⸺d!" she cried. "You *are* afraid of Thompson!"

I started to lurch up after her, making her retreat so quickly that she slipped and fell again, banging her left elbow on the floor.

She began to cry and gather up her clothes. "You dirty skunk," she ranted. "You lousy, no-good son of a b⸺h."

I sat up on the edge of the bed, my upper body weaving, my lower body aching from residual pain in my hip. Reaching out to the table, I picked up the bottle of whiskey and poured myself a glassful.

"Drinking whiskey won't change anything," Susannah said. "You're still a yellow b⸺d."

My voice was soft and trembling as I told her to get out.

"I'll get out," she said, "and *stay* out. B⸺d! You'll be sorry! You can't rough me up and get away with it!"

She sobbed in fury. "That's how God d⸺n brave *you* are!" she said. "Have to beat up *women!*"

"You're no woman," I muttered.

"What?" she snapped. "I can't hear you! Can't you even talk now?"

"You're no woman, you're a whore!" I said.

"And you're a coward!" she responded almost apopletically. "A lousy, stinking *coward!*"

I hurled the bottle at her, missing her by inches, the bottle exploding into fragments on the wall. Susannah's fury vanished and, with a look of dread, she sidled toward the door, her gaze fixed on my face.

"You're crazy," she said, shakily. "You've gone crazy."

I watched her, dull-eyed, as she started to unlock the door.

"Sorry," I murmured. "Not a thing a gentleman should do."

"A *gentleman*," she said contemptuously.

She opened the door and a pair of startled gasps made me tense and squint to see what was there, my sight somewhat blurred by whiskey and the other problem I had not addressed yet.

When I saw who was standing there, I felt the inside of my stomach drop as though I'd just then swallowed an anvil.

It was Agnes, her expression a mirror image of mine: total shock and disbelief.

Susannah stared at her, openmouthed. I stared at Agnes, openmouthed. Agnes was the only one who gave the tableau movement by turning her head from side to side, looking at Susannah, then at me; at Susannah, at me.

I pushed to my feet and Agnes wrenched herself away from the doorway, a sound of revulsion in her throat.

"Don't go!" I cried.

Lurching to the doorway, I started out exactly at the moment Susannah tried to leave. Like some team of amateur clowns, we were wedged together between the two sides of the doorway. "Look out!" I gasped. "Look out yourself!" she gasped back.

I shouldered her so fiercely that she reeled across the room, collided with the bed, and toppled to the floor with a cry of pain and outrage. By then, I was gone, pursuing Agnes, staggering from side to side, calling out her name in drunken desperation. My gait a wildly reeling one, I neared the staircase down which Agnes was beginning to retreat.

"Agnes, wait!" I begged.

I started down the staircase after her, so stunned by dismay that

I didn't even turn back as I saw a couple turning on the second floor landing to ascend.

Seeing me, the woman made a sound not dissimilar to the squeak of a mouse, her eyes rolled back discreetly from the dreadful sight, and she slumped, unconscious in her companion's grasp. I lunged by them, uncaring for their plight, and raced around the landing, calling Agnes's name again.

As I reached the head of the next flight, my hip gave way, causing my left leg to crumple and, with a startled cry, I began to fall.

I saw Agnes stop abruptly to look back at me as I tumbled down the stairs at high speed. She had to press herself against the stairwell wall so I wouldn't carry her along on my juggernaut descent.

I couldn't stop myself, the inertia of my flailing fall continuing until the external force of a wall concluded it, my head and body slamming hard against it. "Bill!" I heard Agnes cry out, horrified.

I heard her rapid footsteps coming down the stairs and looked up at her groggily as she kneeled beside me, her expression one of apprehension.

"Means nothing to me, Agnes," I remember murmuring. Her face began to fade away in darkness then. "Agnes?" I said frightenedly.

Then I fell unconscious.

⊬═─═⊣

My eyes fluttered open and, to my surprise, I saw that I was back in my room. *Had I dreamed it all?* I thought, staring at the ceiling.

Then I sat up, gasping at the pain in my head, clutching, at once, at my skull.

"Bill!" I heard her say.

Turning, gasping further at the pain it caused, I saw Agnes hurrying across the room.

She sat on the bed beside me.

"Agnes," I murmured. I had never been so happy to see another human being in my life.

Ignoring the pain, I clung to her as she stroked my hair. "Shh, it's all right, Bill," she comforted. "It's all right."

"Agnes. Agnes," I whispered, knowing I was close to tears.

She held me for some time, until my bodily and brain pain eased somewhat. Then she drew back from me, smiling; was it teasingly?

It was. "You were a naughty boy," she said.

"She's nothing to me, Agnes, nothing." That was true enough. "Things have been bad here; I was only—"

She stopped my apology by laying a gentle finger across my lips. "You don't have to explain," she told me.

I took hold of her hand and kissed the back of it repeatedly before pressing it to my cheek.

"It's the only time since we were separated, Agnes," I said. "The only time; I swear." I felt I had to stretch the blanket there lest I lose her.

She stood and smiled at me.

"You don't have to explain, Bill," she said, starting to disrobe. "I understand. I understand my Wild Bill."

I watched her, comforted by her presence and desire for intimacy with me, but distracted by the uncomfortable realization that she didn't really understand at all.

"I'm not sure I can—" I began, awkwardly.

"I don't expect it, Bill," she said with a soft laugh. "I just want to lie next to you."

"Please," I said, overwhelmed by gratitude for her acceptance of me, however ill-informed.

She got into bed with me and we embraced. To my astonishment, my manhood made an instant assertion of itself, springing to life. "Bill," she said, "don't hurt your head now."

"I won't," I said, not caring if I did.

Ten minutes later, I was sleeping soundly in her arms, at peace for the first time since I'd retreated from the Bull's Head Tavern.

+>===<+

I sat on a chair, face lathered, Agnes shaving me. I could not have trusted my own hand with the razor.

"I'm surprised at you," she chided. "Letting your appearance go like this. That's not the Wild Bill Hickok I know."

"Well . . . Agnes," I hesitated. "It's been very demanding here. Hays was like a holiday compared to Abilene. The strains, the tensions. You wouldn't believe what goes on here."

"I'm sure it's terrible, Bill," she said. She scraped off whiskers. *"Lord,"* she said, "if *you* have trouble, it *must* be terrible."

"It is," I said, "it *is*. I have to be alert to danger night and day."

"Don't nod, dear," Agnes cautioned me.

"Oh, sorry," I replied.

I closed my eyes with a contented sigh as she continued shaving me. It was quiet for a short while. Then she spoke again.

"Well, at least you won't be alone anymore," she said.

My eyes popped open. What was this?

"I'm going to stay with you," she explained. "The circus can get by without me for a while."

"No," I said, impulsively.

She looked at me, surprised. *"No?"* she asked.

I stared at her in hapless silence, then cleared my throat and braced myself.

"Absolutely not," I told her, trying to sound stern.

"But *why*, Bill?" she asked.

I gazed at her gravely, trying hard to think of a convincing answer.

"Because it's dangerous here," I finally said.

"But that's exactly why I want to stay," she told me. "So I—"

"No," I interrupted. She could not stay, that was certain; I could not allow it. "It isn't safe, Agnes."

She was still for disconcerting moments.

"It isn't," I insisted.

"Bill, are you trying to get rid of me?" she asked.

"Yes," I said. I saw her look. "I mean *no*." I amended. "I mean *yes*!" I said, exasperated. "From Abilene! Not from my life."

She gazed at me in silence, obviously wanting to believe my words but having difficulty doing so. Making matters worse, it was the first moment since we'd met that I grew conscious of the fact that she was a number of years older than me.

I stood up. "Agnes," I said. I took her in my arms and pressed a lathery cheek to hers.

"Don't you understand?" I explained, "Abilene's a powder keg. I have so many things to settle. They're bad enough by themselves. If I had to worry about you, I just couldn't handle them."

Still, she was suspicious.

"I won't be here much longer, Agnes," I went on. "I've had the offer of a better job. In Newton. You can meet me there and stay with me. It won't be long. A few weeks maybe." *How will I get out of this?* I wondered.

"I just don't like it here in Abilene," I lied on. "Oh, I can handle it all right, but why should I go on living like this?" I drew back to smile at her, then had to chuckle as I saw the foamy lather on her face.

Removing the towel from around my neck, I wiped off her cheek. Still that uncertain look remained on her face.

"Agnes," I said.

I kissed her as passionately as I could. She remained unpliant for a few more moments, then abruptly, clung to me with desperation equal to my own. My heart leaped, overjoyed.

"You *do* love me, Bill, don't you?" she asked.

I gazed into her eyes.

"I love you with all my heart and soul," I told her, and I did—and do.

"Oh, Bill," she said.

We kissed tempestuously; and there were tears of happiness in both our eyes: hers I saw and mine I felt.

Dust and Double Death

I opened the front door of the hotel a crack and peered outside.

Seeing no one there, I opened the door for Agnes.

"Are things *that* bad, Bill?" she asked me, sotto voce. "You can't even walk out a door without checking first?"

"You have no idea," I replied, quite truthfully.

We started along the plank walk, my eyes darting in all directions for any possible sign of Thompson.

"Oh, Bill," Agnes said, "you should–"

She broke off as I pulled her underneath the shadow of an overhanging roof. "Stay out of the light," I told her.

"Oh, my," she said.

I repressed my sense of guilt toward her as we continued on.

"You *should* leave, Bill," she said. "It makes no sense to live like this. A little danger, yes; that's your profession. But *this*? You should take that job in Newton as soon as ever you can."

"Yes," I mumbled, distracted, still on the lookout for Thompson.

"Bill, Bill," she murmured, clinging to my arm. She looked at my leg. "That limp is bad," she said.

"Yes," I said, "my old arrow wound. That's what made my leg give way yesterday."

"Oh, my poor Bill," she said. "I had no notion it was so distressing here. I just wish I could stay with you."

"I know, I know," she added hurriedly as I gave her a look. "I just hate to see you have to be like this. It isn't fair."

I managed a twisted smile.

"It goes with the job, love," I replied.

A few minutes later, we were at the stage station. Agnes pressed her cheek to mine as I edged her toward the coach, my eyes shifting constantly, nervously.

"I'm going to miss you, darling," Agnes said.

"I'm going to miss you, too," I told her. "It won't be long, though. I'll write as soon as I know my plans."

"We'll be in Kansas City for another month," she said.

"I won't forget," I promised. "Good-bye, love."

I pressed her into the coach and tried to draw back, losing balance and toppling forward as she pulled me to her for another kiss. I disengaged myself, eyes still darting. "Good-bye," I said with a straining smile. "Good-bye."

"Good-bye, Bill," she said. As she saw me back into the shade again, she added, worriedly, "Oh, *Bill*."

"Don't worry now," I reassured her. "Everything is going to be all right."

As the coach pulled off, Agnes leaning out the window, waving, I exhaled heavily, my shoulders slumping with relief. *Thank God she's gone*, I thought.

When the hand tapped me smartly on the shoulder, I whirled with an astonished cry, clutching for one of my pistols, which I drew so fast I lost hold of it so that it flew away and splashed into a nearby horse trough.

Mike Williams lurched back, almost falling. "Hold it!" he cried.

I staggered, then regained my balance, wincing at the pain in my hip, pressing a hand against it. "What the h———l are you doing?" I demanded.

Williams straightened up, a look of aggravation on his face.

"Just thought you'd like to know," he said, "Ben Thompson

sold his half of the Bull's Head Tavern. Left Abilene this afternoon."

Albeit bathed in cool deliverance, I drew myself erect and looked at Williams with disdain. "Why should that mean anything to me?" I said.

"Oh, C———t," said Williams, turning to walk away. Despite his obvious scorn, I felt a sense of unutterable peace. Drawing in a long, deep breath, I started toward the Alamo Saloon, then, remembering, turned back and, pulling a coat and shirtsleeve as far up as it would go, I felt around distastefully in the murky water of the trough.

+>==<+

After a quick drying and cleaning of the submerged Colt, I left my room and sauntered to the Alamo, ready for a celebratory drink.

Entering the saloon, I strode to the counter and ordered a drink.

It tasted like ambrosia.

"Haven't seen you in a spell, marshal," said the bartender, a goading tone in his voice.

I didn't let it bother me. "I have been indisposed," I informed him.

"That so?" he said.

"Indeed," I replied. "An old scouting wound in my hip."

"Uh-huh," he said.

I poured myself another drink.

"It happened near Fort Riley, several years ago," I recounted. "I was out one day when seven hostiles started to pursue me." I looked down at my right hip. "One of them managed to imbed an arrow in my hip," I said. "I lost considerable blood but—"

I looked up quickly as the bartender started edging off, an uneasy expression on his face.

"What's wrong?" I asked.

I had only a moment to jerk my head around and see Phil

Coe's twisted countenance in the mirror before I was flung around and his right fist hurtled into my jaw. I stumbled backward, skidded across a table, breaking up a six-hand game of poker, and landed on the floor, my hat flying off.

I sat up dizzily and shook my head, just in time to see Coe charging me again. Hauling me to my feet, he snarled, "Beat my girl up, will you?"

"What?" I asked.

He walloped me a second time and sent me flying backward, where I broke up a second poker game as I sprawled across the table, scattering chips, cards, drinks, cigars, and players in all directions.

I staggered up, attempting to remove my coat as Coe ran at me once again, face twisted with rage. He drove his left fist deep into my belly, his right into my battered jaw. I staggered back and fell again, then struggled up, tearing off my coat so quickly that it hit Coe in the face. Lurching forward, I aimed a haymaker at his face, but at that instant, Coe slipped on some puddled whiskey, dropping clumsily to one knee. My violent punch, finding no target, spun me around in a circle. Coe lunged at me and we fell to the floor together, wrestling, grabbing, and kicking like a pair of berserk animals.

"Hickok's feud with gambler Phil Coe started quietly enough," Nichols later wrote, "a minor disagreement over the favors of a certain young lady who—to protect her reputation—remained nameless during their subdued conversation."

"You'll never touch Susannah Moore again!" Coe screamed.

"Susannah Moore?" I yelled. "Susannah Moore means nothing to me!"

"The trifling disagreement was to fester and become inflamed however, resulting in the legendary gun duel at the Alamo Saloon."

Coe had me pinned down to the floor now, panting in my face.

"I'm going outside now," he told me. "Right outside that door. I'm going to wait for you; and when you come out, come out shooting. Understand?"

He banged my head on the floor for emphasis. "You *understand?*" he repeated loudly.

Letting go, he pushed to his feet and started to adjust his clothes, looking down at me.

"If you don't come out in the next five minutes, I'll come in and kill you." He kicked my leg. *"Understand?"*

He turned and stalked away, and the saloon was deathly still, every patron looking either at him or at me.

The batwing doors squeaked loudly as Coe went outside, and every gaze shifted instantly to me. I was, by then, standing slowly, trying to look unconcerned, but too dizzy and unnerved to manage the deception very well.

I moved on wavering legs to my coat, almost took a header as I leaned forward to pick it up, then straightened and donned the coat with as much aplomb as I could muster and looked around for my hat. One of the customers picked it up and brought it to me. I took it with a regal nod. "Thank you," I said, shocked at the revealing tremor in my voice.

I felt for my pistols. One of them was missing and I looked around for it. Another customer picked it up and carried it across the room to me. Him I only nodded at, pushing the pistol beneath my sash.

Turning to the counter, I poured myself a drink, attempting as best as I could to look unruffled despite the shaking of my hand, which caused whiskey to spill on the counter. I tried to raise the glass to my lips, but my hand was trembling so uncontrollably that I couldn't do it.

I felt myself beginning to crumble. I pressed my lips together hard to prevent their quivering. All the years of pretense had fallen away. Dread contorted my expression—as much for the fact that the dread was on display as fear for my life. I could not bear standing there, allowing them to witness my disintegration, yet neither could I make myself walk to the front door.

With a sense of haunted affliction, I turned and, limping badly—my hip was hurting again—I headed for the side door, feeling every eye in the saloon fixed on me.

I opened the side door and went outside. Shutting it, I leaned back, shivering, breath straining through my clenched teeth. Shakily, I reached beneath my coat and drew both pistols. Holding them extended, I began to limp toward the street. It is difficult for me to say these things, as you may well imagine, but I was in utter torment, every lie I'd lived by now revealed, my mind naked before my terrors and my self-contempt.

I stopped and peered around the building edge. Coe was standing just outside the entrance, waiting for me. I felt terror mounting to a peak and knew that I had to deal with it or break entirely.

Lunging from the alley, I shouted "Coe!" and fired both pistols simultaneously, sending two lead balls into his stomach, the impact of them flinging him backward, a look of shock on his face.

I now was frozen to the spot from which I'd fired, knowing that I'd just committed murder.

Then an even more horrible occurrence happened.

Hearing the sound of running footsteps behind me, I whirled in mindless terror and fired both guns at the figure rushing toward me.

"And having catapulted Phil Coe to his maker with one clean shot between the eyes, Hickok, hearing the approach of further enemies, whirled with one astonishingly graceful motion, drew both pistols once again, and delivered three more scoundrels to their just reward."

The figure rushing toward me was my deputy, Mike Williams.

My repeated shots not only killed him but, flying astray, wounded two townspeople who had the misfortune to be standing too close. An official paper was submitted to me shortly after the event.

"Be it resolved by Mayor & Council of City of Abilene," it read, "that J. B. Hickok be discharged from his official position as City Marshal for the reason that the City is no longer in need of his services."

Treading the Boards

⚬═⚬

In traditional drama, tragedy is not supplanted by farce. In real life, no such sensible condition prevails.

In need of income, I agreed to work for a man named Doc Carver, who had signed a contract to deliver one hundred live buffaloes to Kansas City for shipment to Niagara Falls, where they would appear in an exhibition.

This had never been attempted previously and, when I ventured out with the capturing party, the question uppermost in everyone's mind was: What would a buffalo do when roped? A pair of Sioux Indians with the party were dubious about the prospects.

The day we went after our first buffalo is one I am not likely to forget.

After searching for some time, I caught sight of an old bull and rode after it.

The first rope I threw had too large a loop which, unfortunately, slipped back across the buffalo's hump.

The remainder of this sorry incident is best described by an item in the Lincoln *Daily State Journal*.

"The rope on the buffalo's hump gave the animal all the advantage, and with a surge he turned Wild Bill's horse head over heels. The greatest pistol man the West has ever known described an ungraceful arc in the air and landed headfirst on the prairie.

"Getting to his feet, Bill spat grass and buffalo dung from his mouth and watched his horse, still fast to the buffalo, disappear toward the horizon.

"It did not help his feelings when one of the Oglala braves rode up and commiserated with him: 'You ketchem d———n tonka heap gone.'"

Thus occurred my first experience with show business.

My next one was quite different, albeit worse. A momentary mouthful of buffalo dung beats, hands down, the piles of horse manure I was buried under during the theatrical season of 1872–73.

I present same sketchily.

＋═══＋

I held the woman with my left arm whilst, with my right, I fired at some whooping offstage Indians.

"Fear not, fair maiden!" I cried. "By heaven, you are safe at last with Wild Bill, who is ever ready to risk his life and die, if need be, in defense of weak and helpless womanhood!"

The audience erupted with a chorus of cheers and whistles, pounding their hands together.

My career was launched.

＋═══＋

Alone in my hotel room, I lay on my bed, drinking whiskey and reading a book on English history to forget the nonsense of the play I was in.

＋═══＋

The settlers were trapped in the burning cabin, father, mother, and daughter. The father fired two shots through the window, then flung aside the rifle in despair.

"That's the last of our ammunition, Mandy!" he cried. "Them outlaws are going to get us now for sure!"

"*No!*" the daughter cried back, clinging to her mother, both females blubbering pitifully.

Now the father lunged to the window, shaking the canvas wall of the cabin.

"Wait!" he cried, "I see a figure in the distance!" (Pause.) "A man on horseback!" (Pause.) "I believe it's *Wild Bill!*"

Audience cheers, whistles, foot stamping, and applause.

A dreadful imitation of galloping hooves offstage, a flurry of fired blanks.

"See how gracefully he moves!" the father cried. (Pause.) "He's getting closer!" (Pause.) "Closer!" (Long pause.) "He's *here*! Wild Bill is here!"

Cheers. Applause. Whistles. Stomping feet. I charged into the doorway, a pistol in each hand. Drunk, I stumbled on the threshold and sprawled into the room.

The audience roared with laughter.

The beginning of the end.

They had me recount a story about a horse named Black Nell that I'd ridden in the war.

According to the tale, this remarkable equine, at a whistled signal, would follow me into a saloon and climb onto a billiard table, where it stood on all four legs, several patrons sitting on her back. After which, I would mount her and have her bound across the front porch and into the middle of the street in one leap, a distance of some thirty to forty feet. Remarkable creature. She should have been on the stage instead of me.

Finally, I had to stop the account because it was too ridiculous.

They tried to get me to tell how I'd killed a giant grizzly bear single-handed but that I refused to do from the outset.

The gypsy woman lived in a shack on the outskirts of town.

"Good evening," I said as she opened the door. "I'm—"

"Tell me nothing," she instructed me. "I will be given information by my sources."

"Yes; of course," I said.

She led me into a small room illuminated by a single burning candle and, at her gesture, I settled on a chair across from her.

She closed her eyes and made some mumbling noises, then began to chant beneath her breath; it sounded like the chanting of an Indian.

How long she did this I have no idea, but finally she opened her eyes and seemed to look at me, although she may have been looking at visions of which I was not aware.

Then she said, "You suffer."

I felt myself begin to tense at these words.

"You suffer because . . ." She drew in a rasping breath between her teeth. ". . . you *killed*."

I should not have come, I thought. *I don't want to hear this.*

She looked around and murmured, "What?" as though someone had just entered the room and spoken to get her attention.

I sat rigidly, staring at her. *I should not have come,* I thought again.

"Yes," she said. "I understand." As though the new party in the room had spoken to her once again. She nodded. "I understand, do not be upset."

She turned back to me.

"A man is with us," she told me. "His name is Mike. He asks, 'Why did you shoot me when I only meant to help?'"

It seemed as though all breath had just been sucked from me. I couldn't speak, couldn't move.

"You understand?" the gypsy woman asked.

I do not recall how I endured that meeting. Not that I remained with her that long; I left as soon as possible, thanked her, paid her, and departed.

Back in my hotel room, I drank myself unconscious, terrified to fall asleep in the usual way lest the dead come floating to me in a dream and kill me with fear.

+⟩═══⟨+

I stood in the stage saloon, leaning on the counter, declaiming slurringly to a group of men.

"McCanles jumped into the room, his gun . . . leveled to, uh, shoot," I said. "But he wasn't quick enough. My . . . pistol ball went through his heart."

"Can't hear you, Hickok!" someone shouted in the audience.

From the corners of my eyes, I saw the stage manager watching me, grinding his teeth in frustration at my intoxication and inability to remember lines.

"His death was . . . was—" I faltered, cleared my throat, went on. "His death was followed by a . . . *yell* from his gang." I knew my voice was fading, but I didn't care. "I . . . said to myself. Only, uh . . . six shots left and—" I sighed and finished glumly, "nine men to kill."

"Can't *hear* you, d——n it!" screamed an angry voice.

+⟩═══⟨+

Three hours later, snow fell steadily as I stumbled from the saloon and started to trudge along the sidewalk, trying to walk upright, but scarcely able to do so. I moved weavingly through the darkness and the snow, Wild Bill Hickok, Hero of the Plains.

+⟩═══⟨+

It ended on a rainy night in March in Philadelphia.

The set was that of a street, men standing and sitting on barrels and boxes, listening to me as I limped back and forth, in my usual inept fashion, trying to ignore the periodic boos and hisses and insulting taunts from the audience.

"I was . . . in a hotel," I fumbled, "in . . . Leavenworth City and I . . . saw these—loose—loose characters about as I ordered a room. I had . . . uh . . . had considerable money—"

"Can't *hear* you!" someone yelled down from the balcony. I glanced up, wincing at the lights, which hurt my eyes.

"Come *on*, come *on*!" another member of the audience shouted.

"What happened *then,* Bill?" one of the actors on stage prompted. "What happened *after you got the room?*"

I started limping back and forth again, saying, "I had—lain some thirty—"

"Louder!" raged a man.

"I had lain some thirty minutes!" I repeated loudly, mocking whistles and applause greeting my increase in volume.

"—lain for thirty minutes on the bed when . . . as I . . . as I suspected, I heard some men at my door. I . . . I pulled out my revolver and . . . my bowie knife and, uh—"

"—your whiskey bottle!" someone in the balcony yelled. The audience laughed and I looked up, forced to lower my stinging eyes once more because of the spotlight's glare.

"What happened *then,* Bill?" asked an actor.

"I had . . . lain some thirty minutes on—" I started.

"You already *told* us that!" someone shouted.

I stiffened angrily, looking around, then felt a chill run up my back at what I saw moving to the edge of the stage. I peered at the nearest box.

Agnes was sitting there, tears running down her cheeks.

I murmured her name.

"Louder!" cried a number of men.

I stared at Agnes, thinking: *That she should see this . . .*

"What happened after you pulled out your revolver and your bowie knife, Bill?" one of the actors asked me desperately.

I could only stare at Agnes, wishing that I was far away from this agony.

"Did they open the door, Bill?" the actor asked. His voice broke as he added, *"Wild Bill?"*

I could not go on. Even the audience seemed to realize it, for they gradually grew still.

Then, a wondrous moment, ending the excruciating pain.

Agnes stood and extended her arms to me.

With a sob that I hoped nobody heard, I limped forward, climbing into the box, where I embraced her, pressing my cheek to hers, my tear-filled eyes closed tightly. "Agnes," I whispered. *"Agnes."*

"Bill," she murmured.

And in that vast enclosure crammed with people, we were, nonetheless, alone together.

My Attempt on
the Life of Wild Bill

⋆⇥⊙⊂⇤⋆

My abortive effort to assassinate Wild Bill Hickok—at least in a limited fashion—occurred the very night that Agnes came back into my life.

With no attempt at social niceties or courting graces, we retired immediately to my hotel room where I (and I hope she) enjoyed the most fruitful sexual union I had ever known in my life; fruitful because, deeply intermingled with the pleasure of the physical experience were the added elements of gratitude, happiness, and, most of all, love. It is a combination I can recommend most highly or, as Hamlet expressed it, "A consummation devoutly to be wished"—or something on that order.

It was when we were lying together, warm and satiated by our most rewarding act of love, that I essayed to make Wild Bill take the big jump to, at least, obscurity if not the actual wooden overcoat.

"You still haven't told me why you didn't come to Kansas City, Bill," she said, by the use of that name perhaps planting, in my brain, the seed of what transpired.

"Well," I lied (I think I became fully aware of that for the first time), "I had the offer of this play, you see—"

"That awful play," she interrupted. "You aren't going to do that anymore; I just won't let you. It's beneath your dignity. You're too important a man to let them use you like that." (Another seed planted by her comment.)

"No," I promised her, "I won't do it anymore."

"Good," she said, looking grimly pleased. "No wonder you drank. To be made a fool of in that way. A famous man like you."

Another seed. I seemed to sense it germinating in my mind.

"Why didn't you write me, Bill?" she asked. Bill again. The germination continuing.

"I was ashamed of what I was doing," I answered quietly.

It was a beginning.

She didn't sense what was about to happen. Can I blame her? Not at all; I can only blame myself.

"You should have come to Kansas City," she said. "You could have joined the circus as a—guest of honor or something. It would have been much better than appearing in that dreadful and humiliating play."

"I suppose," I answered, secretly mulling, contemplating.

"To hear those stupid people . . . *braying* at you," she said angrily. "At *you*. A man whose boots they aren't fit to polish."

She held me tightly and possessively and we almost made love again, but something kept me from it; a need to express, to reveal, in a word, to *confess.*

"Agnes," I said.

"Yes, darling," she replied.

"The reason I . . . didn't come to Kansas City . . . wasn't the—play. It was . . ." My voice drifted into silence. This was a difficult move to make for me, albeit she was the only person in the world I would even have considered making it for.

"What, Bill?" she finally asked when I did not continue.

I swallowed, very dryly, and set myself for the tribulation I sensed it was going to be.

"The newspaper stories," I began.

"Newspaper stories?" she said.

"About what happened in Abilene."

"Bill," she said, appalled, "you don't think I believed them, do you?"

For an instant of leaping hope, I thought that she already understood.

But then she went on. "Nobody believed them. Everybody knows how newspapers lie. Especially the *Abilene Chronicle.* Obviously, they represent people whose toes you stepped on when you were marshal."

Gently, chidingly, she slapped my cheek.

"Bill," she said, "you didn't come to join me in Kansas City because of *that?* Shame on you. Haven't you any more faith in me than that? Don't you think I know you? Know how brave you really are? Do you think a few newspaper stories could change that? *Do* you?"

Good God, I thought. I had hoped to point out to her that the newspaper stories, especially the one in the *Abilene Chronicle,* which more than intimated murder, had not been overstating the case in suggesting that my killing of Coe had been deliberate. But before I had a chance to do so, Agnes had rallied to my defense and cut the ground right out from under me.

"Well . . ." was all I could respond.

I almost gave it up then and there; the effort seemed too onerous to face. But the need to unburden myself was too overpowering; I knew that it was, literally, as the phrase goes, now or never.

"Agnes," I began again.

"What, Bill?" she asked.

I paused again; it seemed, to me, a long time before I asked, "Agnes, do you love me?"

She sounded surprised if not injured in countering, "Why do you ask that, Bill?"

"*Do* you?" I persisted.

She seemed about to respond in pique, then relaxed. Still

perplexed if no longer offended by the question, she said, "You know I do, Bill."

I paused again. Then, bracing myself, I replied, "My name is James, Agnes. James–Butler–Hickok."

"I know that, Bill," she said, still not understanding.

"What I mean is that I'm not . . ." I drew in a quick breath and finished, "*Wild Bill* Hickok."

"Bill–" she started.

"*James,*" I corrected, cutting her off.

"All right," she said, "I know your name is really James. It's just that I've become accustomed to calling you Bill. It's the name everyone calls you. You never told me *not* to call you Bill."

"I know, I know," I admitted, "but . . . well, it's just a nickname, Agnes. A nickname some old lady gave me years ago; she wasn't even *thinking* who I really was when she gave it to me. But it doesn't mean a thing."

"It does to me," she said.

I felt myself grow tight inside. Was this attempt going to become a total failure? "You know what I mean," I said, hoping it was true.

It wasn't. "No, I don't," she responded. "I *don't* understand what you're saying, Bill–I mean . . . well–" Her voice trailed off, and I knew that she did not elect to apologize for calling me Bill but, rather, was somewhat edgy about me insisting, at this late date, that she call me by my given name.

I wouldn't back off; I was into it, and I intended that she know and understand, no matter how difficult it was for me to do so.

"What I'm saying, Agnes," I went on, "is . . . there is a *real* me and a . . . a *made-up* me. Those stories . . . mostly by Colonel Nichols . . ." I scowled at myself for giving him that undeserved title. "They're *exaggerated,*" I finished.

Agnes smiled. "But I know that," she said. "Everybody does. No one takes him seriously."

"They don't?" I murmured; it was news to me.

"Of course not," she said. "It's the way things are done. They call it yellow journalism."

Another leap of hope, clutched and smashed as she continued. "It doesn't detract from what you've really accomplished," she said. "Just because the stories are exaggerated doesn't mean they aren't fundamentally true, does it?

"You *did* kill seven men at Rock Creek. You *were* a hero in The War Between the States. You *did* turn back that mob. You did kill Dave Tutt in Springfield. You *were* a heroic scout for General Custer, a heroic sheriff in Hays, a *magnificent* marshal in Abilene. Stories can't alter facts, Bill—all right, James."

She smiled with amusement. "You may not have killed hundreds of men and Indians, but you've certainly defended yourself with honor any number of times. Isn't that right." She waited. "*Isn't* it?" she insisted.

I didn't know what to say or think, not knowing whether to feel aghast at how versed she was in my legendary past or to be frustrated by the difficulty I was having getting through to her.

"Well . . . yes," I said, retreating. "Yes; of course." I couldn't let it go at that, however. "It's just that," I continued, "well . . . my reputation. Wild Bill, Prince of Pistoleers. Gun Master of the Border. It's . . . *ridiculous.*"

I felt a tremor of foreboding to see her expression tighten at my final word.

I could not back down, though; not when I had gone so far.

"I want us to be married but—"

"Oh, Bill," she cried, hugging me so tightly her leg thumped against my hip, making me wince. "I want that as well! With all my heart!"

I drew back, trying not to show my reaction to her hurting my hip, and said, "Well, when I've made a decent raise and can afford to ask you for your hand—"

"But Bill—*Jim*—I have the circus, we'd have more than enough to—"

"No, no," I said, feeling thwarted by the sidetracking of what I really wanted to discuss. "I want to make some money first. But that's not the point. The point is—"

"What, Bill, I mean *Jim*."

"*That's* the point," I pounced on it. "This *Bill* thing; *Wild* Bill, in particular. I can't have you marrying me, thinking I'm a—great *hero* or something."

"You're too modest, Bill," she said.

I almost groaned, repressing it with effort. "No," I said. "*No, Agnes.*"

She didn't respond and, once again, uneasiness gripped me. Was I destroying our relationship by doing this?

To my dishonor—at least, my discredit—I went on, conditionally.

"I've killed men, yes," I said. "Dave McCanles and—one other at Rock Creek, *not seven*. Dave Tutt in Springfield. Bill Mulvey in Hays. Phil Coe in Abilene." I swallowed. "Mike Williams in Abilene, that by terrible mistake.

"But *that's it*, Agnes. Not hundreds. Not even dozens. Just the ones I've mentioned. And if you'd seen how—"

My voice would not allow me to go on. The total truth was not only difficult for me to reveal, it seemed d———d near impossible.

"You see . . . Agnes," I said, "I want you to love me."

"I *do*, Bill, I *do*."

I looked at her accusingly. She tried to look repentant, but I could see that she was more inclined toward exasperation. "*Jim*," she said, "I do love you."

"Me?" I demanded. "Or some . . . character who doesn't even exist?"

I knew from her expression that she still didn't comprehend what I was trying so hard—albeit unsuccessfully—to convey.

"I mean—" I started.

"I love *you*, Bill." Was that a scowl? "*Jim*, I love you."

I put my arms around her and held her close. Was I asking too much of her? Was I being unjust? After all, she had committed no crime; she was blameless of fault in all this. It was *my* doing, all mine.

"And I love you, Agnes," I told her ardently. "I love you more than anything else in the entire world. That's why I want you to know the truth about me. So you won't think you're married to some—*fiction*. You know what I mean."

"I understand," she said. But did she?

"I know you do," I said, regardless.

I waited. Then, at last, I had to add, "I've been afraid a lot of times."

"That's only normal, Bill," she said, catching her breath in irritation as she realized that, once again, she'd used my nickname.

Was I lulled by the tone of her voice? I'll never know. But I continued, "I didn't leave Hays because I had the offer of a better job in Abilene. I left because—"

Realization of what I'd been about to say brought me up short. *How far could I go?*

"What, Bill?" she asked. She didn't even react to using the name now; I believe she felt that it was all right to do so since it was the name I was so widely known by.

"Well—" I hesitated. Did I dare?

Self-anger made me go on. I would not give way when I'd come this far. I must not, I resolved.

"I'd arrested Custer's brother and put him in jail," I told her, "and he said he was going to—*kill* me, so . . ."

Impossible; I simply couldn't tell her the naked truth; talk about *cowardice*.

"Well, there was . . . there were seven other soldiers with him and I just . . . I didn't think I could handle eight at once so . . ."

I retreated even further toward a stated ignobility.

"It was the only time, though," I continued. "I mean . . . as you said, I *was* the marshal in Abilene, I *did* scout for Custer, I *was* in the war. The stories weren't *all* made up by a long shot." I wanted to end it now. I knew that it had been a failure and wanted to get out of it as quickly as possible.

"I'm glad we had this little talk," I said. "It just wouldn't be right to have you marry me, thinking that your husband was *The Hero of the Plains*, performance nightly, six days a week, matinees on Wednesday and Sunday afternoon."

"No," she said—very quietly, I thought.

I never brought up the subject again and we have never spoken of it since. I know I *tried* to let her know the truth, but how much she was willing to accept the facts I don't know to this day. I needed her too much to make any more of it, and if she was or still is disturbed by the notions I raised in that talk, she has never mentioned it.

I tried to put Wild Bill to rest—at least in our relationship—but I am not sure whether I succeeded, even in part. Did I, in fact, replace him, in her estimation, with that pitiful impostor I have been on too many occasions in the past? I hope not.

Does she understand at all? Or do I expect too much of her? How could she understand my circumstance when I have never truly managed to do so myself?

Miracles in Kansas
and Beyond

I still loved Agnes deeply but feared that I had done some injury to our relationship by what I'd said during that conversation.

Accordingly, I felt a need to separate myself from her in order to give her the time to adjust and recover from my words. I didn't feel that she really perceived what I was trying to convey but believed that enough had been said to create a cloud of uneasy suspicion in her mind.

For that reason, using the perfectly valid excuse that I was going to seek out a means of income other than the theater, which we both agreed was hardly worth the pain and aggravation to me, we parted company after a few days, promising to correspond and keep our love alive with words.

To be honest, I had the apprehension that I had destroyed our relationship by what I'd told her. This produced a double reaction in me: one of sorrow that I might have lost the one person who could make a difference in my life but also, and almost equally disturbing, that if our relationship could not survive the truth, it was too flawed to pursue in any case.

With these conflicting emotions hovering in the air above my head, I left Agnes and sallied forth. Wrong word there; to sally forth implies an expedition or excursion.

I merely removed myself physically from her company, my emotional tail between my legs.

+⟩━━⟨+

During 1874, a year of miracles for me, I accomplished the following:

I was in New York City being lionized by one and all.

I was visiting friends in Springfield, Missouri.

I was killing Indians out West.

I had a gunfight with two of Phil Coe's relatives and killed them both.

I was, myself, killed in Galveston, Texas.

I was also killed in Fort Dodge, my body "riddled with bullets."

What I really did was somewhat less dramatic.

I took a position leading a party of English hunters whose sole intent seemed to be the extermination of all wild game in Colorado. Their carnage grew so demented that a company of cavalry was dispatched to see to it that the Britishers did not exterminate all the Indians they saw as well. I did not last very long on this adventure, so thoroughly disgusted was I by the mindless butchers, who came close to surpassing the Grand Duke Alexis and his 1872 mass slaughter of the buffaloes.

+⟩━━⟨+

About that time, I began to experience more and more difficulty with my eyes and began to wear tinted glasses to protect them from the glare of the sun.

A visit to a doctor in Topeka elicited his diagnosis that I was suffering with an infection caused by the colored fire used on stage during my theatrical touring. When I asked him if the problem would decrease in time, he could give me no assurance of that; it could, conceivably, get worse in time, he said.

Which, of course, made life a little more delightful than usual.

I took to tucking my hair beneath my hat and that, along with the darkly tinted glasses, served to disguise my appearance well enough; not to mention my enforced use of a cane whenever cold weather brought on rheumatism in my hip. Why I didn't have my hair cut short as I would have liked to, I shall never know. Perhaps a residue of false pride would not allow me to eradicate one of my Wild Bill talismans.

✦━━✦

While I was in Topeka, I had a curious experience.

I went one night to an establishment called the Colorado House to play some poker and enjoy some drinking.

I had not chosen to disguise myself and, as I entered, everyone saw me and began to cheer, immediately making me sorry that I hadn't entered incognito. However, the deed was done, and I was either to accept it or depart; I chose to remain.

While standing at the counter having a drink, a man came up behind me. Seeing his reflection in the mirror, I turned quickly, tensing.

Seeing that, he flinched and drew back, both hands in the air. "I come in peace," he said, his voice so shaky that I almost laughed, but managed to confine my amused reaction to a smile. "What can I do for you?" I asked.

"Sir, a gentleman is playing poker over there (he pointed) who I thought—*we* thought—you might enjoy meeting."

"And who might that be?" I inquired.

"Clay Halser, Mr. Hickok."

I could not prevent a sudden stricture in my chest and stomach muscles. Halser was, in fact, what I was in legend: a genuinely brave, courageous man whose exploits as a shootist and lawman were well-known in the nation, much less the West. *Meet* him? The idea chilled my blood. What if he was really as aggressive as I'd read? Wouldn't his immediate inclination be to try me and add yet another—sizable—notch to his gun?

All this rushed through my head as I stared at the man.

"I wouldn't want to disturb his game," I said as casually as I could.

"Oh, you wouldn't be," the man said eagerly. Before I could prevent it, he had turned and bustled off. Not wanting to be perceived as anxious in any way, I turned back to the counter and poured myself a libation of whiskey, downing half of it in a swallow, grateful for the soothing warmth of it in my stomach.

In the mirror, I saw the man come bustling back. This time I didn't turn to meet him, knowing it to be unnecessary.

"Sir?" he said.

I let him stand a moment, unacknowledged.

"Mr. Hickok?" he asked.

I turned and nodded. "Yes?" I said as though I didn't know why he was there.

"Mr. Halser said that he'd be honored to meet you."

"Honored?" I asked.

"Oh, yes, sir, his exact word," said the man.

I felt the stricture slowly loosening. I grunted as though thinking it over, then shrugged and said, "Oh, very well."

I crossed the room behind him, sensing every eye on me. "Meeting of the Giants!" I saw the blazing headline in my mind. "Two Gun Masters Face-to-Face!" Inwardly, I cursed Nichols yet again for making me think in terms of his overblown journalistic jargon and wondered what Halser thought of the "colonel" since he, too, had received the royal treatment in Nichols's magazine and newspaper articles.

As I neared the table where he sat, a man stood up and, in an instant, I knew a number of things about Clay Halser. He was no imposing giant, being, I would estimate, approximately five foot nine inches in height and built very slenderly. He was not heavily armed, no weapon visible at all, although I assumed that, living under similar circumstances as my own, he had to keep at least one weapon on him for defense.

Mostly, I saw that, if anything, he was in worse physical and mental condition than I was, his hair streaked with gray, his features haggard and ashen, his eyes virtually burned out. I saw in them the same emotional depletion I saw in my own eyes when I looked at myself in the mirror. I had no idea what he had looked like earlier in his life but, to me, it seemed as though he must have lost considerable weight as well, his clothes hanging loose on his frame. As he extended his hand to shake mine, I saw a very visible tremor in it.

"Mr. Hickok," he said.

"My honor, sir," I replied. "I have admired your career."

He seemed genuinely flustered by my words. *"My* career?" he said, incredulous. "Good God, sir. Compared to yours—" He made a scoffing sound as though to relegate his own career to some inferior position.

Two thoughts occurred to me almost simultaneously: one, how prematurely foolish I had been to presume that he would want to challenge me and, two, that I felt a disquieting sense of sympathy, even pity for him. The only thing that might have caused me to react with even more inner distress would have been if I had known his age. I took him, by appearance, to be well in his forties when, actually, he was barely thirty-one.

After our initial handshake, we retired to a corner table where I evoked a smile from him by noting that we both sat with our backs to the wall.

He asked me then if I remembered "hurrahing" him in Morgan City some eternity previously. I told him that I honestly did not, but when he described the incident during which I had treated him with brusque dismissal, I told him I was sorry I had done so. "However," I said, "I imagine that you understand, now, why I acted as I did."

"I do," he said. "Being a cow town marshal is not the most relaxing job in the world."

We enjoyed a mutual chuckle over that. "No, it certainly is not," I agreed with him.

He glanced around the room and smiled at what he saw; a bitter smile, I noted. "You know what they want," he said.

"Of course," I replied. "For us to pull down and blow each other to bloody ribbons."

He chuckled. "I could not have said it better," he responded.

I must say that, all things considered, it was a pleasant evening. Only one thing marred it for me: the fact that I had to maintain, as always, the fiction that my life had been as heroic as his. Not that he presented it as such. Indeed, a more modest man I never met. Still, I knew that all the exaggerated stories about him were—unlike those about me—based on truth. It made a profound difference, although I tried not to show it in any way. I liked him very much and wish, to this day, that our exchange had been as honest on my side as it was on his.

We discussed for a while the interesting parallels in our careers, both born in the Middle West, both on the Union side during the war, both cow town marshals, both known through the bloated hyperbole of Nichols and writers like him.

Both—this we laughed at heartily—appearing in self-exalting plays, required, in essence to play the fool. I suspect our laughter was laced with acid, but we enjoyed it nonetheless.

He told me then—no laughter here, completely solemn—of an incident where he had been convinced he'd seen the ghost of a man he'd killed. I did not respond at first, but felt a prickle of gooseflesh over my body.

When he was finished with his strange and sorrowful story, I told him that I'd read a number of books on Spiritualism and even gone to see a gypsy medium who had told me things she could not have known by normal means.

I told him that there was a woman in Topeka who claimed she could communicate with the dead, but I could see from his reaction that he wished no part of that.

At last, we spoke about the subject that was uppermost in both our minds: our position in the West, the nation, and, for all we knew, the world.

"We are victims of notoriety," I told him. "No longer men but figments of imagination.

"Journalists have endowed us with qualities that no man could possibly possess. Yet men hate us for these very nonexistent qualities.

"Our time is written on the sands, Mr. Halser," I told him. "We are living dead men."

I had never thought about my situation in those terms but, once I had expressed it so, I realized how true it was.

At that moment, it seemed to me that I had nothing to look forward to but death.

My History Concluded

I am nearly finished now with my account. I need not fear that anyone will, ultimately, read it. Even if they came upon it, they would, more than likely, burn it as a somber, boring narrative.

But I will continue, thus wrapping up the ends.

The year 1875 was not a banner one for me. No miracles occurred or were imagined.

Instead, I started down the slope of drink and lechery again, albeit briefly.

I don't know whether it began after my experience with Clay Halser. It may well have, for I never felt more of a fraud than I did from that night on.

In addition, for more than several months I heard no word (of love or otherwise) from Agnes. Because of this, I became convinced that she no longer cared for me; that I had, in fact, turned her away from me with my clumsy attempt at revealing the truth about myself.

In a state of despair, I succumbed to old weaknesses once more. Yet even in this renewed surrender to intemperance, I presented a spurious facade to all I came in contact with, intimating (even overtly stating) that the reason for my dissipation was a melancholy reaction to the closing in of civilization on the free soul that I was. Pure, unadulterated buffalo chips!

I got into the odious habit of joining crowds of tenderfeet at the bar and regaling them with high-blown, windy accounts of adventures with "red fiends" and "white rogues," all the while soaking my inner man with gratis bottles of whiskey.

I reached my lowest point in June of that year when I was charged with vagrancy and a warrant for my arrest was issued. Unable to face this humiliation, I fled the city, returning some months later where, although the charge was still outstanding, I was able to move about once more.

Happily, by that time, I had heard from Agnes once again and was relieved to discover that she still cared for me. As I have indicated, she did not mention our conversation and, gratefully, I did not raise the topic, vowing never to speak of it again.

This made me think, in the fall of 1875, of the concept of preparing these memoirs. I had, through the previous months, accumulated the sum of $1,600 through various means (gambling, involvement in hunting expeditions, etc.), which, while it was certainly not enough to provide a comfortable life for Agnes and me, did provide me with the wherewithal to write these memoirs, the bulk of which I have done. I feel some guilt about not sending part of this money to my aged mother and hope that she has not felt a sense of resentment toward me for my dereliction. As excuse, I can only offer that my main concern was (in addition to preparing this book) amassing enough money so that I could offer Agnes a married life with a decent standard of living. I certainly did not intend to live permanently off her circus earnings.

I did consider accepting one of the many offers tendered to me to write a chronicle of my adventures, but knowing what kind of heroical tommyrot these people would expect, I could not force myself to the task. As I have told you, I actually did keep a journal for a number of years, choosing to incinerate it rather than promulgate its thick-headed absurdities.

So I commenced to prepare my memoirs.

And now we are in 1876, unusual festivities taking place around the country, this being the centennial year of the Declaration of Independence.

⊹⊱——⊰⊹

On March 5, Agnes and I were married at the Cheyenne residence of S. L. Moyers and family, friends of Agnes.

Agnes, being the honest woman that she is, wrote down her true age on the wedding license: forty-two. Being still a gentleman—if nothing else—I did not write down my true age (thirty-nine) but, instead, put down that I was forty-five.

If ever I felt inclined to kill (and you now know how nonexistent that inclination has always been in me) it was because of an article written about our wedding in the Omaha *Daily Bee.*

"Hickok has always been considered as wild and woolly and hard to curry, but the proprietress of the best circus on the continent wanted a husband of renown and she laid siege to the not oversusceptible heart of the man who had killed his dozens of both whites and Indians. The contest was short, sharp, and decisive, Wild Bill went down in the struggle clasping his opponent in both his brawny arms, and now sweet little cupids hover over their pathway, and sugar, cream, and honey form a delicious paste through which they honeymoon."

Indeed! Whoever wrote that drivel should be staked out naked on an anthill on a summer's afternoon!

⊹⊱——⊰⊹

Agnes and I had two fine weeks together sullied only by a somewhat heated discussion regarding our means of income, she stating that she could earn five thousand dollars a year plus all expenses in any number of circuses, me retorting—unequivocally—that no wife of mine would ever work.

As fortune would have it, the discovery of gold in the Black Hills of Dakota a few years earlier had created a nationwide furor, and by the middle of 1875, men were beginning to swarm to the Hills like crazed ants. By April of this year (1876), the mining camp that had become most prominent was Deadwood Gulch. It was to there that I determined to travel, hopefully to make a strike and provide for Agnes for the remainder of our lives and find myself a respectable niche in life.

┼━━━┼

My first attempt to reach Deadwood was to announce that I was raising a company to travel to the Black Hills, not only for safety's sake but to economize on supplies and, reaching the gold region, to comprise an impressive settlement of miners. The fare per person was to be in excess of thirty-three and a half dollars.

Unfortunately, a lack of adequate applicants forced me to cancel this project and, instead, travel to Deadwood in the company of the Utter brothers, Steve and Charley, who own and operate a four-horse shipping company.

I arrived in Deadwood on July 12.

┼━━━┼

The city (probably too grand a name for such a primitive location) sits at the end of the gulch, which is a dead-end canyon.

It consists of one street filled with tree stumps and potholes, hastily constructed frame buildings on either side. The street is, during daylight hours, jammed with men, horses, mules, oxen, and wagons. Saloons outnumber stores three to one and, in general, the lure of gold and the fleecing of men who might find it has attracted every low-grade denizen capable of reaching the community. *Was I one of them?* I wondered at the time.

My eyes had been bothering me considerably and, upon arrival in Deadwood, I felt it advisable to see a doctor. I had seen a number of them in Cheyenne but none had put forth the same opinion as to the cause of my optical affliction.

With this in mind, I approached a burly man unloading a wagon. "Pardon me, sir," I said.

The man turned quickly to reveal as unprepossessing a countenance as I have ever seen, so dirty and odor-ridden that gnats hovered about him.

"You lookin' for a fat lip?" he said.

"I beg your pardon?" I replied.

"Never mind, never mind," he cut me off. "What do you want?"

"Could you tell me where I might find a doctor?" I inquired.

He pointed. "That way, bucko," he answered. "Dr. Kelly, ten doors down."

"Thank you," I said.

"What's the problem?" asked the ugly man. "Dose of the clap?" He chuckled, revealing a set of rotten, crooked teeth with numerous gaps. I backed away, brushing at a gnat attacking my nose. "Thank you again," I said.

"Say hello to Kelly for me," he said. "You won't be the first dose of clap I sent to him."

Upon which, he cackled madly, gurgled, hawked up an oyster, and let it fly, just missing me. "J———s C———t," he said, turning back to his work.

As I walked away, I saw Charley Utter standing nearby, grinning.

"By all that is holy," I muttered to him, "who is that horrible man?"

Charley laughed and answered, "Calamity Jane."

"That is a *woman?*" I said, incredulous.

"If you can call her that," said Charley. "Some folks claim she's a hermaphrodite."

"My God," I murmured.

"I think she makes a better man than a woman," Charley said.

I will say no more about that incident except to comment that, not knowing what dire events may have occurred in this creature's life, I cannot criticize her. At any rate, I do not expect to cross her path again.

For that matter, if I do happen to see her corning, I will most likely cross the street to avoid contact with her.

⊹⇒⋯⇐⊹

Why, after all the doctors I have seen elsewhere, with their multiple diagnoses of my problem, it took a hick doctor in a mining camp to tell me what the problem really is, I have no idea. But it was Dr. Kelly who let me know what was really wrong.

"You want it straight, Mr.—?" he said, breaking off when he reached my unknown last name—not really unknown, I suspect; I think he knew exactly who I was.

"Butler," I told him.

"Ah, yes." He nodded. "You want it straight, Mr. Butler?"

"What is it?" I asked.

"Glaucoma," he said. "Advanced. Looks to me like gonorrheal ophthalmia."

His words stunned me, my first horrified thought being: *Oh, dear God, have I infected Agnes with a disease picked up from whores?*

"How advanced?" I heard myself inquire. It seemed like the voice of someone else.

"You want it straight?" asked Kelly.

"Yes, damn it, *yes*," I replied.

"You could be blind in a matter of months," he said.

I left his office in a daze. I had felt that there was something chronic going on in my eyes, but *that?* The realization was staggering. *Blind in a matter of months.* What was I to do?

Limping along the plank walk, my cane slipped through a crack in the wood and, staggering, I fell clumsily to one side, sprawling into the street, my spectacles falling off, my hat falling off so that my hair (which I customarily pushed up inside my hat) fell loose.

A man stepped over to help me up. "You all right, mister?" he asked.

"Yes," I muttered, standing up.

He looked more closely at me. "Hey, ain't you—?" he began.

"No," I interrupted him and, quickly, picking up my spectacles, hat, and cane, moved away from him as rapidly as possible. As I did, another man joined him and I heard him say, "Sure looks like Hickok to me."

"Hickok!" exploded the second. *Why not climb up on a rooftop and shout it?* I thought angrily. "I thought he was *dead*!"

Hearing the Magic Name, a third man joined the pair and their voices rang out above the noisy bustle of the street, "Did you say *Hickok*?" "Yeah! That's him! Right there!" *"Wild Bill Hickok* in Deadwood?"

So much for incognito.

⊷══⊷

I complete these memoirs sitting on a rough cot in a tent. It is nearly the end of July.

I wonder if it is nearly the end of my life, as well.

When it is general knowledge—as I'm sure it will be—that I am on the verge of blindness, some aspirant, more daring because of my failing eyesight, will go up against me and, unless I can hit him by the sound of his revolver being drawn (an unlikely feat) it will all be over.

Even if that doesn't happen, what kind of life can I lead in darkness?

I have been taking mineral drugs prescribed by Dr. Kelly, and from what I can make out in my hand mirror, it has taken its toll on me. My skin is almost gray, my eyes are dull and lifeless. I look dead already.

I read, a while back, of the death of Clay Halser in Silver Gulch; he was shot down by some adolescent boy who had the good luck (or bad luck as it will probably turn out) of having Halser's pistol misfire on the first shot. God rest Halser's soul; I hope he is in peace, and that, when my time comes, I will be disposed of by a man worthy of the name, not by some ambitious fool seeking only notoriety.

Mentioning that makes me wonder, as I have on more than one occasion, if the souls of the men I have killed still linger about me like that of Mike Williams. I pray to God that they do not and, most of all, that I will never have to see them standing before me, white-faced and accusing.

So I draw near the conclusion of this manuscript. I hope that I have made it clear that I am no more wild than a butterfly and that my name isn't Bill. For that matter, my last name has been misrepresented as well, more times than a dog has fleas; I have been, among other family monikers, identified as Hitchcock, Hansock, Hickock, Haycock, Hicock, Hiccocks, and Hiccox.

To wrap things up: I have come to the final judgment that I am not a man any longer. I am a figment, a concoction, an overblown invention born of low-grade whiskey and high-grade journalistic distortion; of street and saloon gossip and dime-novel bombast.

It is not that I have been a total waste as a human being. I have accomplished *something* in my life; just something less than has been cast abroad. The truth lies somewhere in between the two extremes.

I have written to Agnes and, heaven pity me, lied to her once more, unable to tell her the truth; at least, I can try to hold on to her love at a distance, if not in my presence. I have told her that I never was as well in my life and that we will have a home yet and will be happy even though I know that it will never happen. I bade her good-bye, calling her my dear wife and, after signing J. B. Hickok, adding—a final act of cowardice because I fear to lose her?—*Wild Bill*.

To amuse her (I hope it does) I added a second note written in the style of the uneducated boor so many people believe me to be.

As to the future, God only knows; I do not.

However, as Lincoln put it, "The best thing about the future is that it comes only one day at a time."

Or, as Benjamin Franklin wrote (words I live by nowadays): "Blessed is he who expects nothing, for he shall never be disappointed."

Addendum

I thought I was finished—in more ways than one—but fate (if that is what it was) has intervened, and my tale goes on, albeit briefly.

I was lying in my tent one gloomy, overcast afternoon, much in need of a bath, a shave, and a change of clothes, when footsteps sounded outside. By instinct, I reached for my new .32 caliber Smith & Wesson—my first cylinder-loading pistol—then changed my mind and lay back down. If it was Death's tread I heard, let it be. That may not have been my exact thought, but certainly that was the gist of it.

If it was Death, it cleared its throat outside the tent flap, then inquired, "Mr. Hickok?"

"Who is it?" I asked, relatively certain at that point that it wasn't Death at all but some more prosaic entity.

"John Stebbins, Mr. Hickok," said the voice.

"Who are you?" I asked.

"Stebbins, Post and Company, sir," he answered. "I am here representing the merchants of Deadwood."

Instantaneous disinterest on my part; I did not respond.

He cleared his throat again. "May I come in?" he asked.

"No," I said. I wanted him to vanish.

"Oh," he responded. "Well . . . of course." Another throat-clearing. "We've been thinking, Mr. Hickok," he went on (I knew what he was going to say before he said it), "Deadwood needs a marshal bad and we were wondering if you—"

His voice had faded off by then. I stared into a memory, a gauzy, ethereal remembrance of Agnes standing on a horse's back as it cantered around the circus ring; a vision of the first night I had seen her in performance and fallen in love with her.

I soon realized that Stebbins was still talking. When his words ended with an audible question mark, I said, irritably, "What?"

"I said, would that be agreeable?" he repeated.

"Would *what* be agreeable?" I demanded; Lord, but I'd become a surly wretch.

"Why . . . two hundred dollars a month and half the collected—"

"I'll *think* about it," I interrupted. Anything to get rid of him.

"That's all we can ask, Mr. Hickok," he said. "All we can ask."

He was silent for a few moments before clearing his throat again. I almost groaned aloud. "Uh . . . Mr. Hickok?" he said.

I closed my eyes; obviously the man was never going to leave. *"What?"* I asked.

"There are six men in Saloon Number Ten. Shootists from Montana. A real bad lot."

"So?" I muttered, wearily.

"They say they're going to kill you."

That was adequate to make me open my eyes.

"I just thought you should know," said Stebbins.

"Thank you," I replied, as far from feeling gratitude as any man could be.

"That's all right," he said. He really thought I was grateful. "They said they'd be there all afternoon and into tonight." He cleared his throat. Dramatic emphasis? "Waiting for you," he concluded.

I heard his footsteps moving off. I stared up at the canvas overhead.

"Sure," I said, "I'll go right down and kill them all."

I tried to sleep but couldn't. I sat up, but that was not enough.

I stood and paced a bit. No, not enough by half. Something was rising in me; I could feel it like a dark, acidic liquid being slowly poured into my stomach, then my chest.

I could not remain there. Hastily, I threw on my jacket and, grabbing my cane, vacated the tent. I walked and walked and *walked* until I was alone in the wilderness, limping back and forth like some caged, restless beast.

The more I paced, the more I realized exactly what it was that was rising in me. It was anger and resentment, yes, but mostly it was self-contempt. I picked up a stone and tossed it in my palm as I paced. The rage and hatred I felt toward myself kept mounting and getting hotter until it felt as though the acid in my body had caught fire, its flames a searing pain. My pacing grew more agitated. Back and forth and back and forth.

Suddenly, it all erupted, the fury and disgust flooding upward in me. I stopped and hurled away the stone, screaming at the top of my voice, my tormented howl ringing and echoing off the walls of the canyon.

Across my mind, a rush of scenes appeared; a flash of painful recollections so rapid I could scarcely keep track of them: my boyhood terrors, my panic at Rock Creek, my flight in the war, my unintentional heroics with the mob, my pathetic shooting of Dave Tutt, my dread at Fort Riley and during my scouting days. My ridiculous killing of Bill Mulvey, my fleeing from Tom Custer's rage, my false displays in Abilene, my fear of Thompson, my almost literal murder of Phil Coe and Mike Williams, my humiliating stage experience, my bloated reputation, the lies, the lies, the *lies*.

From the very center of my being—neither shouting it nor raising my voice—I said, *"Enough."*

Unhurriedly, I walked back to my tent and brushed my best clothes, polished my boots; cleaned my pistols; bathed and shaved and groomed my hair; dressed slowly and meticulously. Done, I

looked—albeit ghostly—much like the Wild Bill Hickok of old, that
persona created by others and emulated by me: The Hero of the
Plains.

I pushed the two revolvers underneath my sash (a .32 would
not suffice on this occasion) then left the tent and walked down to
the main street, using, as was customary, my cane.

When I reached my goal, I removed my blue-tinted spectacles
and put them in an inside pocket, glad that it was not a sunny day. I
started toward Saloon Number Ten, then stopped and slung my
cane aside; I would not utilize it. Drawing in a deep breath, I walked
the remaining steps to the saloon without a limp, clenching my
teeth so as not to facially reveal the pain it caused me.

I reached the saloon, took one more chest-inflating breath,
then pushed inside, slamming the batwing doors against the wall.

The six men were at the counter, just now turning as I came inside. Seeing me, they tensed, and I braced myself for confrontation.

When none of them immediately went for his weapons, I
spoke.

"I understand," I told them, "that you cheap, would-be gunfighters from Montana have been making remarks about me. I want
you to understand that, unless they are stopped, there will shortly
be a number of cheap funerals in Deadwood."

I had no idea where the words were coming from, but they kept
on coming, regardless.

"I have come to this town not to court notoriety but to live in
peace," I said, "but I do not propose to stand for your insults. So if
you *vermin* have a true desire to extinguish my life, here is your
golden opportunity."

The sextet stood immobile, staring at me, and a rush of glorious
grit took hold of me; I raised my hands. *"Well?"* I demanded. "Either
fill your hands or get your yellow a———es out of here!"

The six were cowed, I saw with triumphant delight. One of
them actually tried to smile! "We was only joshing, Mr.—"

"Out!" I roared, jerking my left thumb over my shoulder.

I stepped aside and, for the first and probably only time in my life, truly resembled the Prince of Pistoleers (if a sallow-faced one) as the six cowboys (for they were not really gunmen at all) trudged sheepishly for the door, filing by me, one by one. As the last one passed, I could not resist kicking him soundly on the rump, wincing at the jab of pain it cost me but enjoying it immensely. "And don't come back!" I shouted after them.

The patrons of the saloon applauded, cheering. "Hurray for Wild Bill!" one of them cried.

It was my moment. I had waited for it all my life, but there it was at last. I smiled beneficently at the saloon's customers and enjoyed a drink with them.

So now my memoirs are unquestionably done—and with a happier ending withal. I feel a sense of confidence I did not feel before this incident; assurance that I will, in fact, find gold and make a strike toward wealth's security. I will continue taking medication and my eyesight will be, if not restored, at least improved enough to allow me to enjoy the remainder of my married life with Agnes, who I am equally assured, will—in time—come to a better understanding of me. I will not make any further abject confessions to her but will, instead, gradually instill into our life a more realistic atmosphere so that she comes to know me for what I am—at least to a large proportion.

In brief, I feel a sense of positive persuasion about my future. And, on that note, I sign these memoirs,

James Butler Hickok

Afterword

So ends the final entry in these odd, revealing memoirs.

Two days later, Hickok was assassinated.

I have spoken to one of the men who was sitting at the card table with Hickok when Jack McCall moved up behind him and shot him in the back of the head. His name is Captain Massie.

As he describes it, Hickok entered the saloon, the same one in which he had triumphed over the six Montana "gunfighters," Nuttall and Mann's Number Ten, a little after noon. He was dressed in full finery: his Prince Albert frock coat with all the appropriate accoutrements.

A card game was in progress, its players Captain Massie, Carl Mann (the saloon's co-owner), and Charles Rich. Mann signaled to Hickok, who moved over to the table where he was invited to join the game.

He accepted, asking Rich if he would move so that Hickok could sit with his back to the wall, as was his custom. Rich demurred, laughing, telling Hickok that no one would dare come at him after what he'd done two days earlier.

To Massie's surprise, Hickok made no issue of the point whatever but sat down with his back to the room and asked for fifteen dollars' worth of pocket checks, which were brought to him.

As the game progressed, Massie noticed Hickok's peculiar

behavior. He told me that Hickok seemed possessed of some strange, inner calm, as though he had come to some resolution within himself. His smile was faint and almost distant, his voice restrained and modulated. In short, Massie seemed to be telling me, Hickok behaved like a happy man—a man at peace with himself.

"That was a magnificent show the other day, Bill," Massie commented.

"Grand, Bill. Absolutely grand," Mann added.

To which Hickok replied quietly, "A gentleman could do no less."

He regarded his cards, nodding to himself, Massie fancied. Then he said, "I am descended, as a matter of fact, from the Hiccock family of Stratford-Upon-Avon, Warwickshire, England. A noble line."

A moment later, Jack McCall cried, "D———n you, take that!" and fired a bullet into Hickok's brain.

✛═══✛

Having read Hickok's memoirs and interviewed Captain Massie, I am led to the inescapable conclusion that Hickok allowed his death to occur.

How else to explain his casual willingness to sit in a position he had not allowed himself to sit in since his life became constantly in jeopardy?

Captain Massie's description of Hickok's behavior crystallizes my opinion: that he seemed possessed of some strange, inner calm, as though he had come to some resolution within himself.

I believe that he had.

He had proved his courage by confronting the six men—whether they were gunfighters or not is irrelevant. Hickok believed at the time that they were and faced them down, regardless, with a display of mettle he had never demonstrated before—or, if he had, he had certainly never mentioned in his memoirs.

Having displayed this proof of courage not only to the world but, more important, to himself, he had achieved a high plateau of gratification and, more important, self-respect. So much so that his final comments speak of a positive persuasion about his future.

In the several days that had passed since the dramatic incident, I believe that Hickok may have felt a sense of anxiety that he would, in spite of his accomplishment, backslide to his previous state of mind. He knew that he still faced imminent blindness, despite his hopeful words to the contrary. Accordingly, he knew that he could not provide his wife with the company of a full man but would, instead, have to call upon her to take care of him in his sightless condition; a prospect that must have been anathema to his pride. Moreover, he knew that the chances of him making a sizable strike in the Hills were beyond remote.

These things all under consideration, I wonder if he did not deliberately sit in such an unaccustomed position; if he did not—with the near psychic oversense of the professional gunfighter—actually *know* that McCall was moving up behind him to end the conflict of his existence with a single shot.

I believe, in short, that Hickok was ready to die.

Between two pages of his memoirs, I found a scrap of paper on which Hickok had scrawled a brief verse. I do not know if he, himself, had written it or if he had found it in a book of poetry and responded to it because it reflected his thoughts.

Whatever the case, the verse reads as follows:

> *To win a single battle*
> *is not to win a war*
> *And the hero soon discovers*
> *he is still the man he was before*

Frank Leslie